PERFEKT ORDER

The Ære Saga: Book One

S.T. Bende

The Ære Saga
Perfekt Order
Copyright © 2015, S.T. Bende
Edited by: Lauren McKellar
Cover Art by: Cora Graphics

Praise for *Perfekt Order*

"Like macaroni and cheese with bacon, *Perfekt Order* provides the perfect comfort from a hard day. Snuggle up to Tyr and Mia's story of warmth and love mixed with adventure and excitement that will keep you turning the pages until the end."
- Kristie Cook, International Bestselling Author of the *Soul Savers* series

"*Perfekt Order* has everything you want in a book filled with HOT Norse gods: The swoon-worthy hero, the sweet yet strong heroine, the humorous Norse-god sidekicks, and the page-turning suspense."
-Stina Lindenblatt, Author

DEDICATION

To my three gentlemen —

I wished for you upon a star, and all my dreams came true.

CONTENTS

"Serve God, love me, and mend."

-Benedick, *Much Ado About Nothing*

CHAPTER ONE

"CHEESE AND CRACKERS." NEEDLES shot up my pointer finger. I freed the pinned appendage from my bureau drawer and cradled it to my chest, willing the pain to stop. My digit was an unfortunate casualty in an overzealous unpacking spree. Excitement made grace something of an enigma, and today was pretty much the most exciting day of my life.

In the twenty minutes since I'd pulled up to 121 Daffodil Drive in Arcata, California, I'd unloaded the contents of both of my suitcases and done a moderate amount of decorating. The upstairs bedroom I now called home was just a short walk from the school I'd worked so hard to get into—Redwood State University. Now, after three thousand miles of driving and roughly seven thousand calories of road food, I was itching to explore my new neighborhood. I crossed to my little dormer window and looked at the wall of evergreens standing sentry outside. Since my roommates still weren't home, it wouldn't be rude to pop out for a quick run. Five days without exercise left me stiff and cranky, and it seemed prudent to run off a little anxiety before meeting the ladies I'd be living with for the next year. First impressions took a heartbeat to make, but a lifetime to break, and I wanted mine to be impeccable. I threw on my workout clothes and jotted a note to the girls.

Just got in and went for a run. I'll be back by dinner time—can't wait to officially meet you! XO, Mia

I left the note on the table in the entryway and closed the front door behind me.

A quick search on my phone told me there were two main hiking paths that picked up just behind my house. The review of one said it offered "the most pristine ferns this side of Jurassic Park, nestled amidst redwoods too beautiful to be missed." *Winner.* I committed the map of the trail to memory—straight at the end of the pavement, turn left at the top of the hill, and stay north at the fork near the big boulder—pocketed my phone, and jogged toward the forest, taking in the late afternoon air. It smelled of fall, like a pile of newly fallen leaves baking in the warm sun. At the end of the block I turned right, then crossed the street and entered the woods that bordered campus. The air was thicker in here, the dense trees acting as a sieve against the sun's filmy rays. My footsteps padded softly on the dry dirt as I ran up a steep slope. At the top of the hill, I hung left, making my way through the gently swirling fog. The mist was cool—it tickled my nostrils and chilled my lungs as I sniffed the familiar scent of earth and pine. This smell was one of my favorite things about our family camping trips. It was nice to snatch a bit of recognition in an all-together foreign world, and besides green leaves and dirt, there wasn't much familiar about my new home.

To start with, the trees in this forest were much taller than the trees in the forests of New England. Hundreds of feet taller, to be exact. Their trunks were a warm reddish color, and an emerald green moss was draped like a blanket covering the bark from base to lower limbs.

And the air . . .

I skidded to a stop as the trail came to an abrupt end. Since I hadn't seen any big boulders, I must have taken a wrong turn. Somewhere along the way, the air had dropped ten degrees in temperature, and the fog morphed from a soothing cumulus mist to an oppressive cloud of smoke. The backs of my arms prickled. Fear took hold in my gut, gripping my stomach in its iron manacles as my gaze darted around the densely packed forest. Between the hovering sequoias and the intricately woven ferns, the woods were so dark I couldn't see much of anything. But I didn't need to see to know the only thing that mattered—I wasn't alone. And judging by the low snarl coming from the foliage in front of me, my visitor was madder than a wet hen.

"I'm leaving," I offered softly, hoping to placate the unseen creature with a gentle tone. My voice cracked just enough to betray my panic. What was I thinking going into a strange forest alone this close to dusk? Things got hungry at dusk. Big things. Carnivorous things.

God, I hoped whatever was growling was a herbivore.

I waved my arms at my sides to make myself look bigger, and slowly placed one foot behind the other. There wasn't time to think about the blades of terror piercing my gut, or the numbness settling in my hands. All I had to do was make it back to the top of the hill. Then it was a clear shot back into town. Just a little fun run. I could absolutely do this.

With my arms still moving, I inched backward up the

hill. The snarling continued, but I ignored the impulse to flee. The creature hadn't come out of the ferns yet; I didn't want to give it any reason to chase me. Toe to heel, I continued my climb until I was halfway to the top. *Breathe, Mia.* I consciously drew two slow breaths, willing my heart rate to stop its frantic tango.

And then I couldn't move.

Two blazing red eyes emerged from behind a fern. They formed crimson and orange swirls, like the fun-house décor at my boarding school's fall carnival. But there was nothing amusing here. The eyes locked me in place, immobilizing my feet despite the urgent bulletin running across my brain—*run*. I fought against their hold, struggling with every ounce of power I could summon, and lifted one sneaker then the other from their invisible stronghold. Panic willed me forward. I barely registered the grey fur covering an enormous head and the ears framing frightening eyes. I just turned and bolted for the top of the hill.

The beast bolted right after me.

The creature's labored breathing grew louder—it was closing in. My toes pushed against the cushion of my Nikes as I lengthened my strides, working as hard as I could to reach the safety of the clearing. But I still had a quarter mile to go, and the snarling was right at my back.

"Arugh!" I shrieked as the beast's fangs snapped around my arm, pulling it behind me and dragging me backward before releasing its bite. My arm tugged again as the sleeve of my hoodie tore—the fabric must have been attached to the animal's canines. My wrist throbbed as pierced flesh met cold air. Something hot and wet trickled down my fingers, but I didn't dare look; I was afraid of what I'd see.

"Help!" I jerked forward as my sleeve finally ripped away. The moment I was free, I bolted for the top of the hill, putting as much distance as I could between that awful animal and me. My arm was on fire, and I was afraid one more bite would break it clean off. Bile rose in my throat, but I willed it down. *You can freak out later, Mia. Now you have to run.*

I was so focused on reaching the summit that I almost didn't see the man in the shadows. He leapt across my sight line just as I cleared the top of the hill. His intense blue eyes forced me to a stop as they held my gaze for the briefest of moments. The connection was broken as the man's guttural cry bounced off the evergreens, and he flew thirty feet to tackle my attacker. The sound of bodies colliding thundered throughout the forest. I whirled around just in time to see a mass of claws and fists, blond hair and grey fur, as the man and the beast catapulted into the brush. Both were unnaturally large. The creature, whatever it was, had to be ten feet, with the long tail and sharp ears I'd seen on foxes back home. And the man . . . though he wore a hooded sweatshirt, it was obvious he boasted the kinds of muscles not seen outside UFC gyms. He wrenched the creature's head to one side with ease, although I was sure the beast had a few hundred pounds on him.

They disappeared into the woods before I could take a breath. I doubled over as the snap of cracking bones came from behind the ferns, and when I heard the agonized cry of a wounded animal, I dropped to my knees.

Then everything went to black.

CHAPTER TWO

WHEN I OPENED MY eyes, a tiny blond girl knelt at my side.

"Are you okay?" Worry lined her brow as she gently guided me to a sitting position. She couldn't have weighed more than a hundred pounds soaking wet, but she shifted me with ease until I was resting with my back against a mossy trunk. My fingers grazed the back of my head where it throbbed. I glanced at the dry earth, the cage of trees, and the seemingly incalculable amount of green coating the forest from top to bottom. *How did I get here?*

Memories bombarded my addled brain like snowballs in an avalanche, and I scrambled to my feet. I turned my head so fast the end of my ponytail slapped my face. "Where are they? Is the animal still here? Oh God, did it . . ." My chest rose, and I glanced down, preparing myself for exposed bone and torn flesh. But when I took in the sight of my chipped manicure peeking out from beneath the untouched sleeve of my hoodie, my jaw fell open with an audible pop.

"What in Sam Hill. . ." I shoved my sleeve up to my elbow and stared in awe. There wasn't so much as a scratch on the smooth peachy surface. No exposed bone. No blood. No evidence of the life or death battle I'd just endured. Had I imagined the whole thing?

"You saw an animal?" The blond girl jumped up, taking a defensive stance. She couldn't have been more than five-foot, two-inches, with loose waves that bounced as she shifted her weight back and forth. She looked better suited to waving pom-poms than taking on a crazed animal, but I didn't care—I was glad I wasn't alone.

"I was running away, and it tried to bite off my arm. But then this guy came and—oh my god, the guy. Is he all right?" My eyes scanned the forest, looking for any signs of the struggle. The trees, ferns, and lightly swirling mist were still there, but the animal and my savior were gone.

"Are you sure you're okay?" The girl's face softened as she relaxed her stance.

"No!" A lump lodged in my throat and my eyes pricked with tears as I remembered the terrifying sensation of teeth piercing flesh.

"Let's get you out of here." The girl guided me by the elbow with the careful movement one might reserve for a confirmed lunatic. No doubt I seemed crazy, staring at my forearm with a look that wavered between reverent and horrified.

"I'm Brynn." The girl spoke conversationally as she led me back to town. Her voice was lyrical with each sentence ending on a high note. It made her sound as if she was singing.

"I'm Mia. Thanks for helping me."

"Of course." Brynn spoke lightly. "Mia Ahlström, *ja*?"

"How'd you know that?" My eyes narrowed. First a giant beast attacked me, and now a total stranger knew my name. Either someone was out to get me, or I was going insane.

"I recognize you from the picture you sent." Brynn laughed. "I'm your roommate, Brynn . . . the one from Sweden."

"Oh, *Brynn*. I'm so sorry." I flushed. "I should have realized."

"You're pretty out of it, *flicka*." Brynn nodded cheerfully.

"What did you call me?" I knew a little Norwegian from my Grandpa Ahlström, but Swedish was a whole new linguistic beast. *Beast*. I looked over my shoulder and shuddered.

"*Flicka*. It means girl. Let's get you back to the house. Charlotte and Heather can't wait to meet you."

"They weren't home when I left," I told Brynn as we walked toward town. The sky had dimmed considerably while I was passed out—now the last rays of daylight filtered through the thick trees.

"They're going to meet up with us at the party later."

"The party? I'm not sure I'm up for a party . . ." I glanced at my arm again. Not so much as a stitch of pain. *How is that even possible?*

"Just a little gathering. You'll be up for it!" Brynn giggled. "You're looking better—the color's back in your cheeks. You'll be fine by the time we have to meet the girls."

"Did you see what happened back there?"

Brynn shook her head, her big green eyes brimming with concern. "No. I was jogging, and I saw you lying on the ground. You must have passed out while you were running. Has that ever happened to you before?"

"You didn't see the giant animal? Some kind of mountain lion-wolf thing? Or the huge blond guy with massive muscles and a death wish?"

"I must have missed them." Brynn trilled. "Wouldn't have minded seeing massive muscle man, though."

I scratched the back of my neck. So I *was* losing my mind. My brother Jason would have a field day with this story.

"Come on," Brynn bounded ahead, her golden ponytail bouncing high on her head. "Let's call for pizza. I'm starving, and you need to get your blood sugar up."

She bobbed her head, and I jogged tentatively after her. Nothing hurt, so I ran faster, matching her pace. Maybe all the fresh air had got to me. Or maybe I shouldn't have jumped right into a workout after five days in a car. Whatever happened, there most definitely had not been an attack on my arm—it was fit as a fiddle. And pizza and a party would make a *much* better first-day-at-college story to tell my brother than dwelling on a made-up mountain beast. Although standing around with a bunch of strangers, even if it was only a 'little gathering', sounded as appealing as showing up to a test without studying first. *Baby steps, Ahlström. You have to start somewhere.*

I sucked in a breath and kept running. Looked like that somewhere started now.

* * * *

"You're going to do *what?*" My brother's all-American face formed a mask of shock. I rested my iPhone against my mirror and so I could FaceTime with Jason at the same time as I put on my makeup. Multitasking for the win.

"You heard me. I'm going to a party."

"You hate crowds." Jason pointed out the obvious.

"Don't remind me." I repressed a shudder. "My roommate says it's just some freshmen down the block, so maybe it won't be that bad."

"I don't even know you anymore. Does the Math Club know you're going to a party? I thought Friday nights were reserved for Fun With Fractions." Jason's violet blue eyes crinkled in a smile. They were the exact same shade as mine.

"Har-dee-har-har. For your information, math can be fun, too."

Jason snorted. "You keep telling yourself that."

"Aren't you in a *business* fraternity, Mr. High And Mighty?"

"Yes ma'am." Jason nodded. "And Kappa O throws the best keggers on campus. Though I'm sure the Math Club's thrown some real ragers in their day."

I stuck out my tongue and unscrewed my liquid eyeliner. "How's Mama holding up?"

"She's better now that you're safe in Arcata. Letting her seventeen-year-old baby girl drive cross country by herself wasn't easy for her, you know."

"I'll be eighteen in three months," I reminded him. "And she seemed much calmer about my road trip once I installed that GPS thing on her phone so she could check on me twenty-four seven." I drew a line above my lashes, flicking it up at the corner of my eye.

"Speaking of, Dad just disabled the app for stalking on our end, so you can live out your college days in relative peace. He says to tell you *you're welcome*."

"Bless him." I lined my other eye.

Jason adjusted his baseball cap. "So how was the trip?"

"Mostly okay. I blew a tire about halfway through Nebraska and nearly ruined my brand new suede riding boots changing it in the middle of a rainstorm. I was in such a rush to get out of Buckshire, I forgot to weatherproof them."

"Oh, no. You forgot to weatherproof your boots?" Jason put his hands on his cheeks and dropped his jaw.

"Stop it, it's a big deal!" I loved my brother, but Jason knew diddly-squat about shoes.

Jason blinked. "You do realize not everything has to be so serious, right? Some things are just supposed to be fun."

I mulled that over while I curled my lashes. With our chocolate brown hair and athletic builds, Jason and I were obviously cut from the same DNA, but where my brother was playful and outgoing, the quarterback of his prep school football team and consummate life of the party, I preferred a lower profile. My best subjects were math and science—things with concrete, black-and-white answers, since grey didn't sit right with me. My choices had yielded a life that proceeded in an orderly, straightforward manner, which was exactly the way I liked it. A lifetime of meticulous planning meant things rarely ruffled my feathers . . . including my all-knowing, charming, loveable brother. He was the one person I could count on to be honest with me, no matter what, and I adored him for it.

"Jason?" I asked, swiping my first coat of mascara.

"Yes?"

"I'm going to like it here, right?"

"Is Mia Ahlström admitting she's nervous?"

"Don't tell anyone." My cheeks tingled. My inability to hide emotions lived on the border of absurd and mortifying.

"You'll love it." Jason nodded inside the screen. "An entire university full of math geeks? You'll fit right in."

I stuck my tongue out as I swiped on my second coat, then moved to my other eye. "I'm serious. I don't want to be the loner in the corner at a school full of . . ."

"Math geeks," Jason repeated himself. "You'll be their queen."

"I will not hesitate to disconnect you." I pointed one menacing finger at the phone.

"All right!" Jason held up his hands in mock surrender. I turned my attention back to my makeup bag. *Blush, blush, blush . . . ah, there it is.* I snatched up the black compact and dusted off my brush. "Seriously, you'll be fine. You keep the family together, like Meemaw. You won that Junior League award thing for teambuilding last year." Jason was on a roll now, counting on his fingers. "You were head girl at Tottenham Prep, and kept all those underclassmen from killing each other during pillow fights. If you can keep the peace at one of the snootiest boarding schools in the tri-state area, you won't have any problem making friends with some California hippies. Though it'd probably be easier if you lived on campus. Why are you renting a house instead of living in the dorms?"

"You know why." I polished a rosy pink powder on the apples of my cheeks. "I spent forever in a dorm. All those teenage girls breathing down your neck gets a little cloying."

"I think it sounds perfect." Jason wiggled his eyebrows.

"You would."

"So you've got your roommates all sorted and everything?" He ran his hand through his hair.

"Yep. The school matched us based on a personality questionnaire. A sort of *eHarmony* for housemates."

"They do that even if you're not living in one of the residence halls?" Jason asked.

"Redwood does." I shrugged. "It came with the freshman orientation packet. I just checked the box that said 'off-campus housing' and filled out the form. A few weeks later they sent Heather and Charlotte's names and e-mail addresses. A week ago we got another roommate—Brynn."

"Cool name." A sly grin spread across Jason's face. "I'll bet she's some super hot athlete chick."

"She's really pretty," I agreed. "She's from Sweden. She's the only one I've met so far."

"Swedish? Definitely super hot then. I'll be sure to come visit." Jason nodded. "Well, I'm sure you know what you're doing. Start with your roommates, and branch out from there. You'll be fine."

"Thanks, Jase." I quickly lined my lips, then filled them in with a pinky-nude lipstick.

"Hey, listen. I know you've always done things a certain way. You're my little rule follower, and that's great. Usually."

"There's a *but* coming, isn't there?" I smiled. It was impossible to be annoyed with someone who always looked out for you.

Well, not impossible . . .

"But . . ." Jason returned my smile. "Life isn't always black and white. Sometimes you'll find yourself in a situation our upbringing didn't prepare you for. God knows I have. I just want you to promise me one thing."

"What?"

"Break a few of your all-important rules for me. College is full of once-in-a-lifetime experiences. It's the most freedom with the least responsibility we're ever going to have. Stay out late, go crazy at parties, maybe even go on a date once in a while. I promise they won't kick you out of Math Club for having a little fun."

"I have fun." My chin jutted upwards. If Jason didn't think quadratic equations and ski practice were fun, then he didn't have the sense God gave a goat.

"Just live a little. That's all I'm saying."

Since my brother was prone to spouting wisdom worthy

24

of a tiny green Jedi master, I forgave his ignorance surrounding the joy of math. "Okay, Bro-da. Just for you."

Jason chuckled. He looked so pleased with himself that I didn't have the heart to point out he was dead wrong. Sure, math and "chick sports" might not constitute "living" in his world. But I *did* know what life held for me: college, a cutting-edge engineering job, and a "happily-evah-aftah" with a real-life Prince Charming, just like our maternal southern belle always promised.

"Well, I'd better go. Wish me luck at this thing."

"Party on, Mees." Jason held up his hand in a fist. "You've got this.

"Thanks. Try not to break too many hearts this semester, okay?"

"I never make a promise I can't keep." Jason shot me a wink, and I laughed.

"Love you, Jase."

"Love you, Mia."

I turned off my phone and slid it into my back pocket, then took a deep breath and walked purposefully down the hall.

Here we go.

* * * *

When I was halfway down the staircase, I was accosted by a whirlwind of blond curls and vanilla perfume.

25

"Are you ready or what, *flicka*? Charlotte just texted me—she and Heather are already at the party. Let's go!"

Brynn bounced on her tiptoes, her pale green eyes radiating joy and her ear-splitting smile brimming with energy. If she was going to be this chipper all the time, I'd be sure to hit the coffee before our paths crossed in the mornings.

"How do I look?" I twirled.

Brynn eyed me from top to bottom. "Hair—touchably soft. Makeup—subtly sexy. Outfit—chic yet comfortable. You can't go wrong with skinny jeans. You're *perfekt*. And we're missing all the fun—come on!" Brynn grabbed me by the wrist and pulled me down the stairs.

"I just have to grab—"

"You're fine." The living embodiment of cheer bounded for the front door, dragging me behind her. She skipped down the porch steps so quickly, I practically had to run to keep up. How did anyone have this much energy at nine p.m.? Brynn must have been a night owl.

We made our way across the street and onto the lawn of a three-story Victorian. Brynn navigated the sea of students strewn across the grass, making her way toward two girls on the front porch, holding red cups. As we got closer, I recognized them from the pictures we'd exchanged. *Smile on. It's time to meet the roommates.*

"Heather! Charlotte! I got her!" Brynn finally let go of my wrist, and propelled me unceremoniously onto the porch. I stopped myself just before stepping on the shorter girl's black Converse sneakers.

"Sorry," I apologized.

"No worries." The girl waved. She had crimson hair that fell in soft waves around her face. Her boyfriend jeans, graphic tee and green rectangular-framed glasses gave off a hipster vibe. "I'm Heather."

"And I'm Charlotte. So lovely to meet you after all those e-mails, Mia." Charlotte held out her hand, and I shook it. She had silky, black hair that fell in an angled bob to the top of her shoulders, with thick bangs that must have needed weekly trims, and she wore suede ankle boots that were to die for.

"It was definitely a long summer. It's great to meet you both." I nodded at Charlotte's feet. "Fabulous boots."

"I picked them up this afternoon," she confessed. She spoke with the prim cadence of a librarian, but her brown eyes were crinkled in a friendly expression and her smile radiated warmth. From the way she stood—spine straight, shoulders back, hands folded softly at her waist—I guessed she was either a fellow prep school graduate, or had the 'pleasure' of attending cotillion, the South's equivalent to etiquette boot camp.

"Charlotte's obsessed with shoes. She picked up *four* pairs on her Target run, which was supposed to be for laundry detergent." Heather hooked her thumbs in her belt loops. She had the kind of throaty voice I imagined black-and-white film stars must have had, and her words came at their own pace; leisurely, like a jazz melody on a summer afternoon.

"And I came *out* with laundry detergent." Charlotte put her hand on her hip.

"Along with?" Heather pushed her glasses up on her

nose with one finger. She'd painted her nails the same shade of green as her frames. *Fun.*

"Along with a fedora, a new belt and . . . four pairs of shoes." Charlotte huffed. "I do not see the problem with sampling the local merchandise."

"What you sampled was made in China," Heather pointed out.

"Well, then the sales tax boosted the city's economy. Or something. And it's not like I didn't offer to share them with you. *Moi* closet is *toi* closet. That goes for all of you." Charlotte smiled beatifically.

"I could be in for a clothes swap." I nodded. Quadrupling my wardrobe without setting foot in a store sounded like a fabulous deal. "If what we're wearing tonight is a barometer for the rest of our clothes, we've got just about every look covered."

"And speaking of looks . . ." Brynn tilted her head to the side. "Somebody's checking you out, Charlotte."

Our eyes followed Brynn's gesture. On the other side of the porch, two guys sipped from red plastic cups and stared at our little group. Charlotte's perfect posture straightened even more.

"The one on the right is Matt. He brought over the flier about the party. He's from Texas," Charlotte whispered.

"And the hottie on the left was washing his car shirtless in the front yard this afternoon. He's got smokin' arms, and that's all I need to know." Heather pulled her shoulders back, thrusting her chest forward in the process.

"Well, it sounds like you two have work to do. I'll

expect a full report back at the house." I nudged them gently toward their would-be suitors and turned to Brynn with a smile. "What about you? Anyone here catch your eye?"

"Yes." Brynn giggled as she grabbed my wrist and trotted toward the front door. She must have downed one of those energy drinks while I was in the shower. It wasn't humanly possible for anyone to be this perky without chemical assistance.

"Oh good. They did come!" Brynn bubbled. She smoothed the front of her sweater as she walked into the house, and turned around, waving for me to follow her. My stomach dropped the minute I entered the room. Brynn smiled at me, oblivious. "How are my teeth?"

"Um, pearly white. How are mine?" I flashed a grin, but my teeth were the least of my concerns. Sixty people must have been packed into the tiny space, with more spilling over into what I assumed was the kitchen. *Little gathering my left foot.* I shuddered. Jason would have rolled his eyes at my insecurity, but this living room was absolutely packed with flannel-shirted athletes and the co-eds dressed to impress them. RSU students had an awful lot of low-cut tops and generous bosoms. My fingers grazed the top of my V-necked sweater—it stopped a good inch north of my cleavage. *Well, shoot.* If my Prince Charming was at this party, he'd better find clavicles sexy.

Brynn waved across the room, her long blond curls bouncing against her back. Then she clapped her hands together and squealed. "Yay!"

There was no way not to smile. Brynn's energy was infectious. "Who are you waving at?"

"My friends from back home. Come on." She tugged at my hand and practically dragged me into the mob of inebriated college students. "I'll introduce you."

Brynn raced across the living room, expertly dodging red plastic cups and lip-locked lovers. I kept my eyes on the tiny feet skipping in front of me and moved with as much care as possible while being hurtled through what amounted to the ultimate kegger obstacle course.

Since I was staring at the ground, I failed to see the mountain before I plowed into it.

Ouch.

"Whoa. Slow down." Strong hands gripped my shoulders as I tumbled backward. They set me gently on my feet and held tight. I waited for my ears to stop ringing. "Brynn's not the greatest navigator. You okay?"

"I'm fine. I think . . ." I managed to look up and my hand flew to my forehead. Occasionally, I'd fallen hard enough on the slopes to see double, but I'd never imagined an entire person before. The guy holding onto my shoulders *obviously* wasn't real; nobody could actually look like that. He was tall; he probably had a foot on my five-feet, seven-inches. He was huge; calling him a mountain hadn't been much of a stretch. His hands could have circled my waist easily, and biceps the circumference of a baby sequoia strained against his T-shirt. And his eyes . . . they were a midnight blue I thought I'd seen exactly once before. They held my gaze for an endless moment, sucking me into their bottomless depths. I was completely mesmerized, and at the same time I felt as if the wind had been knocked out of me. *It couldn't be him. Nothing actually happened in the forest.*

I ignored the throbbing in my wrist where I'd dreamed the terrifying animal had latched on to my arm, and I tried to pretend Hercules' voice didn't match the deep growl of my imaginary savior. *The imaginary savior I conjured up in my exhaustion-induced delirium.*

My fingers dropped to my cheeks, which tingled in the slightly uncomfortable way they did after a really hard workout. My head swam, whether from the impact of our collision or his touch, I couldn't be sure.

Seriously, he *couldn't* be real.

The stranger's sandy blond hair stood in artfully arranged disarray atop a face that looked as if it had been lifted off a movie star. High angular cheekbones, a strong, square jaw, and pale pink lips with just a hint of fullness were accented by those eyes that seemed to bore right through me. My heart pounded against my chest at twice its normal pace, sending a very clear message to my very addled brain.

Oh, yum.

"How many fingers am I holding up?" Hercules took one hand off my shoulder to flash two fingers. His eyes never broke contact while he assessed my reaction.

"Uh . . . two?" The squeak in my voice betrayed my nerves. Maybe he wouldn't notice the flames bursting off my overheated cheeks like sunspots. I cleared my throat and dropped my voice a register. "Two."

The stranger chuckled. "Well, your vision wasn't impaired by Brynn's lousy leadership."

My knees buckled at the sound of his laughter. When Hercules reached out to catch my waist, the inferno in my cheeks blazed anew. *Get it together, Ahlström.*

"You sure you're okay?" he asked.

"I'm . . . uh . . . I'm great. Thank you." I fought against his magnetic pull and stepped back, raising my voice to be heard above the music. "I'm Mia. You must be Brynn's friend." *The friend she forgot to mention just walked off the cover of* Men's Fitness. The guy was absolute physical perfection—every single one of his abs was clearly visible through the fabric of his light blue T-shirt. Forget the six-pack, there was a bulk-discount-store *case* of muscles underneath that thin layer of cotton.

"Must be," the stranger said lightly. He held out his hand and gave mine a gentle squeeze. "I'm Tyr Fredriksen. And this is Henrik Andersson."

Tee-eer and Henrik?

For the first time, I noticed there were two mountain-sized men standing with Brynn. The second was a few inches shorter than Tyr, with grey-blue eyes shielded by thin silver-framed glasses. He wore his two hundred-plus pounds of muscle on a slightly leaner frame, and his smile gave him the kind of charisma intrinsic in actors or politicians. No wonder Brynn was beaming up at him.

"*Hei hei.*" Henrik nodded at me. "Sorry about Miss Brynn. If you think that was bad, you should see her drive."

"Oh, stop it." Brynn swatted at Henrik. "I haven't seen you for days. Please tell me you haven't been in front of the TV. I promised your mom I wouldn't let you go down the video game vortex. Again."

Henrik patted her arm. "So cute. You think you could stop us."

The way they were built, I was pretty sure a dinosaur driving a bulldozer couldn't stop Brynn's buddies from doing whatever they darn well pleased. But propriety dictated I keep my thoughts to myself.

Brynn rolled her eyes. "Mia, these nerds are two of my oldest friends. Henrik and I grew up next door to each other, and I've known Tyr since grade school."

I tried to picture the dynamic duo as precocious six-year-olds, but came up short.

"Are you guys freshmen, too?" I asked.

Brynn giggled. "Henrik's little brother Gunnar is my year, but this guy here is an old man."

Henrik nodded. "I just started my Master's in Biomechanical Engineering."

"I'm in Engineering too." I smiled. "So is this your first time in the US?"

Henrik glanced at Tyr, who answered after a pause. "We've visited before."

"What are you studying?" I asked him.

"The world." He smiled lazily. My pulse quickened as I tried not to stare at his mouth.

Brynn rolled her eyes. "Play nice, Tyr."

"Says the girl who just catapulted her friend into a total stranger. You're hardly one to talk." Tyr raised an eyebrow.

"No harm. No party foul." I gingerly touched the spot where my cheek had met Tyr's chest bone. Then I held up my hand. "Not even any blood."

Brynn buried her head in her hands. "Ugh. I'm sorry,

Mia."

I patted her back. "I'm fine, honest."

"Let's get you something to drink, Brynnie. You guys want anything?" Henrik pushed his glasses up the strong line of his nose.

"I'm good." Tyr shook his head.

"No, thank you," I added.

"Okay. Catch you later." Henrik led a beet-red Brynn into the crowd, leaving me with Hercules.

"So you're Brynn's roommate?" I nodded. "She may not be very graceful, but she's as loyal as they come." Tyr's voice was as beautiful as his face. Though it had the same singsong lilt of his Scandinavian friends, it was deep and husky—like he'd just woken up.

Double yum.

I pushed that image out of my mind as I met his eyes. "Y'all are great friends, aren't you?"

"Yes." Tyr smiled. "Y'all? Are you from one of the southern states?"

The way he said it was so precise; it was obvious he was translating as he spoke. "No." Heat rushed to my cheeks. "I'm from Connecticut, but my mom grew up in Louisiana. Some of her southern belle rubbed off."

There was no reason to tell Tyr the drawl only slipped out when I was really nervous. Like, standing-in-front-of-a-movie-star-Norseman-in-the-middle-of-a-room-full-of-people-trying-not-to-pass-out nervous. My wobbly voice and fidgety hands probably spoke volumes. It also hadn't escaped my notice that while we talked, *every single female* in the room was sizing Tyr up as if he was every bit the pinnacle of physical perfection. The looks they fired at me weren't nearly so charitable.

A dozen inebriated boys burst through the front door, singing loudly. They swayed back and forth *almost* in time to their off-key tune, and as they did the contents of their plastic cups sloshed violently. At the end of the verse, one threw his arm into the air, sending his beer flying across the room.

Everything moved in slow motion as I watched the cup come straight at me. There wasn't enough time to get out of the way, and I stared in horror, waiting for an hour of primping and a perfectly good cashmere sweater to be destroyed by a single cup of beer. But Tyr swatted it out of the air as it hurtled toward my chest, and the spray of liquid took an abrupt diversion toward the guy standing next to us. Relief washed through me in the second before reality set in.

Wait—did I see that right? A cup of beer just defied the laws of physics? I rubbed my eyes. My five days of travel had clearly messed with my brain.

"Sorry about that," Tyr apologized. The guy wiped splatters of alcohol from his arm and shrugged before leaning closer to the girl he was talking to. From the way she angled her chest up at him, his beer-covered pants weren't going to hurt his chances. "*Uff da*," Tyr muttered.

I blinked. "*Uff da?* That's Norwegian. I thought you were Swedish."

"You speak Norwegian?"

"Not really," I admitted. "But my dad's dad is half

Norwegian, and he says that a lot."

"Ah." Tyr paused for a long moment. "My friends and I speak a mash-up of the Nordic languages—more 'Scandiwegian' than either Norwegian or Swedish. We're Swedish, but we've spent chunks of time in both places, so our language is across the board, you know?"

I exhaled slowly, pressing my hands against my jeans. Between the flying beer and the multi-lingual male model holding my attention, this entire scene was overwhelming. I needed some breathing room.

As if he'd read my thoughts, Tyr tilted his head, and gave me a look that was half invitation, half challenge. "That's about all the indoor fun I can handle for one night. Care to join me outside?" I shot him a grateful look, and he took a step toward the back door. "Let's get out of here."

I nodded.

Tyr grabbed my hand, and a pulse of heat shot from my fingertips to my toes. Butterflies took flight somewhere south of my navel, siphoning all the blood from my head and leaving me with the not altogether uncomfortable feeling of floating across the living room. Tyr was without a doubt the hottest guy I'd ever seen, and he was holding my hand.

Holding. My. Hand.

Dear God, please don't let me pass out. At least let me give this guy my number first. Also, thanks for letting me meet him on a good hair day. Xoxo, Mia.

Without a word, Tyr led me through the throng of jostling bodies, past the speakers blaring a rock song, and out the back door. To my credit, my feet did not betray me—I did not trip once. My mind, however, twirled like a two-year-old in a tutu. The backyard was quieter, with only a handful of students scattered across the lawn. We stopped on the top of the three steps that led from the porch to the yard. Tyr sat down. He patted the stair next to him, and I sat to his right, wrapping my arms around my knees.

"A little out of control in there, *ja?*" Tyr's voice was softer now that we were away from the music.

I nodded, then bit my lower lip. I was afraid of what would come out of my mouth if I opened it. *Thanks for getting me out of that nuthouse. You're hot. You saved my favorite sweater in a touching display of chivalry. Can I touch your muscles? Thanks for blocking that beer. Want to make out?* The possibilities for honesty-induced mortification were endless.

Tyr stared as I nibbled on my lip. His mouth parted, and his eyes darkened a shade. He raised his hand as if he was going to touch my face, then pulled it back. With a sigh, he shifted his eyes away from my mouth.

Breathe, Ahlström. Breathe.

"So, Mia. You're from Connecticut?" I was grateful when Tyr tossed out a softball question.

"Yeah, a town called Buckshire. Pretty river, lots of meadows and open space. Typical small-town America."

"I'm new here. What does that mean?" Tyr stared as a guy and a girl made their way across the yard.

"Just that it's pretty old-fashioned where I'm from. Friday-night movies in the town square, family picnics on Sundays . . . my mom's a homemaker, my dad works in finance in the city. My brother's a Business major at Penn State now, but when we were younger we did everything as a family—hiking, camping, fishing, hunting-"

"Hunting? You?" Tyr gave me a once over. "The tiny thing wearing pearls to a college party? You know how to hold a gun?"

I lifted my chin. "Don't underestimate me. I can go from makeup to mud faster than you can say 'bless your heart.'"

Tyr chuckled. "I'd like to see that."

"Play your cards right, and maybe you will." A smug smile tugged at my lips, and I gave myself a mental high five for finishing an entire train of thought without babbling. *Score one, Mia.*

Tyr raised one eyebrow as he leaned back on his hands and appraised me. His gaze slid slowly down the length of my body then moved back up, pausing a moment longer than necessary at my chest. Heat flooded my neck at the intimacy in his stare. But when Tyr brought his eyes up to meet mine, he didn't look the slightest bit guilty. Instead, he winked and shot me a rakish grin. "Maybe I will."

Oh my goodness gracious. Who did this guy think he was? And more importantly, what was I letting him do to me? I was ninety-nine percent positive it was not appropriate to *actually* pant over a guy you just met.

Not to his face, anyway.

I unwrapped my arms from my knees and tossed my hair over my shoulder. *Fake it till you make it.* "So you're from Sweden?" I leaned back, copying Tyr's pose. I *wished* I felt as cool as he looked. "What's that like? Lots of polar bears? Igloos? You guys travel by dog sled?"

Tyr shook his head, amusement dancing across his features. "You are funny."

"That's the rumor."

"I moved here from Malmö. It's a fishing village on the southern tip of Sweden, sadly lacking in polar bears, but attempting to make up for it with a solid nightlife and extraordinary football club."

"*Football*, football, or *soccer* football?"

Tyr narrowed his eyes. "Soccer football. You realize this is the only country in the world that uses the wrong name for the second-greatest sport in the realms."

"Realms?" I raised an eyebrow.

"Universe," he corrected quickly. *Must be a translation thing.*

"What's the first greatest sport?"

"Rugby." Tyr said it as if it were obvious.

"That's a big deal in my hometown too. The local high school was county champion three years running."

"So you understand."

"Not really. I went to Tottenham, the girls' boarding school two towns over. We didn't play rugby, but we did a lot of skiing. You *do* have that in Sweden, right?"

"*Ja.* The polar bears operate our chair lifts."

"Ha." I nudged Tyr with my knee. The small contact sent a burst of heat all the way to my toes, and I quickly pulled away. It would be harder to keep my cool if I melted into a hormone-induced puddle.

"So you ski?" Tyr asked. I forced myself to stare into his bottomless eyes, the ones that were studying me so intently they might have been trying to see through my soul.

"Um, yes. My team was state champion in Super G last year." Super G—the race faster than Giant Slalom, but with more gates than Downhill—was my event of choice. As much as I liked control, I liked speed more. "My boarding school was close to a half-decent mountain, so we'd run gates locally during the week. But we'd head to Vermont or New Hampshire for the weekends we wanted to *really* ski. You can't beat bulletproof-ice for training, you know?"

"You competed?" The surprise on Tyr's face was as comical as it was insulting.

"I was captain and dry-land training coach, two years running." I resisted the urge to tell him how many pull-ups I could do. He obviously thought I was a total maladroit. After all, I *had* run into him . . .

"And you did Super G?" There it was again—the too-intense stare, as if he was trying to read my mind. "I owe you an apology; I took you for a princess."

"Why?" Between my flaming cheeks and awkward babbling, there wasn't much regal about me right now.

"Fancy shoes, cashmere sweater, pearls? You seem like the kind of girl the birds and bunnies follow around the forest, singing songs."

"You got your entire understanding of American culture from Disney movies, didn't you?"

"Maybe." Tyr's gorgeous smile brought a fresh wave of heat to my cheeks. I tilted my head back and held his gaze, ignoring the urge to hide behind my hair. "Super G's tough.

You must have taken a lot of falls."

"I took a few. But the birds and bunnies diverted a lot of the snow snakes for me."

"Funny. Just for that I'm calling you *prinsessa*."

"Do I get to make up a name for you?" I asked.

"Nope."

"That hardly seems fair."

"Life's not fair." Tyr kept his voice even, but his jaw clenched, lending an edge to his already intimidating presence. He had an intensity bubbling just beneath the surface that made me wonder what exactly he'd been doing back in that Swedish fishing village. Brynn had warned him to play nice—what did that mean? Before I could wander too far down that trail of thought, Tyr's mouth curled up in a half-smile, and my brain went quiet.

God, he was beautiful.

He leaned over so his face was right next to mine, and my heart beat a frantic rhythm. My breath shallowed to sharp gasps. If this kept up I was going to black out. Death by nervous flirting.

"Are you in the same program as Henrik?" I blurted.

"I'm not in school. I'm just tagging along." He ran a hand through his hair and quickly added, "So Engineering for you?"

He was avoiding the question? Sensing his discomfort made me feel a little better. Maybe he was as nervous as me.

I nodded, feeling braver. "I like structure. I like when things add up."

"So you like being in control?" He winked. Nope, definitely not nervous; Captain Cool was back.

"That's not quite what I said."

"It's kind of what you said," Tyr pointed out.

"Well, it's not what I meant. Not at all. Well, not *not at all*—I mean, I like control. Of things, not people. I don't try to control people. Just situations."

"You like to control situations?" Tyr's lips quivered with barely contained amusement.

Abort. Abort. Pull it together, Ahlström. You were doing so well.

"No! That's not what I mean. I just mean I like schedules, you know? And routines. Lists. Totally reasonable things. Like, I go to bed early so I don't sleep through a workout. That's just good sense."

"I see." Tyr chuckled. "You like *perfekt* order."

"Don't you?" I wrung my fingers together as I glanced up. If he didn't, I was *so* the wrong girl for him.

"Yes," he answered seriously. "I do."

I exhaled slowly. *Thank you, God.*

We sat in silence for a long moment. I was afraid to open my mouth after the whole control-freak-debacle.

"So tell me, *prinsessa*," Tyr broke the quiet, "do you like Italian food?"

Was he asking me out? Maybe Tyr *did* have a thing for clavicles! Before I could answer the question that I hoped might be the invitation to my own collegiate happily-evah-aftah, Tyr's phone buzzed loudly in his pocket.

"*Skit*," he swore as he brought the device to his ear. "*Ja?*"

Disappointment flooded my veins, drowning me in its bitter taste. Who took a call in the middle of asking a girl out? Unless maybe he hadn't been going to ask me out. He could have just been asking about my dietary preferences. No, that was just weird. He was definitely asking me out. *Me*, the girl who'd kissed three boys in seventeen years was *this close* to being asked out by a six-and-a-half-foot Swedish dreamboat who looked as if he'd just climbed down off Mount Olympus. But then his stupid phone had to ring. And he had to answer it.

Which was just rude, really.

"*Ja.* I understand. How low are her levels?" Tyr ground his fist into his thigh as he turned away from me. "How did that happen?"

His posture positively seethed dejection—his shoulders tensed, his back hunched, and his head hung low. He must have gotten some truly terrible news. Guilt at my selfishness seeped through the disappointment, and I reached out to touch his arm.

"No. Do nothing. I'll be right there." He turned off the phone and shoved it in his pocket. He swore one more time, then took a deep breath. When he turned around, his expression was hard.

"Tyr?" I asked softly.

"I have to go." He stood abruptly. I scrambled to my feet.

"Is there anything I can do to help?" There was no point in asking if things were okay; they obviously weren't.

The corners of Tyr's eyes crinkled. He reached out to touch my cheek with the back of one finger. My body responded, and I leaned into him, tilting my face into his hand.

Tyr leaned down and touched his lips to my forehead. He inhaled deeply before pulling away. My heart dropped. "You are sweet. But no."

"Oh." I tucked my hands in my pockets and shifted my weight to my back leg. *Bury it, Mia. It's just a guy. One you've only known two minutes.* "Okay."

Tyr looked as if he wanted to say more, but as soon as he opened his mouth he snapped it shut again without a single mention of food, Italian or any other. He stepped down off the porch and walked toward the grass with long strides, then turned and looked back at me. "Take care of yourself."

With that he bolted. He was across the lawn and around the corner of the house before I could blink.

CHAPTER THREE

"SO NOTHING HAPPENED?" BRYNN didn't try to hide the incredulity from her voice.

"Nada. Zip. Zilch." I took a drag of my coffee and stared at my chipper roommate. Even at nine o'clock on a Sunday morning, she looked as if she had enough energy to run a full marathon. Loose blond curls were piled atop a face that looked unnaturally perfect without so much as a lick of makeup, and she sat on the living room floor in seiza position, wearing yoga pants and a sports bra.

"That sucks," Heather chimed in. She was sprawled across the love seat, still in flannel pajama pants and a T-shirt with the periodic table on the front. "Wonder what that call was all about."

"Who cares?" Charlotte waved her freshly manicured hand. "You don't want a guy like that. You want someone who appreciates the awesomeness that is Mia Ahlström: athlete, brainiac, fabulous dresser." Charlotte nodded at my Lulu capris and fitted vest, then pointed to the caddy of polishes on the table. "And a girl in need of a manicure. Come over here and pick your poison."

"Yes, ma'am." I cradled my coffee and moved to the couch next to Charlotte. Her nails now matched her pink silk pajamas. "Hmm. I think French tips, please."

"Classic taste." She pulled two bottles and an emery board, and went to work.

"I want to know how things went down with Texas Matt and the shirtless hottie." I turned my attention to Heather. "What was his name?"

"Jack." Heather grinned. "He's taking me to the beach next weekend."

"Because they already made out in the woods." Charlotte raised a perfectly groomed eyebrow.

Heather stuck out her tongue. "Oh, you're one to talk. You and Texas Matt looked pretty cozy on the porch swing when I got home last night."

Charlotte turned bright red. "You saw?"

"The whole block saw," Heather confirmed.

Charlotte gave a delicate 'harrumph' as she filed my nails to gently squared tips.

"What about you, Brynn? What happened with Henrik?" I asked.

"Henrik? Oh, nothing. We're just friends." She sighed.

"Do you want to be *just friends*?" Charlotte glanced up.

"It doesn't work like that for us. I'm not allowed to date," Brynn grumbled.

"You're not allowed to date?" Heather balked. "How is that even possible? And how would your parents know, anyway? They're in Sweden. Just don't tell them."

Brynn shook her head. "I wish it was that easy. I'm supposed to stay focused on, um, on what I'm here to do. Besides, Henrik sees me as his little brother's classmate. He's one of those guys who gets something in his head and never changes it."

Heather lifted her mug. "I think you just described all men."

"Truth," Charlotte chimed in.

"So what are we going to do today?" I diverted the conversation. "Did the summer orientation week show you what's fun around here? So far, I know there's a forest behind the house and a Target somewhere that calls to Charlotte with its siren song. Brynn, what do you know about this place?"

"Oh, about the same as you," Brynn chirped. Her voice sounded slightly off.

"You okay?" Charlotte looked up from my nails, and I pulled a hand away to take another hit of coffee.

"I'm great! Why don't you two give us a tour today? I haven't seen downtown yet." Brynn folded her hands in her lap.

"We need more caffeine first." Heather stood and padded to the kitchen in bare feet. She came back with the coffee pot, and held it up. "Refills?"

"Yes, please." Charlotte tilted her head toward her cup, and Heather poured.

"Double for me," I added.

Heather filled my cup, then her own. "Brynn?"

"I'm good." Brynn beamed. "I had my cup." She leaned

back into her seiza and perched on her toes. "But if we're going to take a tour, I'd better take a shower first. That six a.m. burn class at the gym was pretty intense. See you guys in half an hour?"

"Uh, it takes me longer than that to look presentable, and we've only got two bathrooms." Charlotte looked up from my hands. White tips now lined my nails, and she'd begun to paint the clear topcoat. "Say an hour-and-a-half?"

"*Perfekt!*" Brynn stood and bounded up the stairs, her curls bouncing atop her head. Heather, Charlotte and I stared after her.

Heather walked the coffee pot back to the kitchen. When she came back into the living room, she brought her mug to her lips. "Did she say she'd only had one cup?"

"I think so." I shook my head.

"Man." Heather set her cup down on the coffee table and rubbed the sleep from her eyes. "It's going to be a long year."

* * * *

Early that evening, we traipsed through the front door of our little house, weighed down with shopping bags.

"That, ladies, was a highly successful day." Charlotte headed up the stairs, carrying a trio of bags in each arm.

"The shoe industry won't know what hit it," Heather teased. "How many did you bring home?"

"I stopped counting after the third pair," Charlotte

called over her shoulder. "Besides, you're one to talk. Those ankle boots are going to look fabulous with your boyfriend jeans."

"I know." Heather grinned sheepishly. She followed me into the kitchen carrying the bags of vegetables we'd picked up at a farmer's market.

Brynn bounded into the room as I set my bags on the counter and started moving perishables to the fridge. "Speaking of fabulous, I'm so excited to try your chicken parm, Mia! Can I help?"

"It's super easy. But here; you do this." I traded spots with Brynn, and she started unpacking groceries. "And I'll work up the dinner schedule real quick."

"I know Mia suggested we trade cooking nights, but you guys should probably know in advance that my skill-set is more boxed hamburger helper and salad in a bag." Brynn handed Heather the produce and nestled cereal boxes in the cupboard.

"You told me that. Don't worry, I won't give you anything you can't handle." I sat at the kitchen table and started sketching on a piece of scrap paper. A minute later, I had an outline. "Where did I put the whiteboard?"

"That thing over there?" Brynn pointed at the white rectangle peeking out of the top of a shopping bag.

"Thanks." I carried my paper over to the bag, and removed the white board and colored pens. It was an erasable calendar, just like the one my mother used in our kitchen. I began to write, filling in each date with meals that could be made from the ingredients we'd bought that afternoon. When I was done, I peeled the stickers off the magnets on the back of the board, and stuck it to the fridge.

"Ta da!" I stepped back to admire my handiwork.

Heather looked up from folding empty grocery bags, and stood beside me. She raised one eyebrow.

"Wow, Mia. That's kind of amazing." Brynn burst into a smile that stretched from ear to ear.

"Thanks." I grinned back. "Will you please get out four chicken breasts, two eggs, and the breadcrumbs? I'll start breading so we can eat soon."

"Sure." As Brynn pulled out items, I cracked the eggs into a bowl and began whisking them smooth. Heather stood, still staring at the list.

"This thing is intense." Heather blinked.

I shrugged. "It's just a menu."

"And a chore chart. And it's color coded."

"The chores are just a suggestion." I flushed. "We can trade later, or come up with another system. This was just how we did it at my boarding school—saved fights, when everybody knew what to expect."

Charlotte came into the kitchen and furrowed her brow at the whiteboard. "This looks scary."

"Mia meal planned," Heather explained.

Brynn held up a frying pan, a question in her eyes. I nodded. "We need that. Add a little oil to it and set the burner to medium, please."

"Deal." Brynn did as I instructed. "What do the colors mean?"

"They're our designated cooking nights, the ones we picked in the car. But we can always switch if our schedules change."

"We can give it a go," Charlotte said agreeably.

"You have a side column for who's doing dishes, and who's cleaning bathrooms, and who tidies common areas on weekends." Heather took off her glasses and pinched the bridge of her nose.

"If it's too much, we can erase that. I'm not trying to push my cleaning schedule on you; we can figure that part out later," I hurried to explain. It had worked for us at Tottenham, but I didn't want to come off as overly pushy.

Heather tilted her head. "Not sure how I feel about a cleaning chart. But can you make me a study schedule?"

"You're pre-Med." I laughed. "I doubt you need my help studying."

"No," Heather agreed. "But I need help organizing my time. I want to volunteer at a clinic, but I'm trying to cram my course work into three-and-a-half years so I can do a semester with Doctors Without Borders before I graduate. And I'm not sure I can carry a full load of classes *and* volunteer."

"Hmm." I battered a chicken breast in breadcrumbs before placing it delicately in the hot oil, then filled a pot with water and set it on the stove. "We can work out a schedule for you tonight. I'm sure we can clear a few hours on the weekend for you to volunteer somewhere."

Brynn bounded to the cabinet and filled water glasses. "What about you Charlotte? What are your plans for the semester?"

"Classes, boys, shopping, more boys, and my internship." Charlotte straightened a spoon on the table.

"You have an internship already?" My brows shot up as I added noodles to the now-boiling water.

"My parents own an art gallery in San Francisco, and they know someone up here," Charlotte explained. "It's super part-time, maybe ten hours a week, but I'm excited."

Well, butter my toast. Classes hadn't even started and Charlotte was already working in her dream field. And Jason thought *I* was type A.

Brynn's phone rang, and she pulled it out of her pocket to check the screen. "It's Henrik. I'll be right back."

"Ooh, Henrik!" Charlotte teased. Brynn turned and beamed at us as she ducked out of the kitchen.

"He's cute," I drawled, as I poured some sauce into a small pan and left it covered on the stove to simmer.

"He's gorge," Heather chimed in. "Just friends, sure."

"Wonder how long that'll last." Charlotte grinned.

"Probably not as long as she thinks." I transferred the chicken to a baking dish, covered it with the remaining tomato sauce, and added a generous amount of cheese across the top before sticking the entire thing in the oven. "Time to parmesan. About four more minutes on the noodles."

"Four minutes?" Brynn poked her head into the kitchen. "Great. Be right back." She ran down the hallway and opened the front door, slamming it shut behind her.

"What the . . .?" Heather walked to the window and peeked outside. "Mmm-hmm."

Charlotte and I crossed to her side and poked our heads around the curtain. Outside, Henrik stood next to a jeep. I craned my neck to see if anyone else was in the car, and tried to ignore the disappointment that settled over me when I saw Tyr wasn't with him. Instead, I watched as Henrik handed Brynn a package. She beamed up at him.

"Aw. He brought her a present!"

"Wonder what it is. Oh. Move." Heather pushed us back to the table as Henrik turned toward the window. He didn't need to see three curious faces pressed against the glass. We could interrogate Brynn when she came inside.

"Act natural," Charlotte hissed. She and Heather pulled out chairs and feigned nonchalance while I gave the noodles one final stir. By the time the front door clicked open, our giggles were somewhat under control.

"I saw you guys." Brynn rolled her eyes as she came into the kitchen.

"Us?" Charlotte batted her eyelashes. "We don't know what you're talking about."

"Subtle," Brynn deadpanned. She grabbed something off the counter and slipped it into her pocket. I was too focused on not burning myself on the noodles to see what it was.

"Serving up in a couple minutes, ladies," I announced.

"Great." Brynn raced up the stairs while I stirred the remaining pasta sauce. By the time I'd plated the pasta and the chicken on two big platters for the table, Brynn was back in the kitchen. She leaned over the counter and held up my phone. "Looks like you missed a call, Mia. Who's Jason?"

"My brother. I'll call him later. Go sit down." I shooed her to the table.

She picked up her water glass. "I'm starving. Can I help dish up?"

"Nope. It's family style." I carried the dishes to the table and winked at my roommates. "Unless you want to tell us what Henrik gave you."

"Uh, nothing."

Knowing prevarication when I saw it, I raised my cup to divert the attention off Brynn. "To college life. And to dinners with new friends."

"Hear, hear," Charlotte agreed.

"*Skål,*" Brynn chimed in. "Cheers."

We clinked our glasses together. It wasn't the Sunday night dinner I was used to—the one with Mama's pot roast, Grandpa's bad jokes, and Jason and me fork-fighting over the last slice of Meemaw's mud pie. But this could be a different kind of family, and, I hoped, the start of a new kind of tradition. After all, Jason always said change was the first rung on the ladder of growth. And so far, Bro-da hadn't steered me wrong.

I winked at Brynn and brought my glass to my lips. "*Skål.*"

* * * *

At zero-dark-thirty on Monday morning, I laced up my running shoes and stepped outside. The air smelled fresh and crisp, like the tang of a freshly picked Macintosh. It was still early enough in the year that there was a sliver of light at this hour, but it wouldn't be long before my morning jogs required streetlights for illumination.

At the edge of our porch, I paused. The prudent thing to do would be to jog through the neighborhood and around campus. I was alone, I hadn't brought the mace I'd promised Daddy I'd keep on me at all times, and I didn't know what kinds of animals might be scouting for breakfast at this hour. Even though a couple of days had passed, the animal/mountain man hallucination was disturbingly vivid. But nothing had actually happened, and it would have been silly to let some weird nightmare keep me from those gorgeous jogging trails forever. Besides, if Google was to be believed, the trails behind my house were really popular hiking spots. People drove from all over California to see this particular patch of Redwoods. If there were a legitimate danger, Hikers.com wouldn't boast so many glowing recommendations.

I'd just follow a different trail this time. No need to trigger any freaky flashbacks.

I hung a left at the end of our driveway and headed toward the woods. The pavement turned to dirt, and my running shoes padded softly on the dusty surface as I inhaled forest air. The redwoods smelled of calm—pine, and dirt, and moss, and earth. The vibe was almost majestic.

According to Google, this particular path should loop through the woods, creating a five-mile track that came out just above campus. As promised, it started as a gentle slope. I lowered my head as I jogged up the hill. It didn't look difficult, but half a mile up, my calves were enveloped in a healthy burn. I ignored the sensation, and distracted myself with the first thought that came into my head. The image of Tyr offering me his hand wasn't particularly helpful, so I focused on circular breathing instead, inhaling through my nose and exhaling through my mouth. When I neared the top of the hill, I glanced up.

And immediately wished I hadn't.

"You have got to be kidding me," I muttered under my breath. A familiar silhouette stood at the top of the hill, hands shoved in the pockets of his hoodie. His back was to me, but his unnatural height, broad shoulders, and air of confidence left little doubt as to his identity. *Cheese and crackers.*

Since I wasn't awake enough to exchange fake pleasantries, I skidded to a stop and took a step back. A twig snapped under my feet. Tyr pulled his shoulders back and turned his head. The hood of his sweatshirt covered his hair, but his piercing blue gaze bore down on me from the top of the hill. His eyes narrowed infinitesimally as he gave a tight nod.

"*Hei hei*, Mia. Going somewhere?"

"Just out for a run." I glanced over my shoulder, wondering if there was any graceful way to hightail it out of the forest.

"Mmm." Tyr didn't move. Instead, he stared into the woods like he was surveying the woods for threats.

"Everything okay up there?"

"Couldn't be better. Why do you ask?" Tyr tore his eyes away from the tree line and looked directly at me. A fresh coat of sweat broke out across my forehead, and I wiped my face on my sleeve. With any luck he'd think I was tired from my run . . . since a lady did not *glisten* at the mere sight of her almost-date.

"You just look so serious," I offered.

"Usually do." He shrugged. "Which way were you headed?"

"Um . . . I was following the Woodside Trail—it's another mile over this hill, then it loops back toward campus."

"No." Tyr's voice was firm.

"No, it doesn't loop back?" I questioned.

"No, you're not going that way. We'll take the Sequoia Trail back." Tyr pointed to his right.

The hairs at the back of my neck prickled. "We? I'm sorry. Did I invite you to run with me?" I tried to keep my tone playful, but I didn't like the way Tyr told me what to do. Or the way he seemed to assume I'd just do what he said. Did girls just blindly follow orders where he came from?

Actually, they probably did. He just oozed the kind of raw power that all but screamed *Thou shalt do whatever I command. And thou shalt be extremely happy about it.*

"Apologies, *prinsessa*. May I join you for a run?" Tyr raised one eyebrow.

"Well, now you're just mocking me. I'll jog alone, thank you very much. Toodles." I marched up the hill and bumped Tyr's arm as I passed him. The contact sent a wave of heat along my side.

"Mia." Tyr's tone was low. "I told you not to go that way."

I whirled around, planting one hand firmly on my hip. "You don't get to tell me what trail to take."

"I do when it's for your own good. Let's go." Tyr jogged thirty feet along the ridge then turned around. "You coming?"

"My own good? Excuse me, who exactly do you think you are?"

"You don't want to know." Tyr met my stare as I sized him up.

"Maybe I don't."

"You just have to trust me, Mia."

I played with the thin gold band I wore on my pointer finger, an heirloom my Meemaw gave me when I graduated high school. On the one hand, I didn't like being told what to do, especially by someone who was pretty much a stranger, and without any kind of an explanation, or so much as a 'please.' But the truth was, I did want to run with Tyr. And that bothered me. Because I was in the middle of proving a very important point about my independence to a man who seemed to have an unfortunately backwards attitude about women—or maybe he just had a backwards attitude about me. Either way, caving at this particular moment seemed like a giant fail for the sisterhood, not to mention a landslide for my personal self-esteem.

But dang it, he'd seemed like a pretty decent guy the other night—one I wanted to get to know better. Plus, he looked really, really good in those shorts.

I raised my chin in a futile attempt to feign control. "Fine. I'll let you run with me. And we'll go your way . . . *today*. But Wednesday I'm taking the Woodside Trail. And you're not coming with me."

"It's a public trail. And I'm usually in the forest about this time."

"Well, next time I won't be so agreeable. This is a one-off, buddy. Don't get used to ordering me around."

"Whatever you say, *prinsessa*." Tyr took off at a slow lope, and I ran after him.

"Why do you care so much what trail I take, anyway?" We hung a left at the big rock and followed the sign pointing to the Sequoia Trail.

"It's not safe."

"You're worried about me?" I shot him a grin as we rounded the corner.

"You don't have the greatest sense of self-preservation." He looked down at me.

"Okay, now you're just being rude."

"A hiker was nearly attacked on the Woodside Trail last week. The rangers only just took down the signs warning about a possibly rabid animal. Didn't your roommates tell you?"

"No." My arm throbbed at the phantom animal bite, and I shivered. Maybe my imagination hadn't been so off after all.

"Well, they should have. It's not safe for anyone to be up there. Especially not someone who runs as slow as you do."

My head whipped up, evil eye at the ready, but Tyr grinned back at me.

"Oh, it's on." I lowered my head and pushed off the balls of my feet. Using all the force I could muster, I barreled through the thick grove of trees. Tyr's easy laugh sounded beside me as he kept my pace. I pumped my arms and pounded the dirt, cold air whipping my face as I moved. My eyes darted to the side. *Dang it.* He hadn't even broken a sweat. "Well, it's easy to run fast when your legs are seven feet long," I muttered.

"Mmm. Tell yourself whatever you need to hear."

"Rude." Realizing my chances of outrunning the Swedish giant were nil, I slowed to a normal pace. Tyr matched my stride.

"Speaking of rude, I'm sorry about the other night," he offered after a moment of silence. "About taking off like that."

"You definitely know how to make a dramatic exit. Everything okay?"

"Not really. But there's not a lot I can do right now."

"Want to talk about it?" I asked.

"No."

That was clear.

"I didn't do something to offend you, did I?" *You know, because you never finished asking me out.* I stared at the twigs beneath my feet as I ran.

"What? No. Nothing like that. I just had some . . . some personal stuff I needed to deal with." Tyr didn't offer anything more, and despite my *excellent* opening, he didn't ask any follow-up questions about any perfectly good first-date suggestions. With a silent sigh, I tabled my disappointment and resolved to live in the moment. Running through ancient redwoods with a superhero clone was definitely a once-in-a-lifetime experience . . . even if it did require bludgeoning my instinct to analyze Tyr's intentions and predict his future behavior. Old habits died hard with me.

We fell into a companionable silence as we made our way through the forest. The only sounds were the morning birds, the occasional falling pinecone, and our soft footsteps. After another mile, we reached the end of the trail. Tyr continued onto the pavement, and I followed.

"You and Brynn live this way." He nodded.

"Yep. Where's your place?" I jogged beside him.

"I'll run you home." That didn't answer my question, but his smile made me forget what I'd asked. The early morning sun filtered through the trees to hit the planes of his face, illuminating his spectacular features in an almost ethereal way. A light sheen lined his brow, and his eyes sparkled against softly tanned skin. His hood was still pulled over his hair, and I wondered if he had bed head underneath that fabric. *Stop, Mia.* No need to put *Tyr* and *bed* in the same sentence. Nothing was going to happen between us. Not even dinner.

"Turn right up here."

"I know where you are." Tyr jogged the three blocks to my house, and I tagged alongside him. He was probably being nice to me because he felt bad about the other night, but I didn't care. It was good to have company.

Especially such attractive company.

"Here we are." I stopped when we got to the front of the little house. Tyr slowed next to me.

"It's nice." He kept his eyes on mine.

"Thanks for crashing my run. Even though you were bossy about it."

Tyr adjusted the hood of his sweatshirt with a chuckle. "Do you run every day?"

"Most weekdays. I swim alternate days, and I take weekends off."

"That's quite an exercise plan. You don't do anything halfway, do you?"

"I try not to," I answered honestly.

"Hmm. Are you going to run in the forest again?"

"I'm planning to." The corners of my eyes crinkled. "Unless a certain bossy-pants is thinking of interfering with my trail run again."

"It's really not a good idea to take the Woodside Trail," Tyr stressed.

"So you mentioned." I reached up to adjust my ponytail. "Maybe you should come keep tabs on me again, to make sure I follow your approved routes."

Tyr's eyes widened a smidge. A half-smile broke out across his spectacular face as he took a step backwards. "Maybe I should. Six-thirty Wednesday morning. This yard. I'll be the one in the hoodie."

My breath hitched. Tyr wanted to see me again. Was he just obsessively controlling and wanted to make sure I did what he wanted? Or was he archaically chivalrous, and wanted to make sure I didn't get hurt? Or, and this was a big *or*, did he actually want to spend time with me? I didn't want to get my hopes up unnecessarily, but if I had any chance at a shot with this guy, I sure as the dickens didn't want to miss it.

"I'll be here," I squeaked.

"Great. See you then." Tyr opened his mouth as if he wanted to say something more, but instead he turned on one heel and raced down the street. He rounded the corner before I could even say goodbye.

We were seriously going to have to work on that boy's manners.

CHAPTER FOUR

MY FIRST OFFICIAL COLLEGE class was one of my general education classes—an Art History course called World Myth in Art. According to the syllabus, we'd start the year with northern European paintings. Though my knowledge of the art world was practically nonexistent, I had Charlotte in class with me. Between her parents' gallery and her internship, Charlotte was already an expert.

We slid into the front row just as class began. Our professor was a pretty woman in her mid-thirties, with light brown hair and eyes that lit up as she went over her outline.

"Okay, class." Professor Kopp looked up from the podium and clicked her remote at the projector. "We're starting our semester with the art and artists of Scandinavia. The pieces in this unit are based in Norse mythology, and while you don't need to have a comprehensive understanding of mythological hierarchy to appreciate the art, it does help to have a basic overview. So let's go over some of the basics. Who's familiar with Norse mythology?" Arms shot up all over the room, including Charlotte's.

"*Beyond* the *Thor* movie?"

Several kids dropped their raised hands.

"Okay. Scandinavia is made up of four of the world's northernmost countries, and that latitude results in long, dark winters. Culturally this has translated to darker folk tales, filled with terrifying monsters and heroic warriors. You'll see this reflected in the region's artwork. For example, this."

Professor Kopp clicked, and a new slide popped up.

"*The Ride to Asgard*, by Peter Nicolai Arbo. A Norwegian painter who lived from 1831 to 1892."

"That's dark," Charlotte whispered, as she clicked away on her laptop.

"No kidding." I stared at the painting. A herd of muddy brown horses ascended from a charred battlefield. The animals and their riders were so monotone, they almost blended together, save for a few blond female riders in the front line. Some carried dead bodies over their mounts, while black birds that looked like ravens swooped over the field. Artistically, it may have been a masterpiece. But it wasn't something I'd put out for company. It positively reeked of despair.

"*The Ride to Asgard* depicts a group of valkyries returning to Valhalla. Do those words mean anything to anyone here?" Professor Kopp asked.

Charlotte stopped her fiendish typing to raise her hand.

"Yes?" Professor Kopp nodded. "Miss . . ."

"Takayama. Charlotte Takayama," my roommate said.

"Go ahead, Miss Takayama."

"Asgard is the home of the Norse gods and the most

revered of the nine realms of Norse mythology, on par with Christianity's version of Heaven. Odin is the head of Asgard. Valkyries are Odin's warrior goddesses. They fly winged horses over Earth, and bring fallen soldiers back to a place called Valhalla. It's Odin's personal hall, and it's a massive structure big enough to house hundreds of fighters. The valkyries train the fallen soldiers to defend Asgard at Ragnarok, the mythological Norse apocalypse."

I blinked at Charlotte. Was all of that in the reading?

"Very good." Professor Kopp smiled. "So in Peter Arbo's painting, these warrior goddesses—valkyries—bring the dead soldiers back to Asgard, the realm of the gods. Those who lived dishonorably might go to Niflheim or Helheim—the Norse equivalent of Hell. Interestingly, the Norse hell is a world of primordial ice, which is reflected in many of the culture's most significant paintings. Now, Scandinavian paintings tend to idolize the upper echelon of their pantheon—Odin the ruler; Thor, God of Thunder; Freya, Goddess of Love; Loki, the Trickster. Ull, God of Winter . . ."

"Speaking of Scandinavians, was that Tyr who dropped you off at the crack of dawn this morning?" Charlotte whispered. "A little early in the semester for the walk of shame, though I have to admire your taste."

"What? No!" I hissed. "He barged in on my run, so we finished our workout together. That's it."

"Finished your workout together, eh?" Charlotte snickered. "That's what they called it at your prep school?"

"Yeah, no. It really was just a workout. But we're running together again on Wednesday."

"Really?" One of Charlotte's perfectly groomed eyebrows shot up. "Did he explain why he took off the other night?"

"Not specifically." I frowned.

"Well, maybe he will next time." Charlotte reached over and squeezed my hand. "That's exciting."

"I know. And kind of terrifying." My stomach was so jumpy after our encounter, I'd barely been able to scarf down a piece of dry toast before class.

"It doesn't have to be." Charlotte kept her voice low. She stared at our professor, typing as the teacher spoke. When Professor Kopp paused to look through her textbook, Charlotte turned to me. "Just try to have fun with it. You're only a freshman once."

I bit back a smile. "You really need to meet my brother."

Professor Kopp brought up a new slide. "Now as Charlotte said, the valkyries from Arbo's painting were charged with training humans to defend Asgard at Ragnarok, the final battle between good and evil. Henry Fuseli depicted Ragnarok in *Thor Fighting the World Serpent*. It ends badly for Thor the Thunder God—Asgard and most of its residents are destroyed, and the world is born anew. Notice the dark colors, the harsh lines, the feeling of desolation Fuseli manages to convey in this painting?"

"All I'm seeing is a giant naked god," Charlotte whispered. My fingers grazed my lips, covering my smile.

"Let's finish up with one of my favorites—Danish artist Lorenz Frölich's *Tor og Loki*. Created in the late 1800s, it shows Thor and the trickster god, Loki, traveling in bridal regalia to a realm called Jotunheim to recover Thor's magical hammer, Mjölnir. One of Jotunheim's frost giants captured the hammer, and refused to give it back unless he could have Freya, the Goddess of Love, as a bride. Freya refused, so Thor and Loki put on dresses and rode Thor's goat-driven chariot down to the icy realm to reclaim Thor's prize." Professor Kopp smiled at the image on the screen. "Who says Vikings didn't have a sense of humor?"

"I'm still thinking about the naked god." Charlotte leaned back in her seat.

"Okay, that's it for today. Read ahead two chapters, and we'll dive into art depicting Muspelheim and Jotunheim—realms of the fire and frost giants—during our next class. You won't want to miss it."

I slid my notebook into my bag while Charlotte powered down her laptop. When she zipped the computer into its case, I stood. "Fire giants and frost giants? They had some dark stories, didn't they?"

"That's only the beginning." Charlotte shook her head.

"How do you know about Norse mythology?" I stepped out of the row and headed toward the classroom door.

"We did a unit on it in my AP class last year. They have some particularly fun myths—and some disturbingly strange ones."

"You'll have to fill me in." We walked toward the entrance of the humanities building. "My grandpa's part Norwegian but he never told me about the myths. And we only studied the Greek ones at Tottenham."

"Would you like to go over notes this week? We can talk about the paintings from the reading, and I'll tell you the stories about the fire and frost giants." Charlotte shuddered. "Crazy stuff."

"Sounds great." I smiled. "I've got my Calc II lecture this afternoon, but I'll see you at home later."

"Have fun." Charlotte waved as she walked toward the student union.

I did a little happy dance and headed to the library to see if I could check out a text on Norse mythology. I had no intention of being caught off guard in class, and preparation begat excellence. My lips pulled back in a smile. This experience was everything I'd worked for. I was officially a college student. My first class was under my belt, and in a few hours, I'd be attending my first lecture in my major. I might have felt way out of my element with art and gods, but I'd be happy as a clam in saltwater in a math class. Roman numerals and Greek letters, cut-and-dry answers . . . I sighed. If everything about life could be as simple as calculus, my world would be just perfect.

* * * *

"*Hei hei* everybody." The voice sounded familiar. I glanced at the back of the Calc II discussion room on Tuesday morning, and saw Brynn's friend Henrik walking up the aisle. He threw his backpack on the table at the front and scribbled his name on the whiteboard in a hasty scrawl. "I'm Henrik Andersson. I'm a grad student in the Biomechanical Engineering department, and I'll be your TA for our breakout section this semester. This is my e-mail address, and these are my office hours. Use them."

To my right, Brynn was positively bursting with excitement.

"Did you know he was the TA for our section?" I whispered.

"Yes," she whispered back. Her freshly painted purple nails dug into her forearms where she squeezed herself, quite possibly to keep from bouncing up and down.

That explained the makeup and fake lashes. And the extra spray of vanilla perfume . . . or three. I covered my grin. There was always looking your best, and then there was this. Brynn might not be allowed to date, but her massive crush was cute as a bug's ear.

"Now who was confused by Professor Antosie's lecture yesterday?" Henrik looked around the room. "Nobody? You all understood everything he said in your first class?"

I glanced at the students to my left, but they all stared at Henrik. Rule number one of Math Club: Don't tell anyone you're confused about Math Club.

"*Perfekt.* Then I'm sure you'll all sign up to be my lab assistants. Two open spots. One unit of elective credit. For my thesis project, I'm developing a robotic arm that operates intuitively by reading brainwaves projected via electrodes. The goal is for the prototype to function as a prosthetic." Henrik leaned against the board and crossed his arms. "Let's work some hypotheticals so I can see who's got the right stuff. Sound fun?"

Brynn squirmed in her seat next to me, and several students nodded enthusiastically. Freshmen weren't usually given access to research projects, so Henrik's project would have a lot of applications—mine included.

We worked through the hour, and passed our notes to the front of the class when the time was up. A handful of students filed out of the room, but the rest of us stayed behind. When Henrik turned from erasing the whiteboard, he treated us to a big grin.

"So you're the fun ones." He chuckled. "You guys have resumes?"

I nodded. Brynn stared raptly at Henrik.

"Great. E-mail them to me this week, and I'll post the names of my new lab assistants when I make a decision. And feel free to get in touch if you get stuck on the homework."

The remaining students started to shuffle out of the room, so I nudged the frozen Brynn with my toe. "You coming?"

"Hmm? Oh, sure!" She scooped up her backpack and skipped to the front of the class. "Bye, Henrik."

Henrik adjusted his glasses. "You down for dinner next week? I'm going to make my mom's chicken picatta, and try out that chocolate bombe recipe from the cookbook you gave me last St. Lucia's Day."

"I wouldn't miss it." Brynn sighed.

Henrik turned to me. "You should come too. Do you like chocolate?"

"Who doesn't like chocolate?" I slung my bag over my shoulder as I stood.

"Exactly. Come over. It'll be fun." He adjusted his glasses. "You settling in okay? Find the good takeout and all that?"

"So far, so good." I nodded at my roommate, who rocked on her toes. "Brynn and I are planning a hike this weekend. There are so many pretty trails behind campus. Have you been out there yet?"

"Well, now that you mention it." Henrik chuckled. "My house —"

"You guys having a party and forget to invite me?"

The back of my neck prickled at the sound of that voice. It was deep, and warm, and smooth, and ridiculously sexy. If the Scandinavian accent didn't give him away, the trace of irony in his tone would have.

Tyr.

Henrik looked behind me and raised an eyebrow. "Play nice, Fredriksen."

"*Hei hei* again, Mia. Brynn."

"*Hei,* Tyr," Brynn chirped.

"Hello." The word lodged in my throat.

Tyr leaned against the door jam in fitted jeans, a black T-shirt, and black motorcycle boots. His arms were crossed, his palms resting on enormous biceps that strained against the thin material of his T-shirt. His dark blond hair was perfectly mussed, and his sparkling blue eyes betrayed an air of mischief. He pushed off the wall and sauntered toward me, casually hooking his thumbs through his belt loops. He stopped so he stood directly across from me, with a desk separating us. I looked straight up to meet his gaze. He was so close. Lord almighty, he smelled . . . intoxicating. Like a redwood grove, and a foggy morning, and . . . spearmint? *Stop it, Mia.* I closed my eyes and ordered myself to focus.

When I opened my eyes again, Tyr was smirking. "What's the matter? Still tired from yesterday's run? I thought you said you were an athlete."

"I'm not tired." My equilibrium betrayed me. I swayed.

Tyr leaned forward so his mouth was next to my ear. His words came in a whisper. "Guess we need to step up the intensity tomorrow."

I shivered. Brynn snickered.

"What were you lot talking about?" Tyr pulled back.

"The girls were planning a hike this weekend." Henrik picked up his books and walked over to Brynn.

"Where?" Tyr narrowed his eyes.

"Where do you think?" I teased. "I hear there's this really pretty creek-side trail just behind campus . . ."

Tyr balled his fists and the veins in his forearms popped up. When he spoke, his voice was low. "I told you no, Mia."

Adrenaline surged through my body, and my stomach churned. "I was *kidding*. Jeez. You sent your message loud and clear—stay away from the rabid animal trail."

"The rabid animal trail?" Henrik stared at Tyr.

"The rangers found a rabid wolf on the Woodside Trail? Back behind the creek? Remember?" Tyr's eyes looked as if they could shoot daggers. When Henrik didn't flinch, Tyr turned to Brynn. "Re-*member*?"

"Oh! The wolf!" Brynn's hand flew to her forehead. "I'm so sorry, Mia! Tyr asked me to warn you and the girls, and I completely forgot. Stay away from the Woodside Trail. There's a—"

"Big bad wolf. Yeah, I got it. Mr. Congeniality over here told me himself. Ordered me to stay away from that neck of the woods, actually." I rolled my eyes at Tyr, ignoring the throbbing in my arm where the phantom animal *hadn't* bitten it.

"I would hardly say I ordered you, Mia." Tyr stared down at me.

"Um, yes. You did. And you weren't particularly nice about it." I tapped my foot. "You didn't even say please."

"I told you it was for your own good," Tyr pointed out. "That's nice."

"And I told *you* you don't get to tell me where to go. You barely even know me."

"If I ask you to trust me, will you?" Tyr asked.

I let out a sharp breath in frustration. "All I'm saying is a little explanation, and in the absence of that, a dose of good manners, can go a long way."

Tyr's eyes twinkled as he leaned forward. Warm breath tickled my ear when he spoke. "Better get used to disappointment, *prinsessa*."

His expression was equal parts sexy and infuriating. My breath hitched as he gave one last wink, then turned on his heel and strode out of the classroom.

"You coming, Andersson?" He spoke without turning around.

Henrik looked from me to the door and back again. A thought percolated on his face, but he just shook his head and slung his bag over his shoulder.

"See you next class. And send me your resumes for the

74

research project."

With that, he walked out of the room, leaving Brynn and me alone.

"Are they always that weird?" I turned to her.

She shook her head with a wry smile. "You don't know the half of it."

* * * *

"Hey, Charlotte, can you come in here for a minute?" Papers and highlighters littered my desk, bed and floor. It was the kind of mess I usually would have deemed unfit for company, but at this point I was too confounded to care about tidiness. And that was saying a lot.

"What's up? Oh, my." Charlotte stepped gingerly over to my bed and pointed to a clear spot. "May I?"

"Go ahead." I swept the sea of index cards to the side, making a bigger space for my roommate to sit. "I read ahead so I could pre-outline for next week's lectures, and I am totally lost in art. Help."

"Oh, honey." Charlotte lowered herself onto my bed and crossed her legs at the ankles. "Of course. What's confusing you?"

"It's the mythology. There are too many characters to keep track of on top of the artists and paintings and themes. I can diagram and spreadsheet and notecard, but I can't memorize all of this if I don't understand why it matters."

"Oh. Well, that's easy enough. Pull up Wikipedia."

Charlotte nodded to my laptop, the beacon of information in a sea of wadded up papers.

"I did that already. Plus I checked out John Lindow's *Norse Mythology* from the library." I handed her a spreadsheet I'd printed. It was filled with notes. "This is a highlighted breakdown of the gods, their functions, and their powers, sorted according to realm of residence. Asgard is in hot pink."

"I can see that. Wow, you are an uber-overachiever." Charlotte shook her head.

"Card-carrying member."

"So what's your question?"

"My question is what does all of it mean? There are like a thousand different gods and realms and battles and stories. It's an entire religion, or it was for the Vikings, and the Nordic cultures that came before them. And there are so many different versions and variations—I'm not sure which ones are right. I don't know how it relates to me, or our society, or Art History, or anything. Right now, they're just facts on a spreadsheet to memorize, but I feel like I should be relating to it if I want to get the most out of the artwork it inspired. I should be *feeling* something when I look at the paintings. I should be connecting to the backstory."

"Or you could just memorize the names of the paintings and the artists like everybody else and get by with a B." Charlotte set the spreadsheet on my bed.

"I can't do that. And neither could you."

"You're probably right." Charlotte picked up the spreadsheet again. "Okay, let's go over the basics. There's way too much on this paper to tackle in one night."

"Fair enough." I closed my laptop and swiveled my chair toward my roommate. "Enlighten me."

"Okay. So the Norse creation story is pretty standard—two opposite realms combined to make something bigger. The fire of Muspelheim and the ice of Niflheim created a giant called Ymir. Ymir fed off the milk of a cow, and created the first humans from his armpits before Odin and his brothers killed him."

"Hold on." I ripped the spreadsheet out of Charlotte's hands. "I didn't read anything about armpits."

"Then you missed the fun part. Anyway, Odin and his brothers killed Ymir and created Midgard—Earth—from parts of the giant's body. His blood became our oceans, his bones our mountains, and every time you pick up a rock, you're touching one of his teeth."

"Ew."

"I know, right? Told you their myths were crazy." Charlotte took the spreadsheet back. "Anyway, Earth was created, some other stuff happened, and big bang boom. We got the nine realms." Charlotte glanced at the paper. "You've got that part on here. Asgard, the realm of the titled gods; Vanaheim, the realm of the next rung of gods; Alfheim, the realm of the light elves; Svartalfheim, the realm of the dark elves—seriously scary monsters, those; Midgard, Earth; Muspelheim, the realm of the fire giants; Jotunheim, the realm of the frost giants; Niflheim, the primordial ice realm; and Helheim, the realm of the dead."

"And then each realm has a ruler, and races, and where do the trolls live? I didn't see a 'heim' for them." I picked up an index card. "Nope. No Troll-heim."

"Trolls are actually inspired by the Sami people of Northern Scandinavia, but that's not the point. What you need to know is that the nine realms were all connected to each other by Yggdrasil, the world tree. It was a living tree that was fed by three prophetic sisters called Norns. Every morning they gave Yggdrasil water taken from the well of wisdom, and that water kept the tree, and consequently the realms, alive."

"I saw the *Thor* movie." I nodded.

"Well, that's a start. Remember the guy with the eye patch? That was Odin. He ruled Asgard, and he gave up his eye in exchange for wisdom." Charlotte smoothed the front of her skirt.

"Did he get it? Wisdom?" I asked.

"Not the kind he was looking for, but he was a pretty smart guy anyway. He had two ravens that he sent on recon missions. They spied on the realms and reported back at the end of the day to tell Odin what was going on."

"And Thor is Odin and Flicka's son?"

"Frigga. And yes. Thor was the God of Thunder, and he married Sif, the Goddess of Beauty. She was also a pretty amazing warrior. She had a son named Ull, who was the God of Winter. And that's the Asgardian royal bloodline, in a nutshell."

I closed my eyes for a moment, committing Charlotte's summary to memory. "What about the other gods? I found at least thirty who seemed to be big deals to Wikipedia."

"There are a lot. The most important were Odin, Thor,

Sif, Ull, Freya—she was the Goddess of Love. Loki, the God of Mischief; Idunn, the Goddess of Wisdom; Balder, the God of Peace; and," Charlotte snickered, "Tyr; the God of War."

"Right. Tyr, the God of War. Because I couldn't have taken up running with some guy named after one of those nicer gods."

Charlotte stretched her legs. "You have to admit, it's funny."

"I'll make no admissions. Tell me more stories."

"It's pretty late." Charlotte handed me my spreadsheet. "And there's a *lot* to Norse mythology. This is just the surface stuff. The actual stories are really dark—murders and rape and destruction and demons. Vikings saw a lot of terrible things in their world, so it makes sense that their pantheon was full of heavy characters. Let's let this stuff simmer for a few days, and we'll come back to it."

With a reluctant nod, I closed my laptop and straightened the pile of papers on my desk. Then I followed Charlotte downstairs and sat at the table while she pulled a gallon of rocky road ice cream out of the freezer. "You're running with Tyr tomorrow morning?"

"I'm running. We'll see if he shows up."

"Hmm." Charlotte took two bowls out of the cupboard and opened the utensil drawer.

"Hmm what? What does *hmm* mean?"

"Well, it's probably nothing, but when I was leaving the gallery tonight, I saw him heading into that Italian restaurant downtown." Charlotte set two spoons and a scoop in the bowls, then carried everything to the table. She set the ice cream carton in front of me.

"Yeah, he mentioned Italian once." I opened the lid and started scooping.

"Well, he wasn't alone." Charlotte bit her bottom lip. "He was with a girl who had strawberry-blond hair."

Oh. My hand froze mid scoop.

"I wouldn't have said anything, except she was hanging on his arm and looking up at him all goo-goo eyed. He had on a big smile, and it kind of looked like a date."

A tiny weight settled in my heart. "I see." Why did this news bother me? It wasn't like I had any claim on the guy. I finished scooping ice cream and pushed a bowl to Charlotte. "Did he seem into her?"

Charlotte shrugged. "I couldn't hear what they were saying, but he looked pretty happy. She was laughing at something he said; had to be an ego boost for him, if nothing else."

The girl. His muscles. His face. Being named after a god. Tyr's list of ego boosters was endless.

"You okay?" Charlotte asked gently. She took the utensil from me and added another scoop to my bowl.

"I'm fine. It's no big deal. Good to know where I stand with him, right?" I stilled the disappointment churning in my gut. Any connection between us was the product of my hyperactive imagination. Obviously, I was just a new running buddy he barely knew. Nothing more.

So why couldn't I get Tyr Fredriksen out of my head?

CHAPTER FIVE

"GOD MORGEN, MIA."

THE husky voice took me by surprise. I wasn't expecting to find anyone sitting on my porch steps. The front door slammed behind me as I spun around. Hopefully my roommates were heavy sleepers.

"You came," I blurted. Then I mentally palmed my forehead. Did I have to sound like a kid on Christmas?

"Of course I came." Tyr's brow furrowed. "Did you not think I would?"

"I . . . erm . . . how long have you been out here?" *When in doubt, deflect.* Jason's old football adage came in mighty handy now and then. Or was that *the best defense is an offense?* My brother had almost as many adages as the green Jedi master from our favorite childhood movie. I didn't call him Bro-da for nothing.

"Just a few minutes." Tyr stood, stretching his impossibly long legs as he walked down the porch steps. "Shall we?"

"Sure." I turned toward the house as I bent down to

double knot my shoe. "Thanks for picking me up at such an
. . . are you staring at me?"

"No." Tyr quickly shifted his gaze.

As I straightened up, I bit the inside of my lip. "Tyr
Fredriksen, you were totally checking out my bootie."

"Do you want to run or not?" he muttered.

"Fine." I jogged toward the sidewalk, nudging him with
my elbow as I passed. "What would Red think?"

"Who?" Tyr fell in step beside me.

"My roommate saw you out with a girl with reddish-
blond hair. Your girlfriend?" I deliberately kept my tone
light.

"You keeping tabs on me, Ahlström?" One corner of
Tyr's mouth turned up.

"No."

But I'd tipped my hand. We ran in silence until we
reached the edge of the forest. Tyr ran ahead of me, then
turned so he was running backwards. Uphill.

"Showoff," I muttered.

"I don't have a girlfriend." He kept his eyes on me as he
ran.

"Oh." I shrugged. Inside I was turning inverted aerials
off a bumps course. "Anything else?"

"Yeah." Tyr grinned. "Race you to the top of the hill."

He turned and sprinted for the peak. I tried to keep up,
pushing off the balls of my feet with everything I had, but
Tyr was taller, stronger, and a whole lot faster than me.

Plus, he'd had a solid head start.

He made it to the top a whole minute before I did. By the time I got there, he stood with crossed arms and a smirk. He wasn't even out of breath.

"No fair." I put my hands on my knees and panted. "You cheated. How did you run so fast?"

"Better athlete than you."

When I glanced up at him, a giggle built up in my throat. "You're totally checking out my bootie again."

"What? No. I'm making sure you're okay. Your face is red."

"Because some cheater just raced me up a hill."

"Fine." Tyr uncrossed his arms. "Two out of three?"

"I have a better idea." I stood straight. "Race you down to the creek."

Tyr stiffened. "I told you, Mia, a hiker saw a wolf down there."

"That was more than a week ago," I reminded him. "Is that going to freak you out forever?" But my arm throbbed. I'd seen a wolf in the woods, too. Correction—I'd imagined one. There was no way I'd been bitten by a giant wolf, saved by a mysterious blond-haired guy who may or may not have borne a passing resemblance to Tyr, and walked away without so much as a scratch. The whole scenario was just preposterous.

Still, Tyr clung to his story about a hiker seeing a wolf. Well, maybe the hiker had the same hallucination I did. The woods *were* pretty spooky in the wrong kind of light.

"Let's not take any chances with you." Tyr set his jaw.

I shoved my hands into the pockets of my hoodie. "You think I can't take care of myself?"

"I think . . ." Tyr paused. "I think you can't be too careful with wild animals. And there are plenty of nice trails we can take instead. Like that one over the hill. Have you been up there yet?"

"No." I didn't mean to sound so petulant.

"Then let's go. It's a five-mile loop, so we'll have to double back to get you home in time for class. But even going halfway out is worth it. Especially in the mornings."

Tyr started to jog and I took off after him. Since he was ahead of me, he'd never know if I snuck a peek at his backside as he ran. Lord almighty, I was a hypocrite.

But it truly was spectacular.

"What's special about the mornings?" I tore my eyes away from Tyr's tush and made myself move into position next to him.

"You'll see."

He didn't say anything more, so we ran through the forest in silence. There was no golden sunlight today, only dim grey light filtering through the trees from an overcast sky. It gave the woods an eerie glow. We ran past a cluster of enormous redwoods, each swathed in a fabric of kelly green moss. When the trail bent to the left, I snuck a glance at my companion. He wore the same grey sweatshirt as he had the last time we'd worked out, but this time the hood was off, exposing a disheveled mass of blond hair. His eyes stared straight ahead with laser-sharp focus, but his lips were curved up in a half-smile.

"What's so funny?" I asked.

"Nothing." He glanced down at me and my insides warmed. If the twinkle in his eye was any indication, he knew just how he affected me. Drawing my shoulders back, I resolved to play it cool. We rounded a corner, and I skidded to a stop.

"Holy mother of pearl . . ." I trailed off.

"Told you it was worth it."

Worth it didn't begin to describe the view. We'd run up a gentle slope, and now we stood at the edge of a ravine. The dusty dirt trail was lined on both sides with logs, and just beyond the logs on one side, the path dropped into a deep canyon. Lush green ferns and thick blankets of moss grew over fallen redwoods, forming an intricate pattern that looked almost deliberate. The ravine was big, maybe fifty yards wide and thirty yards deep, with a thick wallpaper of greenery snaking up the opposite wall. The oversized ferns and fallen trunks gave the forest a primordial feel—as if a velociraptor might streak through the brush at any moment.

"This is incredible," I whispered.

"Say it." Tyr nudged me with his shoulder.

"Say what?"

"*Tyr, you were right.* Go ahead. Say it." He grinned down at me.

"You're ridiculously competitive. You do know that." I put my hand on my hip.

"Takes one to know one."

"Good one." I drew a deep breath, admiring the gorgeous view in front of me . . . and the one next to me, too. *Hmm*. The ravine may have been mysteriously beautiful, but the Swede was beautifully mysterious. It bothered me that I still knew virtually nothing about him. I turned to face Tyr. "What's your story, anyway?"

"What do you mean?" His smile faltered.

"I don't know a lot about you. How old are you?"

"You want to know about me, eh?" Tyr kept his eyes on his knuckles. His fists were clenched so tight that his veins bulged.

"Why wouldn't I?"

He met my eyes and pointed to his head. "Kind of weird in there."

"Try me." I sat on a fallen log and patted the spot next to me, ignoring the way the bark jabbed the thin fabric of my workout pants. Tyr dropped down, and stared into the trees.

"I joined the military after school. Served my term, and followed Henrik here. I'm sorting through a few things while I figure out my next step."

"That doesn't sound so weird." I bumped his arm with my elbow, ignoring the tingling that raced across my skin at the touch. Tyr stiffened, so I pulled away. "Pretty straightforward if you ask me."

"Yeah, well . . ." He trailed off. "Tell me something about you."

"What do you want to know?"

"I don't know. Something not a lot of people know."

I racked my brain, looking for a benign tidbit I'd be

willing to share. My life was pretty low-key; the things people didn't know about me tended to be embarrassing. "Oh, here's one. I am completely tone deaf."

"Tone deaf?"

"Couldn't carry a tune in a basket. Always stuck in the back during elementary school pageants. Was asked to sing quieter in church. And when it's time for the Star Spangled Banner, I lip sync out of respect for my country."

"That's a good one," Tyr chuckled.

"Now you go."

"Huh. Uh . . . I can't cook."

"At all?" I asked.

"Correction. I can cook macaroni and cheese, fry up bacon, and man a grill. But I torch anything I put in the oven, set off the smoke alarm when I try to use the range, and I caught a pan on fire trying to make Henrik a birthday cake. Last time I ever baked." Tyr's mouth settled into a half-smile. His shoulders had relaxed while we traded stories, bringing his intense-factor down a notch. *Thank God.*

I giggled as I pictured Tyr's smoking cake pan. "That's pretty great."

"You again." Tyr rested his elbows on his knees and leaned forward.

"Okay. I *can* cook. Can't paint, can't draw, can't sing, but my art is edible. My mom's a foodie, and she made us amazing four-course dinners every night. My brother, Jason, and I got to help in the kitchen a lot. We were both making roasts, soufflés, lasagnas, you name it by the time we started high school. She wanted to make sure we could take care of ourselves once we were on our own. Jason used to complain about it, but he loves cooking now that he's figured out it gets him more dates." I snickered.

Tyr studied me. "You're very close with your family."

"Of course. They're great." I shrugged. "What's your family like?"

"How about another fun fact?" *Huh?* Why wouldn't he want to talk about his family? "I know you like running and skiing. And cooking. Tell me something that will surprise me about you."

"Um . . . oh. I'm a pretty fierce fighter."

"You? The girl I just schooled on a fun run. You can fight?" Tyr bumped his knee against mine. The familiar burn radiated up my leg, but this time he didn't pull back.

"I can," I squeaked. Then I cleared my throat. "I most definitely can. When I ran my ski team's dry-land training, the girls got bored with the cardio and weights I put them through. So I brought in a mixed martial arts coach to stir things up. He taught us grappling and self-defense and all these fun moves—totally got everyone motivated again. *And* we were able to have some fun with the guys from our brother school when they made fun of us for having slower courses than they did." I giggled at the memory of the boys' captain laying facedown in the snow. He'd called us snow bunnies, so I'd challenged him to a wrestling match. I hadn't hurt anything more than his ego, but he and the rest of the boys had to set gates for *both* courses for the rest of the season . . . and they didn't call us names again.

"Mmm." Tyr leaned over, so now both his knee *and* his

shoulder were touching me. My entire side was on fire. He tilted his face toward mine, and when he spoke his voice came out in a low murmur. "Care to show me sometime?"

"I'd . . . uh . . . I . . ." Oh, hot bejeebus. Tyr's voice was every bit as hypnotic as his eyes. I was being sucked into a vortex . . . a beautiful, blond vortex of Swedish awesomeness, that was equal parts intimidating warrior and overprotective boyfriend. Without the boyfriend part. Much as I wanted to melt into Tyr's touch, I was very much aware he hadn't properly asked me out yet. But I wanted him to. Boy howdy, I wanted him to.

I leaped to my feet so he didn't see me blush. "It's probably getting late. I need to shower before my nine o'clock class."

"Let's get you back then. Ladies first."

Tyr held out an arm, and I jogged past him with a smile. He fell in beside me and we ran back to my street in an easy silence. When we got to my house, I paused. *What now?*

Tyr raised one eyebrow.

"What?" I asked.

"Nothing. Just glad we did this."

"Me too," I admitted.

"We should do it again."

"Okay." *Please just ask me out already.* I pushed the thought into his head and waited.

Tyr stared at me for a long time. His eyes moved slowly from my face, down the contours of my body, then settled on my mouth. My internal aerials resumed, and I wanted to leap into the air and pump my fist. Instead, I stared up at him with wide eyes. This was it. He was going to kiss me. We were finally going to—

"Well, see you around." Tyr nodded as he stepped back. Waves of disappointment crashed over me as he turned on one heel and sprinted back for the woods.

Away from me.

I rubbed my eyes with the heels of my hands, hoping to push down my frustration. Now what?

* * * *

Now nothing. The next few weeks passed without a word. Tyr didn't swing by Henrik's class, he didn't stop by my house, and I didn't see him on my morning runs. I toyed with the idea of taking the Woodside Trail to see if I could coax him out of whatever hidey-hole he was stored up in, but I decided it wasn't worth it. There was that alleged wolf roaming the forest, plus, the idea of an angry Tyr was about as appealing as a root canal.

Besides, I wasn't one for playing games. Either Tyr liked me or he didn't—the hot-cold thing was just silly.

"Arugh!" I threw my pillow at the wall. I was so done thinking about him.

"You okay?" Heather poked her head in my room. She held open a textbook in one hand, and a highlighter in the other.

"I'm great. Just over boys." I closed my window against the late September chill, then walked over and sat on my bed. "Sorry, I didn't mean to break your focus. I know you're working on a paper."

"Believe it or not, I'm *ahead* on my outlining." Heather ran her hand through her hair and exhaled. "But I'd better get back to it. The study schedule you made up for me is going to be a hard pace to maintain. How do you do it? I mean, do you ever take a break? Throw the routine out the window?"

No. No I did not. And it was a source of constant teasing from Jason. "You sound like my brother."

"I'm just saying the routine is all well and good, but it's exhausting. What would happen if this order . . ." Heather gestured around my tidy room, "if it got shaken up a little? Would you be able to handle it? Or would you completely and totally . . . is that a goals sheet taped to your mirror? Does it really say . . . '*Top Five Things To Accomplish Today*?'"

I glanced at the piece of paper above my dresser and flushed. "Maybe."

"Hold up." Heather looked at the ceiling. "Did you hear that?"

"Hear what?" We waited in silence, until a scratching noise came from overhead. It raked hard nails across the surface above us, as if it wanted to claw through the ceiling and . . .

We stared at each other with wide eyes, then bolted for the hallway. Heather dropped her book as she ran.

"Oh my God our house is haunted!" I gripped Heather's arms.

"It's not haunted. It's just an animal. But I really don't want to find out what it is." Heather squeezed her eyes shut.

"What's going on, you guys?" Brynn bounded out of her room, with Charlotte on her heels.

"We have a ghost," I whispered.

"You, of all people, do not believe in ghosts." Charlotte crossed her arms.

"Oh, yeah? Then how do you explain that?" I pointed at the ceiling as the scratching gave way to a scuttling sound, now over the hallway. "Cheese and crackers, it's following us!" I wrapped one arm around Heather, the other around Charlotte, and pulled us all together. I motioned for Brynn to join our huddle. "Brynn, get in here!"

"Cheese and crackers?" Charlotte snickered.

"Seriously, it's an animal." Heather took a breath. "A creepy animal with freakishly long claws from the sound of it. Ew! I just pictured that."

I shivered. "Someone go ask it to leave. Charlotte, you do it."

"I'm not going into the attic. Are you insane?" Charlotte squealed as the scratching moved toward her room. "Heather, you go up there."

The scratching shifted toward the sound of our voices so the clawing came from directly overhead. I lowered my volume, hoping to throw it off track. "No," I whispered. "That thing is following us. It's probably rabid, or full of germs, or I don't know. No. Just, no."

"Oh for the love of Odin!" Brynn groaned.

"Who?" Heather asked.

"Odin. God. Never mind. I'll go see what it is." Brynn marched into her room and came out holding a flashlight. Then she trounced down the hallway and pulled down the string leading to the attic door in the ceiling. The ladder folded down, and she began to climb.

"Brynn! Wait!" I called. "What if it's big? Shouldn't you take a baseball bat or a taser or something?" My mind flashed to the image of an enormous wolf latched down on my arm, and I rolled my shoulders back to still my shiver.

Brynn turned around. "Seriously? You want me to tase a raccoon?"

Charlotte's eyes grew wide. "You think there's a raccoon up there? Those animals are evil. There was this one back home—it would walk right up to us in broad daylight and snatch our food right out of our hands. No boundaries." She stepped closer to me.

Brynn rolled her eyes. "I'm not afraid of a raccoon."

"You should be," Charlotte muttered.

"I want you guys to remember I did this for you the next time bathroom duty comes up on the chore chart." Brynn stepped up a rung. "This buys me two turns, right?"

"I hate that stupid chore chart," Heather muttered.

"You do? I thought you liked the order?" I blinked.

"No, *you* like all that order. I just want to sleep until nine on Saturday mornings; not get up at six to clean the bathroom because some chart tells me I have to."

"I had no idea. I'm sorry, I—" I broke off when the thing in the attic clawed its way down the hallway. Now the noise was headed straight for Brynn.

"Look out!" Charlotte squealed. "It's coming your way!"

Brynn took the last few steps up the ladder. She turned on her flashlight and pointed it through the hole in the ceiling. The scurrying retreated, the scraping now frantic as the creature moved away from the light. "Oh, gross," Brynn moaned.

"What? What is it?" I yelled.

Brynn marched down the ladder and folded it up into the ceiling, looking disgusted. "Rats."

"Ewwwww!" We screeched in unison. Charlotte tucked her head against my shoulder and Heather shuddered. I patted their backs.

"Shh. It'll be okay," I soothed even as I squeezed my eyes shut.

"That's disgusting!" Heather said.

"It's not a big deal." Brynn shook her head, her curls bouncing. "We just need to get an exterminator in here. I'd off them myself, but I'm pretty sure they've moved into the walls and—"

"Ewww! They're in the walls?" I moved Charlotte and Heather away from the side of the hallway.

"I am not sleeping here," Charlotte declared.

"They're full of diseases!" Heather added.

"You guys." Brynn put her hand to her forehead. "They're just rats."

"Just rats." I shuddered. I marched into my bedroom and pulled the pillow and comforter off my bed, and some books from my desk. The scurrying sounded again and I hurried back into the hallway. "Here's what we'll do. We'll camp out in the living room until the exterminator can get here. I'm sure there's a crew that can come in before the weekend. Hopefully we'll be back in our rooms after one, two nights, tops."

"Sounds good to me." Charlotte ran into her room and came out with a pillow and blanket, and study materials.

"You want us to camp out in the living room? Like, all share one little room with no beds in it? And study and sleep there?" Heather put her hands on her hips.

"Do you have a better idea?" I asked.

"I don't know. Maybe. No. But explain to me just how a big kumbaya girl scout meeting is going to fit with the jam-packed *schedule* you mapped out for me." Heather arched an eyebrow.

I stared. "Why are you mad at me? I didn't put the rats in the attic."

"Because." Heather blew her bangs off her forehead. "You think you have the answers to everything. You literally charted out our lives without even asking us, and now you're telling me I have to write a paper and study for a quiz and get all my reading done while sharing one room with three other girls for God knows how many days?"

"When I made the cooking and chore schedules, I told you we could tweak them if they didn't work for you guys," I reminded Heather. "That offer still stands. And actually, you *did* ask me to help make up a study schedule for you."

"Well, I never asked for a cooking schedule. Or to be assigned bathroom duty, or sweeping-out-the-gutter duty, or whatever other asinine chores there are on that thing."

Heather rolled her eyes. "You think you have everything figured out, Mia. You want to shove everyone and everything into your neat little boxes instead of letting them be what they are . . . your friends included. Well, I have news for you. We're not all as perfect as you are."

Whoa. If the clenched jaw and balled fists were any indication, Heather was really upset. I looked to Charlotte to see if she felt the same as Heather, but her wide eyes were the picture of shock. A quick scan of Brynn's body language revealed barely contained tension—her lips were in a tight line, and her torso was angled at Heather. She looked like a guard animal, poised to protect.

If I didn't make things right with Heather, we were in for an extremely uncomfortable year on Daffodil Lane. I folded my hands and stifled my ego.

"Listen, Heather, I'm really sorry. I've always done things a certain way because it's worked for me, and having schedules worked for the girls I lived with at prep school. But I get that it's not working for you, and I shouldn't have pushed my way of doing things on you. You too, Charlotte, Brynn—I thought that stuff was okay with you guys, but if it's not we can drop the charts. Cook our own dinners, just clean whenever." I cringed as the words came out of my mouth, but I pushed on, ignoring the mental image of dirty bathrooms and dish-filled sinks. Friends—and avoiding a war zone—were more important than tidiness. *Just deal with it, Ahlström.* "I'm sorry I upset you. I hope you can forgive me."

I held my breath while Heather stared me down. After a long minute, she unclenched her fists and shook her head.

"It's fine. I'm really stressed out about keeping my

grades up, and this forced relocation put me on edge. Let's just go downstairs and try to finish our homework. If it's too crowded, I'll study in one of the campus libraries until we get the rat situation handled." Heather walked into her room and came out with her sleeping and studying materials. Brynn followed suit, stepping in between Heather and me.

Charlotte and I exchanged a look as we walked down the hallway. *Crisis averted.*

"Consider the cooking and cleaning schedules officially voided," I offered as we all walked downstairs.

"I kind of like the schedules," Charlotte murmured.

"Me too," chirped Brynn. "I like knowing what to expect."

"Seriously? I'm the only one who didn't like hearing 'It's Saturday, your turn to clean the bathroom?'" Heather paused at the bottom of the stairs.

"Well, I don't like it *per se*," Charlotte agreed. "But I do like having a clean bathroom."

"Whatever." Heather rolled her eyes. "I guess we can keep the stupid schedules."

I turned around and put my hand on her shoulder. "I can be a pain. I know. How about you get to sleep on the couch while we're stuck down here, and I take your next bathroom shift so you have more study time?"

"Make it twice and you've got a deal." Heather nodded, and I knew I was forgiven. At least, temporarily.

"Great. Let's get our rat situation sorted as soon as possible so we can all get back to our normal routine." I sized up the living room. "Because Heather's right; a slumber party does not an ideal study environment make."

"Are you . . . really? All this fuss over some tiny rodents?" Brynn shook her head.

"Tiny rodents with razor-sharp teeth," Charlotte pointed out.

Brynn sighed. "Well, I've never been to a slumber party. Where do we start?"

"You've never been to a slumber party?" I asked, as she spread her comforter out on the rug near the couch. "How is that even possible?"

"They're not really a thing where I'm from." Brynn positioned her pillows and sat down with her backpack in her lap.

"They don't do slumber parties in Sweden?" Charlotte staked out a spot across from Brynn.

"Sweden? Uh, no. Not so much." Brynn's voice sounded weird.

"Huh. Well, they're fun. Except when they're haunted by evil rats." I shivered as I set up my makeshift bed.

We waited for the sound of nails in the walls, but the rats seemed to be confined to the attic.

For now.

I tucked my legs underneath me and set my notebook, textbook, and the Norse mythology tome I'd checked out of the library on my blanket. Then I picked up John Lindow's text and found the page titled 'Norns.' My roommates took the hint, immersing themselves in their own studies. We read in silence, interrupted by the occasional turning page.

"Charlotte?" I placed a bookmark on the 'Norns' page and looked up.

"Mmm?" She flipped a page in her own text.

"Why would the Norns be so secretive when they knew they had information that could save the realms?" I asked.

Charlotte looked up in confusion. "What now?"

"The Norns. Did you study them in your AP class?"

"Some, but we focused more on the main gods and realms," Charlotte recalled. "But if we've got Brynn here, she's probably way more qualified than I am to talk about Norse gods."

"Why?" Brynn asked.

"You're from Scandinavia, *ja?*" Charlotte tried for her best Swedish accent, but ended up sounding like Zoolander. "I just figured you guys grew up with those stories."

"True. What do you want to know?" Brynn stretched out on the floor.

"Well, I'm reading about the Norns. This author makes them sound like the Fates since they can predict the future, but instead of weaving they fed the world tree. I guess I'm wondering why they didn't use their gifts to help Odin and the other gods when they knew something bad was going to happen?"

"Because whoever they warned would try to avoid getting hurt," Heather guessed, closing her anatomy textbook. "Which would change the course of the future."

"But they can help stop the bad stuff. They have the

answers. Why not share them?" I challenged.

Brynn shook her head. "It's dangerous to know something good is coming. The gods have a lot of enemies, and if one of them got word of an Aesir or a Vanir—"

"A what?" Heather asked from the couch.

"The gods of Asgard are called Aesir, and the gods of Vanaheim are called Vanir—they're both good guys. And if one of the bad guys found out one of the good guys had a power that could destroy them, they'd go after the threat. Which would also change the future." Brynn shook her head. "Scandinavian mythology is very structured. Every god has his or her role to fill, and every life is fated to complete a specific task. Interfering with those tasks could throw off the balance that the Norns strive to maintain. Because in Norse mythology, without *perfekt* order, there is *absolut* chaos."

Finally. Something in all those stories I could relate to.

"Now the infrastructure of Asgard requires certain gods have information above and beyond the generalized prophecies the Norns hand out." Brynn studied her cuticles. "Like, the Goddess of Love needs to know the prophecies that relate to the future of a potential couple. Say one is destined to fulfill a calling by the sea, and the other is destined to rule a mountain land, it wouldn't be a good idea for her to bring those two together, right? So the Norns give the Goddess of Love access to information that helps her better perform her role as matchmaker. Similarly the Norns would give the God of War access to the prophecies relating to warring realms, or hostile elements."

"So they were secretive with individual destinies, but if

you were the god of whatever, they gave you the information you needed to keep things running smoothly?" Charlotte summarized.

"Exactly. Because so much rests on Asgard maintaining control over the realms, it is a very traditional culture with a patriarchal hierarchy, and Odin rules with an iron fist. Did they teach you that in art?" Brynn asked.

"Nope. They just showed us pictures of a naked god." I winked at Charlotte, and she giggled.

"Well, the titled gods were given their titles at birth, and they hold them for the duration of their existence. On the rare occasion a titled god dies, or elects to retire, his or her title passes down to his heir. So if anything ever happened to Odin, the Alfödr title would pass to his son, Thor," Brynn explained.

"You talk about them like they're real people." I smiled. "They must be a big part of the Scandinavian culture."

Brynn stilled. "Er, *ja*. They are a big part of our culture."

I nodded.

"These sound like military bedtime stories. Where's the romance?" Heather said.

"Order sounds romantic to me," I said. "Though Mama has a slightly different concept of romance. She thinks everyone's life should play out like hers did. She and my dad met at a college homecoming party, locked eyes across the crowded dance floor and fell instantly in love."

"That actually happens?" Heather asked.

"In the magical land of Louisiana, yes." I grinned, thinking of the thousand times Mama retold her love story.

"The southern belle married her Yankee prince, and they lived happily-evah-aftah." I threw my hand across my forehead and pretended to faint.

"Hey, true love is a powerful force. It's worth believing in." Brynn urged.

"Oh, I believe in love," I said. "I just also think it's great that your culture's myths honor the beauty in structure."

"Well, they're about destiny and meaning within the structure, too, on multiple levels," Brynn clarified. "Asgard is actually a really complex society, mythologically speaking, and every god plays a role in the overarching saga of the realm—even the lesser known gods."

"What do you mean?" I asked.

"Asgard has warriors and bodyguards and valkyries and farmers and craftsmen. Non-titled gods play key roles in Asgardian society, not just the blockbuster gods like Thor and Loki." Brynn crossed her legs and rocked back and forth. "Okay, like a Unifier? She minimizes conflict by heading off issues before they come to a head, guiding opposing factions to a neutral resolution, and fostering community."

"Sounds like Mia," Heather grumbled.

"Chore chart-maker for the gods." Charlotte snickered. I stuck my tongue out at her.

"Exactly. On a massive, inter-realm scale." Brynn nodded. "Then there's a Healer—she's able to cure almost any ailment. A Seer is able to predict the future. These kinds of roles are called Keys, and they can be passed through inheritance, or through marriage, if the personality fits the job."

"I don't understand." Charlotte frowned. "I don't remember learning about Keys in my AP class."

Brynn hid a smile behind her hand. "Do you think textbooks can teach you everything?"

Yes. Yes, I do.

"So these Keys could marry into a . . ." I searched for the right word, "a job?"

"Exactly. If someone with a predisposition for, say, bringing people together, were to marry someone with a peacekeeping job, like maybe a high-ranking warrior? Well, then Odin might make the warrior's bride a Unifier, and she'd use her powers to assist her husband in performing his duties." Brynn watched me closely.

"So she'd get to be the woman behind the man? Would she have a choice?" I raised an eyebrow. That sounded kind of backwards.

"It's a pretty big honor, actually. In that specific instance, the warrior god wouldn't be able to perform his job effectively without the Key's assistance. They'd have an extremely symbiotic relationship." Brynn nodded.

"Talk about a power couple," Charlotte mused.

Brynn raised her arms over her head in a yawn. "Boy, I'm getting tired. Must be bedtime."

"I'm not sleeping tonight," Heather muttered. "Stupid rats."

"It's one night." Brynn pulled her sleep mask over her eyes and buried herself under her comforter. "The exterminator will be here tomorrow."

"He better be." I shivered. Bedtime stories or no, this

was one new experience I wouldn't have minded passing on.

CHAPTER SIX

"SO YOU'RE SAYING THEY can't fit us in until next week? That is completely unacceptable." I threw my gym bag over my shoulder and marched out of RSU's locker room. Brynn trailed behind, fluffing her ponytail, not the slightest bit put out. "Why aren't you upset about this?"

She shrugged. "It's just a few rats. I still don't see what the big deal is."

"The big deal is that we're camping out in our living room. Are we supposed to do that for an entire week while we wait for the rats to chew through our walls? Heather's going to kill us all before then." A cute guy walked through the glass door and held it open. "Thank you," I said as I passed him.

"You are welcome, darlin'," he drawled. He gave me a once over, his eyes taking in the bare skin between my sports bra and cropped yoga pants. His look might have made me blush if I weren't so focused on the image of crawling rodents. *Ew.*

"Camping out is kind of fun," Brynn argued. "And we could always go back to our rooms."

"I'm not sleeping up there." I pulled my sweatshirt out

of my bag and slid my arms through the sleeves. I didn't bother zipping it up; the night was unexpectedly warm, even though dusk now bathed the red brick buildings in a purple-ish glow.

"Fair enough." Brynn skidded to a stop, then stood on her tiptoes. "Oh yay. Henrik! Tyr! *Hei hei!*"

My heart thudded to a standstill. *Tyr.* He who still had not called. When Brynn waved, I followed her sight line until I spotted Sweden's Herculean export. He walked toward us wearing black jeans, a black T-shirt, and a smirk.

"*Hei*, Brynn. Hey, Mia." The voice belonged to Henrik; Tyr was too busy staring at my exposed stomach, his eyes moving along the contours of each of my abdominal muscles. Despite my religious workout schedule, there were only four; I was never able to get those last two to pop. Tyr didn't seem to mind. *Stare away, Hercules. See what you're missing.*

"How are you guys?" Brynn chirped.

"We're good. Just heading to the lab to pick up my laptop," Henrik said.

"You left your laptop in the lab? Henrik! You know it's got the breakdown for—eh, you know you shouldn't leave it lying around." Brynn sounded upset. It was sweet of her to worry about Henrik's research project, or whatever other school materials he kept on his laptop, but I couldn't echo her sentiment. My eyes were lost in a deep blue vortex.

Tyr stared me down with an intensity that tripled my heart rate. He stood with his shoulders back and his jaw set, and although his lips turned up, the expression looked forced. Tiny tremors of an emotion I couldn't identify rippled just beneath his perfect exterior. The effect was barely noticeable, but I was so glued to each little nuance that I couldn't help noticing he seemed . . . off. Not that he was ever Mr. Warm And Fuzzy, but just below the usual air of arrogance rested a vulnerability I wasn't used to. His eyes looked at me with almost softness, at the same time as his hands were balled into fists.

Tyr Fredriksen was a study in contrasts. Absolutely striking, impossibly irresistible, infuriatingly frustrating contrasts.

"Mia. Breathe." I didn't realize I was holding my breath until Brynn elbowed me in the side.

"Huh?" I blurted, to Tyr's amusement. The softness disappeared as I toppled over, and in a lightning quick movement, he threw an arm out to catch me. As always, the touch sent a burst of heat radiating through my body, and I pulled my elbow out of Tyr's grasp as soon as I was steady. When I met his gaze, he stared back at me with wide eyes for just a moment before wiping his face clear of any expression.

He was so stinkin' irritating.

"Ouch, Brynn. That was hard!" I complained.

"Sorry." She shrugged, totally unapologetic.

"Kickboxing class ended twenty minutes ago," I muttered.

"You two took kickboxing? Feel like punching someone today?" Tyr raised an eyebrow, once again the picture of calm and collected.

I crossed my arms. "Maybe."

"Anyone in particular?" The amusement on his face was beyond annoying, but I wouldn't bite.

"So Henrik forgot his laptop, but what are you doing here? You're not a student."

"Haven't you figured it out by now?" Brynn gestured to her friends. "They're joined at the hip."

"Twinsies." Henrik held up a fist and Tyr pounded it with his own, the universal sign of male friendship.

"I see." An involuntary chuckle escaped as I watched the bromance play out, but my amusement stopped short when a shiver laced my spine. Despite the warm breeze rustling through the old oak trees that peppered campus, goosebumps danced across my skin. I uncrossed my arms and glanced down to zip up my hoodie, but a low voice stopped me cold.

"Don't," Tyr ordered.

"Excuse me?"

"Don't zip it up." He ran a hand through his tousled hair as he stared at my stomach. "You'll ruin the view."

Next to me, Brynn snickered.

My jaw fell open. On the one hand, it was incredibly forward of him. Who said that kind of thing out loud, in front of other people? On the other hand, it was hard to maintain the appropriate amount of indignation when the cutest boy I'd ever seen had told me he liked my abs.

Bet his abs are to die for . . .

Sparks popped along my cheeks as I hurried to zip up my sweatshirt.

"Sorry about him," Henrik apologized. "We don't let him out much. He likes to get a rise out of people."

"Obviously," I muttered.

"You guys get your rat situation under control?" Henrik asked.

Brynn sighed. "I called the guy you recommended this morning. He can't fit us in until next week."

"You ladies could always come stay at our place. We've got plenty of space," Henrik offered.

Brynn's eyes lit up at the same time as Tyr's smirk disappeared.

"Oh, that's not necessary," I blurted, just as Tyr muttered, "I don't think that's a good idea."

Our eyes met in a mutual understanding. Tyr didn't want to go out with me, and I didn't want to feel underfoot in his house. Spending the night at his place would be more awkward than being caught in white shoes after Labor Day.

"But you were just saying a week was too long to sleep on the living room floor," Brynn argued. "And Heather's going to explode when she hears it'll last another week."

"Why are you sleeping on the living room floor?" Henrik asked.

"Uh, well . . ." I glared at Brynn.

She shrugged. "I think it's all pretty ridiculous."

My eyes scanned the sidewalk outside the gym, looking for an excuse to get away. The way Tyr looked at me was unsettling. "Um . . . well . . ."

"Mia and the girls are scared." Brynn reached up to

straighten her ponytail.

"Really, *prinsessa*? The Super G champ is afraid of mice?" Tyr raised an eyebrow.

"They're *rats*, they're over my bedroom, and I like to sleep alone, thank you very much."

"Mmm." Tyr stared me down, and I flushed.

Oh.

"You do realize the rats are going to make their way to your kitchen eventually, right? I'm assuming you're not as uptight as Tyr, and you leave the occasional crumb on the counter. And your living room floor is probably closer to the kitchen than your bedrooms." Henrik raised an eyebrow.

Oh, crepes. Why hadn't I thought of that? I whirled on Brynn. "There has to be another exterminator. Someone who can fit us in *today*." *Note to self: scrub the kitchen top to bottom the minute you walk in the door.*

Henrik chuckled. "I might know another guy. His methods aren't exactly conventional, but he can rid the house of pests pretty quick."

"We'll take him," I blurted.

"I'll give him a call and see if he can fit you in." Henrik punched Tyr in the arm. "We'd better get going. I have to turn in grades to Professor Antoise by nine. You guys both passed your quiz, by the way."

"Are we talking an A or a B?" I pushed. It was never too early in the semester to obsess.

"I think you both got As." Henrik furrowed his brow. "Or A-minuses—I can't remember. Oh, and you guys got the internship spots. Congrats."

"Fabulous!" Brynn trilled.

My grin was so big my cheeks pinched, my irritation with Tyr and rodent-induced paranoia both forgotten. "Really?"

"Really. Mia, you have a really good resume for a freshman. Volunteering at the Space Center must have been a great experience."

"It was. I mostly just collated data for the scientists, but it was fun getting to read their research papers before they were published." I beamed. "Wow, I'm really excited."

"Great. Can you start tomorrow? I'm thinking Tuesday and Thursday afternoons will work, unless you have classes then." Henrik pushed the thin-framed glasses up his nose.

"I'm free after two," I offered.

"Me too," Brynn chimed in.

"Excellent. See you both in the engineering lab." Henrik offered a wave and turned in the direction of the engineering building. "Tyr! Stop staring at Mia and come with me."

My eyes darted to Tyr as he finally unclenched his fists. He gave me a look that lingered a second longer than absolutely necessary, and held more than a hint of sadness. What did he have to be sad about? The corners of his eyes turned down and his gaze softened, earning a familiar tug from my traitorous heartstrings. The look in his eyes told me more than the sum of all our previous conversations, making it clear my illogical Tyr infatuation wasn't entirely one-sided. *I knew it!* But as quickly as the change came over

Tyr, it was gone. In one swift movement he turned on his heel and walked away. "*God natt*, girls." He threw the words over his shoulder.

"Ni-ight!" Brynn sang back.

Tyr sauntered away with the confidence of a seasoned athlete, as I once again tried not to stare at his unnaturally glorious backside. It was an absolute thing of beauty.

And it was completely out of my reach.

* * * *

"Mia, you're the organizational whiz, right?" Henrik stood behind a lab table in a white coat. He had a tray of neatly organized metal parts on his right. The skeleton of the robotic arm stood on a pedestal to his left, and an intricate diagram outlining the design of the machine was taped to the white board.

"Depends on who you ask." I uncapped my pen.

"Brynn says yes, so I want you helping me test the metal bits for the device. Brynn, I want you to play with the algorithm on the board. Learn it. Love it. Make it your friend. Mia, these are all yours." Henrik held up a small bolt. Behind his glasses, his eyes were bright—he looked like a kid who'd just discovered he'd been locked in a candy shop overnight.

"Aye aye." Brynn saluted. She grabbed her notebook and started scribbling.

Meanwhile, I dragged a stool over to Henrik's table and started examining nuts and bolts. "What do you need,

Captain?"

"I like that." Henrik scratched his chin. "Yep, you ladies can call me that from now on."

"I think it was a one-time deal." I picked up a screw and held it between my fingers. My French tips looked dangerously close to fading—better ask Charlotte to touch them up.

"Well, the option's out there—feel free to call me Captain. Or Cappy. Whichever feels right to you."

"Did you have a job for me or not?"

"Right. So I'm toying with mobility this week. Which size parts will allow for the highest degree of flexibility and the lowest amount of resistance? Got it?" Henrik picked up a pair of tweezers and turned to the arm.

"You want it flexible and pliant, solid but light—stable, more or less?"

"Yes. And it's just about mechanics at this phase; the electrodes come next."

"It'll be one of the first prostheses that don't require manual operation—are you working from a pre-existing model or developing new technology?" I asked.

"It's . . . new technology," Henrik paused. "Microelectrodes will allow it to read brainwaves."

"How is that possible?" I stared.

"Implant them in the left motor cortex, connect them to the arm via a computer, and the computer—"

"The computer runs the algorithm that translates the signal the brain sends to the arm," I interrupted. "Henrik, that's brilliant!"

"Thank you. Tell a friend. Now get to work on some configurations based on that diagram." Henrik pointed to the board. "The parts in the bin are sorted by size and mass, so if you set them up the way Diagram B suggests, I can plug them in for trials."

"Sounds good." I examined the diagram closely, then set to work choosing the pieces I'd need to make the smallest configuration.

"Did you come up with a name for it yet?" Brynn looked up from her notebook.

"As a matter of fact, I did." Henrik lowered his glasses down the bridge of his nose and peered over the top. "Ladies, I'd like you to meet Fred."

"Aw!" Brynn's dimple popped. "That's perfect!"

"You named the arm Fred?" I asked.

"I happen to like that name. You have a problem with it?" A small V formed between Henrik's brows, and his glasses slipped down a quarter inch.

"Not at all. Very traditional name." I bit my cheek so I couldn't laugh.

"Fred was his childhood dog," Brynn explained. "He was a Malamute, *ja?*"

"*Ja,*" Henrik confirmed. "Best friend I ever had."

"What am I? Chopped lutefisk?" Brynn stuck out her tongue.

"Oh, *sötnos*. Don't be jealous."

"You guys are going to have to teach me Swedish." I

chuckled. "What's it like there, anyway?"

"In Sweden?" Henrik stared intently at the arm. "It's nice. Good hiking, you'd love the skiing, and there are lots of outdoorsy things to do. Tyr and I have a little lake cabin outside Malmö we use for fishing trips."

"I'll bet it's beautiful. Have you been to their cabin, Brynn?" I picked up the pliers and tightened a bolt.

"*Boys only*, blah, blah, blah." She glared at Henrik. "You guys let Gunnar go with you but not me?"

"He's an expert fisherman, can shoot an animal at a hundred yards with a crossbow, and knows how to gut and grill a reindeer. Sorry, *sötnos*, no chicks allowed."

"Whatever, Henrik," Brynn huffed.

"You wouldn't like it anyway. No cell reception. No Internet in that part of the realm. You know that."

"Realm?" There was that word again. First Tyr used it, then Henrik. Weird translation? "You mean country?"

"Hmm? Right. Country. It's too remote for Internet service. No towers. Nothing." Henrik's eyes glazed for a second before zeroing in on Brynn. "We don't even have a TV, Brynnie. How would you watch your *Project Runway* reruns?"

"No Internet?" Brynn dropped her pen in mock horror. "No television? However do you survive?"

"Every once in a while a man needs to unplug." Henrik swung the arm around; his Fred now had a solid range of motion.

"Not me," Brynn muttered.

"Do you and Tyr go to the cabin a lot?" I kept my eyes on my work.

"I go a fair amount. Tyr, not so much."

"Why not?"

"He's a pretty busy guy, Mia." Henrik seemed to choose his words carefully. "He doesn't get a lot of free time."

"He's not doing anything now," I pointed out. "He's not enrolled here, and he's not working."

"Oh, he's working. He's just not doing the kind of job you're going to see." Henrik paused.

"What does that mean?" I asked.

"It means that Tyr's a complicated guy."

"I figured that much," I muttered. If Tyr's stereo silence up until last night hadn't clued me in to his issues, his general hot-and-cold attitude surely would have.

"Don't be like that." Henrik leaned on his forearms. "Tyr's complicated, yes. But he's loyal. And honest. And incredibly protective of the people in his life. Once you hit his inner circle, you're locked in for the rest of your existence. Stick it out, Mia. He's worth getting to know."

My neck grew hot, and I ducked behind my hair. What made him think I wanted to get to know Tyr?

"It's totally obvious you guys like each other," Brynn offered by way of explanation. "You couldn't stop staring at each other last night."

"Yeah. Well, he could have called me if he wanted to." I sighed. "Guess I wasn't a great running partner."

"Trust me, Tyr would love to spend more time with

you. He's just been busy. Freya's in town, and—ouch!" Henrik rubbed his shoulder and glared at Brynn. "Why'd you throw a bolt at me?"

"Because you are unusually dense, you nitwit." Brynn glared back.

"Freya? Right. Friend of his?" My fake-casual tone fooled no one. She must have been the strawberry-blonde Charlotte saw out with Tyr.

"Yes, Henrik. Explain Freya." Brynn shot eyeball-daggers.

"Oh. Uh, Freya's Tyr's best friend. She's from where we live." Henrik tapped his finger on the tabletop.

"They're best friends?" The fake-casual tone went up an octave.

"*Ja.* They've been friends forever. Do everything together. Kind of irritating, really. Ouch!" Henrik rubbed his other shoulder and glared at Brynn. "Enough!"

"Freya and Tyr really are just friends, Mia. There's nothing there." Brynn probably thought she sounded comforting.

She didn't.

"Yeah, he mentioned her once." I nodded, then I blurted out the thought pounding in my head. "Freya's the redhead, right?"

Brynn launched icy beams at Henrik, but he was oblivious to her stare. "Yeah. Long hair, about six-feet tall, legs for days. Total *baben.*"

Baben had an obvious enough translation.

117

"Gods, you are so stupid!" Brynn exploded.

Henrik looked at my flat expression and quickly backtracked. "Not that Tyr's ever seen her like that. Honest, Mia. She's like a sister to him."

"So the total *baben* has been in town how long?" I squeaked.

"Three weeks." Henrik shrugged.

Three weeks. She'd shown up, Tyr had run with me one last time, and then he'd all but disappeared.

"Fan-freaking-tastic," I muttered.

"Don't write him off, Mia. Freya's not what she sounds like." Brynn tried to reassure me.

"I'm sure she isn't," I grumbled. The pieces were coming together, and the picture they were forming didn't look so great for me.

Not that I cared, one way or the other. I had way more important things to think about than some guy.

* * * *

Thursday was my night to cook, so I headed to the grocery store after we'd finished up in the lab, intent on making a dinner so amazing I'd be forced to forget about Tyr and the *baben*—at least for a couple of hours. Since I hadn't talked to my brother in almost a week I called Jason on the way, clicking over to speaker when he answered.

"Well, if it isn't the brains of the family." Jason's smile came through the phone.

"Hey, Jase. How's that big ivory tower?"

"Studying hard. What about Math Club? You guys getting into trouble?" Jason chuckled.

"You know it."

"What's going on with that dude you mentioned a while back?" Jason had a memory like a steel trap. Leave it to him to bring up the one thing I *didn't* want to talk about.

"Oh, Tyr. Things didn't work out with him." I tried to keep the hurt out of my voice.

Jason put off the appropriate amount of indignation. "I'll come beat the crap out of him if you want me to."

"Thanks, Jase, but I'm okay. Onward and upward, right?"

"Hey, that's my line."

"I get all my best lines from you," I teased. "Hey, I'm about to run into the store. I just wanted to say hi. Miss you, big brother."

"I miss you too. Say hi to the trees for me."

"Will do. Give Mom and Dad hugs when you see them this weekend." I pulled into a parking space.

"Deal. And Mees?" Jason added.

"Mmm?"

"Don't stress about the loser. You're smart and cute and a pretty cool chick. The right guy will come along."

"Thanks, J." Sometimes he could be so sweet.

"But say the word and I'll kick his butt. Later, Mia." Jason signed off.

I hummed to myself as I walked into the store, my heels clicking on the linoleum. Jason always knew how to make me smile. I grabbed a hand basket and made my way through the vegetable aisle until I found the first item on my shopping list. My hand was halfway to the asparagus when I heard the familiar voice.

"*Hei,* Mia."

I turned on one heel and came face-to-chest with Tyr. He wore slender-cut jeans with his black leather jacket, and his characteristic half-smile tugged at one corner of his mouth.

My heart thudded to a standstill.

"You're everywhere."

"It's starting to seem that way." He didn't look any happier about it than I felt.

"Sure is. Well, see you." I threw a cluster of asparagus in my hand basket and walked away.

"Are you mad at me?"

Seriously?

Tyr followed me down the aisle, where I grabbed two packages of capellini, a jar of chicken stock, and marsala cooking wine.

"Nope." I pasted on my finest fake smile and scooted down the next aisle. I threw basil, oregano, and seasoned sea salt into my basket, and held my smile until my jaw twitched as I strode toward the self check-out. *Play it cool. You'll be out of here before you know it.*

Tyr furrowed his brow. "You're acting strange."

"Just in a rush. It's my night to cook dinner."

Tyr stood at the station next to me and scanned his groceries. Three frozen pizzas and a bottle of dishwasher soap . . . not that I was watching. When he was finished, he pulled a black AmEx out of his wallet and swiped it.

"Is that a—"

He tucked the card back in his wallet before I could finish. "Want me to carry your bag?" he offered.

"What? Uh, no. Thanks." I hurried out of the store in clipped strides. Tyr followed. Of course, his motorcycle was parked two spots over from my Audi. He really was everywhere.

"Mia, wait," he called as I threw my bag and my purse into my car.

"Sorry, I've got to go. Dinner." I slammed the door closed with a tight wave and peeled out of the parking lot. This was *so* uncomfortable. I might have been naïve about boys, but I knew enough to figure out I was barking up the wrong tree when it came to this one.

CHAPTER SEVEN

FROM MY ROADSIDE PRISON, I channeled every ounce of decorum my mother had drilled into me and *didn't* scream. But I wanted to. Stupid deer. If it hadn't jumped in front of my car, I wouldn't have swerved and hit that pothole. And if I hadn't hit that pothole, I wouldn't have blown a tire. Again. Now I was stuck on the dirt shoulder, with a bag of groceries that might not make it home in time to fulfill their destiny as tonight's mind-blowing supper.

Stupid, stupid deer.

I'd just have to let my roommates know dinner was going to be delayed while I changed my tire. I rifled through my purse until my fingers wrapped around my phone. When I pulled it out, I made the underwhelming discovery that this particular section of wooded road had no cell reception.

Well, wasn't that just the berries.

I fumbled with the door and stepped out of my car, gearing up to change the flat, but before I even reached the back of the car, I stopped in my tracks. My jack wasn't in the trunk. It was in the garage, where I'd left it after I'd cleaned it. It was all muddy from my mid-rainstorm-tire-change on the drive to California, so I'd scrubbed it down and forgotten to return it to my car. I climbed back into the Audi and fought the impulse to cry. For somebody with impeccable attention to detail, this kind of slip-up was unacceptable.

My cheek sought solace on the steering wheel, and I closed my eyes. I was psyching myself up for the two-mile walk home when I a knock at my window made me jump. I turned my head and opened one eye.

This was just not my day.

A vision in a black leather jacket winked at me. Casually disheveled hair, pale pink lips, the square jawline with more than a hint of stubble because he couldn't possibly be bothered with something as trivial as shaving when he had a drop-dead gorgeous "best friend" to entertain.

The berries, the berries, the berries.

My finger tapped a button, lowering the window. "Stop following me. It's creepy."

"Need some help?" Tyr tilted his head, barely contained laughter brimming from irritatingly beautiful eyes.

My head met the steering wheel. *Hard.* The ensuing honk made me jump. "Go away."

"And leave you stranded? What kind of gentleman would that make me?"

"You're no gentleman." I didn't bother looking up. The day couldn't get any worse, so I decided to tackle the Tyr situation head on. Running away hadn't gotten me far. *Thanks a lot, deer.* "Why didn't you ever call me?" It shouldn't have bothered me so much. I fought to remember which of Jason's adages applied here. Two runs does not a relationship make . . . or something.

"Because." Tyr chuckled. "You never gave me your number."

I didn't?

"And besides, I'm trying to do right by you. You might be the kind of person bunnies follow around the forest, but I'm definitely not. If you knew the *skit* I bring to the table, you'd avoid me like the plague."

I sized Tyr up with a steady look. "Maybe. Maybe not. I'm tougher than you think I am."

"Mmm." Tyr reached out as if he was going to touch my cheek, but he pulled his hand back so quickly I barely registered the movement.

"I am," I insisted, cringing at how pathetic I sounded. As my fingers inched for the window switch, Tyr's hand shot out to cover mine. Electricity prickled up my arm, making me jump. Tyr's lips parted slightly, and he withdrew his touch, looking drawing a shaky breath.

"Look, Mia—" Tyr began.

"Please, stop. I just want to go home and cook dinner." I opened the door and stepped out of the car. My heel sunk into the mud, and I nearly fell over trying to wrench it free. Tyr put his hands on my hips to steady me, and that heat shot through me again. It settled in my abdomen, a warm pulse radiating down to my thighs. My eyes widened, and I looked up at him. He stared down at me with an expression that bordered on nervous, and quickly dropped his hands. *What in the world does he have to be afraid of?*

"I can take care of myself. Now if you'll excuse me . . ." I faltered. My mind told me I needed space from this guy to clear my head; to stop thinking about him; to figure out what was right for *me* when it came to Tyr, since he was clearly doing what worked for *him*. But my heart was afraid that if I walked away, I'd never be this close to him again. And for some irrational reason, the thought of being away from Tyr made my heart ache.

What is wrong with me?

As I pondered my illogical vulnerability, something snapped inside of Tyr. His eyes were hard now, his voice cool. "If you had any idea what was really going on, you'd let me drive you home. You don't always have to be so stubborn."

Whoa.

I leaned back on one heel, jutting my hip out to the side and folding my arms across my chest. "Well then, enlighten me. What's *really* going on? Because you've done a whole lot of talking without saying anything that makes a lick of sense. The way I see it, what's *really* going on is some overbearing guy who somehow manages to avoid me whenever it suits him, and show up everywhere I go when I *don't* want to see him, is keeping me from cooking a really delicious dinner."

I reached into the front seat and grabbed my purse and the bag of groceries, then slammed the door and stomped past Tyr, bumping him with my shoulder.

"Where do you think you're going?" he asked.

"Home." One of my roommates could give me a ride back to my car—with my jack—in the morning.

"It's two miles away. You're wearing heels."

"I'm aware." I stomped down the dirt shoulder with my head held high.

And then I stepped in another hole.

My ankle burned from the painful twist. My purse slipped off my arm and my groceries flew out of my bag as I launched forward. But before I hit the dirt, solid arms wrapped around me. Tyr held on tight and set me gently on my feet. I tried to step away but he didn't let go. His arms circled my waist from behind, and he rested his chin on the top of my head. I leaned into him and tested the weight on my ankle. It hurt, but it would be okay.

My cheeks seared as I realized the position I'd put myself in. Tyr's chest was hard against my back, and my stomach was white-hot where his forearms were wrapped around me. I rested my head against Tyr's torso and closed my eyes, breathing in his woodsy smell.

"Let me take you home," he murmured into my hair. "You can't walk on that ankle."

I snapped back to reality. At the moment I might have been in his arms, but he had a *baben* waiting for him at home. "No, thank you. I'm fine."

"It's just a ride, Mia. What's the big deal?"

The big deal was I felt way more than I should for a guy who'd made it abundantly clear he just wasn't that into me. And whom I barely knew.

I stepped out of his arms and turned around, and my ankle wobbled. Darn it. He was right. I couldn't walk home. "Fine," I caved. "You may drive me home."

"Gee, thanks." Tyr propped me against my car and bent to pick up the groceries and purse I'd dropped when I fell. He fastened them to the back of his bike, then took his helmet off his handlebars and set it on top of my head. "Wear this. You need it more than I do."

"Harrumph."

Tyr scooped me up in his arms and set me on the back of the motorcycle. He swung one long leg over the seat, and settled in front of me. "Hold on to my chest."

"No thanks," I muttered. Being this close to him without actually *being close* to him was painful enough. If there truly wasn't going to be anything between us, I didn't need to know how good it felt to be snuggled against him. No point making things harder than they already were.

"Safety first, Mia." Tyr turned to face me. "If you don't hold on, you'll fall off. Have you ever ridden on a motorcycle before?"

"No," I admitted. The helmet made my voice sound funny.

"Then it's doubly important you hold me. We're not that far from your place, and I can go slow, but for the love of Odin, don't fall off the bike to prove some point. Last thing I need is you getting hurt again."

Well, when he put it like that . . .

Tyr turned around and brought the steel beast to life. I flung my arms around him at the sound of the engine, and tried not to moan at the way his stomach muscles tensed under my arms, or the way his chest vibrated in a sigh when I touched him. He was probably going on a date after he'd dropped me off, where he'd laugh about this whole thing

127

with Freya. I didn't need to embarrass myself any more.

Tyr wrapped one hand around mine, squeezing so I held him even tighter. Then he gently eased the motorcycle onto the road. I rested my helmet against his back and closed my eyes, feeling the vibrations of the bike through my body all the way to my skull, and ignoring the panic I should have felt at riding what my mother referred to as a "death trap." Being on Tyr's motorcycle didn't feel dangerous. It felt good—my body pressed against Tyr's, the engine thrumming beneath my legs. It was easy to imagine this was our normal, that we rode together and touched and hung out and laughed. In this one moment, everything between us felt right.

But it was only one ride, and it was only one moment. Tyr wasn't mine, and he probably never would be. Too quickly, he eased the bike onto Daffodil Drive. He pulled to a stop in front of my house, and I reluctantly released my grip on his abs. Tyr climbed off, lifted the helmet from my head and placed it on the handlebar, and scooped me up in one arm. My cheeks burned as he tucked a strand of hair behind my ear without a word, then held my grocery bag and purse in his free hand. He walked up my front path, without moving to put me down.

"It's okay, I can—uh, I can walk," I stammered. He hadn't stopped staring at me, and his proximity was overwhelming. Every nerve in my body pinged to attention.

"We'll see about that." Tyr's voice sounded as shaky as I felt. He waited until we reached the porch before lowering me to my feet. He didn't take his hand off my waist as I put weight on my ankle. "You need me to call a healer?"

"In America we call them doctors. And I think it'll be

fine." I drew a wobbly breath and took my bags from his arm. "Uh, thank you for the ride. You've probably got stuff to do, so . . ."

"Yeah." Tyr's eyes darted to the street. "Well, if you need anything else, I'm around."

"Okay." I watched as Tyr walked backwards to the curb. He climbed on his bike and lowered his helmet over his head, without seeming to break eye contact. After half a minute, he nodded. He revved the engine and took off down the street, leaving a trail of rubber in his wake, and a hollow feeling in my gut.

* * * *

"Sorry again about the late dinner," I apologized to my housemates. Being kept waiting was one of my pet peeves; I felt awful doing it to anyone else.

"Stop apologizing." Charlotte dabbed the corner of her mouth with a napkin. "Wow, that was delicious, as always."

"I'm glad you liked it. Hey, would anyone be willing to drop me off at my car on the way to school tomorrow? I've got a spare tire in the trunk, I just need to grab my jack out of the garage so I can change it." I folded my napkin and put it next to my plate.

"*Självklart*." Brynn nodded. We stared. "Of course," she translated. Then she passed a plate of brownies; my mea culpa for the late meal. "Oh, I forgot! Henrik's other exterminator guy called. He has an opening this weekend, but we're going to have to stay somewhere else while he works. I guess he's some kind of a rat whisperer, and he needs all the human energy out of the house so he can communicate with the rats and trap them humanely before he ushers them to their new home."

"You hear the words as you're saying them, right?" I asked.

"He *communicates* with *rats*?" Heather stared. "And I thought Portland people were weird."

Brynn shrugged. "It sounds crazy, but Henrik says the guy's good. Honest."

"Well, if Henrik says it's true . . ." Charlotte giggled.

Brynn put a hand on her hip. "Do you guys want the rats gone or not?"

"Gone." Heather and I spoke in unison.

"Good. So prepare to clear out tomorrow afternoon. The rat guy says we can come back Sunday."

"It takes two days to clear out bad rat juju?" Heather snickered.

Brynn raised an eyebrow. "If you want your private study space back, I suggest you stop mocking the rat guy."

Heather held up her hands. "Fair enough. I turned in my paper, so I'm heading to San Francisco with Charlotte this weekend anyway. I've never been."

"You two are still welcome to come with us," Charlotte offered.

I shook my head. "Thanks for the offer, but I can't. I have a lit paper due on Monday. I need the library this weekend. Maybe I'll just stay at a hotel."

"Don't be silly." Brynn waved her hand. "Henrik said he'd be happy to have us both. He owes me, anyway."

"That's okay. I'll find something else." Brynn didn't need me getting in the way of whatever might be going on between them. Another Jason-ism—*two's company, three's a crowd*. And there was no way I wanted to spend two nights in Tyr's house.

"You don't really have a choice," Charlotte pointed out. "The Antiques Festival is this weekend. All the hotels in town have been booked out for weeks."

"And by 'all the hotels,' you mean both of the hotels." Brynn fingered a blond curl. "I love this little place."

"Seriously?" I asked.

"Seriously," Charlotte confirmed. "But you really are welcome to come with Heather and me. San Francisco's gorgeous this time of year. Some days are actually sunny."

"I'd love to, but I have to work on my paper." I bit the inside of my cheek while I imagined staying out of Cupid's way for two days. Shouldn't be that difficult, since Cupid clearly had no problem steering clear of me. And without another viable option, I really didn't have much of a choice. "Are you sure the guys won't mind if I stay at their place?"

"The guys?" Heather asked.

"Henrik lives with Tyr," Brynn explained.

"Oh. Oh!" Charlotte's mouth settled in an *O*. "Oh, honey. Forget your paper. Just come to San Francisco with us."

"It's going to be a quarter of my grade. I need to write in the lit library so I can look stuff up." I sighed. "Thanks for inviting me, though."

"And we probably won't even see Tyr. He's hardly ever around the actual house," Brynn added.

"Really? Where does he go?" I asked.

"Oh, around." Brynn waved her hand. "Somewhere. I don't keep tabs on him or anything. Besides, Henrik will probably keep us busy working on Fred out in the garage or something." Brynn rolled her eyes. "He's such a *nörd*."

We stared again.

"A nerd," Brynn translated.

"Well." I nibbled on my bottom lip. Henrik was a good guy. Tyr might not be around all that much. And it wasn't like I had a lot of other options. "Okay. Thanks, Brynn."

"Don't mention it." She bounced in her chair. "This is going to be great!"

"So everybody's set?" Heather glanced around. We nodded. "Awesome. Come Sunday night, no more rats."

"The house is going to feel so empty without them," Charlotte joked.

"Thank the maker," I muttered.

"Oh my gosh, Mia. You are going to die for Henrik's kitchen. Did you know he loves to bake too?" Brynn giggled.

"Henrik? The big dude?" Heather interjected. "He bakes?"

"Oh, *ja*." Brynn nodded. "His pies are legendary. I'll bet he'll make his grandmother's Dutch apple crumble."

I raised an eyebrow. Heartbreaker Hercules underfoot or no, Henrik baking his grandmother's dessert was something I most definitely *had* to see.

CHAPTER EIGHT

THE NEXT AFTERNOON, I threw my suitcase in the back of my freshly re-tired Audi. Brynn climbed into the passenger seat and checked her appearance in the mirror.

"You look great," I reassured her.

"*Takk.*" She breathed. "Thanks. Head back to the main road and go toward the forest," she instructed. "The guys live in the hills."

"That's right. They're super outdoorsy." From what I'd gathered from Henrik, their woodland activities put my family camping trips to shame.

We drove another mile and turned into the hills. "Left up here." Brynn pointed. "And then just head through that grove of trees."

"There's no road."

"I know. It's *galen* back here, right?" Brynn stared out the window.

"*Takk? Galen?* Seriously, Brynn. If we're going to make it through the year together, you have to teach me some Swedish."

"Sorry." She laughed. "*Takk* means thanks—that word's actually Norwegian. And *galen* means crazy in Swedish. We kind of mash up our languages."

"Tyr mentioned that. And yeah. It's totes *galen* here." I followed her directions, pulling off at the forked tree when she told me to.

"It's about half a mile up ahead."

We drove until a light shone in the distance. After another minute, I could see it came from a house. The building was massive—almost as big as my parents' place in Buckshire, but with a rustic country charm. Towering redwoods may have dwarfed it, but the two-story structure was still fairly substantial. Large, shuttered windows offset a grey stone façade. A crimson door with a wrought-iron knocker popped against the beams of the rail encasing the vast porch, and the makeshift driveway that circled in front of the house led to a four-car garage.

This house belongs to some twenty-something exchange students?

"Here we are!" Brynn chirped. "Cabin sweet cabin."

"This is nothing like a cabin." I craned my neck over the steering wheel to stare at the house.

Brynn shot me a curious glance as she opened her door. "This isn't cabin-y to you?"

"Unless *cabin* is Swedish for *stately manor*, then nope." I stepped out of the car and grabbed my bag. "Are all the houses like this where you guys live?"

Brynn shrugged. "Yeah."

Interesting.

"*Hei hei*, girls. Welcome to the *hus*." Henrik opened the

crimson door of his palatial 'cabin.' In loose jeans, a Chili Peppers T-shirt and an open flannel shirt, he was frat-boy meets mountain man. The silver-framed glasses he adjusted with one hand added an intellectual edge.

"*Hei!*" Brynn ran the rest of the way to the porch and skidded to a stop in front of Henrik.

"*Hei sötnos.*" Henrik cuffed her shoulder. I still didn't know what that word meant, but it must have been a good thing; Brynn's smile lit up the entire forest.

"Thanks for letting us stay with you, Henrik." I made my way to the front door, then handed him my hostess gift—a white box wrapped with a red ribbon. "I made these for you; I hope you like red velvet."

Henrik's eyes lit up. "I do. Are these cupcakes? Cookies?"

"Cookies," I confirmed. He held open the door so we could step into the house. "My maternal great-grandmother's recipe."

"*Takk*, Mia. We'll have them for dessert." Henrik followed us into the house, holding the box. "Well, welcome to our humble home. For the weekend, anyway. Will it do?"

If by 'humble' he meant perfectly understated, he'd hit the nail on the head. Someone with an impressive attention to detail had chosen colors and fabrics to create a restful yet rustic vibe. The entry had a soothing beige and white color scheme, with white wainscoting covering the bottom third of the walls. An informal living room was to the left. It could have been the feature story from last month's *Modern Country Home*, with a dark leather sectional couch, low iron lamps on mahogany end tables, and an entertainment center anchored by the predictable oversized flat-screen. A fireplace sat in one corner, covered in the same grey stone as the outside of the house.

"I had no idea you were into design." I shook my head. "The grey houndstooth throws are a particularly inspired touch."

Henrik nodded at my compliment. "I'm not, but I'll take it. We just called Pottery Barn and told them to ship whatever would work for a hunting cabin. We're dudes. We don't decorate."

Seriously? I was familiar enough with the contents of the Pottery Barn catalogue to know they were not cheap. *Henrik and Tyr's families must be pretty well off.* At the thought of Tyr, adrenaline shot through my veins. I looked around to see if the house's other occupant was home.

"Tyr's not here." Henrik correctly interpreted my glance. "He'll be back later tonight."

"No biggie." I feigned nonchalance. He'd given me a ride. We could totally co-exist.

Oh, who was I kidding? Between the would-be lovebirds making eyes at each other and the guy I couldn't have running underfoot, this was going to be the most uncomfortable forty-eight hours of my life.

"Relax, Mia. Everything's going to be fine." Henrik gave me a reassuring pat on the shoulder and sauntered down the hallway. "How about a tour, and then we can order pizza? I'm famished."

"Okay." My voice sounded feeble.

"You're staying in here, Mia." Henrik ducked into a doorway just off the hall and I followed. A queen-sized sleigh-bed stood in the center of the room, swathed in plush cream bedding. Wrought-iron lamps stood on matching nightstands, bookending the headboard, and thick blue curtains hung from black rods, pulled back to let in the late afternoon light. Henrik pointed to the en suite. "Bathroom's in there, and towels are on top of the sink. Let me know if you need anything else. Come on." He walked out of the room and we followed him up the stairs.

"Brynn, you're over here." He pointed into an open doorway. Brynn's room had a four-poster bed and navy bedding, with windows that looked out onto the front of the house. "I'm across the hall, and Tyr's down at the end. The office is back here." He pointed. "But stay out of there. Scary man cave."

"Afraid we'll play with your iPads?" I teased.

"Mmm. Something like that." Henrik chuckled.

Brynn hung back and spoke in a quiet voice. "Seriously, though, stay out of the office. Tyr's weird about his technology." She didn't blink.

"Duly noted."

"Kitchen's downstairs." Henrik shot Brynn a look before jogging down the staircase. "Help yourself to anything in the fridge. Plates and glasses are up here." He pointed to the spotless glass cabinet containing rows of meticulously organized white plates and sparkling cups.

"It's obvious an engineer lives here." I admired the attention to detail.

"Thanks, but this is all Tyr's doing. I have no problem

with mess, but it drives him insane. Sometimes I move one of the glasses, just to see how long it takes him to notice. He won't say anything, but when I go to check, he's always realigned everything so it's *perfekt*." Henrik snorted.

"Sounds like somebody I know," Brynn teased me.

"Order can bring a tremendous sense of calm." I raised my chin. "Especially in a kitchen."

"Yeah, well, maybe you two can bond over your organizational OCD. Sort the pantry according to box size or something. Playing house might get you two to lighten up already." Brynn giggled. My neck prickled as I pictured doing something so domestic with Tyr.

"I . . . erm . . ."

"Seriously. Just relax." Brynn skipped after Henrik. "Besides, we're only here for two days. What's the worst that could happen?"

* * * *

Later that night, we sat in front of the television. Brynn snoozed on Henrik's shoulder while I worked through *Much Ado*. Henrik clicked back and forth between the Oregon/Washington football game and an extreme skiing competition somewhere in South America.

Henrik looked up from the couch. "How's the reading, Mia?"

"Fine, I guess. I just don't understand why Hero couldn't *tell* Benedick to ask Beatrice out. If she knew Beatrice would say yes, why all the deception?"

Henrik shrugged. "Sounds like everybody was too pigheaded to see what was right in front of them. And Hero just wanted to make sure her cousin wasn't being a total idiot and sabotaging her own chance at happiness. Come on, you telling me you've never tricked someone into doing the right thing?"

"Maybe." I smiled. "My brother *might* be a little stubborn."

"And speaking of stubborn." Henrik rolled his eyes at the sound of Tyr's motorcycle in the driveway. My stomach churned as I looked to the window, where the swoop of a solitary headlight confirmed Tyr's arrival. Every muscle in my body went on lockdown. "Things cool between you?"

"Cool enough." I shrugged.

"Tyr comes off kind of rough at first. But underneath he's a good guy. He's just got baggage you couldn't even begin to understand."

"He mentioned that," I admitted.

"He did? That's a big step for him. He's a pretty guarded guy; he's had to be with what he does." Henrik adjusted the blanket over Brynn's legs. She smiled in her sleep.

"He's military?" I asked.

"Is that what he told you?"

"Yes." Why had Henrik put it that way?

"*Ja.* He's military. He's never been in a position where he's been allowed to get close to anyone. He doesn't know how to do it."

"What about Freya?"

"That's different." Henrik shrugged. "She's like a sister to him."

Right. The *baben* was hot in a sisterly way.

At the sound of the key, my eyes darted to the door. I gripped my book so hard my forearm cramped.

"*Hei hei,*" Tyr's voice bellowed from the entry.

"In the living room, *kille.*" Henrik shot me a reassuring look. "The girls are here."

"Mmm." Tyr walked into the room in fitted jeans, a white T-shirt, and a thin leather jacket. He held his helmet in one hand and raked the other through his hair. My stomach fluttered, and an irritatingly familiar tingle ran up my spine. *Stop that.*

"Hi." I jumped up nervously.

"*Hei.*" One corner of Tyr's mouth turned up.

"The rat whisperer guy says we can go home Sunday night. I'll spend most of my time in the library, so I'll hardly be here at all." The words poured out of my mouth at light speed. I sounded like a total dimwit.

"Be here as much as you like." Tyr took off his jacket and hung it in the hall closet. When he came back, I tried my best to look nonchalant.

Tyr looked me in the eye as he lowered himself onto the L-shaped couch. "Good to see you," he said simply. "How's the ankle?"

"All better. Thanks." I sat back down on the loveseat and settled under my blanket. With a conscious effort, I unclenched my fists and attempted to breathe normally.

I totally failed.

"Mia made us cookies. Try one." Henrik nodded at the empty plate. "Oh . . . guess I ate them all."

"Typical. Did Henrik show you around?" Tyr ran his palms over his thighs.

"He did."

"Do you need anything? Toothbrush? Towels?" Tyr offered.

"No, thanks. I'm good."

Tyr looked at my hands. My book was positioned in front of me like a shield. "What are you reading?"

"Um . . ." I glanced down. "Oh. *Much Ado About Nothing.* I have a paper due Monday."

"Huh. Can't say I've read that one." Tyr shook his head.

"Neither have I," I admitted. "In fact, I should go to bed and finish reading it. Thank you for letting me stay here. See y'all in the morning."

I jumped to my feet and moved for the hallway.

"Night, Mia. Help yourself to anything you need," Henrik called after me.

"Okay. Thanks." I hurried toward the guest room. Recessed lighting bathed the walls in a dim glow as I padded down the hardwood hallway. When I was just outside the bedroom, I heard a deep voice behind me.

"Wait." Tyr must have followed me out of the living room.

The butterflies in my stomach commenced an Olympic-level trampoline routine. When I'd settled them enough to turn without throwing up, Tyr stood two feet away. He looked adorable, his thumbs hooked in the pockets of his jeans, his head tilted to one side, and a lost expression on his face.

"Yes?" I asked.

Tyr stared at me with a focus that took me by surprise. He took a step closer; heat radiated off his chest. Our eyes locked. No matter how much I told myself to stop thinking about this guy, I couldn't ignore the pull I felt to him. He was charming, and gorgeous, and dangerous, and completely and utterly unattainable.

Falling for him would be extremely imprudent.

Squaring my shoulders, I drew myself up. "Yes?"

"I just wanted to say . . ." Tyr took another step. Now we were less than a foot apart. I took a deep breath and inhaled the intoxicating scent of spruce and sweat. *Bad idea, bad idea, bad idea.*

"What did you want to say?" I forced myself to meet his gaze.

"I wanted to say, uh . . . it's nice to see you."

"You already said that." I spoke calmly.

"Then I wanted to say this." He bent down and brushed my forehead with his lips. Oh, hot bejeebus. A current flowed from my face down my spine, and settled in the base of my belly. My skin felt as if someone had shoved me in a slow cooker and turned it on high. And if the burning in my cheeks was any indication, I must have been redder than a tomato patch.

"Oh." My weight shifted to my back foot. Tyr looked unsteady, the question on his face clear. Did I want more?

Well, did I?

That wasn't an easy question. The only thing I knew was that I couldn't possibly think with my head when he looked at me like that, and I wasn't about to hand over decision-making duties to my heart. Not when it came to Tyr.

"Night," I mumbled, as I darted into the guest room and closed the door behind me.

But not before I'd caught the twinkle in Tyr's eye. I'd inadvertently issued him a challenge, and something told me he wasn't about to turn it down.

* * * *

An hour later, I was pillow-deep in the plush sleigh-bed, staring at my book. I'd spent forty-five minutes trying to read the last act, but I hadn't registered a word. Needless to say, the quiet knock on the front door made me jump. *Who knocks on doors in the middle of the woods this late?*

When nobody answered, the knock came again. It was firmer this time.

"Tyr?" A voice called. It was a female voice. A musical one.

The sound of silence echoed from upstairs. Awkwardness washed over me like a wet blanket. Whoever this visitor was, I doubted she'd want to be greeted by a pajama-clad co-ed. Maybe Tyr couldn't be bothered to greet his guest, but at least Henrik should come answer the door.

The knocking continued in an insistent rhythm.

"Tyr, it's Freya. Open up."

Friends my foot. If Freya was just a good chum, she had no reason to be knocking on his door this late at night. I'd been right about their relationship. That lying son-of-a . . .

I was done being lied to. The covers couldn't come off fast enough; I flung them aside and stomped down the hall with all the grace of an irate rhino. The doorknob was cold in my hand as I wrenched it open and got my first look at Freya. *Oh, fantastic.*

The chill shot up my arm and settled on my heart like a frost blanket— *baben* didn't even begin to cover it. Standing opposite me was an extremely beautiful, and extremely surprised, supermodel. She had waist-length strawberry-blond hair and perfectly applied makeup. And though she was dressed casually in mid-calf boots, skinny jeans, and a fitted fleece, she exuded the kind of glamour I'd never achieve. I was girl-next-door pretty. Freya's ethereal beauty had been lowered from the heavens so all the men of Earth could worship at her feet like an army of lovesick puppies. And she got to be BFFs with the one guy at Redwood who'd caught my eye.

Life was so unfair.

"Oh. Mia. *Hei hei.*"

"You know my name?"

"Of course." Freya's smile brightened. "It's nice to see you here. Does this mean you and Tyr are together?"

"Us? Oh. No. My house is being, uh, de-ratted, so I needed a place to stay." And then, because I just couldn't help myself, I added, "I'm sorry, who did you say you are?"

"I didn't." Freya's eyes sparkled as she held out a perfectly manicured hand. She'd done a twist on the classic French—her bases were pale pink, her tips silver. Even her nails were perfect. "I'm Freya. Tyr's friend."

"Hi." I shook reluctantly. Freya had a surprisingly firm grip.

"Is Brynn staying here too?"

"Brynn's in the upstairs guest room."

"Interesting." Freya put her hands in her jacket pockets.

"So . . . did you want to go up and see Tyr?" The words lodged in my throat. If there was anything between him and me, a beauty queen had no reason to be on his porch at this hour.

"I think it'd be better if you went up and told him I was here. Would you mind terribly?"

"Um . . . okay. Come on in." I held open the door. Freya stepped into the foyer. Her long legs moved in seamless steps; she looked as if she were floating.

Geez, she was beautiful. She was graceful. If she got hold of my Meemaw's cookbook, I wouldn't stand a chance.

"Do you want me to get Henrik or Brynn, too?" I asked. *Or instead?*

"No. Just Tyr." Freya smiled sweetly.

Dang it.

"Be right down." I jogged up the stairs without looking back. When I reached the second story, I paused. Tyr's was the one on the end. Stepping lightly on my toes, I padded down the hall and knocked softly. "Tyr?"

My knees buckled when Tyr opened the door. The T-shirt was gone. He was in a loose pair of charcoal grey sweatpants, nothing else.

Five years of mandatory etiquette training failed me miserably; there was just no way not to stare. He was inhumanly gorgeous.

Tyr's body was unlike anything I'd ever seen. He looked like the live model for one of the paintings from Art History. *Norse God of Bodybuilding*, by Thorson Larson Bjornson.

"Thank Odin you're okay." Tyr's voice was husky, as if I'd woken him up. He pulled me into his arms and hugged me, hard. Had he turned nuttier than a fruitcake in a pecan factory?

"Of course I'm okay." Better, now that my face was pressed against a bare chest that was hard as a plank and smelled absolutely divine. But why in the world was the king of stand-offishness *hugging* me, of all things? I hadn't taken him for a hugger. "Are *you* okay?"

"I am now." Tyr exhaled slowly, then leaned back to hold me at arm's length. "You're not hurt?"

"Why would I be hurt?" This interaction made zero sense.

"I just thought . . ." Tyr shook his head. "It was a dream. *Förbaskat* realistic dream."

"Nope. I'm fit as a fiddle." I shrugged. Then I forced myself to step back. Being this close to a half-naked Tyr was a really, really bad idea. The man was hotter than blue blazes in July.

"Um, you have a visitor. Your *friend* Freya is downstairs." I crossed my arms.

"Freya?" Tyr leaned against the doorjamb and touched his jaw. His fingertips grazed the unnecessarily sexy touch of stubble kissing his skin. "What's she doing here?"

"No idea." I shrugged. "Is she a frequent late-night guest?"

"Mia." Tyr rubbed his neck. "It's not like that."

"Whatever," I muttered, turning on one heel.

Tyr's fingers wrapped around my bicep. He spun me back and pushed me gently against the wall. With his hands on my arms and his chest inches from my face, it suddenly got very difficult to breathe.

Tyr leaned in so our noses practically touched. I stood frozen, drawing ragged breaths. Every nerve in my body felt like it was on fire as my chest rose and fell, pressing lightly against his with each intake of air.

"Look at me," Tyr commanded.

My eyes moved up his body with agonizing slowness. Tyr's gaze bored into me with a focus that wiped any remaining breath from my lungs. He rested one forearm on the wall next to my head, maintaining eye contact as he spoke.

"Do you want me to show you how *un*interested I am in Freya? Because right now, she is the absolutely furthest thing from my mind."

"And what exactly is on your mind?" I whispered.

"What do you think?" Tyr breathed into my ear.

"Not me," I blurted out. "You avoid me, remember?"

"Yeah. I do." Tyr's breath was warm against my skin. "Because you're so *förbaskat* fragile, and I don't want you to get hurt. But it's stupid to stay away from you when that monster is—"

I stilled. "Monster? What are you talking about?"

"Nothing." Tyr rested his forehead against mine. "Nothing's going to hurt you. I just had a bad dream."

"Maybe you need to rest. You're not acting like yourself." *You're being sweet, attentive, concerned. Where's the real Tyr?*

"Did you ever think that maybe I'm acting exactly like myself, because I'm tired of doing the right thing?"

I turned my head so I could look at him. "Um . . ."

"That's not helping me focus." Tyr released my other shoulder and brought his hand to my face. He ran the pad of his finger along my bottom lip, tugging it free of my teeth. "Better."

"Your friend is waiting for you . . ." I pressed my back against the wall, grateful for its support.

"So?" he murmured. He ran his nose along my jawline, and I whimpered. *How embarrassing.* "Listen, I'm obviously failing at keeping my distance. But there's something I need to tell you before this can go any further."

"Yes?" I breathed. Tyr brought his nose up my cheek and rested his forehead softly against mine. Our lips were so close . . .

"I—"

Just then, a musical voice rang from the first floor. "Tyr! I really have to talk to you."

I squeezed my eyes shut. The supermodel's timing could not have been worse.

Tyr pounded his fist against the wall. "Be down in a minute," he called through gritted teeth.

"It's kind of a big deal," Freya called back. "Code red. Outside. Now."

That sparked something in Tyr. He shot to attention, his back ramrod straight and his hands fisted at his sides. "I'm sorry, Mia. I need to go."

"Okay." I let out a breath I hadn't realized I was holding.

Henrik poked his head out of his bedroom door. "I heard code red. Do you need me to—" he broke off as he noticed me standing there. "Oh, *hei* Mia. Fancy seeing you outside Tyr's bedroom door. In the middle of the night. In your pajamas."

My cheeks felt as if they were on fire. "Hi Henrik," I muttered.

Henrik turned his attention back to Tyr. "Should I wake Brynn up?"

"No. I'll head out with Freya." Tyr tilted his head toward me. "You and Brynn just hang out here."

"Will do." Henrik yawned, then opened his door all the way and crossed to sit on his bed. "Check in when you get home, *ja*."

Tyr nodded, and turned to me. "This shouldn't take long, Mia. Wait up for me?"

His eyes looked adorably hopeful. He stroked my cheek with the back of one finger, and gave me a soft smile as I ducked my head. "Sure."

"I'm sorry." Tyr apologized again. He ran into his bedroom and threw on a T-shirt, hoodie and sneakers, then joined me in the hallway. He placed a hand on the small of my back and guided me down the stairs. When he got to the bottom, he growled at Freya. "This better be important."

"I wouldn't be here if it wasn't." Freya's jaw was set. She glanced at Tyr's hand on my lower back, and the corner of her mouth twitched. "I'm sorry, Mia. I won't keep him long."

My cuticles became the subject of infinite fascination. "I have some reading to catch up on. Nice to meet you, Freya."

Freya nodded, and turned on one heel. "I'll be on the porch," she called as she walked outside.

I edged toward my room, where my Shakespeare text lay on the unmade bed. Tyr grabbed my arm and spun me around. He pulled me close, so our chests were pressed together, then he lowered his mouth to my ear. "I'll be right back," he whispered.

"Okay." I swayed on my feet.

With that, he brushed his lips against my cheek, then followed Freya out the front door. I stood, too charged to move, until the sound of their footsteps faded into the forest.

CHAPTER NINE

THE HAND ON MY cheek interrupted what was fast becoming a *very* pleasant dream.

"Let's get you comfortable." Though the voice was low and warm, I shivered as I opened my eyes. It was as if my subconscious had willed him there; Tyr knelt next to the loveseat, looking positively delicious. His tight black T-shirt clung to his chest with a light sheen of sweat. Blond hair pointed in every possible direction, and his lopsided grin made my insides melt. The dim glow from the lamp hit him from behind so he looked like an angel.

"Hey," I mumbled as I struggled to sit up. A crick in my neck stopped me cold. "Ow."

"Hey yourself. You fell asleep reading." Tyr chuckled. "And lodged Billy Shakes in a pretty lousy angle. Here." He took the book off my shoulder and set it on the coffee table, then he pressed two fingers to my neck. "Is this where it hurts?"

I nodded slightly as pain spiraled down my back. "Yes."

"Mia, Mia, Mia." Tyr sighed as he began to massage the knot. "Who gets hurt reading?"

I searched for the appropriate response and gave up. His fingers were *amazing*.

"Did you just get home?" If the clock on the mantel was right, he'd been gone three hours.

"Yeah." He rubbed in small strokes away from the knot. I groaned. The pain was gone, replaced by pulses of absolute relaxation.

"Everything okay?" I murmured.

"Not really. But we're working on it."

I wanted to ask what he meant, but instead I closed my eyes and leaned my head to the side. Tyr was doing a rolling thing with his knuckle that compromised my ability to form words.

"Mmm . . ." At the moment, I was not exactly the brightest bulb in the marquee.

Tyr's fingers slid down to my shoulders, where a treasure trove of tension awaited. "You did a number on your back, *prinsessa*. Lean forward just a little."

I did as I was told, and Tyr slid in behind me on the loveseat. I shivered again.

"You cold?" He leaned forward and pulled the blanket up to my lap before resuming his ministrations. I relished the feeling of strong fingers stroking my shoulders. When I let out an involuntary moan, Tyr tensed behind me.

After a moment, the kneading resumed. "You know, you're pretty cute when you sleep."

My body molded against his. *Good God. This is heavenly.* "Oh am I?"

"Lean *forward*, Mia. I can't massage you when you're this close. Not that I mind you there . . ."

Oops.

He pressed his thumb into my shoulder blade, and I let out a yelp. "Just give it a minute." He kept a firm pressure on the spasming spot. Sure enough, the pain eased. Tyr rubbed a slow circle until the ache was gone, then made his way up my neck. When he trailed his fingers along the base of my hairline, I gripped the arm of the loveseat.

"Ah. So *that's* your weak spot." He rubbed it lightly. The sensations radiating from that one tiny patch of skin were debilitating. But much too soon, he pushed me away, gently extricating himself from the loveseat. He cracked his knuckles and grinned.

"Where are you going?" I whispered.

"It's late. We both need to get some sleep."

"O-oh. . ." My disappointment painted the word over two syllables.

Tyr gently took my book in one hand while he held out the other, palm up. When I stood, he tucked my arm through his and walked me to my room.

"I've got something to take care of tomorrow, but I'll be home by five. Can I take you to dinner?" he asked.

"You mean like on a date?"

"Yes, like on a date."

Um . . . I played with the ends of my hair. "I'd like that."

"You hesitated."

"No, I didn't." I protested with a head shake.

"You totally hesitated. You don't trust me."

"It's not that . . . okay, it's a little that," I admitted.

"That's okay. You probably shouldn't trust me."

"Why not?" I tugged my hair. Was he saying he was a jerk?

"A lot of reasons." Tyr nudged my fingers, and I set my hair free. "The only thing you need to know right now is that I'm not going anywhere. And if you decide to let me in, then hold on, *prinsessa*. Being with me is one Hel of a ride."

A tremor ran through me as I processed Tyr's words. *Oh, my God.*

"So what do you say? Dinner tomorrow night?"

"Um. Well. Here's the thing. I kind of promised Brynn and Henrik I'd cook lasagna tomorrow night. I really want to play in your kitchen. I've never used an actual Viking brand range," I gushed. "Yours has six burners and a griddle and touch-sensitive gas adjustments and an oven that heats in under a minute. It's just . . . wow. But if you'd rather go out, we can do that instead."

Images of the ultimate cooking machine danced in my head while I waited for Tyr's response.

"You'd rather host a dinner party than let me take you out?" Tyr chuckled. "That's a first."

"Well, having a guy pass on my legendary lasagna would be a first for me. And I'm not saying I couldn't handle the rejection but, you know, it's not the best opening move to crush a girl's culinary spirit."

"I hope I never crush your spirit. Culinary, or otherwise." Tyr spoke so sincerely I didn't doubt his words.

"So . . ."

Tyr handed me my book. "So you cook dinner for the motley crew. I'll pick up dessert, and we'll kick Brynn and Henrik out if they annoy us too much. It's not the most conventional first date, but since you've got feelings for my stove, it'll have to do."

"I'd apologize, but I'm not even remotely sorry. It's a seriously sexy stove." My tone was light, but my hands gripped my copy of *Much Ado* so tight I was surprised it didn't tear. It took every ounce of composure I had to *not* bounce up and down on my tiptoes.

"Maybe if I'm good, you'll talk about me the way you talk about my stove," Tyr teased.

"You should be so lucky." I winked.

"You're trouble, *prinsessa*. See you tomorrow night."

He kissed the tips of my fingers, then he jogged up the stairs while I did my darnedest not to stare at his positively breathtaking behind.

I closed the bedroom door behind me and leaped into the downy sleigh-bed. I rolled on my back and kicked my feet in silent celebration.

Tyr asked me out!

* * * *

When I woke up, Tyr was gone, and Brynn and Henrik showed no signs of coming out of their rooms. But the kitchen offered a fresh pot of coffee, a loaf of sourdough and a toaster that very well might have been manufactured by NASA. I made a quick plate of toast, then I grabbed my backpack and headed to the library. By nine, I was tucked away at a corner table, *Much Ado* in one hand and a soy latte in the other. By noon, I'd outlined my paper, and by two, my first draft was completed. My plan was to sit on it for a few hours before I made any changes, so I headed to the store to pick up the ingredients for lasagna, then headed back to Tyr's place.

"Hello?" I called as I opened the door to the cabin with the spare key Henrik had leant me. "Anybody home?" I poked my head into the living room, the kitchen, the laundry room, and even dared a peek up the stairs. Nobody was there. I set down the grocery bag and pulled out my phone to text Brynn.

Where are you?

In town. Back for dinner!! Can't wait for lasagna!!

I'm prepping it now, then going for a walk before I get back to my paper.

'Kay. Have fun!!

After I slid my phone in my back pocket, I carried the groceries into the kitchen to start dinner. The range was even easier to use than I'd imagined it would be. The gas burners cooked the ground beef and onions to savory perfection, and Henrik's oversized pots held the wide noodles with room to spare. Usually I had to snap them in half, but tonight's dish would be an aesthetic, and hopefully culinary, masterpiece.

When I put the covered dish in the fridge, I noticed a cake box from the local bakery. Tyr must have picked up and delivered dessert while I was out. With a smile, I headed into the forest behind the house. I wandered aimlessly through the grove of giants. Lush, reddish trunks sprang up at random intervals along the damp earth, shrouding the forest beneath a leafy green canopy. My fingers brushed a low-lying branch of needles; I was surprised at how silky they felt. Green moss circled the base of each tree and snaked along the edge of the path. I trod carefully, knowing it would be easy to lose my footing.

When I reached a small clearing, I found a fallen tree and settled beside it. A cacophony of birds provided an afternoon serenade, so I leaned back against the log as I took in the prehistoric beauty surrounding me. With the towering redwoods and lush green ferns, it was calm, restful, and absolutely spectacular—a piece of nature untouched by time.

As I sat, a deer made its way across the small clearing. It walked gingerly, silent hooves padding on the mossy earth. A muted thud sounded in the distance, and the animal's ears perked up. There was an electronic beep, as if someone had locked a car remotely. It sounded out of place in the woods. The beep rang again, and the deer took off, leaping through the trees and bounding gracefully over a small hill, then it disappeared from sight.

Once the deer was gone, there was silence. I checked my phone—I still had time before dinner, and enough curiosity to get a cat in big-time trouble. In ten seconds flat, I was on my feet, heading deeper into the woods, toward the sounds.

It didn't take long to find the small cottage. The one-story structure was hidden within a thick grove of trees. It had a wraparound porch and large, curtained windows.

Judging by the amount of lace on the windows and the birdfeeders attached to the overhang, I guessed the home belonged to a sweet elderly couple who sat on the porch swing every afternoon sipping tea and talking about their grandchildren. I wondered how many they had. Four? Maybe five?

I walked out of the trees, heading toward the cottage door. If these sweet little old people were Tyr's closest neighbors, it was just good manners to see if I could bring them some leftover lasagna in the morning. There would be plenty after tonight; I'd made enough to feed a small army.

I'd just stepped onto the porch when I heard footsteps on the far side of the clearing. The elderly couple had a visitor. Maybe that was one of their adorable grandkids, coming around the corner of the house . . . wearing a bulletproof vest.

What?

I dropped to the ground so the vest-wearer wouldn't see me, and rubbed my eyes. Maybe this was another hallucination. I counted to ten, hoping the sweet toddler grandson from my imagination might replace the guard. Nope. The forest was devoid of cherubic children. And now that I was on this side of the house, I noticed the shiny black Hummer sitting in the dirt drive. It was the old-fashioned kind the army used, not the fancy new models kids drove around Buckshire. And on closer inspection, those lacy curtains in the house were drawn firmly shut. Except the window nearest me—its curtains were parted just enough to let in a sliver of sunlight.

What was this place? A drug den? Should I call the police? Logic demanded I turn around and run as fast as my feet could carry me. But what if it wasn't drugs inside that house? What if the vest-wearer was holding someone hostage? What if someone was trapped in there?

I'd been raised to look out for people who needed help, and right then I was overwhelmed with the feeling that there was someone in that house who needed me. I pulled my phone out of my pocket to call nine-one-one, only to discover I'd wandered into another dead zone. *Seriously, Arcata? Would a few more cell towers be such a bad thing?* I slid my phone back into my pocket and silently drummed my fingers on the porch. Walking away would be the smart thing to do—I could call the police from Tyr's house just a few hundred yards away, where the good people of the telephone company saw fit to provide cellular service. I'd just take a quick peek in the window so I could give the police an idea of what they'd be walking into. Then I'd hightail it out of there. Looking out for the underdog was one thing—there was no need to get myself killed in the process.

I waited until the vest-wearer moved to the south side of the structure, then I jumped to my feet and crept to the closest window—the one with the gap in the curtains. I pressed my face to the glass, squinting until the room came into view.

All hope of seeing those imaginary grandparents vanished.

The room was set up like a medical ward. A queen-sized bed sat in the center, with the arm rails and raised back of a hospital bed, but the plush linens and downy comforter of a Ritz Carlton suite. A ghostly-white girl lay on the bed, her pale complexion offset by the dark circles under her eyes.

She looked fragile, and helpless, and young—she couldn't have been any older than me. Four women moved between the bed and a cluster of monitors—at least, I thought they were monitors; I couldn't see the screens, only images that reflected what appeared to be a body scan, and a series of numbers. The women wore long-sleeved, white robes that gathered at the neck with an ornate silver clasp, and they spoke calmly amongst themselves, occasionally keying something into the monitor.

I leaned in to pick up on their conversation, but as I pressed my ear to the glass, a clammy hand covered my mouth. My neck cracked as I was wrenched away from the window and dragged across the boards of the porch. Fear and pain fought for dominance in my brain, but I shoved them both in a corner while struggled to find a way out of this.

"On the ground!" My captor shoved me onto the dirt. My palms broke my fall just before my face hit the earth.

Oh, God.

"Arms behind your back," a second voice ordered. "Cuff her."

Rough hands grabbed my wrists, and my cheek hit the ground. Handcuffs clinked at the same time as cold metal slapped against my skin. Three clicks, and I was trapped. I took deep breaths, ignored the searing pain in my kneecaps, and willed myself not to freak out. But my heart pounded in my chest, my breath came in sharp gasps, and my face burned from its close encounter with the dirt.

Cheese and crackers. CHEESE AND CRACKERS.

"Stand up and don't turn around." The guard dragged

me to my feet. He jabbed something cold against my neck. I didn't have to look to know what it was.

So much for not panicking.

"Um. . ." My legs wobbled. I'd never been held at gunpoint before, but breaking down wasn't going to be an option. It wasn't like I didn't know how to defend myself—bringing that martial arts coach into the dry-land training mix suddenly seemed like the best life choice I'd ever made. Whoever my captors were, they probably wouldn't expect me to struggle—one did have a *gun* trained on me. But complying wasn't a survival strategy. I did *not* want to go wherever these guys would take me next. Fighting back would be terrifying . . . but whatever they had in store would be far worse.

Here goes nothing.

I whipped my leg in a low circle and struck the guard holding me. He dropped his weapon, and I toed it out of his reach before turning to plant a solid heel to his face.

"Arugh!" he cried out as blood spurted from his nose.

I tugged at my handcuffs and discovered the chain was just long enough. I tucked each knee to my chest and climbed back over my hands. With my fists in front of me, I turned to assess the second guard. He stood five feet away, with his hand on his holster and his mouth slightly open.

"You little—" He drew his gun and my stomach dropped.

"Enough! Everybody stand down," a deep voice thundered from the porch. I whipped around to assess my next assailant. When I caught sight of his face, I froze.

The man stormed across the porch, down the steps, and over the dusty earth. He grabbed my upper arm. "What do you think you're doing?" His voice was low . . . and unbelievably angry.

"Tyr?" I gasped.

Tyr's eyes blazed. The hand that wasn't gripping my arm balled into a fist. Every muscle was tensed, and he positively radiated fury. "What are you doing here?"

"I'm—I was taking a walk and I heard—well, there was this deer and—ouch!" I twisted my arm out of his grasp and stared at my bicep. "That hurts!"

"You need to leave. Now." He marched me toward the Hummer.

"No." I dug my heels into the dirt. "Not until you tell me what's going on. Who is that girl? You're not holding her against her will, are you? Because so help me, I'll go to the police and—stop pulling me! I'm not getting in that thing. Whose car is it anyway?"

"Any more questions?" Tyr glowered down at me, still holding my arm.

"Are you hurting that girl?" I spun free of his grip.

"No." Tyr's fists were so tight, the veins in his forearms pulsed.

"Well then, what is she doing in there?" I wanted to put my hands on my hips, but the handcuffs were completely inconvenient. "And for the love of all that is holy, will you please take these things off me?"

Tyr fished around in his pocket and pulled out a keyring. He undid the cuffs and I rubbed my wrists.

"You need to get out of here in case he comes back." Tyr moved toward me, but I stepped out of his reach.

"In case who comes back? What is going on in that house? Why did that guard pull a gun on me?" My pitch climbed as I spoke. "He pulled a gun on me! I deserve some answers."

"Mia," he pleaded. "I have to get you out of this clearing. Now."

We locked eyes in a silent power struggle. Tyr was so angry, tremors of rage radiated off his chest. I squared my jaw, squinting into midnight blue orbs that practically spewed daggers. I should have run away screaming—I barely knew Tyr, and here he was in the middle of what looked like a military operation, holding an unconscious teenager in a cabin protected by lethal force. But I wasn't about to blink. If there was one value I was taught, it was to look out for people who were weaker than you. If the girl in that house needed help, then I would figure out a way to help her.

"I'm not backing down," I pointed out.

"Obviously," Tyr muttered.

We stood toe to toe for another ten seconds. Finally, Tyr's shoulders dropped. "Why do you have to be so stubborn? We can talk. But you *have* to get in my car. I don't want you exposed."

"That's your car? What happened to the motorcycle?"

"Get *in*, Mia," he pleaded.

"Okay." I stomped to the Hummer, and waited while Tyr unlocked the door. Before I could reach for the handle, a hand shot out from behind and opened it for me.

"Get in," he repeated. He whipped his head from left to right as he lifted me into the cab. *What is he looking for?*

"I'm going," I complained. The door slammed behind me and Tyr appeared in the driver's seat before I could turn around. I glanced out my window. The forest looked darker through the shaded glass. What did Tyr need with tinted windows, anyway? "Tell me about the girl."

Tyr dropped his head against the steering wheel. "Your life will be a whole lot easier if you just let me drive you home."

"Is she being held against her will? Because I should probably warn you, I'm not going without her if she is." I crossed my arms.

Tyr raised his head a fraction of an inch. A hint of a smile played at the corners of his eyes. "I can see that."

"So what are you doing to her?" I pushed.

"I'm trying to keep her alive." Well that explained the white robed women—they must have been nurses.

"If that's true, then why isn't she in a hospital? She looks sick. She should be in an ICU."

"That *is* an ICU. At least it's our version of an ICU. Western medicine isn't going to help her." Tyr kept his eyes closed.

"Why not?" I asked.

"Because she's not like you. She's . . . special."

"Ignoring that dig, that girl looks *sick*, Tyr. Whatever your ICU is doing isn't enough. She needs a real hospital.

I'm calling nine-one-one." I pulled out my cell phone before I realized this corner of the woods was a reception-free zone. Frustration clouded my vision.

Tyr snatched the phone out of my hands and threw it in the backseat. "I told you. They. Can't. Help. Her."

"Oh, and you can?" I reached for my phone but Tyr grabbed my hands. He held tight.

"I don't know if I can. But the best team of healers in the realms is working on her. And I have security making sure nobody gets anywhere near her. Well, apparently anybody but the world's nosiest co-ed."

"And why would you do that? Who is she?" I tried to pull my hands away, but Tyr held on tight. "Oh my gosh—is she your girlfriend? Your girlfriend's dying and you asked me out. That's so . . . so . . . common."

"Common? That's the meanest word you could come up with?"

"It's the meanest word I want to say out loud. But I'm thinking a much worse one about you right now."

"Well, you shouldn't be. The girl in that house isn't my girlfriend."

"Then who is she?"

Tyr met my eyes. "She's my sister."

CHAPTER TEN

"SAY SOMETHING," TYR GROWLED.

"You have a sister?" The words tumbled out. "And she's in a coma in a secret cabin in the woods behind your house? Surrounded by armed guards?"

"More or less."

"Do your parents know she's here?" I asked.

"Our parents are dead."

"I . . . I am so sorry." Mortification settled over me like wet wool. "I had no idea."

Tyr's shoulder lifted, as if shoving off my sympathy.

My world turned on its head. Things like that didn't happen in real life. And they certainly didn't happen to people I knew. In that moment, everything I thought I'd known about Tyr flew straight out the window. "What happened to them?" I asked softly.

"I was young when they were killed. I don't wallow." Tyr gripped the steering wheel.

"I—I'm sorry." I reached out to touch his hand.

"The same monster tried to kill my baby sister, Elsa, a few weeks ago." Tyr's knuckles were white.

"Why would he go after your sister?"

"It's complicated." Tyr rubbed his palms on his jeans. "Listen, Mia, if you're going to be in my life, you're going to have to fly blind in some areas. Can you handle that?"

"Probably not, but it's moot. Do you even want me in your life?" He'd been so hot and cold since we met, I honestly didn't know the answer.

One corner of Tyr's mouth turned up in his signature half-smile. "Yes."

"Oh." *Oh!*

"But letting you into my life means putting you in the middle of a living nightmare. And I mean it when I say there are things I am not going to be able to explain to you."

"You said last night you wanted me to trust you," I reminded him. "And trust is founded on honesty. How do you expect me to trust you if you're not going to tell me the truth?"

"I'll always tell you the truth," Tyr corrected. "I just won't be able to answer everything you want to know. Does that sound fair?"

"Fair, yes. Doable for me? Not so much."

Tyr chuckled. "Henrik told me you had one of *those* minds."

"Excuse me?" Indignation colored my tone.

"The inquisitive ones. It's why you chose engineering,

ja? So you could make order in a chaotic world?"

My fingers played with my grandmother's ring. "That's actually really perceptive. I'd never thought about it that way, but yes. That makes sense."

"Well *prinsessa*, there's nothing orderly about my life."

"Besides your kitchen cabinets."

"Right." Tyr sighed. "Mia, you have to understand. I wake up every morning and wonder what kind of *skit* I'm going to deal with that day. I'm not complaining; I signed on to this life. But I'm not sure you're going to want to."

"How do you expect me to make an informed decision if you're not going to answer my questions?"

Tyr closed his eyes. "How about a compromise? You can ask *one* question now, and you have to hold the rest until tonight. I'll answer as much as I can, but you have to accept there are some things about me you might never understand."

My mind spun, trying to compartmentalize the list of things I suddenly wanted to know about Tyr—who he was, how he'd dealt with losing his parents so young, how he wasn't losing his mind worrying about his sister, how Henrik and Brynn fit into all of this? How I fit into all of this . . .

"Is Elsa going to be okay?" I wrung my fingers in my lap.

Tyr's eyes dropped. "I hope so. I've got the best medical team in the cosmos working around the clock. When I found her, he'd left her for dead—maimed within an inch of her life, and barely breathing."

Bile swirled in my gut as my brain fought against that image. "Did you call the police? Do they have any leads?"

"It's not that easy. Things don't really work like that where I'm from."

"Police don't go after murderers in Sweden?" There was no way that was true.

"You already asked your one question," Tyr pointed out.

"But this is a relevant follow-up. And more than that, a totally legitimate response to your statement."

"The less you know about all of this, the better. If the killer thinks you're involved, he'll come after you, too."

"Why?" Icicles traced a pattern along my vertebrae.

"He picks off people who are important to me. My parents and sister weren't his only victims, though Elsa was the first target he left alive."

I squeezed my fingers so hard a knuckle popped. "Why would he do that?"

"It's who he is. I used to think I could change him—if I showed him there was another way that he'd choose a different path. But I should have known I wasn't that powerful. And now he's become what he was born to be."

"You know him?" I asked softly.

"He was practically family."

"Oh, Tyr." This time I took his hands in mine. He'd lived a horror I couldn't begin to imagine. "I am so sorry."

"I can't change what he's done. But I can protect the people I care about moving forward." Tyr raised an eyebrow. "So you need to stay away from all this before he comes after you. I'm not sure I could handle you getting hurt, on top of everything else."

The icicles burst, spreading a chill across my back that left me shaking. What would happen if the killer tracked me down? Would I end up like Tyr's sister . . . or worse?

"Told you it was some messed up *skit*." Tyr squeezed my hands. "Are you okay?"

"Not even a little bit," I answered honestly. "But I'm here. I'm sorry you've been going through this." Embarrassment flooded my face. All this time I'd thought he didn't call because he was into Freya, but as his best friend, she'd probably been his lifeline while he'd been trying to keep his sister alive and fighting off some crazed killer.

"Can I meet her?" I asked tentatively. "Elsa?"

Tyr ran his hand through his hair. "That'd be nice. But go straight in the house. And when we're done, I'm taking you home immediately. If it was him I saw in the woods earlier, I want to make sure he doesn't see you again."

"Again?" When had he seen me before?

But Tyr just stared straight ahead, so I opened the car door. Tyr was at my side before my feet hit the ground. "How do you *do* that?"

"Let's move, Mia. I don't want you out in the open longer than necessary." Tyr scooped me in his arms and raced toward the house. The guards stared as we moved— one still dabbed at his bloodied nose. *Ouch.* By the time Tyr closed the front door behind him, I was breathless, and more than a little flushed. Thankfully, the entry was empty—the nurses must have been with their charge in the other room.

Tyr leaned against the closed door. "We made it."

"Made it," I said back. It was hard to form words when I was cradled in his arms. I felt like the heroine in a regency romance novel.

"So . . ." Tyr stared down at me. My heart thudded against my ribcage.

"So . . ." With tentative fingers, I reached for his hair. I touched the strands just above his ear, then trailed my way down his jawline. A light stubble broke through the hard plane; the rough hairs tickled the pads of my fingers. I hesitated, then moved one finger to his mouth, tracing the line of his bottom lip. He stiffened.

"Sorry." I pulled my hand back.

"Don't be." He grinned. "But I was under the impression you wanted to meet my sister."

"I do," I insisted. I swung my legs over his arms, and he helped me stand. "But is there a landline in here? I need to call Brynn so I can ask her to put the lasagna in the oven, and somebody confiscated my phone. Plus, apparently there's no reception out here."

Tyr smiled. "Your mind never slows down, does it?" He walked the few steps to a small desk by the living room window, lifted the receiver of a telephone and held it out to me while he dialed.

"Never," I confirmed. When Brynn answered I asked her to cover the lasagna and bake it at 375 for forty-five minutes. She sounded unaccountably giddy when I told her I was at Elsa's with Tyr, and wished us a 'fabulous time.'

"All sorted?" Tyr asked when I hung up.

I nodded. Tyr twined his fingers through mine and pulled me toward the hallway. I glanced at the enormous hand wrapped around my own. It was warm, and strong, and oddly familiar. It fit mine perfectly.

Tyr knocked softly on the door. He poked his head in without waiting for an answer.

"*Hei*. It's me. I brought a guest. No need for the security check on this one." He pushed the door open, providing a clear view of what I'd struggled to see through the window.

A stark white room held a store of medical equipment. The robed nurses exhibited an air of competence and grace, their matronly expressions set in neutral masks. One injected Elsa with a long needle, then stepped aside. The white-clad caretaker kept her head low as she walked by Tyr. My eyes darted to Elsa—she wore a long, silvery-blue robe, and a strange rectangle hovered over the bed.

Tyr gripped my hand. "A moment, please?"

All four women stepped out of the room while Tyr pulled me to the side of the bed.

"Mia, this is my little sister, Elsa." He gazed at her, and I followed his eyes. Elsa looked like a life-size child's doll. Her eyes were closed; thick black lashes rested against unnaturally-pale cheeks. Blond waves flowed from the top of her head down to her stomach, where her hands lay folded neatly across her slender waist. Despite being in a coma, her eyelids were powdered with a silvery shadow that offset the dark circles under her eyes. She had a smattering of freckles across her tiny nose, and her pale pink lips were fixed in a small smile.

"She's so beautiful. Who would hurt her?"

"A monster," Tyr growled.

"What's that?" I nodded to the rectangle hovering over Elsa.

"It monitors her vitals." Tyr reached up to press a corner of the rectangle, and a series of numbers and symbols flashed across the suspended screen. "She's holding—no changes since you snuck up on us outside."

"Sorry about that."

Tyr lifted my chin with one finger. "I'm sorry you found out. I don't like you being any more involved with this than absolutely necessary. But selfishly, it's nice to be able to share this with you. And Elsa would like knowing that you came to meet her. She loves mortals."

I shot him a puzzled look.

"You know what I mean." Tyr shook his head, obviously rattled. "People. She loves people. Sorry, translation."

His accent was so faint, sometimes I forgot he was from another country.

"Right." I turned toward the bed. "Can I talk to her?"

Tyr nodded. "She'd like that."

"Hi Elsa." I kept my voice cheerful. "I'm Mia. It's nice to meet you. Your brother's kind of a pain sometimes. So's my brother. We can talk about them when you wake up."

Tyr put a hand on my back and rubbed softly. "She's tough—she's like you that way. But he found her in a weak moment and almost broke her. Henrik and I barely got to her in time. Freya suggested I bring her here—it's so remote, we didn't think he'd find her again. I got her stabilized, and now it's just a waiting game. We're hunting for a cure but so far, the best we can do is keep her from getting worse." Tyr's shoulders slumped.

"Hey." I cupped his cheek. "She's going to be okay."

"Thanks." He bent to kiss my forehead and a pulse shot from my face all the way down to my toes. While I fought for breath, Tyr leaned over his sister and kissed her cheek. "Be back soon, Else. Hang in there for me."

Then he turned for the door and tugged my hand gently. "Let's get you home."

When we walked in the hallway, three of the white-robed women rushed back in to tend to their patient. Tyr stepped aside for a hushed conversation with the fourth nurse before returning to my side.

"She's doing better today. Hopefully it's an upward trend."

"I'm sure it is." I squeezed his hand and followed him to the Hummer. He turned the car around and drove through the forest, weaving effortlessly through trees despite the apparent absence of a road.

"So what exactly is your job?" I couldn't hold in the rest of my questions any longer. "I thought you were in Arcata to figure out your next steps after you left the military?"

Tyr glanced over as he drove. "You don't miss much, do you?"

My fingers tapped my temple. "Steel trap. Answer the question."

"I'm actually still involved with the military, but my role is hard to explain." Tyr thought for a long moment. "Here's the problem. I have a job I won't be able to talk a lot about. I'm going to disappear for days at a time, and I won't be able to tell you where I've been or why I left. I'll show up with nasty injuries, and the only thing I'll be able to tell you is that I'll be okay. My job requires that I mitigate damages whenever possible. I'll be overprotective and overbearing, but it's because I know things I couldn't begin to explain to you, and I don't want you to end up on life support with my sister." He reached across the console and put a hand on the back of my neck, rubbing softly behind my ear. His words sent a chill dancing across my skin but a second later, I melted into the touch.

"I'm not always going to be able to answer your questions, but I can promise I'll always take care of you. I'll never betray you, and I'll make sure that whenever you're with me, you're safe. And if you still want to date me, I'd like to actually take you out. Like, outside of my house, and you're not allowed to cook. What do you say?"

I hesitated. It wasn't an ideal situation, given my need for *all the details* in every single situation, ever. And it wasn't at all the way I'd imagined starting my first college relationship, if that was what this was going to be. It seemed like a stereotypically dimwitted chick move to blindly follow some guy who openly admitted to being secretive, angry, and oh yeah, fending off a killer that stalked everyone who got involved with him. But despite every lick of common sense screaming *RUN*, I didn't want to. This might not have been what Jason meant when he'd told me to live a little, but if anyone was worth taking a leap of faith for, it was the Swedish dreamboat.

I made up my mind. For the first time, I was ignoring what I *should* do and following my heart.

Even if it landed me smack dab in the middle of a world of hurt. Or worse.

"Okay." I nodded. "I'll be patient. Well, I'll try, anyway. Patience isn't my strong suit."

"Good." Tyr exhaled, the corners of his eyes crinkling with his smile. "So where do we go from here?"

I checked the clock on the dashboard. "How about dinner?"

CHAPTER ELEVEN

TYR'S HOUSE WAS BATHED in the warm glow of sunset when we pulled into the drive. He came around to open my door, then lifted me out of the car with ease. He left his hands around my waist a moment longer than necessary. It was a familiar gesture, and I stepped back.

"Why, Mia Ahlström. Did I make you blush?" Tyr's telltale half-smile was as adorable as it was infuriating.

"No," I lied.

"Pity. You ready?"

Tyr offered his hand, and I stared at the way the filtered light reflected off his fingers. His question hung in the air, a palpable tension crackling between us. This was it. Not exactly the traditional dinner party, but *our* dinner party nonetheless. And even though I'd been handcuffed, held at gunpoint, and found out my would-be suitor was harboring a very dark secret, *this* was the part of my day that scared me the most. It was the moment I took a chance on a guy I barely knew. A guy who, from what I could figure, was a member of the Swedish secret service, and might disappear on assignment at any moment, taking my heart right along with him. A guy my roommate recently admonished to 'play nice,' and who, by his own admission, might never be able to fully open up to me. A guy who seemed like an extremely imprudent boyfriend choice . . . if that was even what this was going to be.

Break the rules. Jason's words rang in my head as my pulse thundered in my ears. *Okay, big brother. But you better know what you're talking about.*

I put my manicured hand in Tyr's slightly calloused one. He twined his fingers through mine and squeezed lightly, then planted a kiss on the top of my head.

We walked up the porch and Tyr opened the front door. "After you."

When we stepped inside, we were greeted by the mouthwatering smell of fresh lasagna. *Sweet niblets, Ahlström, you can cook!* Tyr closed the door behind him and took my hand again, leading the way to the kitchen.

"That smells amazing. I know Brynn didn't make it," Tyr ribbed.

"Ha. Ha." Brynn stuck her tongue out. "Putting it in the oven counts as helping. It smells great, Mia."

I waved at my friend. "It's my Meemaw's recipe."

"You going to share it?" Henrik whirled around, salad tongs in hand and Kiss The Cook apron around his chest. He glanced at my hand, still wrapped in Tyr's, and broke into a saucy grin. "Well *hei*, you two."

Brynn caught on immediately. She leaned against the counter, looking every bit the proverbial canary-eating cat. "About bloody time."

I tried to pull my hand away, but Tyr held tight. "Come

on, baby. Let's set the table."

My insides leaped in a dance worthy of admission to the Bolshoi. I followed Tyr to the cabinet and took the stack of plates he handed me, all the while running the words over and over in my head. *Come on, baby.* The nickname rolled off his tongue in that soft, lilting accent, as if it was the most natural thing in the world to say. My heart thumped joyfully, and I hugged the plates to my chest.

"You okay, Mia?" Henrik glanced over the top of his glasses.

"Never better." I practically skipped to the table and began distributing plates, while Tyr set out knives, forks, spoons and linen napkins. Henrik carried the salad over, while Brynn set the lasagna on hot plates.

"Oh. I forgot the garlic bread." Brynn jumped up and ran to the oven. She used an oven mitt to remove a foil-wrapped loaf of sourdough before bringing it to the table.

It was smoking.

Tyr opened his mouth, no doubt to make a snide remark, but when he saw Brynn's expression his jaw snapped   shut.

"Sorry guys," she muttered.

Henrik patted her hand. "I always liked crispy bread, *sötnos.*"

He offered me one of the slightly less charred slices from the center of the loaf. He did the same for Tyr as Brynn doled out lasagna, and I dished up the salad. Soon we were happily eating.

"Mmm . . . sourdough." I took a bite. "It's so nice

living in California."

"The patriot in me feels compelled to point out that gingerbread is superior to sourdough. And it's best made in Sweden." Henrik cut into his pasta.

"Tell me more about where you guys are from."

"What do you want to know?" Tyr took a bite. "This is delicious, Mia."

"Thanks," I demurred. "I don't know, what was it like growing up together?"

Tyr and Henrik exchanged a glance. Tyr spoke first. "It was . . . interesting."

"Interesting?" Brynn snorted. "It was a regular riot. I lived next door to the Andersson boys. Tyr and Elsa grew up a few properties away until—well, they were always nearby. I don't have a single memory that doesn't involve Tyr and Henrik beating each other senseless with sticks, swords, numb chucks—"

"Nunchucks," Henrik corrected.

"Whatever. They basically spent first through sixth forms beating the living daylights out of each other."

"All in good fun." Tyr leaned back. He set his utensils across his plate.

"Do you want seconds?" I held up the serving spoon.

"Maybe later." He winked at me.

"Didn't your brother beat on his friends growing up?" Brynn took a bite of salad.

"His friends. Me. Jason was a bruiser for a few years there." Tyr bristled, but I just laughed. "Oh, don't worry about it. My dad taught me a few choice moves. Let's just say Jase's friends *loved* the story about how Jason lost his first tooth when he tried to rough up his baby sister."

Brynn leaned in. "Siblings fight. Guess that's why Tyr and Henrik were always at each other."

"You guys are brothers?" My eyes darted between the two. *Nice gene pool.*

"No. But the Anderssons took Elsa and me in when our parents were killed. We lived with Henrik and Gunnar from the time we were all in secondary school. They're family." Tyr shrugged.

"Where's your brother live now, Henrik?" I asked.

"He just moved to Wales—he left home around the same time we moved here. He's starting graduate school at Cardiff University with his wife, Inga, and their best friend, Ull."

"Your brother's still in school and he's already married?" I blurted out.

"*Ja.* Well, he and Inga have known each other forever. And we're a pretty traditional family." Henrik ignored Tyr's snort.

"They *are.*" Brynn glared.

"Is their friend . . . did you say his name's *ooo-hl?*"

"Ull," Henrik confirmed.

"Right." These Swedes and their names were going to be the death of my pronunciation capabilities. "Is their friend Ull married, too?"

Henrik let out a laugh so loud, I guessed I'd asked the

182

wrong question. "Ull's a confirmed bachelor. He's far too set in his ways to make room for a girl. Though if Inga had her way, she'd have him married off yesterday. She's *helpful* like that."

"Hmm. Well, it sounds like your brother's in a happy place over there in Wales. And I think it's great all of you were so close growing up, and that you're such good friends now, sibling rivalry and brotherly brawls aside. I hope Tyr didn't beat you up too badly when you were younger." I winked at Henrik.

"For the record, I was the one beating *him* up." Henrik puffed his chest.

"You wish." Tyr rolled his eyes. "Only reason I never broke any of your bones is because I promised your mom I wouldn't hurt her baby."

"You want to arm wrestle? Right now. You, me, no rules." Henrik tossed his napkin on the table.

"It's on, Andersson. Loser buys the replacement table." Tyr clenched his fist and set his elbow down.

Replacement table?

Brynn let out a wolf whistle. The boys turned to stare.

"Can we *please* press pause on the testosterone fest, and maybe finish dinner?" Brynn glared.

"Right. Sorry, Brynn." Tyr sat back in his chair.

"Yeah, sorry." Henrik shot Brynn an apologetic look.

I tried to hide my disappointment. Two six-foot-plus Swedish dreamboats arm wrestling might have been the high point of my college experience.

Later, I loaded the plates into the dishwasher while Tyr washed the pans and Henrik dried them. Brynn swept the floor, whistling the whole time. We had a good rhythm going as a foursome.

"What do you guys want to do now?" Tyr dried his hands on a dishtowel. "Want to watch a movie? Or would you rather play a game?"

Brynn and Henrik exchanged a glance. "We're actually pretty tired. I think we're gonna head upstairs for the night."

Tyr rolled his eyes. "You are completely transparent. You know that?"

"You're welcome." Henrik grabbed Brynn and hustled out of the kitchen. I could hear her giggles all the way up the stairs.

"Not exactly subtle. Though they are effective." Tyr crossed the room in two large strides and backed me against the counter. He put his hands around me on the granite surface, pinning me in.

The atmosphere in the kitchen went from zero to sixty in half a second.

"Um . . ."

He was so close. His scent filled every square inch of my head, scrambling my brainwaves. He leaned in so his torso pressed against my chest. I clung to the counter for support.

"We're alone. Finally." Tyr's breath was cool against my skin.

"We've been alone before," I squeaked.

"Details." He ran his nose down my jaw. My eyes rolled

back. He was going to have to stop touching me if he wanted me to be able to form a coherent sentence.

I stared at him with wide eyes. He looked back at me, fire emanating from his azure stare. My breath caught. Before I could register what was happening, he cradled the back of my head with one hand. He fisted my hair and brought his mouth down, crushing his lips over mine. It wasn't a gentle first kiss; it was forceful. Demanding. Possessive.

Coherent sentences were so overrated.

Tyr tugged my hair and my head fell back, making my jaw go slack. He took advantage of my vulnerability and probed my mouth, exploring every surface with his tongue. I met each gentle push with one of my own, tasting his unbelievable sweetness. He pulled back and nipped at my lower lip, then sucked gently on the sensitive skin. He brought his mouth down to my jaw, grazing the skin with his teeth before settling on the hollow of my neck. *Oh, hot bejeebus.* He drew lazy circles with his tongue, then moved to my collar bone, following the line down the V-neck of my shirt. When I shivered, he lifted his head to examine my eyes.

I tentatively reached up to touch his cheek, running my fingers along the stubble on his jaw. It tickled.

"You okay?" he murmured.

"Yes," I whispered, stroking the strong line of his chin. I brought my other hand up to his chest and touched the taut surface with the pads of my fingers.

"You sure?"

"Positive." I stared at his chest, stroking the muscles

with my thumb. When I looked back up, his eyes were closed.

"You want to watch a movie?" he offered.

"Do *you* want to watch a movie?"

"Not particularly. But it seems like the gentlemanly thing to ask."

"Well, if you're being all gentlemanly, how could I say no?" I teased.

Tyr put his hand on the small of my back and guided me to the living room.

"Pick your poison. We've got a pretty good selection. I'll go make popcorn." He opened a drawer, and I picked through the DVDs, while the sound of popping kernels came from the kitchen. When I found a winner, I held it up triumphantly.

"Here." I grinned as Tyr came back into the room.

"Of course you picked Henrik's chick movie. Well, in it goes." He popped the disc into the player, then got comfortable on the sectional. "Come here, baby."

He patted the seat and I curled up against him. He tucked the houndstooth throw around us, and set the popcorn on his lap, then wrapped an arm around my shoulders and rubbed my shoulder with his thumb.

"Comfortable?" he asked.

"Extremely." I lay my cheek against his chest and picked up a kernel of popcorn.

Tyr kissed the top of my head softly. "What is it with girls and this movie? Brynn loves it, too. She makes us watch it all the time."

"*The Princess Bride* is a classic," I explained. "Adventure and villains and camp and heroes and romance. That fantastic old hag. And a man who'd do anything to be with the girl he loves. He never gave up on her—ever. And she loves him to the end of the earth and back again. It's hopelessly charming, in every conceivable way."

"You mean every *inconceivable* way?" I could hear Tyr's smile.

"Good one." I giggled. "Now hush your mouth. It's starting."

"Did you just hush me?"

"Shhh." I took another piece of popcorn.

"She hushed me," Tyr muttered. But he didn't say anything else as the opening sequence rolled. I snuggled closer, breathing in his now-familiar smell. It felt good, watching a movie, tucked under his arm.

It felt right.

Tyr pulled me against him, and laid his head on top of mine. I closed my eyes, relishing the closeness. And before I knew what was happening, my focus started to drift. The movie became a soothing babble of background noise. The last thing I remember before I fell asleep was Tyr's mouth against my hairline, murmuring something that made absolutely no sense.

"*Förbaskat, Mia. Jag kunde falla för dig.*"

* * * *

I woke up early and pulled a ballet sweater over my camisole. Tyr must have carried me to the guest room while I was sleeping. Had he watched the rest of the movie first? The idea of Tyr watching the ultimate chick flick on his own made me giggle as I walked to the kitchen in bare feet, intent on brewing coffee. If I could find the right ingredients, I'd whip up a proper breakfast while I was at it. The pristine Viking range called my name.

When I had the coffee brewing, I turned to the refrigerator. A quick examination turned up eggs, milk, cheese and greens. A spinach frittata would be easy enough to pull together. I found a mixing bowl and a whisk, and moved to the island to begin chopping. As I scraped the leaves into the egg mixture, a pair of strong arms circled me from behind.

"Morning." Tyr leaned over and pressed his cheek against mine. The stubble tickled my skin.

"Morning." I set the cutting board down so I could turn in his arms. They were warm, and hard, thick muscles peeking out from the sleeves of a grey T-shirt. My palms lay flat against his chest as I lifted my head. Tyr brought his mouth down, claiming my lips in an intense kiss.

He pulled back. "Next time, I pick the movie. I can't believe you fell asleep."

"In my defense, it was kind of a big day." I pushed him away and turned back to my eggs. "Attacked at gunpoint, meeting the family, working on my paper . . ."

"Is all of this too much for you?" Tyr sounded serious. I looked up to find him studying my face.

"I'm fine. Just needed some sleep. And now I need to

finish my paper—I kind of forgot about it last night."

"Want any help?"

"No, thank you. I think I've got a decent first draft. Just need to tweak it a little and hopefully it'll be good enough." I poured the egg and cheese mixture into the pan and popped it in the oven. "Do you like frittata?"

"Does it involve bacon?" Tyr peered at the oven.

"Not this one. I didn't see any in the fridge."

"There's some in the garage fridge. Give me a sec." He walked out of the kitchen and came back a minute later with a large package of meat. The griddle was hot thirty seconds after he turned it on. That range was amazing. He opened the bacon and placed enough for a small army on the steaming surface.

"If you're going to stay here, you need to know the ground rules. Rule number one: no breakfast is complete without bacon. Coffee?"

"Yes, please."

Tyr crossed to the coffeepot, where I'd set out four clean cups. He filled one and offered it to me. "Cream?"

"No, thanks. I like it black."

"So do I." He handed me the cup and poured one for himself.

"Do I smell bacon? You know what goes great with bacon? My famous Swedish pancakes, that's what. I'll just whip up a batch and . . ." Henrik sauntered into the kitchen, followed by a cheery-eyed Brynn. A devilish smile broke out across his face as he came to a stop at the island. "Well, lookie what we have here. The picture of domestic bliss.

Looks like you two have the cooking covered. Wonder what else you'll have covered by—"

"Behave, Henrik." Brynn swatted him. He gave me a saucy wink.

"Just for that you can get your own coffee." Tyr jerked his head at the pot.

"Mmm. Coffee." Brynn practically skipped toward the caffeine. Her endless energy without the aid of stimulants was truly mind-blowing. She poured two cups and added a generous heaping of sugar to hers, offering the unsweetened one to Henrik. *Ah, that's the secret to her perkiness. Sugar.* Then she sat at the kitchen table. "So what's on the agenda today?"

"I need to finish my Shakespeare paper. So I'm headed to the library. What are you guys up to?" I took a sip from my mug.

"Henrik wants to see the new James Bond movie," Brynn offered.

"You still haven't seen that?" I was incredulous. I figured all guys went to those things on opening day.

"Nope. I've been slaving away in the engineering lab. My assistants don't work hard enough for me to take a movie break."

"Right." Brynn rolled her eyes.

"Speaking of, do you think you could come in this Wednesday afternoon, too?" Henrik pushed his glasses up his nose. "I'd like to have Fred functional in a month, and I want an extra brainstorming session so we can figure out how to make it happen."

Tyr tensed. "What's the rush?"

"Just thinking it'd be a good idea to speed things up."

A deep V formed between Tyr's eyebrows.

What did the deadline on our lab project upset Tyr? And why did he and Henrik suddenly sport matching frowns?

"Henrik, can I talk to you? Outside?" Tyr stalked out of the kitchen.

"Pardon us, girls. We'll be right back." Henrik glanced at Brynn before rushing out of the room.

"That was weird." I walked over to the oven. The frittata looked firm, so I carried it to the table to cool, then took the bacon off the griddle and set it on a plate of paper towels. "Are they always that secretive?"

"Pretty much." Brynn laughed, but the lines around her mouth looked more tense than joyful.

What was going on?

The boys strode back into the kitchen just as I was serving the frittata. Tyr rubbed his forearm while Henrik wore a smile that didn't quite reach his eyes.

"Everything okay?" I asked casually. I hadn't forgotten our conversation yesterday—if something was wrong, I wasn't supposed to push. But boy, howdy, did I want to.

"Everything's great." Tyr picked up the coffee pot with a tight smile. "Who needs a refill?"

The matter was clearly closed. Despite my overwhelming desire to jump in and fix whatever was wrong, I followed my friends and sat down to eat. Tyr and Henrik started a heated debate about their favorite soccer teams. Tyr was loyal to Malmö. It ticked him off that Henrik rooted for Stockholm.

"They're not rivals, man. We never actually beat you guys."

"It's the principle. Who doesn't root for their home team?" Tyr took a fierce bite of bacon and Henrik laughed.

"Do you guys want to go to the movie with us?" Brynn changed the subject.

"I'll go if Mia goes." Tyr picked up his coffee cup. "But it doesn't count as the date I promised you. Hanging out with these two isn't what I had in mind."

"Rude." Brynn stuck her tongue out.

"Paper." I shook my head. "Shoot. That looks like a fun movie."

"We weren't planning to go until three-thirty. You think you'll be done by then?" Brynn checked the clock over the stove. "It gives you a few hours."

"Maybe." I chewed my lip. "That could work, actually. If I go get ready now." I jumped up and carried my plate to the sink. "Should I meet you guys there?"

"No, come back here. I'll drive us." Tyr followed me to the sink and brushed his lips against mine. When I stood on tiptoe to prolong the kiss, Henrik cleared his throat.

"We're still here," he pointed out.

"Right." Heat flooded my cheeks. "See you back here this afternoon."

"See you." Tyr winked at me. "But I still owe you a date. You won't have any papers to write on Friday night, will you?"

My pulse raced. "I'd have to check my schedule, but I think I'm paper-free on Friday."

"Good. We can double with these troublemakers today, but I want you all to myself next weekend." Tyr leaned down and whispered in my ear. "I've got something in mind I think you'll really like."

"Oh do you?" I blinked up at him, praying he couldn't hear the pounding of my heart.

"I do." Tyr quickly brushed his lips against mine before stepping back.

"Sounds great," I squeaked before scurrying out of the kitchen.

Suddenly I couldn't wait to get to the library so I could finish my paper and get a jump on next week's reading. The sooner I finished my work, the sooner I could see Tyr again.

I'd never been more motivated to study in my life.

CHAPTER TWELVE

"I'M READY. SO WHERE are we going? You were so cryptic all week."

I stared at the shiny black motorcycle parked outside my house. It was Friday night, the night of our first official one-on-one date, and my pulse pounded a rhythm that was equal parts nervous and excited.

"I thought I'd give you a little peek into my world, and hopefully show you a great time all in one move. What do you say?"

I tugged at the wrists of my open leather jacket as I eyed the motorcycle. "I say I'm glad you told me to wear pants."

Tyr let his eyes run down my flowing pink top before settling on the contours of my black skinny jeans. They hugged my curves in all the right places, and judging by Tyr's appreciative stare, the extra squats I'd done this week had paid off. "So am I," he said.

"Okay." I drew a deep breath through my mouth and exhaled slowly. "Let's do this."

"Are you nervous to ride again?"

"No," I answered quickly. *Yes.* Accident statistics ran

through my brain like the stock market ticker at the bottom of a television screen, reminding me of all the reasons getting on a bike was a bad idea. My eyes drifted to my Audi parked just behind the motorcycle—the winner of the highest safety-rating awarded the year I turned sixteen, and therefore the most suitable vehicle for my parents' youngest offspring. None of that mattered.

The Audi couldn't offer a ride where I was pressed firmly against Tyr's body, the wind in my face and an engine rumbling between my thighs.

"Come on." Tyr held out his hand and we walked side by side to the bike. He dropped my hand and picked up a helmet. "You wanna put this on yourself, Miss Super G?" he quipped.

"Ha." I cuffed his shoulder before taking the helmet out of his hands. As I slid it over my head, I sent a silent prayer that I wouldn't have helmet hair by the time we got wherever it was we were going.

"You look hot."

"Oh." The temperature inside my headpiece doubled. "Thank you."

Tyr gave me a wink and put on his own helmet. The Swedish bad boy was a far cry from the Yankee prince my mother hoped I'd fall for, but for the time being he was *my* prince, whatever that meant. And Lord, if he wasn't sexy as all get-out. Even if it meant getting my heart stomped into a million pieces, I was *so* following him anywhere he asked me to. At least for tonight.

"Hold on tight. We're gonna let it go."

I threw my arms around his waist and held myself

against him. A growl resonated from Tyr's chest. "On second thought, we could always stay in."

"Drive, Fredriksen."

Tyr squared his shoulders as the bike roared to life. Before I could get my bearings, we were flying through the otherwise quiet neighborhood. Being pressed up against him was as exhilarating as it had been the first time. Only this time, I wasn't bemoaning the fact that Tyr could never be mine. In this moment, and hopefully at least a few more, he was.

Tyr pulled into a parking lot and turned off the engine. He climbed off the motorcycle, and hooked his helmet on the handlebar, then held out his hands. I gripped them tightly and scooted down the side, setting one foot on the ground before I tried Tyr's cool leg-throwing-over-the-bike trick.

Turns out that trick was best done by people *not* wearing three-inch heeled boots.

"Whoa. You okay, *prinsessa?*" Tyr caught me as I tumbled.

"Never better," I muttered into my helmet. It never failed to amaze me that I could fly down icy hills on five-foot planks, but I couldn't walk across a lawn without tripping. Tyr slid his hands around my waist and squeezed lightly as he set me on my feet. When I was steady, I pulled the headpiece off and handed it to my date. "How bad is my hair?"

Tyr raised an eyebrow. "You're worried about your hair?"

"Of course I am." I bent at the waist and tipped my

head down so I could fluff it with my fingertips. When I straightened up, Tyr was laughing. I planted my hands on my hips. "Hey buddy, hair is important to girls. And helmets are *not* hair-friendly. That's why skiers wear braids."

"You look great, Mia. Don't worry about your hair. Besides, the earphones are going to make it less floufy, anyway."

"Floufy? You use the strangest words sometimes. Wait, what do you mean earphones?"

Tyr pointed, and I turned to the building at the edge of the parking lot. "Skeeter's Shooting Range and Grill? Shut the front door!"

"You're smiling." Tyr sounded relieved.

"Heck yeah, I'm smiling. This is an awesome date."

"You said your family was outdoorsy, and that your dad taught you to shoot. I thought you might like coming here."

"I love that you brought me here." I stood on my tiptoes and pulled his head down so I could kiss his cheek. "This is going to be great."

"Mmm. Agreed." Tyr laced his fingers through mine. "You ready?"

"You have no idea." *Finally*, I was in my element.

We walked across the parking lot. When we got to the range, Tyr held the door so I could step through. "Thank you," I murmured.

"Any time."

We showed the clerk our driver's licenses and signed our waivers, and Tyr carried the rifles to our stations while I brought our goggles, headphones and ammunition. We each attached our target to the wire, and sent it down to the end of the range. Then Tyr turned to me with his telltale half-smile.

"You know how to load a rifle, right, *prinsessa?*"

I pointed the rifle at the target, cocked it and inserted the magazine, pushing until I felt it catch. "Like this?" I fluttered my lashes.

Tyr's eyes darkened a shade. "You have never been hotter to me."

"Wait 'til you see me shoot." I lowered my goggles, secured my headphones, and set my focus on the target. With six quick pulls, I'd sent a half-dozen bullets through the paper man's heart. Keeping my rifle pointed at the target, I turned my head to Tyr. "Am I hotter now?"

"*Förbaskat*, Mia. I want to take you home so bad." My headphones distorted the volume of Tyr's voice, but the desire in his eyes spoke volumes. *Holy mother* . . .

"Nope. I'm having a good time." As I lowered my head to aim, I willed my pulse to calm down.

"I promise I'll show you a good time at home," Tyr growled.

"Stop it. I'm trying to focus." I fired again, this time obliterating the center of the target's head. When I'd depleted my ammunition, I set the .22 on the counter and recalled the paper. It returned with a set of matching holes in its head and heart. I pulled it off the clip, and handed it to Tyr. "For you. So you'll always remember me."

"Oh, I don't think I could *ever* forget you. A mortal girl

in leather and heels, holding a gun with deadly accuracy."

"A 'mortal girl'? We really need to work on your pickup lines, foreigner."

"Uh . . . yeah. The translations don't always come so easily, you know." Tyr grabbed the paper from my hands and folded it before slipping it in his jacket pocket, and loading his own rifle. He lowered the goggles over his eyes but didn't bother with the earphones. I tried not to stare as he shot, but the sight of a godlike Swede firing at the thin paper man was unbelievably sexy.

This was *so* the greatest date ever.

Tyr caught me ogling as he turned back around, and one corner of his mouth turned up. "Like the view?"

"Uh . . . erm . . . doesn't the noise bother you?" I tapped my earphones, avoiding the question.

"Not much bothers me, baby."

"Really? Because when I first met you, you seemed pretty uptight." I reloaded my rifle and pinned another paper to the clip. When I saw it safely down the range, I glanced at Tyr. He was grinning.

"This from a girl who has a daily goal list taped to her mirror. Oh, I know about that. Brynn tells me things."

Raising my chin half an inch, I ignored his laughter. "Studies have shown that a visual affirmation is a highly effective tool in goal setting, and in fact, increases efficacy by more than two hundred percent."

Tyr held up a hand. "All I'm saying is people in glass houses shouldn't call other people uptight."

"Are we here to talk or shoot things?"

"Gods, you're sexy."

With a wink I turned back to my target. Three rounds and two targets later, my arm was getting sore and my date was getting hungry. When I set my gun down, he followed suit and removed his goggles. "What do you say we head to the 'and grill' section?"

"I say absolutely. I'm hungry."

We returned our gear to the clerk, and headed to the restaurant adjacent to the gun range. It was cleaner than I'd expected, with a vibe that was much more hometown diner than bar and grill. Photos of the local little league teams lined the walls, along with high school football and basketball pictures. A case of trophies sat in the corner, and behind the bar was a row of flat screens showing football, baseball and hockey games. Clearly Skeeter sought to appeal to all sports-minded audiences.

"Have a seat wherever you like." The bartender gave Tyr an appreciative onceover as she filled a pitcher of beer. He nodded, and pointed me to a window seat.

"Booth okay?" he asked me.

"So long as they serve the burgers over there, I'm good."

We crossed the room and sat on opposite sides of the dimly lit table. A waitress appeared shortly with our menus. She slowly recited the specials to Tyr, holding her chest in a way that suggested she'd be happy to serve him something *off* the menu if he'd be so inclined. But Tyr kept his eyes on me, waiting until I'd ordered my cheeseburger to turn to the waitress and ask for the same. She cast one more hopeful glance at my date, but when he ignored her she shot me a glare that could have frozen lava and stalked away. I tried not to think about what she might do to my food.

"You're good with a gun. Better than I thought." Tyr reached across the table and held my hand.

"Gee, thanks."

"You know what I mean. You said your dad taught you to shoot, but I didn't realize he taught you to *shoot*. I thought mortal girls were more . . . more helpless, I guess."

"Not me." I shrugged. "My parents were big on life skills. Mama taught us to do our own laundry, sew and cook when we were pretty young, and Daddy taught us to set up the tent, shoot, fish, and change a tire. They wanted to know when they sent us out in the world, we'd be prepared for anything."

"They had to know they couldn't prepare you for *everything*." Tyr stroked the back of my hand with his thumb.

"True." I shivered. "But darned if they didn't try. What about you? What was your childhood like before . . ." I didn't finish the sentence. *Before your parents were murdered.*

"Not quite like yours." Tyr squeezed my hand. "Even before, I had a lot of responsibility at a very young age. My family is . . . there's a lot that's expected of us. It was always understood I would follow in my father's footsteps and join the military. When he died, his job should have fallen to me, but I was too young to manage the responsibility. Odin took the job over until I came of age, and then he passed it over to me."

"Odin? Is he a friend or an uncle or something?" Was every Swede named after a Norse god?

"Odin? Uh . . . a friend. Kind of a grandfatherly figure. If your grandfather happened to be a six-foot killing machine." I raised an eyebrow and Tyr squeezed my hand lightly. "It's a joke, Mia. He's just really intense."

"Oh. Right. So now you're doing the job your dad and this Odin guy had?"

"I oversee all major threats to my . . . country, and I protect its most sought-after treasures. If they fell into the wrong hands, it would absolutely devastate the peace we've worked to build."

Tyr's statement raised a cluster of concerns. What was Sweden doing entrusting it's national security to a guy who was barely old enough to vote? And why had they given him time off to come to the States? I studied Tyr's face as he frowned. "Are you okay?"

"I'm fine." He raised my wrist to his lips. He sucked softly on the sensitive skin, and I let out a quiet sigh, my laundry-list of questions momentarily forgotten. Blood pooled deep in my belly, and my cheeks tingled with prolonged anticipation. When Tyr spoke again, the movement of his lips resonated against my arm. "I'm hungry."

Oh. My. God.

The waitress chose that moment to appear with our food. She dropped my plate in front of me with such force a french fry bounced onto the table. But she placed Tyr's carefully in front of him, lowering herself slowly so her cleavage was positioned as close to his face as decency would allow. "Anything else I can bring you?" she drawled.

"Mia?" Tyr raised one eyebrow.

"We're good, thanks." I shot her my sugary-sweet smile. She glared at me and stomped off.

"I do *not* think she likes you very much." Tyr chuckled as he pushed his plate toward me. "Here. Trade. I don't want to know what she did to yours."

"You don't have to eat it," I protested. But he held up a hand.

"Take the cheeseburger, woman."

I slid my plate in front of him, gratefully. "Thank you."

"All in the name of romance, *prinsessa*."

"You're not half bad at the romance bit, Fredriksen."

"So I hear." He chuckled. He picked up a fry and took a bite. The intensity in his eyes while he chewed made me pause. There was obviously more to Tyr Fredriksen than I might ever know. As I bit into my burger, I ran through every possible scenario. He was a mutated super-warrior. He could predict stock trends and print his own money—it would certainly explain the fancy house and designer furnishings. He was a superhero. The ideas continued as we talked and ate, and even as Tyr paid the bill and we walked to the motorcycle, each possibility increasingly more bizarre than the last. But my obsessive train derailed completely when I again climbed onto the motorcycle and wrapped my arms around Tyr. It was on the back of that bike, my arms wrapped around my date, that my mind jumped onto an entirely different track. And it didn't shift focus until after Tyr dropped me off, with a long, lingering, front-porch kiss.

* * * *

That Friday night date was the start of my new normal—my somewhat bizarre, definitely unexpected, ridiculously fabulous, normal. The next week, Tyr picked me up when I finished at the engineering lab, and we headed to his place with Henrik and Brynn to cook dinner together. It became our Tuesday and Thursday night tradition, and we'd alternate my heartier Southern meals with Henrik's lighter Scandinavian ones. Weekends were for hiking, watching movies, or hitting the beach. We'd bring picnic dinners over to Elsa's, who seemed to respond to the company; several times when I was there, her vitals spiked with marked improvement, and once I even saw her mouth twitch in a smile. Her condition was improving steadily, and there had been no mention of any more dangerous sightings in the woods. I was no closer to figuring out exactly what Tyr's job entailed, but the upside of spending so much time with him was that his secrecy didn't bother me as much as it used to. He was letting me into his life as much as he was able, and I was learning to make peace with the fact that his mysteries would unravel themselves in due time.

At least, I seriously hoped they would.

On a Friday afternoon in late October, Henrik, Brynn and I were pulling an extra session in the lab. Henrik bent the prosthesis' finger back and forth and grinned at me.

"What?" I handed him the solvent and he poured some over a swab before wiping down the robot.

"I'm just glad Tyr got over himself and started dating you. He's been decidedly less obnoxious since you came into the picture."

"You said it." Brynn looked up from her notebook, where she'd made great headway on the algorithm. "Dating you has brought out a kinder, gentler, less irritable Tyr."

Brynn and Henrik looked at each other and burst into laughter.

"What's so funny?" I asked.

"Can't explain. But if you'd known him all your life like we have . . ." Brynn gave in to a fresh bout of hysteria.

"Sorry." Henrik wiped his eyes. "Hand me that wrench, would you?"

I did as instructed and tried not to feel left out.

"And speak of the devil." Henrik winked. "Tyr says you guys have plans tonight."

"He said to dress warm. Any idea where he's taking me?"

"Yep. I helped him pack up."

"Pack up? Are we going away?" I tried not to panic. I wasn't sure if I was ready for a sleepover. Tyr had been opening up more about his life before Arcata, and he was sexy as sin, but I still didn't know if I was ready to sleep with him. I *wanted* to, I wasn't made of stone, but he had this whole secret world with his sister and his job that I couldn't begin to understand. How could I let him in on that level without understanding exactly what made him tick?

"You wish you were going away," Brynn teased. "Tyr's hot. Soooo hot."

"He's okay." Henrik muttered.

"He's more than okay. You're hot, too. But you're an intellectual hot. The brains, the wild hair, the glasses— definitely a bookish hot." Brynn conceded.

"Which is sometimes better than the non-bookish hot," I offered, relieved I still had some time to decide whether I wanted Tyr to be my first . . . well, my first everything.

"Charity will get you nowhere. Work harder, ladies. Fred isn't going to finish himself." Henrik adjusted his glasses and attached a tiny screw to the arm.

"We're still calling it Fred, are we?" I exhaled, relieved the focus was off me.

Henrik bristled. "Yes, we are. Fred was a very special dog."

"Okay. Truce." I held out my hand, and he took it.

"Truce. Oh, and Mia? You're welcome for the marshmallows."

He grinned as I blinked. What the heck did that mean?

CHAPTER THIRTEEN

"YOU LOOK AMAZING, *PRINSESSA*."

Tyr stood on my porch with a handful of purple peonies. He was perfection in fitted jeans, a grey Henley, and his leather jacket. He let his eyes linger over the neckline of my tight sweater before holding out the bouquet. Score one, LaPerla.

"Thank you." I took the flowers. "These smell great."

"So do you." Tyr wrapped his arm around my waist and dipped me back, planting a feather-light kiss on my lips. My head spun as he pulled me up. He eyed me levelly. "You gonna make it?"

I laughed. "You're trouble."

"You have no idea."

"Let me just go put these in water." I darted into the kitchen, and put the peonies in a slim vase. It would have made sense to have a vase waiting at the door; Tyr rarely showed up empty-handed. Still, it took me by surprise that the bad boy who employed a team of armed guards for protection was sweet enough to bring me flowers. Tyr wasn't turning out to be at all what I'd expected. He was much more thoughtful than he wanted people to believe, at least from what I'd seen during the last few months. Something told me I'd only scratched the surface.

As I walked back through the front door, Tyr held out his arm. He walked me to the street where the gleaming black motorcycle waited.

We made it to town in record time, and by the time Tyr slowed to the speed limit, my heart was pounding a beat worthy of a college-bowl-game halftime show. He must have felt it through his jacket, because he reached around and pressed me against him with one hand, then slid the same hand slowly down to my behind. He gave a firm squeeze and returned his hand to the handlebar.

Oh, hot bejeebus.

We kept our speed low as we moved through downtown. The little shops lining the quaint street were picturesque in the cool night. Couples strolled casually in and out of the diner, and I wondered if we were going to one of the three restaurants in town, but when the light turned green, the bike revved again.

We passed through the main hub, and Tyr took the road that led down to the beach. *The beach!* Now his suggestion to dress warm made sense. The shores of northern California were downright chilly at night.

Tyr brought the bike to a stop and swung a long leg over the side. He wrapped his fingers around my arms and guided me off the seat. When he pulled off his helmet, his grin lit up the whole beach. It would have been buzz kill to mention my legs were the consistency of Jell-O.

"Thought I was going to lose you for a minute back

there." He lifted my helmet from my head and hooked it to the seat. I fluffed my hair while his back was turned.

"Uh-huh." I straightened up. "And you thought you'd secure me by fondling my tush?"

"Kept you on the bike, didn't it?" Tyr winked. He pivoted with his shoulders pulled back, his eyes combing the beach so intently, he could have memorized the specs on each grain of sand. Although his back was to me, I heard the low rumble of his voice a half-second before I saw the light. It appeared overhead, then whirled around in a blur, encasing the beach in a pale green bubble. My squeal echoed across the sand as the illusion disappeared.

"What in the name of all that's good and holy was that?" I blurted.

Tyr turned around. "What?"

"That!" My finger jabbed at the air. "That . . . crazy light thing?" Tyr's litany of cryptic comments ran through my mind like a newsfeed on fast forward. "Hold on. You mumbled something just before it happened. Did you do . . . whatever that was?"

"What are you talking about?" Tyr furrowed his brow.

My words tumbled out. "Did you do that?"

Tyr placed his hands on my shoulders and squeezed. "Baby, if you saw some crazy light thing, it was probably the meteor shower. It starts tonight, remember?"

"This didn't look like a meteor shower. It looked like a Northern Lights thing. Like what you guys get in Scandinavia."

Tyr shook his head. "Arcata's not far enough north for

that kind of atmospheric phenomenon."

"You're avoiding the question." I waited.

Tyr sighed. "Listen, baby. I need to make sure the guy hunting my sister doesn't come after you. Henrik thinks he saw him in the woods again today, so we're being extra careful. That's all you need to know."

"Why can't you tell me what I saw?" Ignoring the shiver that crept up my spine, I let irritation at Tyr's secrecy trump my fear at Elsa's attacker being close. Again.

"Because it would take too long, and dinner would get cold. Come on." Tyr grabbed a bag off the back of the bike and slung it over his shoulder. He laced his fingers through mine and tugged me toward the sand.

My mind swam with questions, percolating to the point of being overwhelming. If the light hadn't been a bad thing, why wouldn't Tyr just tell me what I'd seen? Did he have some hidden flare gun, or illegal fireworks? How would either of those keep Elsa's would-be killer away? And why did so much of his life still have to be such a big secret?

"Tyr." I broke our silence as we rounded an outcropping of rocks and entered a small cove. "Do you trust me?"

"Implicitly," he swore.

"Then why won't you tell me what just happened?"

Tyr sighed, and pulled a small plastic tube out of his pocket. It looked like a lighter. "Because I don't want you to laugh at me. I know you think I'm overprotective. I haven't forgotten our first run together."

"You *are* overprotective. This is not news."

"Regardless." He held up the lighter. "Henrik designed this. It's a kind of refractor. It bends light in a fifty-yard circumference around the spot it's activated, so anyone *outside* its reach can't see what's happening *inside* its reach. Meaning if Henrik really did see the guy hunting my sister today, we don't have to worry about him seeing you with me right now."

"Seriously? Henrik made that?" I stared at the device. "He's a genius."

"He likes to think so." Tyr shrugged, putting the refractor back in his pocket. "So that's it. I trust you. Henrik's a nerd. We're safe from the bad guy in here. Now can we please eat dinner?"

"Of course." *Thank God.* My imagination had started to come up with some pretty unbelievable explanations for Tyr's strange behavior, none of which were all that comforting. Leave it to the Math Club and Henrik's obsession with technology to set order to my mental chaos.

"Good." Tyr tossed his bag on the sand, then pulled out two blankets and an array of food. He laid one blanket on the sand and started unpacking dinner: focaccia sandwiches with turkey, avocado, and cheese, and a steaming foil container, plates, forks and napkins.
    "What's in the foil?" I sat on the blanket.

He lifted a corner of the lid and I breathed in the scent. "Mmm, mac and cheese." It wasn't the boxed variety. This looked as if it had been made from scratch. It even had breadcrumbs on top. "Is that . . . bacon?"

Tyr winked.

Oh, yum.

Tyr sat next to me and held out the second blanket. He wrapped it around my shoulders before handing me a plate. He piled food on top and passed me a bottle of sparkling water, then filled a second plate for himself and raised his own bottle to mine. "*Skål*. Cheers."

"Cheers." We clinked bottles and took a drink, then I tucked into the food. "This is amazing. It's so savory. I'm impressed."

"You don't have to sound so surprised," Tyr said wryly.

I took another bite. The cheese was the perfect mixture of tangy and smoky—Gouda was my favorite. "You should do more of the cooking from now on."

"I don't look nearly as good as you do in an apron. Besides, you like to be in control in the kitchen." Tyr leaned over with a lascivious grin. "It's hot."

I ducked to hide behind my hair, but Tyr tucked the strand behind my ear.

"You're *så förbaskat* beautiful, Mia." He let the words linger. When I finally broke eye contact, every nerve in my body buzzed.

My fingers trembled as I picked up my sandwich. Tyr did the same, and we chewed in silence, staring at the waves crashing ten yards away. When we finished eating, I pulled my knees to my chest and rested my head on Tyr's shoulder. He wrapped an arm around me, gently massaging my lower back. I closed my eyes, trying to commit every detail of this moment to memory.

"How's Elsa?" I ventured.

Tyr let out a breath. "She's having a rough day."

"Oh, Tyr." I circled his waist with my arms and squeezed. "What happened?"

"I have no idea. She was doing well for a while."

"I know. Last week, she had more color in her cheeks. It almost seemed like she was just sleeping." I nuzzled against his chest.

"Yeah." Tyr rested his chin on the top of my head. "Her vitals have been volatile since yesterday. Her doctors don't know what's wrong—none of her treatments have changed, and her internal injuries have been stabilized for weeks. It doesn't make any sense."

"Is there anything you can do?"

"I'm doing everything I can." Tyr's agony came through in his voice. "I just don't know how much longer she'll be able to hold out. Her cell counts are . . . she's not doing great."

"I'm so sorry," I whispered. "Do you want to go see her right now? I'll go with you."

"No. I went this afternoon. Henrik's with her now. I think my energy was actually making her worse. I get pretty upset when she takes a dive."

"I'd be exactly the same if anything ever happened to Jason." I squeezed Tyr's waist again and his mouth brushed the top of my head.

"Just be careful, okay?" Tyr's lips moved against my hair.

"Always am," I promised.

Tyr lifted my chin with a finger and kissed me softly. When he pulled back, his eyes were considerably lighter.

"Help me find some driftwood. I thought we'd make s'mores. I've never had one before."

"Do you even know how to make them?"

"Henrik gave me some pretty detailed instructions." He rolled his eyes, and I laughed.

"Let me guess—step one, build a fire with birch strips configured in the perfect teepee shape, covering exactly four pieces of wadded-up newspaper for kindling. Am I close?"

"Frighteningly so." Tyr held out a hand to pull me up. "Help me look for those birch strips, will you?"

"Yes, sir."

We strolled along the beach, hand in hand, pausing to pick up pieces of driftwood that looked reasonably dry. When we'd collected enough to start a small fire, we headed back to our blanket. Tyr arranged the wood in a small pit and pulled the lighter out of his back pocket.

"I thought that was the magic light bubble thing?" I questioned.

"It's multi-functional." Tyr flicked the trigger, but the breeze snuffed the flame. His brow furrowed, and he tried again. And again. He stuck his tongue out of the corner of his mouth and bit down, glaring at the lighter.

I let out a giggle.

"This funny to you?" He looked up.

"Yes," I admitted. Seeing my cool, capable Hercules bested by a piece of plastic was priceless.

He didn't swear. Didn't throw it into the surf. Instead, in

true Tyr fashion, he simply returned to his task, manipulating the tiny device long after it was obvious the thing wasn't going to cooperate. It was a matter of pride at this point, and I knew things well enough to know he wasn't backing down. He might have been the only person on the planet more stubborn than me.

Though it looked like that lighter had a leg up on both of us.

"Why don't you go grab the bag while I work on this? The marshmallows are in there." Tyr nodded toward the blanket.

"Fair enough." I turned and walked the short distance to the blanket. By the time I came back, Tyr had managed to start a small fire.

"How'd you do that? And so fast?" Usually a fire smoldered for a while before the logs caught. After a lifetime of camping, I was no pyro-novice.

"You know I'm good with my hands." Tyr raised an eyebrow.

I swatted him. "Seriously. There's no way you got a fire going that fast."

"You calling me a liar?" Tyr pushed himself to his feet and took a step toward me. I paused. It did seem like a silly thing to lie about.

"Um. No?"

"More conviction, please." Tyr took another step, his eyes glinting.

"No. Absolutely not. Nope." I dropped the marshmallow-filled bag and started backing up.

"I'm not believing you." Tyr stepped over the bag. He was closing the gap.

"I'd never call you a liar. Ever." I held up my hands.

"Too late." Tyr took one more step, and I bolted down the beach, running in the soft sand. The ocean roared to my right, and Tyr's footsteps thundered behind me. Before I knew it, he'd caught up; his thick arms wrapped around me from behind and swung me in a circle. When he set me back on my feet, I was dizzy, lightheaded, and laughing hysterically.

"You are so much trouble," I said, for the second time that night.

"You have no idea," he muttered.
"You keep saying that."

"Trust me." Tyr looked down at me, desperation in his eyes. I realized that he was trying to communicate something important. His words reverberated through my head. They were more than a passing comment—they were a pledge. And a plea. Tyr was laying his soul bare, exposing his deepest wish in two words. *Trust me.*

I blinked up at him, struck by the truth that had snuck up on me somewhere between our first run and our first grilled cheese, between the late-night phone calls and the picnic visits with Elsa, the evenings falling asleep in front of a movie and the mornings jogging in the forest. Tyr had eased himself into my life so seamlessly, I couldn't imagine my world without him in it.

And I didn't want to.

In that moment, I made a conscious choice. "I trust you," I whispered, marveling at the truth of the words. I put my hand in Tyr's and stared up at him. His face broke into a beautiful smile as he scooped me up and wrapped his arms below my bottom, so we were eye to eye. My heart thudded.

"Do you really?" Tyr asked.

"I do."

With that, Tyr shifted me to one arm, and lifted his hand. He wrapped his fingers around the back of my head and crushed his mouth to mine, kissing me with a force that sent my poor heart into overdrive. Blood rushed out of my head on a breakneck journey south as I wrapped my legs around Tyr's waist and held on tight. His palm caressed my bottom, softly at first, but increasing in pressure as he pulled me closer to him. His mouth moved to my neck, and he gently sucked his way to the neckline of my top. This would have been a *really* good night to have borrowed that deep V-neck in Charlotte's closet.

"Say it again," he growled into my neck.

"I trust you," I whispered.

"Oh, Mia." Tyr buried his face against my skin, and my breath caught as I made another choice. I was ready to show Tyr the depth of my trust. In the most important way I knew how.

Oh cheese and crackers. It was an enormous decision—I'd kissed three boys in my entire life, and I'd certainly never slept with anyone. These were really deep waters, and I was sure Tyr had swum in them plenty of times before. But I'd never felt like this about anyone; there wasn't anyone else I wanted to be my first.

Suddenly s'mores were the furthest thing from my mind.

I lifted Tyr's face and stared into his eyes. "Can we go home? To your place, I mean?" I asked.

Tyr watched me levelly, then set me on my feet, stalked back to the blanket, packed up our picnic, and snuffed out the fire. The whole circuit took less than a minute.

He took my hand and walked me to his bike without a word, placed the helmet on my head and gave me a determined stare.

"Hop on."

We pushed the speed limit on the streets of Arcata, and when Tyr hit the forest he let loose. My arms squeezed his chest so hard I was afraid he wouldn't be able to breathe, but we got to his house in record time, and he lifted me off the bike with minimal effort. He didn't put me down until we were inside the foyer, and from the look in his eyes, letting me stand was just a formality.

My mind raced.

Tyr flipped on the lights, closed the front door behind him, and took my coat. He crossed to the hall closet and removed his own jacket while I fidgeted with the wrists of my sweater.

Tyr closed the door and turned to me. In five long strides, he was at my side. He wrapped one arm around me, pulling my lower back into his waist, while his other hand gathered my hair into a low ponytail. He tugged gently, and brought his mouth to my neck. His tongue was hot on my skin, its languid movement drawing a fiery trail downward. I threw my hands around him, reaching up to finger the soft hair at the back of his head. As I did, he licked a slow line up my jaw, then crushed his mouth against mine. His tongue pushed past my lips, gently moving in a maddening dance that left me squirming.

And then I heard the voice.

"Tyr! Get outside *right now*!" Freya pounded on the front door.

"For the love of Odin!" Tyr thundered. He pulled back just enough to look into my eyes. "Don't move. That's an order."

"Aye aye." I saluted breathlessly.

Tyr didn't take his hand off my waist as he reached for the door. He wedged it open just enough to poke his head through, all the while holding me tight against his side.

"What?" he hissed.

"That." Freya pointed at something just beyond the driveway.

"You're going to have to be more specific. And come back tomorrow. Because as you can see—"

Just then I heard a boom. It sounded like a clap of thunder let loose nearby. With a flash of light, something big and furry crashed against an invisible screen at the edge of the trees. Then it burst through, careening toward the house, and snarling through bared teeth. Freya dropped to a crouch, as if she were preparing to jump.

"*Skit!*" Tyr swore. He released his hold on me so fast I barely had time to gather my footing. He raced to the door next to the coat closet and entered a code into a keypad I hadn't realized was there. The door sprung open. Tyr ripped out two futuristic handguns and a crossbow. Then he sprinted out of the house.

"Stay inside, Mia," he commanded. I stood inside the front door, too shocked to move.

Tyr launched himself off the porch, flying a good twenty yards. He met the creature midair, their bodies entwining in a deadly dance, but instead of dropping to the ground, they stayed suspended two stories high, a blur of fangs, fur and fists. Something about the animal seemed familiar, but I didn't have time to process the thought because a bluish light emanated from somewhere between my boyfriend and the beast. It grew brighter as they struggled—almost like the light fed off their energy. Tyr grabbed the creature's ears and wrenched its neck. I heard a sickening crack, but the animal seemed unaffected. It just snarled and slammed its head against Tyr's shoulder.

His crossbow fell to the ground with a clang. Tyr grabbed for one of his guns, but the beast swatted it away with one enormous paw, and Freya swore from the porch.

"He's only got one left," she muttered. "Double *skit*."

"I can help. I'm a good shot. Give me one of those guns." I darted for the closet, but Freya ran inside and grabbed my arm.

"Those guns are not for mortals. This isn't something you can help with, Mia. Not yet, anyway."

Did she have to sound so patronizing? And what was with the mortal thing? Who taught these people their English?

"Look, you might be his best friend, or whatever you are to each other, but you're not the only one who cares about him. He needs help. I'm an excellent marksman. Give me a freaking gun." Something let out a growl from outside, sending goosebumps up my arms. "Now, Freya!"

"Sorry, Mia. No." Freya sprinted out of the house and waved her hand at the doorway. She turned to the woods with a gasp as the beast lunged at Tyr. Sure, jumping in the middle of that fight would have been dumber than using the good scissors to cut chicken, but did the beauty queen really think I was going to stand by while the guy who owned my heart was mauled to death by some wolf on steroids? I ran for the open door, and cried out when my face struck an invisible surface. *What the . . .?* Freya looked back at me, sympathy in her eyes. I shook off the dull ache in my now-tender nose, and moved for the porch a second time, only to be stopped again by something I couldn't see. There was some kind of a shield filling the doorway, keeping me from getting outside. *Hold on.* Freya had waved her hand. Did she have one of Henrik's lighters, too? Did she use it to block me? Was she insane? Now I was trapped in the house, and the only thing I could do was watch helplessly while a horrific battle raged outside.

"Freya!" I shrieked. She was going to have some *major* explaining to do.

"Sorry, Mia." She ran a hand through her strawberry locks. "Tyr would want me to make sure you stay safe." With two graceful strides, she jumped high in the air and flew the twenty yards toward the altercation. *How is that even possible?* She landed on the creature's back and started tearing, sending tufts of fur floating to the ground. The animal roared, and Tyr reached for his gun. He fired a series of laser beams into the animal's neck, but it didn't flinch. Instead, it grew very still, and gave Tyr a steely-eyed stare that left frost in my heart. Then it disappeared in a puff of smoke.

My face was pressed so hard against the invisible barrier at the door, I'd lost feeling in my nose. My fists pounded helplessly against the unseen shield like a pitiful, angry mime.

Tyr and Freya remained floating above the ground. Did the laws of physics not apply here? There was no way Henrik had invented something that could make them do *that*. Were they doing it on their own? And if they were . . . there was no way they were . . . were they even human? Mortal? What the hell was going on?

Freya saw me gaping and muttered something to Tyr. He glanced over his shoulder with a grimace, then put his gun in his back pocket and glided slowly to the ground. He didn't break eye contact as he walked steadily toward me, pausing at the steps leading up to the porch. He held out his hands, palms up.

"Mia," he murmured.

That was when I realized I was shaking, though with anger at being kept in the dark, or shock that the guy I thought I knew could fly, I hadn't yet decided.

Tyr took two tentative steps onto the porch and stopped. He took in the way my body was pressed against the invisible barrier of the door, hands balled in tight fists by my face as if I could push through it with sheer willpower. My eyes were wet, my chin was quivering, and I stood on my toes, ready to bolt as soon as someone lifted the block.

"Hey," Tyr whispered softly. "It's okay. It's just me."

I shook my head violently. There was no reconciling the

man I'd been dating for the past couple of months with the man I just saw fly, battle a monster, and fire off a laser. Not to mention the mysterious weapons closet he'd never mentioned—it didn't take a rocket scientist to figure crossbows and space guns were the tip of the iceberg in there. And the best friend who thought it was a good idea to lock me in the house like some simpering girlfriend had another thing coming. I was a girlfriend, yes, but I didn't simper. I was tougher than she knew, and I was about to show her.

"You want me to stick around?" Freya came up behind Tyr.

"You," I cried. "I don't know what you are, or who taught you appropriate social behavior, but you are a major piece of work. It is not okay to lock people in houses."

Tyr's mouth twitched, but he didn't smile. If he had, I'd have thrown something at him, door barrier or no.

"I'm sorry, Mia. I really am. And I know that looked bad, but you have to believe I did it for your own good." Freya held up her hands.

"For my own good? What is it with you people and those words? I don't need you two protecting me. I can take care of myself, *thank you very much*. I could have shot that thing down, or at the very least distracted it. But your best idea was to lock me in the house with one of Henrik's techy-lighters?" My voice had risen at least an octave. It wasn't dignified, but I was well beyond caring.

"Henrik's techy-lighters? What's she talking about, Tyr?" Freya turned to Tyr. He tilted his head, looking confused.

"The techy-lighters." I glared. "You know, the ones that

made that bubble that kept the bad guy from seeing us on the beach, or wherever." Freya stared blankly at me. "Tyr has one in his pocket. Show her."

Tyr slowly pulled the lighter out of his back pocket. He and Freya exchanged a glance. They seemed to be having a silent conversation.

"See? The techy-lighter. Sorry I don't know its *proper* name. That's what you used to lock me in here, right? Right?" I waited for Freya's confirmation, but she was silent. Tyr tucked the lighter back into his pocket, and Freya tore her eyes away from his.

"Mia, you and I can talk later. I'm truly sorry for upsetting you. I won't lock you anywhere again." She turned back to Tyr. "I'm going to leave you two alone. I won't be any help here. Call me if he comes back. I'm sorry he got away."

She was just going to leave? Just like that? And what did she mean, he got away? The creature had disappeared in a puff of smoke. I'd seen it. Surely he was dead, right?

"Step back, Mia." Freya waved her hand at the door, and I pushed my hand through. The barrier was gone. She nodded at me and ran into the forest. I stared at the spot where she'd disappeared until I couldn't hear her footsteps.

"Can I come in?" Tyr asked. His hands were still open—maybe to prove he was unarmed. Not that it mattered much—a guy who could fly and battle a creature that size wouldn't need a weapon to debilitate me.

I gave him my finest stink eye.

"Please, baby. Let me explain."

My eyes darted wildly between the forest and my boyfriend. There was a beast in the woods, but there was a man unaffected by gravity on the porch. One who had most definitely lied to me. I wasn't sure which unnerved me more.

What I really wanted was to understand; understand how Tyr had done what he'd done; understand how he and Freya seemed human enough, but obviously weren't; understand how that wolf was so powerful; understand how, if Tyr was an alien or a superhero or a mutant or whatever he was, how we could possibly have any kind of a relationship; understand why everyone but me had Henrik's absolutely awesome lighters.

"I'm coming inside." Tyr walked slowly, palms up, and stepped through the door. Then he walked backwards to the closet, where he hung up his crossbow and the two space guns. He shut the door gently, entered a code that I assumed locked the room, and closed the cover on the keypad.

I still hadn't moved.

"Can I touch you?" he asked.

I nodded. Tyr slowly moved to my side. He took one of my balled fists and pulled me from the door.

"No more secrets," he vowed. He pulled the lighter out of his back pocket and threw it off the porch. "Henrik didn't make a special lighter. This is all me."

He held out one hand and muttered something in Swedish I didn't understand. Light shot from his hand and I spun around to follow its trajectory. It hit what looked like a clear screen at the edge of the woods, and traced an arc around the house in a half-dome, encasing the property in a silvery coating. Tiny spots floated gently from the dome, like thousands of luminescent snowflakes, and soon the ground around the house was covered in a glittery powder. Tyr snapped his fingers and the powder disappeared. Everything was as it had been—it was as if the whole night had never happened.

My knees buckled as the room started to spin. Tyr caught me just before I hit the ground. He swept me up in his arms and carried me to the couch.

"Okay, *prinsessa*. Time for the talk."

He tucked a heavy throw around my legs and sat next to me. He kept one of his shoulders an inch from mine. I cautiously turned my head to appraise him. On the outside, nothing had changed. His eyes were the same midnight blue, his jaw the same perfect square, and the enormous arms folded calmly across his chest were the same ones I loved to curl up in.

But everything felt different. I realized I had no idea who this man actually was, where he came from, and what else he was capable of. The only thing I knew for sure was that I needed answers. *Real* answers, this time. No more secrets.

I drew a shaky breath and spoke the words that would change my life forever.

"Who are you?"

CHAPTER FOURTEEN

"MAY I?" TYR HELD out his hand.

I nodded.

He traced my palm with the pads of his fingers. "I might have understated my position when I told you I was in the military."

"I figured."

"I serve the Alfödr in a military role."

"The all father . . ." I froze. "You're in the Mafia?"

"No." Tyr chuckled. "That's the godfather. I serve Odin, the Alfödr. Father of all. Ruler of the gods."

"So you're in a—religious organization?" In other words, a cult. I'd learned about those in sociology class. *Members suffer from deep disillusionment.* I slowly extricated my hand and placed it in my lap. Tyr's brow furrowed, but he let me go.

"What? No. Let me try again." He looked at the recessed lights, then brought his gaze back to me. "Here's the thing." He took a deep breath. "I'm a Norse god."

"Of course you are. Look at you." Talk about stating

the obvious.

"No, Mia. I'm a Nordic deity. Literally. I serve the realms as God of War. I live in Asgard, under Odin's command, and oversee protection of the nine realms via termination of hostile elements. I'm an assassin by profession, immortal by nature, and I have a small legion of enemies with a price on my head." He watched my face, presumably for a reaction.

I stared blankly. Either he had a really weird sense of humor, or being so good looking had given him a god complex. I'd learned about those in sociology, too. "Is this supposed to be funny?"

"Not even a little bit."

"Then what are you doing?" Tyr's hands circled my wrists. He laced his fingers through mine and held on as if his life depended on it.

"I'm being honest with you."

"You expect me to believe you're the Norse God of War. That isn't funny. It's just weird."

"Then how would you explain what you saw outside?" Tyr waited as I worked through my thoughts.

"I don't know," I admitted. "Atmospheric phenomenon?"

"Do you believe that?"

No. An atmospheric phenomenon wouldn't produce the kind of pressure inconsistency that elevated certain items within its reach, but not others. But what Tyr had suggested wasn't exactly believable either.

"You're telling me you're a god? And you expect me to

take you seriously?" That request was utterly absurd. There weren't gods in real life. They were the stuff of myths—characters in storybooks and movies. The real world had people and animals and the occasional vacuuming robot. But it most definitely did *not* have gods. And it absolutely did not have gods who went out with human college girls.

"Well, you've kissed me. What do you think?" Tyr winked. Then he looked down at our clasped hands and frowned; mine started to tremble so hard they became a blur.

"No more jokes. Are you telling the truth?"

"I swear on my sister's life," Tyr vowed. "I am a god. And a rather good-looking one, if I say so myself."

CHEESE AND FREAKING CRACKERS. He wasn't kidding. Either he was completely delusional, or I'd been about to give my virginity to an honest-to-goodness *god*.

In through the nose, out through the mouth. In through the nose out through the . . . oh, who am I kidding? There was no way to breathe my way out of this panic attack. My boyfriend was a god. *A god. A GOD.* What the hell was I supposed to do with that? The existence of mythological deities did not fit into my black-and-white world-view, and dating one most certainly did not factor into my five-year plan. *Holy mother of pearl.* I was a living, breathing, glittery supernatural teen movie in the making. Only I wasn't the swooning co-ed anymore. Now I was barely holding it together.

"You're a god?" I whispered.

"Yes," Tyr answered. Again.

"Are you going to hurt me?" I asked.

"What? No. Why would you even ask that?" He squeezed my hands softly, then brushed one finger against my cheek. For the first time, I didn't lean into the contact. Everything about him felt the same—his touch still made my skin burn, and the searing look in those steely blue eyes had my heart racing. But absolutely everything had changed. *Everything.*

"Because. This is some seriously scary stuff."

"It doesn't have to be scary. We're the good guys." He rubbed his thumbs along my temples, and my hands went still.

"We? There are more of you?"

"Of course. There's me, Henrik—"

"Henrik, too?"

"Henrik too. Brynn. Freya."

Holy Lord. Half of my social circle is in on this?

"There are hundreds of us. We fight for *ære*—it's a Norwegian word meaning—"

"I thought y'all spoke Swedish."

"Scandiwegian, remember? Since we represent all of the Scandinavian countries, we try to cover all of the bases." Tyr's smile was tight. "And *ære* means honor; glory; virtue; the greater good. We exist to protect the nine realms, and we're willing to die to do it." He paused. "Baby, you're turning white."

"Right." With painstaking effort, I forced a breath in and out. "Wait, gods can't die. They're gods. You're gods. Oh, God!" This was insane. *Insane.* My boyfriend was someone straight out of a dark fairytale.

And he wasn't Prince Charming.

"Gods can die, Mia. Being immortal does not mean being immune to death. It means we continue living until we are killed. We do not fall ill, or die of old age as mortals do. Our bodies age extremely slowly."

"How slowly?" I blurted. Something told me my collegiate-looking boyfriend had lied to me about his age. *Among other things . . .*

Tyr furrowed his brow, in the universal facial expression of mental math. "I believe . . . approximately one fiftieth of the rate a mortal does. So while you might easily live for fifty years before looking old, I could live twenty-five hundred before assuming that same appearance."

"Awesome." I squeezed my eyes shut as I jumped from my seat. "That would make you what, a thousand years' old right now?"

"Almost." Tyr stared at me. I stared back. This was all so *complicated*. My brain worked through a million thoughts at once, but processed none of them. I started to pace in front of the couch.

"You're a god."

"Still yes."

"And you can do . . . god stuff?"

"Yes," Tyr repeated.

"What kind of stuff? What are your powers?"

"It's kind of involved." Tyr ran a hand through his hair. "I can fly, which you saw; create protective shields; my hands are pretty solid weapons—they can project debilitators and enchantments. I have some extrasensory abilities that help me scope out dark spirits and bad auras. I can conjure things and dispense of things, and I have some healing abilities; all pretty run-of-the-mill defensive stuff. It's not that big of a deal."

"Excuse me, it is an *extremely* big deal." I stopped pacing and shoved my finger in Tyr's face, my left hand on my hip. "You are an immortal deity traipsing around a college town, protecting your sister and fighting off homicidal wolves like some frat-boy/boy-scout mash-up. Which, according to Jason, is another total myth. If what you are and what you're doing isn't bat-poop crazy, then I don't know what is."

Tyr's mouth twitched. "Did you just call me bat-poop crazy?"

"You lied to me. You don't get to laugh at me." I tugged at my hair.

Tyr reached up to grab my hand. "I'm still me." A corner of his mouth turned up in a rakish grin, and for a moment I was mesmerized by his brilliant smile; his piercing eyes; the way his stubble highlighted the strong line of his jaw when he spoke. "And I never lied to you, except about the lighter thing. I did move here from Sweden; I was disabling a portal between Midgard and one of the dark realms. I did grow up with Henrik and Brynn; the Anderssons took us in, and Brynn lived next door. And I did lose my parents to the wolf. I just omitted a few facts."

"Big ol' facts to omit," I muttered. "What are you doing here? Why aren't you in heaven?" I tried to reach for my hair again, but Tyr held onto my hand.

"It's called Asgard. It's as beautiful as a lot of mortals imagine their heaven will be—big rolling hills, grassy meadows, a weeping willow with leaves made of real silver, castles . . . but it's not a particularly peaceful place. Our realm is under constant attack, and most of our residents train to fulfill military roles. We have a structured army, much like humans do, with soldiers and commanders and colonels and an elite team, all of which report to me. The only military figure that ranks above me is Odin."

Oh Lord almighty. He actually was the *god* of *war.*

"Stop pulling away from me. Come here." Tyr raised an eyebrow, and I reluctantly sat down. What I really wanted to do was run home to the little house on Daffodil screaming like a banshee, but there was a massive wolf outside . . .

Shut the front door. There was a massive wolf outside. And an enormous blond guy in here. Things slowly clicked into place, the pieces of the puzzle finally forming a whole picture.

"In the woods," I whispered. "My first day here. A wolf *did* attack me. You were there. I didn't imagine it. Oh my God, the wolf outside is the wolf that came after me." I started to shake again.

"You didn't imagine it." Tyr held me as I trembled.

"But I was hurt—he bit me hard enough to hit bone. Why wasn't there any blood?" I touched my forearm.

"You sure you want to know?"

"I'm pretty sure nothing you can tell me will shock me more than '*I'm a Norse God, prinsessa.*'"

Tyr snickered. "Nice accent."

"Whatever. Tell me why I wasn't hurt."

"I had Freya heal you."

There was no way I'd heard that right. "Excuse me?"

"I had to deal with the wolf, and I knew you were pretty torn up. I summoned Freya, she dropped in via the Bifrost—"

"The what?" I asked.

"The Bifrost. It's the rainbow bridge we use to travel between the realms. Heimdall guards it, and directs it to wherever we need it to go." Tyr ran his hand along my shoulders. "You need the blanket again? You're still shivering."

"I'm fine. Just in shock that my boyfriend travels by rainbow, that's all."

"It's not all it's cracked up to be." Tyr grabbed a throw off the edge of the couch and tucked it around my legs. "The motion sickness takes centuries to get over."

"I'll try to remember that." I pulled the blanket up to my waist. "Next time I'm catching a rainbow bus or riding my rainbow bike or . . . Freya seriously healed me?"

"She did. The wolf was in a right state, and I needed to get him away from the human population, so I summoned Freya. When she saw you bleeding out, she knew what to do. Brynn arrived a few moments later, so Freya left you to help me subdue the animal. Unfortunately, we lost him when he ran through a portal."

I blinked. "He went back up the rainbow tunnel?"

"Bridge," Tyr corrected. "And no. That was the plan—we were hoping to ship him back to Asgard's prison. But when I called for Heimdall to open the Bifrost, the wolf took off. He managed to open a portal of his own, and he disappeared."

"Is that what you were afraid of that day I found Elsa's cabin? Were you afraid someone had come out of some portal close to there?" I tucked my knees to my chest. "You acted like something was going to jump out from behind a tree any minute."

"I'd thought I saw the wolf in the woods that afternoon, but Henrik did a sweep later that night and didn't find any residue."

"Residue?" I paused. "Residue of what?"

Tyr frowned. "When the wolf disappeared that day, the first thing I did was make sure you were okay. Freya had healed you as well as I could have, so I left you in Brynn's care and went to inspect the portal the monster escaped from. It contained heavy traces of dark magic. The wolf doesn't have magic—he only has brute strength. Which meant something evil on the other side of that portal helped him escape. Someone with a lot of dark power is working with him. It's not ideal."

Tyr wrapped one arm protectively around me, and used the other to stroke the knots in the back of my neck. I flinched as he rubbed a particularly tender spot. He pressed softly into the knot, and the pain eased.

Well no wonder he was so good with his hands. He was divine.

"Are they trying to kill you?" I whispered.

"I don't think so. I think they're trying to break me."

"Break you? Why?"

"Because I'm the first and last line of defense between the monsters of the underworlds and Asgard. Whoever's helping the wolf must know that I carry a lot of guilt about what that monster has done—he would have been executed centuries ago if I hadn't intervened. And I think they're hoping that guilt eventually drives me mad. If I were to turn against my realm, or even just abandon my post, there would be a clear path to Odin, and to the throne. An open seat at the head of the cosmos," Tyr explained.

"If you've got these bad guys after you, then why are you here? Shouldn't you be in Asgard, protecting the . . . the throne?" Was I even saying this right?

"I'm here to protect my sister. Asgard should have been the safest place for her, but the wolf got to her there. Freya and I guessed he was working with someone on the inside, so we moved her to the sleepiest town we could find in the most remote realm in the cosmos."

"Why Earth? If the wolf can come and go so easily, wouldn't she be safer somewhere else? The realm with all the elves, maybe?" They'd seemed pretty fierce in that *Lord of the Rings* movie.

"Because for the most part, Midgard—Earth—flies under the radar. It doesn't have enough evil for the jotuns, fire giants, or dark elves to bother coming here. The light elves rarely leave Alfheim, and the dwarves have no desire to leave their realm. We thought Midgard would be the best place to hide her." Tyr shrugged. "We thought wrong. But even though the wolf was in the woods that day he attacked you, he still hasn't found Elsa's cabin. And he shouldn't have found this house, either. I had no idea anyone could breach the defenses I set around this place; I've cast new enchantments that should hold him off."

"The glitter blizzard?" I worried my bottom lip. If Tyr's old protections hadn't held, why did he think this sparkly new one would?

"It's a little more serious than that, but yeah. The glitter blizzard." Tyr stroked my hair. If the concern in his eyes was any indication, he was trying to soothe me.

Keep stroking, Hercules.

"So that animal you were fighting, is he the one who . . . did he . . .?" I didn't know how to ask the question.

"He killed my parents, yes."

"But you said your parents' killer was practically family." Recognition clouded my eyes at the same time as empathy rooted in my gut. "Was that animal your pet?"

"In a way. His name's Fenrir, and he's a wolf. My wolf. He's the son of Loki and a giantess."

My mouth turned down as I mentally flipped through my Art History flashcards. *Loki, Loki, ah! Loki.* Loki was the dark spot on Asgard's otherwise spotless family tree; the black sheep who took pleasure in causing pain and destruction for the rest of the gods. And while the books suggested Loki was largely misunderstood, from what I could see, his actions suggested he needed a serious schooling in morality.

And possibly a prescription mood-stabilizer.

"When Fenrir was born, our prophets predicted his treachery would end Asgard. Odin wanted to kill him, but I begged him not to. He was only a puppy, and it felt wrong to let him die for a crime he hadn't yet committed. Odin put him in my care, with the stipulation that Fenrir would be locked up the minute he stepped out of line. I was young then, maybe the equivalent of a six- or eight-year-old human child, and I was determined to save Fenrir. I raised him and tried to teach him right from wrong. Spent as much time with him as my training would allow."

"What happened?" My heart tugged.

"He couldn't beat his nature. He was born of darkness and bred to hate the gods. I wasn't strong enough to break him. He snapped and murdered my parents, then went AWOL. I put out a kill order on him when I took my title, but around that time the Norns prophesied the gods would use Fenrir as a bargaining tool at Ragnarok—apparently his continued existence is a prerequisite to avoiding total Asgardian annihilation. When he heard that, Odin overrode my command and issued a capture order on the wolf instead. Then Fenrir attacked Elsa. We've been trying to bring him in him since."

"Oh, Tyr." I breathed. "I'm so sorry."

"So am I. There is nothing normal about Fenrir, even by immortal standards. He is diabolically smart. He's callous, and conniving, and cruel. Despite everything I tried to teach him, he's taken the worst parts of each of his parents, and turned into this heinous being. He may look like a wolf, but inside he's a calculating mastermind. I'm not kidding, Mia. He's become a monster—or maybe he always was, and I was just an idiot. I don't know anymore. My scout in Muspelheim has seen Fenrir with the fire giants twice now. He may be working with them, but it's equally possible he's conspiring with one of the dark elves, or Jörmungandr."

"With who?" I wrapped my arms around my knees.

"The Midgard Serpent. There's a sea snake that literally circles your world."

Tyr didn't blink. He wasn't kidding.

"That's absurd. We'd see something like that in satellite photos. And no scientific journal has ever mentioned a world-circling snake."

"He's cloaked, Mia. You think Odin would let mortals know about something like that?"

"Oh." I shivered. Tyr moved his hand down my side and rubbed slow circles along my back with his thumb. Anxiety battled with pleasure in my frontal lobe.

"So what do the Norns say about Fenrir? Besides his being a beastly bargaining chip?"

Tyr pressed his lips together in a tight frown, almost as if he was pushing down the sadness that percolated in his eyes. "The Norns say Fenrir's the most calculating demon the realms have seen in centuries. But that he's more useful to us alive than dead."

"That's it?"

"We get a big picture explanation, a lot like your fortune cookies."

"*A wondrous package is coming your way*? That's what my last one said."

Tyr snickered. "Your fortune came true, baby."

"Knock it off." I smiled, in spite of myself. "Does it bother you not to know more?"

"The Norns say sharing the details would take the joy out of living, but I disagree."

"Exactly. They have all of this information, and they don't do anything to help the good guys." On this we were in sync.

"Details are data. They can be processed, planned for. The more I know about a given situation, the more I can manipulate it for the protection of the realms. I get special access to a few select files because in my case, knowledge literally is power. And my special access is what tipped me off to the hack."

"The hack?" I asked.

"Someone hacked the Norns' security and stole the files disclosing the fates of the Aesir."

"The Aesir?"

"The gods of Asgard are the Aesir. The gods of another friendly realm, Vanaheim, are the Vanir," Tyr explained.

"Right. Hold on, someone hacked your files?" I raised a hand. "What kinds of security do gods have? Like, cauldrons and spells around your computers? Or your file cabinets?" What technological level of data storage were they dealing with in Asgard?

"Not at all." Tyr moved his thumb along my shoulder in a circle, but my muscles were unyielding. Was a massage supposed to make all of this okay? "Asgard's technology is rather progressive. The Norns keep their prophecies listed in a digital tablet coded in a system. They only allow a handful of titled gods to access it. The tablet's locked in a safe that requires a retinal scan to access, and the whole thing's domed by lasers. Then we use magic to protect the entire system—if anyone without access gets within twenty feet of the dome, the atmosphere surrounding the safe shifts, and the prophecies implode."

It all sounded like some futuristic action film. "Jeez. Y'all are thorough." Also creepy. Who made things implode?

"That's the plan. Anyway, one day when I was still training, I went in to confirm a portal to Svartalfheim couldn't be opened again. Some of the files were missing— my parents' and Elsa's prophecies, among them." Tyr's head fell. "Fenrir, or whoever he's working with, must have had something to do with it."

"Are you okay?" I asked gently.

"This just makes me sick. It's my fault he's causing all this destruction." Tyr made a fist. "But I'm going to make it right. If it's me he's ultimately after, he'll be back. Henrik and I are getting ready."

"How?"

Tyr cleared his throat. "As much as I want kill Fenrir, the Norns' prophesy rendered that option moot. Strategically, I know he'll be more than just a bargaining chip for us. He'll also be able to provide intel—let us know who he's working with, and who they're targeting."

"You can communicate with the wolf?" That sounded insane.

"I can."

"Jeez . . ."

Tyr watched me carefully, concern in his eyes. I probably looked like I was going crazy. *Maybe I am . . .*

"Fenrir's grown into a monster I can't control, and if he's going to live, then he needs to be restrained. We convinced the dwarves to make a fetter for us—a magical rope that can hold the realms' most powerful animal."

"Seriously, dwarves? Like in *Snow White*?"

Tyr grimaced. "I wish. These dwarves don't sing, and they don't mine diamonds. They're vicious and conniving—the most deceitful kind of manipulative. You have to be careful dealing with them. But they're extremely hard workers—they've made some of the most powerful weapons in Asgard. And they've promised that if I bring them the right ingredients, they'll make me a chain that can hold Fenrir. We can lock him away somewhere he won't be able to hurt anyone ever again."

"So you're gathering the ingredients? That's what you're doing when you disappear?" Tyr's story began to fall into place.

"Correct."

"How many more do you have to find? Ingredients, I mean?"

"Just two left. Bear's nerves and fish breath." Tyr shrugged. "Piece of cake."

I shifted my weight so I could face him. "You hear how insane this sounds, don't you? How are you so calm about all of this? Why aren't you freaking out?"

"Baby, I'm God of War. What do you think I see at work?"

I wrung my hands together.

"Hey." He lifted my chin with a finger. "Don't be scared. I've got this."

"Bear's nerves and fish breath? And the killer wolf will

242

be out of commission. Oh, and you're an immortal war god with about nine hundred and eighty-three years on me. But 'don't be scared'?" My stomach churned. This entire situation was so overwhelming, I felt nauseated.

"The ratio wasn't exact. It's more like nine hundred years on you, tops. But otherwise, yeah. Don't be scared. You want to help me collect the rest of the ingredients? It'd be nice to have the company."

My brow furrowed. As much as I wanted to be okay with all of this, the truth was, I wasn't. At least, I wasn't yet. My analytical mind needed time to decompress.

"I think I'm going to need a little bit of time to think about all of this before I jump in with both feet. You're asking me to take on a life I know nothing about. And as much as I like you, I'm honestly not sure if I can do that."

My heart pounded as Tyr took in my words. When he released my chin, his eyes were downcast. "I understand. You need some space from me."

"A little," I admitted. "You've given me a *lot* to process in a *really* short time. Yesterday you were my boyfriend, from some sleepy little fishing town in Sweden. Different, maybe, but still human. And today you're the Norse God of War, using some rainbow bridge to travel across nine realms and battle evil monsters. It's kind of . . . kind of . . ."

"Unbelievable?" Tyr nodded. "Your brain can't compartmentalize me, can it?"

"No." I shook my head.

"And it's driving you crazy, isn't it?"

"Pretty much."

"Mmm. Can you compartmentalize this?" Tyr put both hands on my face and pulled me close. He kissed me with a force that left me breathless. He ran one hand along my neck and down my arm, leaving a warm tingling in his wake. But when he reached the spot where the wolf bit me, everything turned to ice.

Tyr raised his head when I stilled. "You okay?"

I shook my head, and started to sob.

"Mia." Tyr wrapped both arms around me. "Why are you crying?"

"Because," I wailed. "I really, really, really like you."

"I really like you, too."

"And I don't want the giant wolf to kill you!" I blubbered, wiping my nose on my sweater. "This is all just . . . just . . ."

"Oh, baby." He held my face in his hands. "I'll always take care of us. You get that, right?"

I nodded.

"Come on. I should take you home. You're probably exhausted. And I doubt you want to stay here."

"Okay," I whispered.

"Don't worry about any of this, all right? Henrik and I have this house under control. And Brynn will make sure you're safe back at your place."

"Brynn can do that?" I asked.

"Brynn's one of Freya's top battle goddesses—she's a valkyrie."

CHAPTER FIFTEEN

"WHAT THE HECK?" I flung open the door to Brynn's room and stormed inside. She lounged comfortably on her bed, nose buried in *Pride & Prejudice*.

"*Hei hei* to you, too." Brynn lowered her book.

"You're a goddess? A freaking battle goddess?"

"Shh!" Brynn jumped off her bed and raced to the door. She poked her head in the hallway before it shut behind her.

"Oh, they're not home. Stop glaring at me. If anyone gets to be mad, it's me." I crossed my arms. "How did you never mention this before?"

"I couldn't tell you. And besides, there wasn't a good time." Brynn lifted her chin.

"Don't even try that one. All the late night mani-pedis, the walks to campus, those afternoons in the lab—never, not once, could you have mentioned that you're *not human*?"

"Why'd he tell you? Something big must have happened." Brynn walked to the edge of her bed. She patted the mattress, and I sat down next to her.

"Giant wolf attacked the house," I muttered.

Brynn's eyes widened. "Is he—"

"Everything's fine." I waved my hand. "Tyr and Freya flew around the driveway with their space guns. The wolf disappeared. Freya went home. Tyr brought me here. Everything's hunky-dory. Except my boyfriend and my roommate are *immortal warriors*."

"Pretty awesome, right?" Brynn beamed.

My head dropped in my hands. It had been a ridiculously long day.

"Did he show you the flying thing? Only some of us can do the flying thing. I can't do it, didn't get the gene." Brynn bounced on her knees next to me. "Isn't it cool?"

"Uh—"

"And the 'space guns'? Henrik and I made them. They're nano-molecular particle accelerators."

"Meaning?" I raised my head.

"They'll make you implode. So awesome, *ja*?"

What was it with these people and imploding? "Why are you still bouncing?"

"Because I'm so excited you know!" Brynn tucked her knees under her on the mattress. "Now we don't have to keep up that stupid 'neighbors from Sweden' story. So dumb. It was Henrik's idea. I *told* Tyr you could handle the truth. You're fiercer than you let on."

"Thank you?"

Brynn rolled her eyes. "You know what I mean. You come off sweet and delicate, but you're tough as nails. All *keep calm and carry on*, like you people say."

"British people say that," I corrected. "Americans are more *pull yourself up by your bootstraps; knuckle down; steel magnolias forever.* That kind of thing."

"Close enough. So do you have any questions? About us, I mean."

"Do you want me to start at the top of the list or the bottom?" I fingered the edge of her bedspread.

Brynn looked like a kid on Christmas morning. "I know it sounds kind of crazy, but we're really not that different from you."

"Except you're divine. From another world—realm, whatever. Defy laws of physics, have weird space weapons, and you can never, ever, die. Except . . ." I trailed off. *Except when you're murdered.*

"Did Tyr explain immortality to you?" Brynn asked. I nodded.

"How old are you?" I asked tentatively.

"Not that old. In mortal years, maybe . . . I think eight hundred and forty-nine?" Brynn leaned in, her face practically bubbling with joy. "My birthday's next July."

"You're going to be eight hundred and fifty?" I tried not to balk. *And that's young?*

"Big one, right? I'm thinking Disneyland. I've never been there." Her hands flew to her cheeks. "Ooh, ooh! Would you go with me?"

"Um, sure. Maybe we can get you a senior discount."

"Ha." Brynn shifted so she sat cross-legged. "Well, now

we can talk. So here are the rules. Ask me anything you want to know about us, or Asgard, or what we do, or whatever. But you can't ask me about Tyr's ex-girlfriends— there were some nutters, and frankly, they aren't worth mentioning. Don't ask me to explain the deal with him and Freya—they're BFFs, and they've never even thought of each other romantically, so you don't need to worry about it."

I raised an eyebrow.

"Oh, come on. It's super obvious she freaks you out."

"I thought my boyfriend's best friend was a supermodel. Turns out she's a goddess," I muttered. "That's just not normal."

"She's great. Trust me. So, what do you want to know?"

"I don't know. Start with the basics. Did you ever really live in Sweden?"

"Yes." Brynn nodded. "We haven't actually *lied* to you about anything. We lived in Malmö for a while. Tyr had to locate and dispel a portal to Jotunheim that someone managed to open off-shore. But before Malmö, there was Trondheim, Norway. Another portal issue, this one to Muspelheim. And before Trondheim, there was Asgard."

"Explain these portals. Are they like what Fenrir came here through?"

"Yes. You know about that?" Brynn blinked.

"Tyr said someone with dark magic opened a portal and sent him home."

"Right. Well, Asgardians are pretty powerful—we usually travel by Bifrost, our rainbow bridge, but if we're in a pinch we can open a portal; that's kind of like a wormhole that takes us wherever we need to go. Well, during the last fifty years, somebody from one of the *bad* realms, like Muspelheim or Jotunheim or Helheim—"

"You guys have a lot of heims."

"We do," Brynn agreed. "So somebody from one of those places has been using dark magic to open portals to the Scandinavian countries. We don't know why they're targeting that region, and we haven't figured out who's doing it. But every portal we've found has residue of dark magic, meaning something evil is opening them. Surtr, the leader of the fire giants in Muspelheim, has heaps of dark power. And Hel, the ruler of the underworld, has all kinds of black powers. She's a total nightmare."

"The ruler of the underworld is a girl?" I smoothed the bedspread. The fabric felt soft against my fingertips. I wondered if Brynn had brought it from Asgard. *Wonder what the thread counts are up there. Jeez.*

"Of course. Who else could manage that many evil spirits? You think some guy would have the patience for all the bickering that goes on down there?" Brynn shrugged. "Her dad's Loki. He slept with a giantess and made three monsters—Fenrir, Jörmungandr, and Hel. She's hands down the worst of the three."

The wolf, the snake, and the keeper of the underworld are siblings?

"Is Tyr going to be mad that you're telling me this?" I leaned against the headboard.

"I'm not afraid of Tyr. Besides, he knows you're going to need to know all of this eventually, since you're going to end up with him when all this sorts itself out."

"Pardon?" My mouth dropped.

"Don't look so surprised. Freya sees you two together. So it's totally happening."

"Freya what now?" My voice jumped an octave.

Brynn sighed. "The whole situation is really complicated. And Tyr would probably rather tell you himself."

"Spill it, valkyrie." I crossed my arms and stared.

"Oh. Oh, fine. But don't freak out."

I gave her *the look*. "All things considered, I think I am well past my freak-out point today, *thank you very much*. Talk."

"Fine." Brynn sighed. "So here's the deal. Freya has been looking for a match for Tyr for-freaking-ever. He has this weird complex and doesn't think he deserves to be happy, so he'll hook up with girls but he won't get serious about anybody, because he thinks he'll just destroy their spirit or get them killed, whatever."

"I gathered that," I murmured.

"Right. Well, the Norns told Freya there's a prophecy about who Tyr's going to end up with. Apparently he's destined to be with a girl *not of Asgard*."

"What does that mean?" I asked.

"It means he's not fated to be with a goddess. He's fated to be with someone from another realm. It could be a light elf, or a mountain giant, or . . ." Brynn waggled her eyebrows.

"Or a human?" Did that mean Tyr and I could actually

be . . . *fated* to be together?

"Or a human," she confirmed. "But the prophecy doesn't say *which* human. Something that specific would take away Tyr's agency, you know? The Norns are supposed to guide, not dictate. So it was up to Freya as Goddess of Love to lead Tyr in the direction of a good non-Asgardian match."

"Hold on. Freya's Goddess of Love?" I gaped.

"Yep. Also head of the valkyries. Anyway, she knew Tyr needed to get out of Asgard to protect Elsa, so she found a handful of girls who met her *very* specific qualifications—you included—and planned to introduce all of you to Tyr and hope he'd fall for one of you. But then Fenrir attacked you, and Tyr's always been a sucker for a damsel in distress. The fact that you happen to fit the profile of his ideal match from both Freya's standpoint, and the prophecy, well . . ." Brynn shrugged, finally taking a breath. "Sometimes things just have a way of working out."

Except my 'ideal match' was an immortal battle deity, and I was an Engineering undergrad. Romeo and Juliet had nothing on us in the star-crossed lovers department.

"Why is Freya so keen to match up Tyr? Did Tyr know what Freya was up to? That she'd lined up a bunch of girls for him to meet?" In other words, had I inadvertently entered the world's most bizarre dating competition? One where nobody bothered to ask me if I wanted to participate?

"Oh, gods, no. He didn't know anything about the whole dating plan when Freya suggested he bring Elsa to Arcata—he only knew it was wooded, remote, and close to one of our safe houses. Freya's filled him in since, and he's none too thrilled he moved realms in part to satisfy her matchmaking needs. He's resisted every match Freya's tried to pair him with." She elbowed me in the arm. "Guess you're too irresistible, even for the bachelor god."

"There were other girls . . ." My brain whirred.

"There were." Brynn spoke matter-of-factly. "In Freya's mind, any one of them could have been a match for Tyr, but based on your profile, and your unbelievable stubbornness, we thought you had the highest likelihood of winning him over. It's why Freya moved me in here, instead of with one of the other girls. You were our best bet, and in the event you accomplished what we hoped and captured Tyr's heart, we knew you'd require protection immediately. Possibly sooner."

The words made my blood chill. She hadn't been wrong about needing protection. Fenrir's attack came within an hour of my arrival in Arcata—before I'd even met Tyr. But that wasn't the only thing Brynn said that left me unsettled. "Wait. I was your best bet for what?"

Brynn's eyes filled with moisture for just an instant before she blinked it away. "Tyr's got a lot of darkness in that pretty little head of his. We're afraid if he loses one more person close to him, he could snap. And if that happens, we need to make sure someone with a strong unifying spirit is with him, to keep him grounded. You're amazing at bringing people together; you know that, right? You'd make a great Unifier. That positive energy is what he's going to need if, Odin forbid, we lose Elsa. We're counting on you to keep him on our side. Because if the God of War goes dark. . ." Brynn's eyes turned down and she bit her bottom lip. She looked absolutely gutted. "Well, it wouldn't be pretty."

I cradled my head in my hands and breathed slowly. The immortals of Asgard were counting on me to keep their war god from falling into darkness. Because according to the Goddess of Love, I was his best match.

It would take years to process all of this.

"How does Henrik play into everything?" I rubbed my temples.

"Henrik is Tyr's bodyguard." Brynn pulled an emery board off her nightstand and started filing.

"Sweet, goofy Henrik . . . with the glasses always slipping down his nose . . . the guy who bakes . . . he's the God of War's bodyguard?"

"The glasses are for show. He thinks it makes him blend in. Please." Brynn tossed her hair. "Do you think we have to worry about vision? We can see five times farther than mortals. In the dark. Some of us have X-ray abilities."

How was that even possible?

"Why does the God of War need a bodyguard, anyway?" I asked.

"Who do you think the dark elves go after first when they move to debilitate Asgard? God of War. Take out the leader, it's super easy to pick off the followers. It's Combat 101." Brynn went back to her nails.

"So why did Freya send you?"

"To protect you." Brynn looked up.

"Of course. You're here to protect me . . ." Suddenly

Brynn's ability to head fearlessly into a rodent-infested attic made sense. She probably saw a lot worse things as a valkyrie. *Yeesh.*

"We were worried the fire giants might follow us here—there was this revolt happening when we left. That's why I wasn't there to look out for you the day you arrived in Arcata—sorry about that, by the way. But the giants ended up not being an issue."

"What exactly is a fire giant?" I pulled my knees to my chest.

"A really, really evil monster." Brynn put down her file. "Trust me, you don't want to go to Muspelheim."

"Have you been there?" I asked.

"Of course. We visit all the realms in our training. Our primary function as valkyries is to bring fallen soldiers back to Asgard. The only requirement is that they be of solid moral character, so most are human soldiers, but occasionally we'll find a diamond in the rough in one of the other realms. Anyway, we take half to Odin to defend the realm, and give half to Freya to disperse as she sees fit. I have no idea how she handles her job. Being warrior goddess of love sounds good on paper, but in reality they're such different functions, you know?"

"Huh." I paused. Maybe whoever said all's fair in love and war was talking about Tyr's bestie. "So what exactly are your duties? You bring dead soldiers to Freya and Odin. Anything else?"

"I'm Tyr's second." Brynn rested her head against her pillow.

"His second what?"

"His second bodyguard. Henrik's his primary. Tyr's got all kinds of fancy weapons at his disposal, but Henrik likes to kill with his hands. He's the one you need to watch out for."

I closed my eyes. My TA was a trained assassin, and my perky little roomie was a valkyrie. Jason was right—college was definitely *not* turning out the way I'd imagined.

"There are a lot of scary monsters in the realms, Mia. We can't afford to take chances with the lives of our charges."

"Doesn't that make you nervous? Killing people?"

"Monsters," Brynn corrected. "I've never killed a human. And not really. All gods and goddesses have extensive combat training from primary school on. Drop us in just about any situation and we've got it covered. Perps very rarely survive."

"This is unreal." Gods and monsters and perps and realms . . . my-black-and-white world crumbled into a million shades of grey. I examined my cuticles, wondering if I should be nervous about being alone with a trained assassin.

"Now that Fenrir's back, Tyr will probably order me to protect you full-time."

"Why?" My hands gripped the bed.

"Because." Brynn looked at me as if I was a few needles short of a haystack. "Fenrir's going after the people Tyr loves. Duh."

My hair flew as I whipped my head back and forth. "Tyr doesn't love me. We've only known each other a couple of months."

Brynn rolled her eyes. "For a math genius, you're unusually unobservant."

"Whatever," I muttered. This wasn't a conversation I was ready to have with myself, much less anyone else. And especially with someone other than Tyr. We had a pretty heavy State of the Union talk ahead of us, and I wasn't about to have it with someone else, first. "So you and Henrik are here to protect Tyr. Tyr's here to protect Elsa. Fenrir's out to hurt pretty much everyone." I paused. "What about Elsa? Besides being Tyr's sister, how does she play into all of this? She's not a war god too, is she?"

"Oh, gosh no. She's way too valuable to allow in combat. She's a High Healer, someone who can perform *extremely* improbable healings. She's got super intense magic. Well they both do, from what I understand." Brynn wiggled her eyebrows. "Like I said, you'd make a great Unifier if you and Tyr make it permanent."

My head felt like I was on an out-of-control carousel.

"You look exhausted." Brynn patted my hand. "Why don't you try to get some sleep? I'll be up for a while if you have any more questions."

I couldn't imagine getting any sleep tonight, let alone having some job in Asgard. And a future with Tyr.

"I think I'm all questioned out for now. I should probably go think about all of this. Thanks for talking." I stood and walked to the door, opening it slowly. When I stepped into the hall, Brynn called out.

"I'm here if you need anything. *Anything.*"

"Thanks." I gave a small wave, then walked into my room and flopped face-down on my bed.

My boyfriend was an immortal warrior, my roommate was a valkyrie, and whoever married Tyr might be the key to intergalactic peace. And it could very well be me.

CHAPTER SIXTEEN

I DIDN'T GET ANY sleep Friday night, and I spent all of Saturday going back and forth on whether I could handle being with Tyr, now that I knew what he was, and what was expected of him . . . and what was expected of the girl he ended up with. Tyr had only just come into my life, and up until last night, I'd thought he might become a semi-permanent fixture. But now . . . now I realized he wasn't at all what I'd believed him to be. How could I be in a relationship with someone who'd pretended to be something they weren't? But then, how could I walk away from the first guy I'd ever fallen this hard for? Tyr made me feel things I'd never felt for anyone, ever. Which was problematic, considering I'd been ready to sleep with him, and our entire relationship was built *on a lie*. Or was it? Technically, Tyr had never outright lied to me. Everything he told me about his friendships with Brynn and Henrik, his life in Malmö, and even about his parents and his sister had all been true. He'd lied through omission, which was pretty lousy, but he'd always changed the subject when things got too complicated, or too close to the truth.

The truth.

The truth was, Tyr was an almost one-thousand-year-old Norse God. G.O.D. Apparently he was a very important one, because he had a big-deal job. And if I understood correctly, he was a totally unflappable killing machine. My first real boyfriend was an immortal assassin, tasked with defending the universe from perma-destruction.

What had I gotten myself into?

Could I really be in a relationship with Tyr, knowing everything that would come with it? He was a god—*a god*. He'd live forever, or until something killed him. He'd look twenty years old for at least the next couple of centuries. He'd always have monsters and demons and evil elves and giant dogs trying to kill him, and if I chose to be his girlfriend, and maybe someday his wife, all those creatures would come after me, too. I'd have to take a whole new kind of self-defense class, which would have been exciting if it didn't involve fighting Hel. Literally. A perky blond bodyguard would follow me around twenty-four hours a day, and even if she was one of the best friends I'd made at Redwood, I'd still have no semblance of privacy. I'd have to lie to my parents and Jason; that one bothered me the most. Tyr didn't just go traipsing around telling humans what he was. Being with him would mean keeping his secret and secrets were a rare breed in the Ahlström household. Eventually my folks would want to meet Tyr, and then what would I do? Bring him to Connecticut and hope he won them over with his charm? He was a stickler for bringing flowers, a point that would earn him favor with my Southern mother, but what would happen if we dated for a few years? My dad would expect him to propose. Would he want to do that? Would *I* want him to do that? And what about children? We were from different planets, or realms, or whatever; could we even *have* kids together? Would Tyr want to? What if we did get married? What would happen in three decades when I had crow's feet and the occasional grey hair, and Tyr still looked like a twenty-year-old frat boy? How would we explain that?

My head pounded from all the questions, and by late Saturday afternoon I couldn't take it anymore. I called the one person whose advice had never steered me wrong.

"Hey, Sis." Jason answered on the first ring. "Shouldn't you be out with that dreamboat of yours? Tire?"

"*Tee-er*," I corrected. "And yeah. I should be. But we sort of had a disagreement last night. So we're spending the day apart."

"Trouble in paradise? Last time we talked, things were good. In fact, I believe a certain little sister of mine was asking me how soon was too soon to do the deed." I could practically see Jason's eyebrows waggling through the phone.

"Jason! I did *not* ask you that." I would never ask my brother that question . . . but I might have hinted at it.

"Doesn't take a rocket scientist to know that's where you're heading, if you're not there already. And if you're there already, I don't want to know. Because then I'd have to come and kill the dude."

"Ew. I am not having this conversation with my brother." I shuddered.

"In that case, what was your disagreement about?"

I chose my words very carefully. "He kind of kept a big secret from me about his life back home. He didn't lie; he just omitted something kind of important. And I'm not sure how I feel about it."

"Do you want me to come kick his ass, or do you want relationship advice?"

"Definitely the latter. Depending on how it works out, maybe the former too." I smiled. Jason always had my back.

"Huh." Jason paused. It was a testament to his Yankee-Southern manners that he didn't ask me to share Tyr's secret, though he did have to cover his brotherly bases. "Is the secret something that would hurt you?"

I paused to consider that. *Would it?* "No," I decided, truthfully. "If anything, it's going to make sure I'm always safe." From everything. Ever. Unless one of the monsters got to me. Then I'd be dead.

"Is the secret something that requires you to compromise your morals? I assume he's not asking you to join him in a life of crime or something, or you'd be running the other way."

Tyr was wrapped up in a life of crime, all right, but he was the one fighting it. "Don't worry. My morals are intact."

"Hmm. Is it something that changes the way you feel about him? Does it fundamentally affect what you know of his character? Because last I checked, you were halfway to falling in love with this guy. A little soon for my tastes, but you're a girl. I forgive you."

I sighed. "I'm not in love with him. Not yet. But yeah, I could see it getting there someday. And the secret doesn't exactly change his character, but it does change how I see him. Not in a good or a bad way, it's just different." *So very different.*

"Got it." Jason sighed. "Listen, Mees, it sucks the guy

kept something from you, but if it's not a bad secret, he probably had a reason for waiting until now to tell you. And if the secret doesn't change how you feel about him, I say live a little."

"That's your advice for everything."

"That's my advice for everything *with you*. Life's short, Mia. You only get one shot at it, and you only get one shot at being young, too. This is the time to make those impetuous decisions. Stop notebooking this—"

"What?" I asked.

"Notebooking this. Don't try to tell me you don't have at least half a notebook filled with pros and cons of whether to drop the guy over this."

"I filled three-quarters of one since he told me his secret," I admitted.

Jason laughed. "Well, stop. You've sounded really into Tree—"

"Tyr," I corrected again.

"—really into Tyr for months. Throw the notebook away and follow your gut on this one. You're smart. Your instincts won't steer you wrong."

"That simple, huh?"

"Yep. But remember if he hurts you, I'll come straight out there and end him."

"I love you, Jase." I smiled.

"I love you, Sis. I've got a date, otherwise I could talk longer. You okay?" he asked.

"I will be. Go have fun. Bye."

"Bye." Jason hung up.

I dropped my head into my hands. I'd done everything I could think of to make an informed decision about whether or not to stay with Tyr. I'd filled a quarter of a notebook with pro and con lists, another quarter with all of the "*what ifs*" I'd come up with while I *wasn't* sleeping, and had a third section containing potential solutions to our human/god dating quandary. But I was as confused as I'd felt when I saw Tyr fly. Nothing good ever came from making an emotional decision, and clearly I couldn't rationalize my way through this one. Maybe more facts were necessary. And if that didn't help, a cup of coffee would be nice.

I picked up my phone and called Tyr.

"*Hei hei.*" He answered on the first ring.

"Hi. Can you come over? And bring coffee?"

"I'll be there in ten." His voice sounded scratchy, as if he was as exhausted as I was. Well, good. If I had to lose sleep over this situation, he could too.

Of course, he probably didn't have the thick purple bags under his eyes that I did. Being a god sure had its perks.

When Tyr pulled up to Daffodil Drive, I was already sitting on the porch steps, a fresh coat of concealer masking my purple raccoon rings. Tyr got out of his car carrying two cups of coffee, and walked in clipped strides up our path. His hair was out of place, his jaw looked tense, and I noticed small lines around his eyes. "*Hei.*" He held out a cup at arm's length.

"Thanks." I took the liquid caffeine, and patted the stair next to me. "Have a seat."

Tyr sat stiffly, his back straight as he lowered himself onto the step. He stretched out his long legs and stayed unnaturally still.

"I'm not afraid of you." I rolled my eyes. "You can move."

"I just don't want to overwhelm you." Tyr leaned over and brushed his lips against my hair.

"I'm pretty sure we passed the *overwhelm* point somewhere between *'I'm a god'* and *'the monsters of the underworld want me dead.'* But thanks for thinking of me."

"Mia—" Tyr's voice broke.

"Wait. Before I decide whether this is a life I can sign up for—for however long—I have to ask you a few questions."

"Shoot." Anxiety colored his tone.

I took a sip of my coffee and glanced down at my notebook. It was filled with pages of worries, and I opened my mouth to recite the first one. But then I looked at the guy sitting next to me. Large hands gripped his cup so tightly it looked as if it was about to explode and send hot coffee flying everywhere. Ramrod straight posture was compromised by the elbow bouncing almost unnoticeably at his side. His jaw was locked down so hard, I was surprised I couldn't hear his teeth grinding. He hadn't called me since last night—he'd given me the space I'd asked for. But it was adorably obvious he was as stressed out about my decision as I was.

I closed my notebook and pushed it aside.

"Okay." I turned toward Tyr so our knees were

touching. "Number one. Is there anything else you're keeping from me? And do you plan to keep secrets from me in the future?"

"No," Tyr answered quickly. "I mean, there are lots of things about Asgard I haven't explained to you yet, but I'll answer any questions you have. I promise."

"You better. I'm someone who requires *all* the facts before making an informed decision."

To his credit, Tyr did not smile. He simply responded, "I understand."

"Brynn said something last night about there being a lot of darkness inside you. What was she talking about?" I clenched my coffee cup.

"Do we have to get into this?" Tyr ground his jaw.

"Yes."

"All right. I'm not pure Asgardian, like the rest of my colleagues. I have giant blood in me." Tyr watched me carefully. "It means my temper isn't as mild as the rest of the Aesir, and occasionally I struggle to stay on the side of the light. We can talk more about it if you want to, but the short story is that my family tree is crooked. It's not something I'm proud of."

Well, that sure accounted for the broad shoulders. And the height. *Cheese and crackers.* He was a god *and* a giant. Could this relationship get any stranger?

Follow your gut. Jason's advice echoed in my head. Did I believe Tyr was a good man—er, god? *Yes.* Then what did it matter if he was a god/giant, or the tooth fairy? He was giving me total honesty, bizarre as it was, and the least I could give him back was an open mind.

"Fair enough. Number two. If we do proceed, and if we end up staying together for a while, how are we going to deal with our age difference? Obviously I'm going to age at the normal human rate. And you're going to age at . . . one fiftieth of that rate? So in twenty years I'll look thirty-eight, but you're still going to look like you're in college." I waited.

"I thought about that last night." Tyr leaned forward slightly. "I'm going to like the way you look at every age, but I understand you might feel weird being with a twenty-year-old when you're fifty. Or eighty."

"Eighty?" Shut the front door, he wanted to be with me that long?

"Just working through scenarios," Tyr explained. "Odin would have to sign off on it, but there might be magical options we could use to keep you at your current appearance, if that's something you want to do. Our Goddess of Wisdom, Idunn, has apples that give us our immortality. If she adapted the formula for human use, they should be able to mitigate mortal aging processes. Or Odin might have a spell to keep you from aging beyond a certain point. He's manipulated human genetics before; I'm fairly positive it's within the realm of his powers to do this kind of thing."

I shivered. These waters were so deep, I needed two life preservers. "Okay. So we have options. We can discuss them later. Number three." I paused. "Do you *want* to be with me?"

Tyr took our coffees and set them on the ground, held

my hands between his, and met my eyes with a look that made me forget my notebook filled with concerns.

"Yes, Mia. I want to be with you."

"Why?" I pressed. "You can be with anyone—god, elf, fairy princess, whatever. Why did you choose me?" I wasn't fishing for compliments. It literally made zero sense that this six-and-a-half-foot Swedish—correction, *Asgardian*—dreamboat would waltz down from his cloud, look around Earth and say to himself, *That brunette over there. Mia Ahlström—she'd be a great gal pal while I'm on vacation. I'll ask her out.* I mean, I was a great catch, but there had to be a whole lot of attractive options when you had the *whole entire cosmos* at your disposal.

"Oh, Mia." Tyr sighed. "Why not you?"

"Seriously?"

"Believe me, if I could stay away I would." Tyr held my gaze.

"Gee, thanks."

"You misunderstand. I never meant for you to get mixed up in all this. Fenrir hurts the people I care about—and they're immortal. Can you imagine what he could do to a human? When he attacked you in the woods, I thought it was an unfortunate coincidence; you weren't someone I cared about, or even knew, and so I figured once you recovered from your injuries you'd be safe."

"Huh."

"Hear me out. You didn't mean anything to me the day you were attacked. I didn't know Freya led me to you until *after* we met at that party. I didn't plan to talk to you that night, but Brynn made sure I didn't have a choice. And once we started talking, I realized I actually liked you. I tried ignoring you, partly because I was ticked that Freya butted into my personal life again, and partly because I didn't want you getting involved in all the crazy, but we can see how well that worked out." Tyr shrugged. "And then you showed up at Elsa's cabin and turned my world on its head."

"What do you mean?" I asked.

Tyr paused. "I've always sorted my life into neat compartments, and that day you barged in and knocked them all on their sides. Suddenly, my work life was mixed in with my personal baggage, and instead of hating it like I always thought I would, I was happy because . . . well, because I had somebody to share that part of my world with. Somebody I could actually be vulnerable around. It was the first time I'd ever let my guard down and shared that . . . that pain . . . with someone I cared about." Tyr drew a shaky breath. "I liked letting you see that side of me. It made me feel like I wasn't all alone."

"You're not all alone. You have Henrik and Brynn. And Freya," I pointed out.

"True. But technically I'm Henrik and Brynn's boss. I try not to get overly emotional around them. And Freya and I talk about surface things. She might be one of my oldest friends, but I'm not one of those guys who wants to talk about what's bothering him. Or I wasn't, before I met you."

My cheeks warmed. "I'm glad you want to talk to me," I admitted.

"Me too." Tyr leaned forward to brush my forehead

with his lips.

"I obviously like you. And I don't think I could break up with you, even if I wanted to. But dang it Tyr, this is complicated. How is this going to work? Is this even allowed where you come from?" I gestured between us. "This can't be natural."

"It's as natural as we want it to be, baby." Tyr waggled his eyebrows and I groaned.

"You know what I mean."

"We're not the typical couple, true. And this isn't exactly encouraged back home. Odin doesn't promote inter-realm cohabitation. But he lets me have a little more leniency than most of the council." Tyr stroked my hand with his thumb. "And I'm certainly not going to let a little thing like you being from another realm stop me from seeing where this goes. That is, if you want to take a leap with me."

If you want to take a leap with me. The world was spinning. And underwater. The world was spinning underwater. While upside down.

Breathe, Mia.

"Tell me what you're thinking now," Tyr probed.

"That falling for you isn't exactly turning out like I'd expected," I confessed.

"I'll never hurt you, *prinsessa*. I might disappoint you, I know I'll confuse you, and I'll sure as Helheim frustrate you. My life doesn't fit into any of your neat boxes. I'm okay with that, but I know it's going to be a while before you can be. But Mia Ahlström, I swear I'll do everything in my power to make you happy, every single day that we have together. What do you say?" Tyr leaned back to study my face.

Well, when he puts it like that . . . My anxiety ebbed. Tyr was being completely honest with me. He couldn't give me a normal relationship, but he wanted to give me all that he could. What he pledged was his absolute commitment— one hundred percent of himself, no matter how scary things got. How could I walk away from that?

"This is a little bit overwhelming. And a lot bit terrifying. But I like you too much to walk away," I admitted. "Whatever we've got going here, I'm all in."

"Really?" Tyr's face lit up in a look of genuine joy. "Oh, thank Odin. After I didn't hear from you all day, I thought you were done with me." He shook his head, bent down and pressed his lips against mine. I responded instinctively. My hands flew to his hair, my fingers wrapping in the tousled strands. He ran his tongue along my bottom lip and I sighed, giving myself over to the sensation. A warm burn started in my belly and radiated to my extremities. I no longer wanted to compartmentalize anything—not what Tyr was, not what he was trying to do, and not the impossible things I'd seen last night. I just wanted to be as close to him as humanly—or godly—possible. I climbed on his lap and straddled him, pressing my body against his. He grabbed my hair with one hand and pulled my head back, bringing his mouth to my jaw. I groaned and he moved lower, kissing a line down my neck. He ran one hand down my arm, sending the familiar heat along my skin. Spreading his palms across my back, he pulled me against him, holding on like he might never let go.

I hoped he never would.

The wolf whistle from the water polo players' house across the street ruined what was fast becoming a *very* memorable moment. I immediately buried my head in Tyr's chest, and he leaned back with a laugh. "Can I take you on what's probably going to be the weirdest date of your life tomorrow?"

"Weirder than the night I found out my boyfriend was a Norse god?" I asked, willing some of the heat to drain from my cheeks. *Stupid water polo house.*

"Possibly. The clock's ticking, and I need to get two more ingredients for the rope. Tomorrow's fishing day. What do you say?"

"I say get ready to be schooled. Yours truly holds the Ahlström family record for biggest catch." Jason was still sore about that.

"You are one amazing woman." Tyr pressed his lips to mine, and pulled back. "Come on. Let's order a pizza."

"It's only four o'clock," I pointed out. "You might qualify for early bird specials, but us teenagers eat at regular hours."

"Have you eaten yet today?" Tyr asked.

"Well, no." Come to think of it, I was starving.

"Didn't think so. Come on." He stood and held out a hand. I placed mine in his, and picked up my notebook before leading him into the house. He was already dialing the pizza parlor and placing an order for delivery. *What's that* he mouthed, pointing at my notebook.

"This?" I stared at the pages filled with my befuddled scrawl. A few hours ago, making sense of everything had seemed so important. I'd needed to know where this was going, how it would end, and how we'd tackle the seemingly insurmountable obstacles we had ahead of us. But a girl could get glad in the same britches she got mad in. And Jason had been absolutely right. Letting go of my rigid structure, trying new things, even just accepting things for what they *were* instead of what I wanted to *make them be* . . . it felt right. Crazy, impulsive, maybe even stupid, but right. And saying goodbye to Tyr would have been all kinds of wrong, even if it meant I didn't have a concrete five-year plan. Oh, God. I didn't have a five-year plan. *In through the nose* . . . That was okay. I'd only lost the plan with respect to this relationship. I could still have the plan for my major, and my career, and my fitness routines. It would be baby steps for me. I led us to the kitchen and threw the notebook in the trash.

"Okay, thanks." Tyr hung up his phone. "Pizza's here in twenty. What is that?" he asked again, now pointing to the trashcan.

I stood on my tiptoes and kissed his bottom lip. "It's something I'm ready to let go of."

"Fair enough." Tyr kissed me back, wrapping an arm around my waist to lift me closer to him. I might not have known where things were going to end with us, but I sure as heck liked exactly where we were.

And that was good enough for now.

CHAPTER SEVENTEEN

"YOU READY FOR A day on the lake?" Tyr slammed the trunk of the Hummer and picked up his tackle box. As always, he was unimaginably gorgeous in dark denim, a black T-shirt and a zip-up hoodie. He wore the requisite black boots, and a baseball cap with a picture of the Death Star sat low on his forehead.

The irony wasn't lost on me.

"Absolutely." I carried two fishing rods in my right hand, and laced fingers through Tyr's with my left. He looked down at our hands with a slow smile.

"I like you next to me, you know that?" He stopped to plant a leisurely kiss on my lips, the kind that made me forget where I was. It still blew my mind that this spectacular creature and I had found each other, but I was not about to look a gift horse in the mouth.

"I like it too." I stood on tiptoe to draw out the kiss, but Tyr squeezed my fingers and turned to stare at the water. I reluctantly followed suit.

We'd driven an hour outside of Arcata to a quiet lake surrounded by redwoods. The water was still and blue, and thin clouds stretched across the early afternoon sky. A handful of cabins lined the opposite shore, and the only roads in and out of the lake were dirt. There wasn't a freeway within ten miles. It was relaxing, and rustic, and incredibly romantic.

"Come on. We've got work to do." Tyr tugged on my hand, reminding me why we were here. I followed him to a wooden dock, where a sleek boat was tied to one end. He walked me to the edge and held out a hand. "Hop in."

"Does its owner know we're here?" I asked cautiously. I wasn't quite ready to add grand theft boat to my otherwise immaculate rap sheet.

Tyr laughed. "It's mine. Brynn drove it out this morning."

"Oh." My eyes widened.

"I see what you're thinking." He rolled his eyes. "It's not *that* extravagant."

"Most people in these parts have rowboats." I pointed to the line of modest boats lining the neighboring dock.

"I'm not most people." Tyr grinned. "Now hop aboard, skipper."

"Yes, sir." I saluted before stepping onto the rocking boat. It was designed for speed, all sleek and white and streamlined. But it was also extremely lux. Plush leather seats lined the small sitting area, and three steps led up to a little cabin. "Ooh, can I go up there?"

"You can go anywhere you want. Bed's to the right."

I blushed.

My fingers gripped the railing as I walked. Wearing ballet flats with my skinny jeans had been a good call. The boat rocked gently from side to side; it took me a minute to get my bearings.

"What do you think?" Tyr breathed in my ear. He'd come up right behind me, and snaked his arms around my waist.

I jumped at the touch. "It's nice."

It was. The driver's seat was behind me, ensconced behind a clear window. A small kitchen was to the left, with a tiny cooking area and an intimate table laid out for two. And to the right was the promised bed. It was much too large for the space, easily a full king.

Tyr caught me looking and growled. "Want to test it out later?"

"Would that be before or after we catch the magical fish?"

"It can be whenever you want, baby." Tyr ran his nose along the curve of my neck. When I whimpered, he gave a reluctant sigh. "But not now. We need to push off if we're gonna be back by nightfall. I don't want to drive through these woods after dark."

"You're such a tease."

"Get that cute little butt deck-side. Now."

He pinched my backside and I scampered down the stairs, rolling my eyes as I dutifully donned the fluorescent orange life vest he pulled from one of the benches. "This is just lovely."

"Safety first." He snapped my vest in place. "Do you want to ride inside the cabin or out here?"

"I'll stay out here if you don't mind. I haven't been on a

boat in a while."

"Then sit down and hold on. I drive fast."

"You do everything fast, don't you?" Driving, running, flying . . .

"Not everything." Tyr raised an eyebrow and my pulse spiked. He leaned over the boat and released the moorings. When he'd wound the ropes and put them inside the bench seat, he ducked into the cabin. I took my seat.

"Pushing off."

Tyr expertly steered the boat into open water, picking up speed when he was a safe distance from the shore. The wind brushed my face as I tilted my head back. It was cool in the early afternoon sun, and the thrum of the engine was oddly relaxing. Tyr steered the boat in a slow arc across the lake, taking a handful of unnecessary turns that nearly launched me off my seat. My hands gripped leather as I glared at the cabin. The laughter in Tyr's eyes let me know his navigational skills were deliberate. When I wagged my finger at him, he just winked.

There would definitely be payback.

Tyr slowed the boat when we reached a secluded cove near the opposite shore. The sun was behind the mountain, so we rested in the shade. Tyr climbed out of the cabin and picked up his tackle box and both fishing rods. He handed me a rod as he took a seat beside me. He rested the other on his lap, then opened the box.

"You know you're on my list, buddy." I raised an eyebrow.

"Oh, I'm scared." Tyr nudged me with his shoulder, and

I laughed. "You usually bait your own hooks?"

"Sure." It was my least favorite part of fishing, but it had to be done.

"Not today." Tyr grabbed my hook and returned it with a worm.

I batted my eyes. "Such a gentleman."

"No problem. Want me to help you cast, too?"

I laughed. "I think I've got that part."

"Cause I'm more than happy to assist you with your form." Tyr dropped his rod. He wrapped his arms around me from the side, and held my hands between his. His proximity was overwhelming.

"Well, aren't you just all kinds of helpful today? But I've got this, Fredriksen." I nudged him away and cast my rod, easily sending the fly ninety feet. At its splash, I turned around with a coy smile. "Did I do okay?"

Tyr's mouth was slightly open. "Great Odin. You're as good at fishing as you are at shooting."

I lifted a shoulder and turned back to the water. "Like I told you, makeup to mud in the time it takes you to say *bless your heart.*"

Tyr came up from behind and wrapped his arms around me again. He leaned over so his breath tickled my ear. "*Prinsessa,* if you weren't standing in my arms, I wouldn't believe you were real."

"I could say the same to you." I was on a half-million-dollar boat in the arms of a smoking hot Norse god, trying to catch a fish so we could use its magic breath to trap a homicidal wolf. By all accounts, I was the realest part of this bizarre situation. "Besides, I like fishing. And until you prove me wrong, I'm going to tell people I'm better at it than you."

Tyr chuckled. "Good luck with that. Now we're gonna catch as many as we can—shoot for a dozen."

"Does it matter what kind of fish we catch?" I asked.

"No. I only need to bring in *the breath of a fish*. Any fish."

"Okay." I nodded.

"Just so you know, I've never tried extracting breath, so I might screw it up the first few times. When you catch one, throw it in this bucket." Tyr picked up a silver pail and dipped it in the lake so it filled with water. "We'll aim to keep them alive, but the ones that don't make it get to be dinner. Sound good?"

"Yes." I bit my tongue and narrowed my eyes as I waited for a tug on my line.

Tyr baited his own hook and cast, then stood quietly on the deck while I tried not to stare at his perfect profile. Thankfully, my line began to twitch.

"I think I have something." I reeled the line slowly, and soon a wiggling trout dangled from the end of my rod. Tyr guided the fish into the pail and gently removed the metal from its mouth. It turned fast circles in the small space.

Tyr baited my hook again and picked up his rod. "Now catch another."

We set to our task, bringing in fish after fish. When there were ten swimmers in the bucket, Tyr put down his pole.

"Let's call it for now, and see if I can make this work."

"I'd like the record to reflect that I caught six of those fish. That's two more than you, Fredriksen." I nudged Tyr with my toe.

"Well played, baby. But I was distracted by your killer butt when you bent over to check your line. Next time, I'll have better focus."

"In your dreams."

"Exactly." Tyr winked. Then he squatted next to the bucket. He stared into the water for a long time, his fingers lightly resting on his forehead.

"How do you catch fish breath, anyway? Do you know what you're doing?" I hovered over Tyr's shoulder.

"Not exactly."

He grabbed a fish with two fingers. It flopped wildly. Tyr held out his open hand, and a thin mist floated from his palm. It engulfed the animal, cocooning it in a light green casing. Tyr touched the top of the casing with one finger and pulled back. The fish fell to the ground dead; the casing cracked open.

"Did that work?" My voice was half an octave too high to sound natural.

"No."

Tyr picked up a second fish. He held out his hand, and this time a stream of water shot at the creature. The water froze on impact, surrounding the fish in a block of ice. Tyr studied the block, turning it in his palm. He muttered something in a language I didn't understand. The ice floated above his hand, the fish suspended in mid-air. Tyr pointed a finger at the animal, sending a red beam of light at its mouth. The fish's eyes bulged, but otherwise it remained immobilized in ice. Tyr drew the red beam back with his finger. Just before it reached his hand, it emitted a burst of flame. Tyr jumped back, smoke coming from his finger. The fish fell to the floor.

"It's dead," I whispered unnecessarily.

"I'm aware," Tyr muttered, and my heart opened a little bit more. Tyr might have been a god, but there were still things that didn't come easily to him. Watching his struggle made the distance between our worlds felt slightly less infinite.

The third fish exploded. The fourth fish disappeared. By the time Tyr picked up the fifth fish, a thin sheen had formed on his forehead. He stuck his tongue out of the corner of his mouth and bit down as he waved his hand over the creature. It stilled in his palm. He used two fingers to brush a lavender mist over the animal, and when it was sealed in the casing he tapped it nine times. On the last tap he drew his finger back, and a pale blue vapor rose from the fish. Tyr's eyebrows raised.

"You did it?" I guessed.

"You sound surprised." His voice was dry.

I watched as he produced a small vial. He directed the vapor into the capsule, and sealed it tightly before putting it into his pocket. *Did he just command a magical mist into a bottle?* This was by far the most fascinating date I'd ever been on.

"One ingredient down, one more to go." The corner of Tyr's mouth turned up in a half smile. "So we've got a few fish left. Debone now or back at the house?"

"Excuse me?"

"The fish. Do you want me to debone them here or back home? We'll fry them up for dinner and—" He broke off. "*Skit.*"

I followed his sight line to the edge of the forest, where a large wolf was partially hidden behind a redwood. The wolf's eyes locked on mine and he pawed at the ground, like he wanted to charge. I could have sworn his eyes flashed red and his nostrils flared.

It couldn't be. We're in the middle of nowhere.

I whirled to face Tyr, hoping for reassurance. He threw our fishing gear onto the deck in a frenzied movement, ripped open one of the benches, and pulled out a massive crossbow.

"Mia, get in the cabin. Now."

I was frozen to the deck. My legs wouldn't move.

"Go now!" Tyr barked. My stomach fell. It was a tone I'd only heard once before; the night Fenrir changed everything.

My eyes drifted to the forest, where a snarling beast left me shaking.

"Should I take the fish or—"

"Get inside!" Tyr exploded. He raised his hand and a beam of light shot across the boat, striking me in the chest and pushing me into the cabin. I landed unceremoniously on the bed and jumped to my feet as Tyr forced the cabin door closed with a second beam. My heart hammered as I raced to the door, ready to fight at my boyfriend's side. I jiggled the knob but it wouldn't budge.

"Tyr Fredriksen! Open this door right now! Let me do

something to help you for once, or I'll . . ." What? What would I do? I was on the middle of the lake, stalked by a killer dog, and magicked in a room by a Norse deity who seemed to think the best way to defend me was to lock me in places. I pressed my face against the glass, and wished he'd trust me to defend myself. I might not have had magic lightning hands, but if they had a spare stun gun lying around, I could have debilitated the animal faster than I could have reeled in another fish.

Tyr didn't seem to need my help. On the other side of the glass, he loaded the crossbow and fired off a shot. He quickly fired off two more without blinking. His face was fierce—jaw locked, brow furrowed, and eyes practically shooting sparks. He exuded an air of authority that reminded me of exactly who he was.

And of how much was at stake.

I kept my face against the window. My throat clenched as Tyr fired another round of arrows into the woods. The wolf evaded each shot, crouching as if he wanted to pounce, but the boat was a good hundred yards from the shore; there was no way he'd make it that far.

"*Skit.*" Tyr swore loud enough for me to hear through the glass. He threw the crossbow down and held his hands straight out. He pointed at one of the hundred-foot redwoods, then made a swiping motion with his arm. The tree broke in half and crashed to the ground. Fenrir looked up with a start and ran to the water just as the tree fell. It landed exactly where the wolf had been standing.

Fenrir crouched again, keeping the boat in its sights. This didn't look right. There was no way any wolf could . . .

It hit me like a freight train with busted brakes. Fenrir could do anything. He'd killed Tyr's immortal parents. He'd hurt Elsa. He'd broken through the allegedly impenetrable defenses surrounding Tyr's house. And now he'd tracked us from Arcata to the backwoods of Humboldt County. What were we going to do?

My eyes sought out Tyr's for reassurance, but he offered none. His expression was dangerous, his features contorted in fury. Underneath the rage, his eye twitched. He chanced a glance at the cabin, and when his eyes locked on mine his expression broke my heart.

Tyr was afraid. For me.

He waved his hand at the shore, and a ten-foot wave rose from the lake. It would have taken the wolf under if Fenrir hadn't leapt in the air. The animal flew toward the boat in a narrow arc, closing the distance between us with alarming speed.

"Look out!" I shrieked, hoping Tyr could hear me inside the locked cabin.

Tyr picked up the crossbow and lined up his shot. My pulse quickened—there was no time for Fenrir to alter his trajectory. The arrow struck the wolf mid-chest and sent him falling into the water. He floundered, his jaws snapping open and shut as he struggled to make his way back to shore. The boat rocked as Fenrir's movement stirred the waves, and I struggled to stay upright with the sway.

"Imprison him, Henrik," Tyr commanded.

Henrik?

Without warning, a figure fell from the sky, landing in a low crouch near the water. Henrik stood on the sand, his broad shoulders stiff, and his hands balled in tight fists. Before I could wrap my mind around what I'd seen, Henrik let out a cry and leaped from the shore. He flew over the water, heading for the floundering wolf. Fenrir raised his head when Henrik was still ten feet away. The wolf gave a feral growl that echoed around the lake. Just before Henrik could wrap his arms around the beast, it disappeared. Henrik flew headfirst into the spray, coming up empty-handed.

What the hell?

"Let me out of here!" I pounded on the door, but Tyr didn't look at me. "Tyr Fredriksen, you turn around and open this door right now, or so help me I will . . . I will . . . I will mix your coffee mugs with your water glasses in those pristine kitchen cabinets of yours!"

Tyr turned with an expression that danced between amused and horrified. He twirled a finger at the door and it flew open. Without wasting another breath, I ran out of the cabin and glared at Tyr. "Stop locking me in places. I'm not as helpless as you seem to think I am."

Tyr didn't answer me. Instead, he barked an order. "Henrik, secure the boat. We're getting out of here. He was too close to Mia."

"We are so talking about this later," I muttered.

"I'd expect nothing less," Tyr murmured. He pulled me to his side. My thick life jacket acted like a buffer between us as he wrapped a protective arm around me and waved at Henrik. The other god flew toward the boat, landing lithely on the deck. Tyr held his crossbow in one hand, and me in the other, while Henrik cast what looked to be enchantments from both ends of the boat.

"Good." I shivered.

Tyr's mouth was set in a firm line. "I picked this lake because it was so remote. How did he find us way out here?"

"He must have tracked Brynn when she brought the boat this afternoon." Henrik finished his spell and came to the center of the deck. "You okay, Mia?"

"I didn't just dive headfirst into a freezing lake. Are *you* okay?" I countered.

"I'm great. Just pissed." My normally jovial friend emitted tremors of anger. "I'm sorry, *kille*. I've been scanning the area all afternoon. He only just showed up when you saw him on the shore. He must have transported."

"Transported?" I asked.

"Used a portal to jump realms. Wherever he's coming from, he's found a way to enter Midgard undetected." Henrik slung his bow over his shoulder.

"What does that mean?"

Tyr's eyes softened as he turned into me. He pushed a strand of hair off my face and cupped my cheek in one massive hand. "It means Fenrir has forged a direct line to this realm. He can show up without warning."

Henrik let out a sharp breath. "You want me to swap positions with Brynn?"

"Yes. Effective tonight, Mia's your primary." Tyr narrowed his eyes at the spot where the wolf had been. "Move her into the cabin. I don't want her out of your

285

sight."

My head whipped back and forth between Tyr and Henrik. "What are you talking about?"

But they continued talking as if I hadn't said a word.

"I'll send Brynn to pick up her things. We can't let her out until we trap him." Henrik stared through me as he spoke.

"Can't let me out of where? Y'all better not lock me in anywhere again. It's seriously not okay that you keep doing that." My words fell on deaf ears.

"Make sure Brynn puts some kind of enchantment on her house—it's the first place Fenrir will go, and we don't want him picking off her roommates. Odin has enough messes to deal with right now without two dead human girls." Tyr spoke over my head.

"What is going on?" I stamped my foot.

"He got my family; he's not getting my girl."

"Will somebody tell me what's happening?" I pleaded.

Tyr looked down like he'd just remembered I was there. He reached up to stroke my face and shook his head. "Sorry, *prinsessa*. There's been a change of plans. You're moving in with me."

CHAPTER EIGHTEEN

"I'M DOING WHAT? ARE you insane?" My tone was unladylike, but the situation called for it. A guy couldn't just order a girl to move in with him. Maybe they did that kind of thing in Asgard, but not in twenty-first century America. And certainly not with me.

Tyr ignored my glare. He drove to shore in total silence, despite my increasingly loud protests. It only took a minute to reach the water's edge, but I used every one of those sixty seconds to voice my objection to his Plan Mia's Life For Her stratagem. Who exactly did he think I was? I was a Super G champion, not some simpering damsel in distress.

I drew my shoulders back and lifted my chin. "In case you didn't notice, buddy, I am a woman. Not a chattel. You can't just order me around like some *thing*. If you want me to live with you, you have to date me for a really long time, profess your love, talk to my father, because he's uber traditional and really quite sensitive when it comes to these things, and *ask me* if I *want* to live with you. Not order me. Ask me. There are social rules for this type of behavior, and you, buddy, are *breaking all of them*. Are you even listening to me?"

But he wasn't. He pulled up to the shore and jumped to action. "Henrik," Tyr barked. "Enchant the dock. Protective spell. Then bring the car as close as you can. The vial with the fish breath is in my pocket, so at least something good came out of this. I'll cover Mia, and we'll head back together." Tyr tied the boat to the pier and picked up the bucket with the remaining fish inside it. He wrapped an arm around my shoulder and began to guide me onto the dock.

"I can walk on my own, *thank you very much*." I wrenched my shoulder out of Tyr's grasp, unsnapped my life jacket and shoved it into his hands. With a sharp turn I stormed down the dock, marching a foot ahead of him. It was easier to be upset with Tyr than it was to think about the terror I'd felt when the wolf had attacked again. My insides churned at the memory. There just wasn't anything about this moment that was okay.

"It's clear," Henrik shouted. He'd pulled the Hummer right up to the dock, and moved from the driver's spot to the backseat. "Hurry."

Tyr and I hustled the short distance to the truck. He leaned into the truck to hand Henrik the fish before turning to help me in the passenger's seat, but I'd already climbed in on my own. Tyr crossed to the driver's side, closed the door and fastened his seatbelt. He hit the accelerator and the truck peeled backward, making a big "U" on the dirt. He raced through the redwoods, heading for the highway. Trees flew past at a frightening speed, but Tyr's steady hand kept the vehicle on course. He was determined.

"You going to talk to me now?" I crossed my arms.

Tyr kept his eyes on the road. "About what?"

"I'm not moving in with you."

"Yes, you are." Tyr drove.

"No, I'm not. That's something couples decide together. Maybe not in whatever boondocks part of Asgard you come from, but in these parts, that kind of thing isn't a unilateral decision."

Henrik snorted from the backseat, and Tyr shot him a look. "Fine. Mia Ahlström, would you please move in with me?"

I shot him a fierce look. "Now you're just being patronizing."

"I'm not patronizing anyone. I'm trying to play along. Because at the end of this conversation, Brynn is getting your stuff and moving it to my place. This isn't a negotiation."

"You don't get to tell a girl she's going to move in with you." I recrossed my arms and turned to Henrik. "He doesn't get to tell me I'm moving in with him!"

"He does, actually." Henrik didn't even try to hide his amusement. "He's the God of War. Even Thor doesn't get to question him."

"Maybe that title means something in Asgard, but around here, you can't just order people around. There are steps to observe. Rules to follow. And besides, I'm not ready to live with you. I don't even know your middle name."

"It's Ragnar." A corner of Tyr's mouth twitched.

"Oh. Well." I tapped my foot. "That's a really nice middle name."

"Thank you. Now, is this argument over?"

"No. I am not moving in with you. I like you too much."

"That makes no sense." Tyr reached across the console to hold my hand. "You like me. I like you. You're the only girl I want to be with, and you're the only girl I've ever asked to move into my house. I don't see what the problem is."

"Ever? You're, like, a thousand years' old. Seriously, you've never lived with a girl?"

"Nope. I like my space."

"Oh. Well. You're not living with me because . . ." It was hard to maintain the right amount of indignation when he was touching me. "Because you're doing this for the wrong reasons. You're not doing it because you want to live with me; you're doing it because a killer wolf god is after me, and your macho alpha gene is kicking in. This is an impulse decision, not a rational one."

Tyr shrugged. "I do want to live with you. And my alpha gene is always kicking in. They don't have to be exclusive."

"But if we live together, I want it to be because we both want to, not because we're afraid of something." I pounded my fist against my thigh. It was like talking to a rubber wall. Everything I threw at him bounced right off.

"Listen, baby, I get that you're scared. There's a lot to be scared about right now. But you don't ever need to be scared of this." He placed my hand over his heart. "This isn't going to change. You mean more to me than you know, Mia Ahlström, and I'll do whatever it takes to protect you. Even if it means pissing you off."

I held very still, debating Tyr's offer. *Pros: Spend freshman year living under the protection of the Norse pantheon. Increase likelihood of surviving bizarre wolf attacks. Catch nightly glimpses of the Norse God of War in his pajamas. Cons: Um . . .* My brain was stalled on the mental picture of pillow talk with Tyr.

"You don't have to share my room. You can have the upstairs guest room. But I need you close; at least until we trap Fenrir. Then, if you want to leave, I won't stop you."

He kissed my fingertips with a smile, but I heard the strain in his voice.

The truth was, if I moved in with Tyr, I'd be happy as a chipmunk in an acorn tree. And that would make it that much harder to move on someday when he had to go back to Asgard. Tyr was constantly taking care of me—the sweet dates, the early morning runs, the surprise visits at school. He 'mysteriously' showed up after class to walk me to my car, and his secondary bodyguard just happened to be my roommate. Whether it was Freya's interference, or Tyr's protective nature, I'd been looked after since the day I arrived in Arcata. So much for my college independence; I'd left my parents' home to be guarded by the gods.

And now they wanted to move me into their cabin. Because they didn't think I could defend myself from their evil wolf.

"Tell me what happened that day in the woods. I need to know why Fenrir attacked *me*, and not one of the other girls Freya picked for you."

"How do you know about Freya's girls?" Tyr shot me a glance.

"Brynn explained everything the night I found out what

you are. So why me? Why didn't he trail someone else and attack them?"

"Honestly?" Tyr tapped the steering wheel. "I have no idea. With the hack on the Norns' security, he had to know I was fated to be with someone who might be a mortal; though the prophecy that I'd end up with someone *not of Asgard* could just as easily have been about a Vanir, or a light elf, or, Odin forbid, a mountain giant. I guess because Freya had bought into the idea my partner would be human, Fenrir was willing to, too. That day, you were running on a path that led directly to my house, so maybe he thought you were going to see me. And I never met the other girls, not that I know of, anyway, so I don't know what they looked like. But Fenrir should have known me well enough to know that I'd be attracted to you." Tyr winked. "I've always had a thing for leggy brunettes."

"So he tried to kill me because I was jogging toward your house, and because I'm your *type*?" My voice squeaked. "That's crazy."

"It could have been a hundred other reasons. We'll probably never know." Tyr shrugged. "But I came out of my house when I heard the growling, and I got to you in time to help. Just know that I was taking care of you then. And I'm trying to take care of you now." Tyr leaned forward slightly. "You said on the beach that you trust me. This would be a really good time to prove it."

We'd have a heck of a lot to talk about after all this went down, but his expression was so adorable, it only took two minutes of stewing before I resolved to meet him halfway.

"Okay. Here are my terms. I will move in with you as a trial. One week. If, after one week, we feel it's too much too soon, you will let me move back to my house without any guilt or judgment or weirdness. And I'll follow whatever rules you need me to so you feel like the wolf won't get to me. I won't go jogging by myself, or go to the store late at night, or whatever. But if it's making things awkward with us," *or if I feel like I'm too attached to handle it when, someday, you have to move back to Asgard full time,* "we stop right away. Deal?"

Henrik snickered from the backseat. Tyr and I both glared at him.

"Sorry. I've just never seen anyone barter with him before. Barter with Freya, yes. Idunn, for sure. But never with Tyr." He doubled over laughing.

"Do we have a deal?" I asked again, ignoring the peanut gallery.

"What happens if I say no?"

"Then I go back to my house and carry on with my life like there's no crazy wolf chasing us, and you just have to deal with it. I'll call my brother if you try to abduct me and make me stay with you, and you do *not* want to tick off Jason. He threatened to end you if you broke my heart, just so you know."

"Oh he did, did he?" Tyr smiled.

"He did. So do we have a deal?"

"Fine. Deal." Tyr nodded. "Now stop distracting me, both of you. If there really is a portal in these woods, Fenrir might come back—and he might bring friends. We know he's working with someone, it's only a matter of time before whoever it is shows up."

I shivered and squeezed Tyr's hand. We drove in silence for a few miles before I worked up the nerve to ask.

"What kind of friends does a killer wolf hang out with?"

"His siblings."

"That's right. The wolf has a brother that's a snake." I remembered, but it still seemed absurd. "And their sister is Hel." While I played with the wrists of my sweater, I wondered what other human euphemisms were about real people.

Tyr kept talking. "Odin knew Jörmungandr was going to be a major problem, so he threw him in the ocean of Midgard. The serpent got so big, he bit onto his own tail and held on. But his jaw locked, and he hasn't been able to free himself. Remember, when Jörmungandr lets go of his tail, your world's gonna end."

"So if Fenrir brings Jorga . . . Jomug . . . forget it. If he shows up with the snake, there's going to be some kind of apocalypse?" I pressed my palms against my thighs.

"Pretty much. But you can sure as Helheim bet they're gonna try and kill you first."

Well, that pretty much sucked. Suddenly my brother's *live a little* advice wasn't looking so hot. A shudder wracked my body. I hadn't given a lot of thought to how I might die, being seventeen and in peak physical condition from downhill training, and all. And it wasn't like there was an ideal way to go. But death by giant wolf god and/or snake monster weren't exactly top of my list.

"Get over here, *prinsessa*." Tyr held out an arm, and I scooted as close as the console would allow.

"I'm still mad at you for trying to order me around," I clarified. "This doesn't mean you're off the hook for your seriously backwards bonehead move."

"Trust me, I know. And I also know all of this is intimidating. You're tougher than you look, and I appreciate that you haven't jumped out of the window to get away from all the crazy. But I'm not going to let anything happen to you. Not today, not next week, not ever. I'll fight to the death to make sure you're safe. You get that?" He spoke with a vehemence that left me slightly awed.

"Yes," I whispered. His stubble tickled my lips as I leaned over to plant a soft kiss on his cheek as he drove. When I pulled back, he settled me neatly under his arm.

"Now hold on." He narrowed his eyes and stepped on the gas as we hit the freeway. "It's gonna be quite a ride."

* * * *

When we got to Tyr's house, he jumped out of the Hummer with his arms outstretched. He muttered something I couldn't understand, and a shimmering bubble appeared. It covered the house, stretching in a twenty-yard radius around the structure.

"You've made that before. What is it?" I climbed out of the car, now safe inside the golden sphere.

"Protective casing." He murmured again, this time aiming his hands at Elsa's cottage. "This should keep Fenrir away until we relocate to the northwest compound."

"I'll check on your sister, then meet Brynn at the girls'

house." Henrik glanced at his phone. "Forse ported over so he could look after Elsa. You just worry about Mia."

We're relocating? And who's Forse?

"Call immediately if anything's off at the cottage," Tyr ordered.

"You know I will." Henrik handed Tyr the bucket of fish, jumped into the driver's seat, and peeled the Hummer out of the drive.

"Inside, Mia." With his free hand, Tyr lifted me in a fireman's hold and sprinted into the house.

"I am capable of walking on my own," I pointed out from my position on his shoulder.

"Yeah, but you can't run as fast as I can." Tyr slammed the door behind him and placed the bucket on the ground. I squirmed until he set me on my feet.

"Why don't we race *without* you using your super speed? Then we'll see who's faster." I planted my hands on my hips.

"Great. Tomorrow. Right now, we've got a few things to take care of." Tyr darted up the stairs with otherworldly speed, slammed some doors, and returned to the first floor in the time it took me to draw two breaths. He circled the downstairs rooms in two seconds, and skidded to a stop in front of me. "It's clear."

"That's really freaky, you know that?"

"It's efficient. Now let's get you something to eat. Mac and cheese okay? I'm not really in the mood to fry up those fish anymore." Tyr headed toward the kitchen.

I picked up the bucket, then called out. "Tyr. Wait."

He pulled off his baseball cap to rake his fingers through his hair as he turned around. "What's up, baby?"

"It's going to fall." I pointed to his pocket. The vial with the fish's breath poked out of the top.

"Jeez, thanks." Tyr tossed his hat on a side table and grabbed the vial. "I forgot all about this. Better put it away."

"You do that. I'll put the fish in the kitchen."

We walked down the hallway together. At the end, I turned right and deposited the bucket on the counter—we could freeze them to cook later. When I returned, Tyr had removed a mirror from the wall. He turned the dial on the safe hidden behind it, and the door swung open. When the jar was safely in the vault, he sealed it shut.

"The rest of the ingredients are here. All except the bear's sinew."

"When are we going to track that down?" I asked as he re-hung the mirror.

"*We* aren't. It's too dangerous." Tyr tried to lace his fingers through mine, but I pulled away.

"You're going to have to stop underestimating me at some point. I've already proven I can outshoot and out-fish you. Who knows? I might just be an exceptional bear tracker." I crossed my arms.

"Wouldn't doubt it. But I can't have you out in the woods with that dog lurking around. I'll take care of the bear." Tyr reached for my hand again, but I stepped back. He gave me a long look. "You can be mad at me all you want, *prinsessa*; it's not going to change anything. You're staying here until I know you're safe. You might as well make yourself comfortable."

With that, Tyr walked past me into the kitchen. I stood in the hallway and resisted the impulse to stomp my feet. Instead, I took several deep breaths, and followed the world's most irritating deity, gearing up to give him another piece of my mind.

But when I saw him leaning against the open refrigerator door, shoulders drawn with tension as he moved milk, butter and cheese to the island countertop, my rebuttal ebbed. He was in the middle of a living hell, and I was upset over a temporary living situation.

I shook my head. *Pick your battles, Ahlström. His day's going way worse than yours.*

"Here." I crossed to the cabinet and pulled out the grater, knowing full well Tyr was making his special brand of comfort food. "Let me help. I'll grate the cheese."

Tyr's shoulders sagged with relief as he handed me the block of cheddar. "Thank you, Mia." He kissed the back of my head as I began shredding. "I'm sorry about all of this. I swear I'm doing everything in my power to set it right."

"I know you are." I moved the cheese along the blades. "But you don't have to do everything by yourself all the time."

Tyr's laugh was dry. "How about I let you help me dissect the nerves after I bag the bear. Sound fair?"

"Hardly. But I'm assuming you're done negotiating for the day?"

"You assume correctly." Tyr pulled some bacon out of the fridge and tossed it onto the counter. "I'll leave as soon as the stars come out. It's easier to smuggle a bear around the woods in the middle of the night than it is during the day. You never know who's watching."

I shivered. "You think someone besides the wolf is watching you?"

"Who knows? Luck favors the prepared, right?" Tyr dropped a stick of butter into the pan, then whisked in some flour. A whole stick of butter? No wonder his mac and cheese was so good.

I set the grater in the sink and handed Tyr the cheese as he filled a pan with water and brought it to a boil.

"That's why I've got everything I need for the dissection set up in the garage."

"Serious?" I blinked.

"Serious." He added milk, cheese, salt and pepper to the flour mixture, then poured the noodles into the pan of water.

"It's like the bloody Batcave around here."

"You wish," Tyr teased. "After we eat, I want you to take a shower and get comfortable. Brynn should have left a change of clothes for you."

"When did she do that?"

"Henrik messaged her while we drove home." Tyr shrugged. "He should be here soon with the rest of your stuff. After dark, I'll go sedate the bear. We'll extract the nerves, double check all the ingredients are in the safe, and we can both be in bed by ten-thirty."

"Easy as that, huh?" My stomach flopped. So many things could go wrong between now and then.

"Easy as that." Tyr came over and sat on the stool next to me. He took my hands in his and kissed each palm in turn. A pulse shot up my arm and went straight to my lower abdomen. Bear hunter. Immortal warrior. Superhuman kisser. God. This man was unreal.

When the timer eventually beeped, Tyr stood to remove the dish from the oven. He doled out generous portions and returned to the island with two heaping bowls.

"Now eat up, *prinsessa*. We've got a long evening ahead."

* * * *

Henrik didn't come home that night. He didn't answer his phone, either. Tyr filled his voicemail with messages, each more frantic than the last. While he buzzed around the room, doing that still-unbelievable flying thing in his panic, I pulled out my phone and texted Brynn.

Where is Henrik?

A moment later, I got a response.

With me. There's a bit of a situation. We have it under control.

I typed quietly.

Tyr's freaking out.

Brynn's response made me giggle.

Must be a day ending in "y." Tell him we've got this. Do whatever you have to do to get the rest of the ingredients, NOW. Tell Tyr I said ingredients are Code Orange. I'll send Henrik as soon as I can. Bye!!

Tyr stopped moving at the sound of my laughter. His eyes fell to my phone. "What is it?"

"Henrik's with Brynn. Apparently there's a situation, but they have it under control. She thinks you should do the bear thing right away, though."

"I'll get Freya to stay with you. Let me call her." Tyr brought his phone to his ear and began a heated conversation. "What do you mean you're still securing the northwest compound? I thought the reinforcements were almost finished?"

There was a long pause.

"I see. And Forse? He hasn't left Elsa's has he?" Tyr's eyes closed. "All right. I'll figure something out. Take care of things there."

He shoved his phone in his back pocket and squared his shoulders.

"Freya's busy?" I kept my tone light to offset the heaviness in my gut.

"I'm not going. I won't leave you here by yourself."

"I'll be fine. Put an extra spell on the house or give me one of your fancy space weapons or something." I shot my brightest smile at Tyr, and he flinched.

"Maybe I can get Brynn to—"

"You want me to trust you? That works both ways. I can take care of myself," I said gently.

Tyr's eyes softened. "I know you think that. But this monster . . ."

"Isn't going to get within a hundred feet of me. I've shot plenty of guns." I pointed at the secret space-gun closet. "Just give me one of those."

Tyr glanced at the closet, then back at me. He crossed to the door and opened it. He reached in and handed me a rifle. "Fine. But the fancy space weapons are too risky. Do you need a refresher on how to use this one?"

"You've seen me shoot. I'm better than you." I winked.

"In your dreams." Tyr kissed the top of my head. "I don't like leaving you, Mia. The bear can wait until Brynn and Henrik get back."

"Maybe. But if it matters, Brynn said to tell you the ingredients were Code Orange."

Tyr froze. "Let me see."

I handed him my phone. His face turned white as he read the text. "*Förbaskat.*"

"Go." I nudged him through the front door. He stood on the porch, casting enchantments in a wide circle. A thick lavender bubble formed around the property line, anchored to the ground by a swirling black mist.

"I'll be back in a few minutes." He typed on his phone and squinted at the screen. "There's a black bear fishing a hundred yards south of here. This shouldn't take long."

"There's an Asgardian app for bear tracking?"

"There's an app for everything."

"Well, I'll be here." I kissed his cheek and pushed him off the porch. "Go."

Tyr stared at me. "Are you sure you're okay with this?"

I picked up the rifle and held it at eye level. I took aim at a rock just inside the left edge of the property, and fired off a shot. The rock exploded in a spray of tiny shrapnel.

"I'm good," I assured Tyr.

"Great Odin, you're so beautiful right now. If I didn't have to . . ." He tore his eyes away from me and jogged into the forest. He yelled over his shoulder as he ran. "I've got plans for you when I get back."

"Hurry home," I called after him. Then I went back into the house and locked the door.

And I waited.

CHAPTER NINETEEN

THIRTY MINUTES LATER, I stood in Tyr's garage, huddled over the sleeping body of a live bear. The animal exhaled softly as Tyr made an incision in its upper deltoid. Tyr's tongue poked out of the corner of his mouth as he worked. If the situation weren't so dire, I would have teased Tyr about his tic.

"Pass me the smaller scalpel." Tyr held out his hand. He hadn't been kidding—there was a full laboratory setup in his garage. Next to the motorcycle he'd arranged a sturdy operating table, complete with complicated lighting apparatus and medical machines I'd never seen in a human hospital.

In the middle of it all lay eight feet of sleeping bear. His thick black fur popped against the matte metal table, and his paws were so massive I was sure he'd take us both out with one swipe if he knew he was being operated on.

"You're sure he won't wake up, right?" I kept my voice low while I searched through the tray of surgical equipment. When I found the small scalpel, I handed it to Tyr.

"Pretty sure." He grinned. He bent to kiss my cheek

before returning to the bear's shoulder. "You can go inside if you're scared."

"No way." I shook my head. "I want to help you."

"I love that about you." Tyr looked up. "You're something else, Mia. I'm sorry for all of this. I never meant to put you in danger. I swear if anything happens to you . . ."

Tyr turned his attention to his work. He didn't look up again.

I moved closer and put my hand on his back. His muscles were knotted under my touch, and my gut tugged as I thought about everything he'd experienced. From losing his parents to the childhood pet he'd asked to keep alive, to bearing responsibility for the security of *the entire universe*, Tyr had shouldered more in his lifetime than I could possibly fathom. It was heartbreaking.

"I'm sorry," I whispered.

"For what?" Tyr kept working.

"For everything you've been through. Losing your parents. Fighting for Elsa. Being betrayed by Fenrir. Protecting your realm. All of it. I can't imagine how hard it's been. I'm sorry."

"I chose this life." Tyr shrugged. "I knew what was involved."

"But you were born into your title. Right?"

"I came into it through my parents when they adopted me, yes. But I could have walked away. It's happened before. Vanaheim is filled with birthright titleds who passed on their posts. I knew what being God of War would entail once I came of age and the job was explained to me, and I stayed on to take it. I own that choice, so don't feel sorry for me. Feel sorry for the gods who died looking out for me."

Tyr reached for a long pair of tweezers and continued his operation. I stood just behind him, my view slightly obstructed. Since he was doing fine without me, I rubbed his back softly. "Are you talking about your parents?"

"My parents," he confirmed. "And my bodyguards."

"Henrik's not dead."

"No. But the four guards I had before him are." Tyr didn't look up.

"Oh. Oh, Tyr." I rested my cheek on his shoulder blade. "I'm so sorry."

"The only thing they did wrong was choose to work for me. It's why I turned Henrik down for so long when he applied for the job. But he's the best at what he does, and Odin finally overruled my objection. I've had more hits on my life than any other god. Being involved with me is suicide."

"Are we still talking about your bodyguards?"

Tyr put his tools down and turned to face me. His normally stoic eyes looked moist. Too moist.

Was he going to cry?

"Immortal beings have died because of their association with me. I'm terrified . . . terrified that they'll kill you, too."

"Fenrir's not going to get me." I lifted his chin with my finger. "You're going to get that rope and trap him, remember?"

"Fenrir's just the beginning. I have enemies you can't even imagine. Serpents, and dragons, and an eight-legged horse with a manic crazy streak—a legion of demons that would do *anything* to hurt me. Once they get wind of you, you'll be a sitting duck. And the fact that you're human . . ." Tyr rubbed his eyes and the moisture disappeared. "You're so easily dispensable."

"You really think I'm that helpless?"

"Against the monsters of the underworlds, yes. You want to know why I didn't ask you out the night we met? Because regardless of what I wanted, you deserved to be protected. Walking away was the best way to make sure you were safe."

"So what happened? Why did you change your mind?" My voice broke. Some part of me was afraid that if I asked, he'd change his mind right back.

"My birth father slaughtered a village of light elves, and I decided if I couldn't protect the realms' most innocent creatures from a monster that dark, then I could at least protect you. But the more time I spent with you, the guiltier I felt for bringing you into the *skit* that is my normal. So I backed off again. I couldn't decide what was better for you—being without my protection, or being without my baggage."

I blinked. "What did you say?"

"I wanted to protect you. I wasn't there when the elves were attacked, and look what happened. Seemed like keeping you close was the only way to make sure you were safe."

"No." I paused. "The other thing."

"Oh. My birth father slaughtered an entire village of light elves."

"Oh my God, Tyr. So he's the 'crooked' part of your family tree you alluded to?" I ventured.

"Yes. My parents are dead. Fenrir killed them. But they adopted me when I was a baby. My birth father is still alive." Tyr paused. When he spoke again, his gaze didn't quite meet mine. "Remember when I told you I wasn't pure Asgardian? I'm a halfling. My birth father is a giant. And he's not a great guy."

"Oh." *Oh.*

"My parents, the ones who raised me as Elsa's brother, they were some of the kindest beings I've ever had the privilege of knowing. But from a genetic standpoint, I'm half monster. I've spent the better part of my existence fighting against my instincts so I can live up to my parents' hopes for me. But if you had any idea what I was born to be—" Tyr broke off. He turned to face the table and went to work on the bear.

I touched Tyr's back. His muscles felt like smooth stones, but his anger was so palpable the tremors radiated against my fingertips. I kept my voice soft as I spoke.

"Someone once told me that we don't become what we observe; we become what we *believe*. I know you were born to be exactly who you are right now—protector of your realm; defender of creatures who are weaker than you; the guy who loves his friends and sister with a loyalty very few people possess. No matter what you think about yourself, you have a kindness that I find sexy as all get-out. Your parents—your *real* parents—raised one heck of a man. And

I'm proud to know him."

"Fenrir and I aren't that different. We're both born of monsters. Both raised to be better than our nature would have us be. But my love wasn't strong enough to overcome Fenrir's darkness. Who's to say my parents' love was enough to overcome mine? What would happen if you were the one at my side when I lost it?" Tyr kept his hands on the operating table. His shoulders shook.

"I'm willing to take that chance."

"But you're not safe with me, Mia." Tyr whipped around, with pleading eyes.

"That's because you guys keep locking me in places whenever something bad happens. You said it yourself— I'm a lot tougher than I look. You might as well teach me how to channel it."

"How?" Tyr whispered.

"Stop treating me like I'm helpless. Let me use one of your super space guns the next time something goes down. Teach me your uber-self defense. Give me the chance to be a part of your life, instead of just watching you live it from inside a glass case."

Tyr stared at me. "Is that how you feel? Like I don't let you into my life?"

"Yes. I get that you're trying to protect me, but I've never wanted to be that girl who hid behind a man when things got tough. Those girls didn't go into Super G."

The corner of Tyr's mouth turned up. "I see."

Sensing the opening, I pressed on. "I'm not saying throw me to the wolf and cross your fingers. I'm just saying if you gave me the tools, you might be surprised at what I could do."

Tyr's voice cracked. "That's scary for me."

"I know." I swept my hand around the garage. "But this is scary for me. Nothing about any of this is familiar, or normal, or even remotely logical. And in case you hadn't noticed, I really like logic."

"I know you do." Tyr cupped my cheek with his palm. "You win. We'll do some combat training tomorrow. Even though I really don't like the idea of you fighting anyone, I don't want you to feel like I'm shutting you out of my life."

I brought my hand up to meet his. "I'm not going anywhere. And nothing's going to hurt me, so long as you give me the tools I need to take care of myself. You can stop worrying."

Tyr's eyes met mine with a wistful smile. "I don't think I'll ever stop worrying about you. But I can promise I'll never stop fighting to make sure you're safe. And I promise when Fenrir's captured, I'll take you away from all this."

"Like on a vacation?" My face broke into a grin—that meant Tyr wasn't going to catch the first rainbow bridge back to Asgard when the whole Fenrir situation was over. We could actually enjoy normal couple time together . . . even if we were far from a normal couple.

"Anywhere you want. Just the two of us," Tyr vowed.

I stood on my toes, kissed his bottom lip, and turned him around to face the sleeping beast.

"Get the nerves and let's finish this," I instructed. "Everything is going to be just fine. You'll see."

Tyr picked up the scalpel. He winked over his shoulder before he made his next cut. "Good thing you're always right."

* * * *

A little more than an hour later, I sat in Tyr's kitchen, staring at a jar containing nine live bear nerves. Somewhere in the forest behind Tyr's house, a bear was waking up, wondering why its right shoulder felt just a little bit lighter.

The bear would never know what happened to it. Before Tyr had carried the creature back to the forest, he'd wiped its memory clean.

He'd wiped its memory clean.

Tyr had held a hand over the bear's head, mumbled something I didn't understand, and just like that the animal had been relieved of any memory it had created during the last twenty-four hours.

If Tyr could do that to the brain of a three-hundred-pound beast, I could only imagine what he could do to me. The entire situation was unnerving. No pun intended

Now, Tyr placed a steaming cup of chamomile in my hands, and took the seat next to me at the kitchen table. "Thought you might need this."

"Thanks." I stared into the golden tea.

"Something wrong?" Tyr slid an arm around my shoulders.

I shrugged, refusing to meet his eyes. The tea traced a warm path down my throat to my stomach. It instantly brought my stress level from ten to eight.

"I know something's on your mind, baby. Hit me." Tyr kept his hand on my upper arm and pulled back just enough to stare me down. The color of his eyes was absolutely mesmerizing.

"Mia?" Tyr spoke softly.

"Are you going to do that to me?" I blurted. "Wipe my memory clean?"

Tyr eyed me levelly. "It depends."

"On what?" I gripped my teacup so hard, my knuckles cracked.

"On whether you experience something so traumatic, you wouldn't be able to recover without a cleansing. If that happened, then yes. I'd wipe the memories. I did a partial wipe on you the day you were attacked in the woods."

"You did what?" I shrieked.

"It was necessary. You started to wake up while Freya was healing your arm. When I got back to you after Fenrir escaped, you were coming to, and you were screaming. You were in a lot of pain. I wiped your memory from the moment you blacked out until after Freya finished her healing, and she and I were out of sight. Brynn stayed with you until you woke up."

"That is not okay. Why would you do that?"

"I told you." Tyr's expression lacked the appropriate amount of remorse. "You don't need to suffer on my account. You were attacked because Fenrir believed you were associated with me, and you were in a lot of pain. You didn't need to remember what you were going through."

"I don't want you messing around in my head." I didn't blink.

"I know you don't. And under normal circumstances, I wouldn't dream of invading your privacy like that. For what it's worth, I didn't snoop around when I was in your head. I just wiped the experience and got out. I don't like reading people's minds, you know."

"Wait, you can—oh, cheese and crackers. You can read minds too?" My head throbbed. I pushed my tea to the side, wrapped my arms around my face, and rested my forehead on the table.

"Hey." Tyr rubbed my lower back. "Why does that upset you?"

"Because," I moaned. "You know what I'm thinking? Like, all the time?" When I'd ogled his backside, compared him to a Greek god, thought about . . . *doing things* . . . he'd been listening in. This was beyond mortifying.

"I don't monitor your thoughts, Mia, but I would if I needed to. If Fenrir had captured you, and I needed to find you, I could have listened for your mind and tracked you."

"You've *never* listened to my thoughts?" I cautiously lifted my head.

"Well, maybe one time." The corner of Tyr's mouth lifted in a smirk. "But I figured you wouldn't be too happy if you found out, so I didn't do it again."

"Oh, God. What did you hear?"

"A gentleman never tells." Tyr grinned. "But like I said. It won't happen again."

"How does it work, exactly—reading someone's mind?

Do you have to consciously do it, or do you just hear voices?" I propped my chin on my hands, curiosity trumping embarrassment and fear.

Tyr chuckled. "I have to consciously do it. It's not a science; I can zero in on one person and follow their specific thoughts, or I can take a scan of a room and get general vibes—you can tell from someone's thought pattern whether they're up to no good."

"Really?"

"Really. But it's easier to scan someone's aura and assess them that way. It won't tell me what they're planning to do, but it gives me a read on their moral compass." Tyr gently rubbed the knots in my lower back.

"Did you ever do that on me?"

"Of course. The night we met."

"What did you see?" I held my breath.

"You, baby, are refreshingly uncorrupted." He raised an eyebrow. "At least, for now."

My fist connected with his shoulder a lot harder than I meant it to. My knuckles stung. "Sorry."

Tyr shrugged. "I can take it."

"Back to the mind reading—have you always done it?"

"Since I took my title, yes. Odin gave my dad the ability after the war against the fire giants. That battle started because Loki abducted a giantess, and her father launched the attack on Asgard. Odin thought one of us should have seen what Loki was up to. My dad lost two of his best friends in that battle."

"That's terrible." I twined my fingers through the silky strands of his hair, and gently rubbed his scalp.

Tyr closed his eyes. "Odin lost someone close to him that day, too. It was the impetus he needed to give the war god the ability to read minds."

"Why'd he give it to you guys? Why not someone else?"

"Because if anyone needs to know what's going on behind a false smile, it's the God of War. Now, when I enter any room I automatically do an aura scan. Nobody's betrayed Asgard without my seeing it coming in almost a hundred years."

My eyes bulged. Sometimes I forgot how long he'd been around.

"My age bothers you, doesn't it?"

"No," I lied. Tyr gave me a look. "Okay, a little. It's just weird to think my boyfriend's so . . ."

"Good looking?"

I glared at him. "I was thinking *experienced*."

"Nice spin." He rolled his eyes.

"You're reading my mind right now, aren't you?"

"I promised I wouldn't. How about we make a deal?" Tyr rubbed my hip with one hand, and held my wrists in the other.

"What kind of a deal?"

"A two-part deal. There may come a time when you're in some kind of trouble. Most people who get close to me ultimately are."

"Tyr—"

"I can't fix what's happened, but I can fight for you. Obviously Brynn, Henrik or I should always be looking out for you. But if, Odin forbid, someone ever takes you away from us, promise you'll think my name as hard as you can. Scream it in your head if you have to. I'll hear you. And I'll find you."

I shivered. "I can do that. Now what's the second part of the deal?"

"I promise I won't ever listen in on you. I don't want you feeling like you have to censor your thoughts around me."

"Done." I kissed Tyr's nose and his eyes drooped. "You're tired."

"Exhausted," he admitted. "Let's go to bed."

Oh. My. Lord.

My whole body tensed. Who knew four words could carry so much weight? *Let's go to bed.* Did he want me to share his bed? Or was I supposed to sleep in the guest room? A few days ago I'd been ready to be with him for the first time, but then he'd dropped the I'm-a-god bomb. What did I want now? Oh, who was I kidding? I knew what I wanted. At least, I thought I did. Did he want it too? Oh god, what if he didn't?

"Brain out of the gutter, *prinsessa*." Tyr chuckled.

"You promised you wouldn't read my mind!" I howled.

"Didn't have to. You should see your face." He grazed my chin with one finger. "Now, up to my room. We need to sleep, and I can't do that right now if you're not in my arms. In the morning I'll take the ingredients to the dwarves. They should have what they need to make the chain. Henrik and I can work on our plan to catch Fenrir after that. But right now, I'm about to pass out."

Tyr punctuated his statement with a huge yawn.

Stop over thinking everything, Ahlström.

"Okay." We walked into the hallway hand in hand. Tyr opened the mirror to check on the ingredients in the vault.

"Everything's there," he confirmed, before shutting the mirror and leading the way upstairs. He kept a firm grip around my palm as he walked past the guest room, and into his bedroom.

My heart thudded against my ribcage.

"Henrik's not back with the rest of your stuff yet. Here." Tyr dug around in his dresser and pulled out a pair of Redwoods sweats and a grey T-shirt. "These okay?"

"They're perfect." I eyed the open bathroom door. "I'll just go change in there."

"Why?" Tyr mumbled, his shirt half over his head. Eight exquisitely defined abdominal muscles framed by obliques—actual, visible obliques—stared me down. They were spectacular. The ribbed surface of his chest called to me, making something stir deep inside. Blood drained from my face, and I licked my bottom lip while Tyr pulled his shirt the rest of the way over his head, then threw it next to the clothes hamper. *Typical guy.* "Mia?"

"Hmm. What did you say?"

"I asked why you'd go change somewhere else. You can just change here." Tyr pulled off his pants. Now he stood in front of me wearing nothing more than a pair of black boxer-briefs. He had thick thighs that strained against the cotton fabric, his muscles stretching down long legs. His underwear rested low on his hips, and clung tightly to the contents underneath.

Oh hot bejeebus, the man was a god. In every conceivable way.

"Stare as much as you want, *prinsessa*. It's all yours."

My head snapped up and the blood returned to my face in a rush. *Oh my god. This is mortifying.* "I wasn't staring at you. I just, erm . . ."

"Relax. I don't mind. But now it's your turn. I showed you mine, you show me yours." Tyr winked.

My hands clutched my makeshift pajamas as my pulse pounded in my ears. Accepting Tyr as a god had been a cakewalk compared to what I was about to do.

CHAPTER TWENTY

"WHAT'S THE MATTER, BABY? It's not like you've never been in your underwear in front of a guy before." Tyr crossed the room and gently tugged the pajamas out of my hands.

"Actually, uh . . ." My cheeks positively blazed.

Tyr held me at arm's length as recognition dawned. "Really?"

"I went to a girl's school." I shrugged. "I had dates, but never anything long-term. That seems like the kind of thing you do with someone you're serious about, you know?"

Tyr watched me without blinking, his expression unreadable. After half a minute, I couldn't take it anymore and averted my eyes. Obviously he'd done this, probably a jillion times over a thousand years. Standing there in his underwear was no big deal to him.

But it was a huge deal to me.

"Say something," I mumbled.

Tyr pulled me to him and pressed my back with his palm. My face rested against his chest, and I inhaled the smell of spruce and pine that was so divinely Tyr. His scent, combined with the absolutely to-die-for feeling of being held against his naked chest, was almost enough to make me forget everything we'd been through. *Almost.*

"Let's just get some sleep. It's been a really long day." Tyr's voice made his chest vibrate against my cheek.

My eyes stayed locked on the ground. "I disappointed you," I whispered.

"What?" Tyr pulled back so he could look at me. "Gods, no. Why would you think that?"

"Because . . . because . . ." *Because you're an immortal sex god and I'm a virgin.*

"Baby, listen to me." Tyr tucked a finger under my chin and lifted my head so I was forced to meet his gaze. "You did not now, nor have you ever, disappointed me. I just don't want to pressure you into something you're not ready for. And it's not like I don't have the time to wait."

"You're not upset that I'm a *virgin*?" I whispered the last word. It made me sound so lame.

"Not at all. I didn't realize I'd have the pleasure of being your first." Tyr winked. "Nice choice, holding out for a god, by the way. You're going to have one Hel of a ride."

"Tyr!" My palm made a loud noise against his bicep as I swatted him. Tyr wrapped long fingers around my wrist and held my hand in place.

"Seriously, we don't need to rush into anything. Much as I would love to throw you on the bed and show you exactly what you've been missing out on, I'm looking forward to doing a lot of other things to you first. Starting with this." Tyr released my wrist and wrapped his fingers under the hem of my cardigan. He pushed further, lifting the T-shirt underneath. The pads of his fingers brushed the skin of my abdomen, and I inhaled sharply. "Relax, baby. It's just clothes." I exhaled, and raised my arms. Tyr met my gaze, and waited until I nodded. Then he gently tugged the layers up, over my head and tossed them on the ground. When he'd finished, he ran his palms down the sides of my bra, along my ribs, and stopped just above my hips. "See? No big deal."

Right. Standing in my bra with the Norse God of Hotness in his bedroom was no big deal. And my Meemaw cheated at cards. *Snort.*

My breath shallowed as Tyr pulled me closer. He kissed a line from my ear down to my shoulder, pressing the washboard that doubled as his stomach against my belly. His skin was hot against mine, something I registered at the same moment as something deep in my abdomen burst into flames. *Breathe. It's just clothes.*

"Now these." Tyr knelt down and slowly unzipped each of my boots, removing them with unnerving slowness before tossing them to the side.

"And these should probably come off, too." Tyr rose so he was on his knees. He wrapped both hands around my waist and brought his mouth to my belly button. It was warm, and soft, and my abdomen practically exploded at the touch. My eyes were locked on Tyr's unruly hair as he licked a languid trail around the contours of my stomach, outlining the softly-defined muscles and pausing just above the top of my low-cut jeans. He took the waistband between his teeth and gave it a tug. At the same time, he glanced up at me with his telltale half-smile. I sucked in a jagged breath. He'd managed to undo the button and turn my heart into a jackrabbit on Red Bull in one singular movement.

"Oh my god," I whispered.

"Yes?" Tyr responded with a grin. Then he ran his nose along the line where my stomach met my pants, and slowly unzipped my jeans. He hooked his thumbs inside the band, and tugged. I lifted one leg, then the other, as I shimmied out of my pants and stood there in nothing more than my bra and panties. Thank the maker I'd worn the lacy white set. Between God's generosity and the wonders of the underwire, my girls were being displayed to their maximum advantage.

But it was my bottom half that seemed to hold Tyr's attention. The lacy scrap of fabric barely covered the essentials, and Tyr's hands palmed my backside as he raised himself up from the floor. He gave a gentle squeeze, sending a tremor shooting up my spine. The blood in my belly pulsed violently. *Hot bejeebus.* If it felt like that when he touched me there, what was it going to feel like when he . . . he . . .

I swayed on my feet, and Tyr swooped in to lift me in his arms. "You okay, *prinsessa?*" he asked, concern evident in his eyes.

"Never better," I murmured. Despite my ragged breathing and lack of equilibrium, it was true. I was out of my element in every conceivable way—hunted by a killer wolf, stripped to my undies by a smoking hot Norse deity, and about to spend the night in the bed of the God of War. But I'd never felt more alive. Apparently, following my heart was a lot more exciting than following my schedules.

Tyr shifted me to one arm and pulled back the covers with the other. He lowered me onto the soft mattress and climbed in beside me, tucking his impossibly long legs under the down comforter. He pulled me closer and threw the blankets over me, then nestled my body against his. We lay skin to skin, the borrowed sweatpants forgotten. My entire body vibrated with anticipation. As much as this intimidated me, I couldn't wait to see what would happen next.

"Good night, *prinsessa*." Tyr stroked the muscles in my lower back as he kissed my forehead. He lay his cheek against my hair, cupped my bottom with his palm, and said softly, "Sleep well."

What? That's it?

"Good night?" I hadn't meant the words to come out on a question, but the squeak in my voice betrayed my disappointment.

Tyr tilted his head so he pressed his forehead to mine. Our eyes met, the question dancing between us. It hung in the air for a long moment before Tyr gave me his trademark half-smile. "Not tonight. You're exhausted, and probably overwhelmed. It's been forty-eight hours since you found out I'm immortal, got attacked by a wolf with a grudge, and were invited to move in with the greatest guy in all the realms."

"Were ordered, more like it," I corrected. But Tyr slid his leg between my thighs, and a thousand nerve endings I hadn't realized existed sprung to life. The sensation wasn't the slightest bit unpleasant.

"Details," Tyr murmured, brushing my lips with a soft

kiss. "Point is, you've had enough change for one day. And much as I want to play with all of this . . ." he squeezed my bottom, "I'm going to be good for once in my existence and let us both get some sleep. There'll be plenty of time for me to blow your mind later." He slipped his tongue inside my mouth and swept it lightly over mine. His palm squeezed again, bringing my hips into his. The thousand nerve endings did a frantic tap dance, and I felt a slow build in the base of my stomach. My hands stroked Tyr's chest, and I kissed him back, moving my lips against his with a pace that built to match my desire. But when I shifted to climb on top of Tyr, he rolled away with a groan.

"Mia, you are not helping me be good."

"Who said I wanted you to be good?" I murmured.

"You'll thank me in the morning. When all of this sets in, and you realize what an enormous two days you've had." Tyr rolled back so he faced me. He stroked my cheek with one finger. "Baby steps, *prinsessa*. There's a whole world to explore between this" —he kissed my lips softly— "and this." He pressed his hips against mine, and I let out an involuntary moan. He tilted his head to whisper into my ear, "And I don't want you to miss out on a single thing."

"Okay," I whimpered, excitement building at the idea of all the *single things* Tyr might be talking about.

"Now go to sleep, troublemaker." Tyr tucked an arm around me and stroked the small of my back. His kiss was sweet, his lips lingering just long enough to leave me lightheaded.

"Night," I whispered. My fingers trailed a line along the stubble of his jaw, down his neck, and came to rest on the hard planes of his chest.

And then I fell asleep, wrapped safely in the arms of the God of War.

* * * *

"Where do you think you're going?" Tyr stood by the front door with his arms folded across his chest. In dark jeans and a navy blue Henley, he was so delicious I wanted to jump into his arms and beg him to finish what we'd started the night before. But Art History started in less than thirty minutes, and I'd need a lot more than half an hour for him to do what I was hoping for.

"I'm going to class." I held up the backpack Henrik had brought sometime in the middle of the night, when he'd delivered the rest of my things. "Why are you still here? I thought you were going straight to the dwarves to deliver the ingredients after breakfast."

"Apparently Hreidmar is not accepting visitors at this time." Tyr's eyebrows made a small V.

"Hreidmar is . . .?"

"The dwarves' leader. And he's busy. I spoke with his servant while you were brushing your teeth."

"You did?" I tried to move around Tyr, but he was impassive. "How'd you do that? Doesn't he live in another realm?"

Tyr reached into his pocket and pulled out his iPhone.

"Let me guess. There's an app for inter-realm FaceTime,

too." I shook my head.

"Henrik developed it a few years back." Tyr stuffed his phone in his pocket and recrossed his arms. The wrinkles between his eyebrows deepened. He looked *really* stressed out.

"Well did you explain that you sort of need this chain, like, yesterday? On account of the satanic wolf attacking and all?" I moved for the door again, but Tyr stepped to the side, blocking me.

"Mmm. Something like that. And yes, he's aware. But you don't push dwarves. What I'm asking is a big favor, and they don't tend to do things out of the goodness of their hearts." Tyr frowned.

"What do you mean?"

"Don't get me wrong; dwarves have made some remarkable treasures for Asgard— Thor's hammer, Mjölnir, is one of them. But they do so on their own terms, and in their own time. And their gifts always come at a great price." His arms still crossed, he rubbed lightly at his right elbow.

"What's the price going to be for the chain?" I tried to reach around him, but Tyr stared at me and leaned against the door. There was no getting past him now.

Tyr's fingers tightened around his arm. "Why don't we go back to the kitchen? I'll make another pot of coffee."

"Because I'm going to be late for class," I reminded him. He just blinked at me, the poster god for overbearingness blocking my path to a timely exit. "Tyr, I really need to go."

"I don't think so." Tyr reached behind him and turned the deadlock. "You're not leaving this house."

"Excuse me?" There was no way to keep the incredulity out of my voice. Just because he was having a standoff with some dwarf king didn't mean he got to boss me around. Again.

"I said you're not leaving this house. There's a homicidal canine just waiting for you to set one foot outside the protection."

"Are you crazy? I'm not missing class. There's no way I'll be able to keep up if I start ditching lectures." My fingers gripped my backpack so tight, my knuckles cracked.

"I'll forge you a sick note and you can get notes from someone. What classes do you have today?" Tyr didn't move.

"Art History and Calc II. Both of which are really complicated. I'm not skipping."

"Charlotte can give you her art notes, and Henrik will pass you in Calc II. Solved." Tyr looked unaccountably pleased with himself. Bless his heart, the poor thing was delusional. The whole wolf deal must have gotten to him.

"That's not going to work for me," I said sweetly. Rule number one dealing with crazy people: kill them with kindness. "Charlotte's super smart, but I'm already kind of lost in Art History, and I need to be there to understand the pieces. And I don't want to just *get* a pass in Calc II because I'm dating my TA's roommate. I want to *earn* an A so I don't fall behind for the next series of equations. Math classes build on themselves, and I'm planning on going to a top graduate school. Now, if you could kindly let me through the door, I would very much appreciate it." I reached for the deadlock.

"Forget it, Mia. It's not happening." Tyr flexed his arms. At six and a half feet, and what looked like a solid ton of muscle, he should have been intimidating. But he was standing between me and my academic future. Hell hath no fury like an Ahlström facing mediocrity.

Forget killing him with kindness. If that god made me get a *B*, I'd just plain kill him.

"Oh, it's happening." I glared at him. "I agreed to live with you; I didn't agree to give up my entire life. Look, I've done a pretty decent job compromising. I didn't push you when you wanted to go off bear hunting without me. I didn't go ballistic when your BFF locked me in the house so the two of you could wrestle the crazy wolf. I'm living in your house, even though it's *way* too soon to even think about a step like this, and even though my parents would freak out if they knew I'd moved in with a guy I'd only been dating a few months. But dang it, Tyr Fredriksen, I will not skip class for you. That is just asking too much."

We stood, locked in an angry stare-down, neither of us willing to budge. He might have been revered and honored in Asgard, but right now he was pushing my very last button.

"Fine. You may go to class." Tyr finally surrendered. "But I'm coming with you."

"You're not enrolled. What are you going to do there?"

"I'll watch you." He grabbed his keys and his wallet, pulled his leather jacket out of the closet, and unbolted the front door. "After you."

I stared at him as he opened the door, then I walked onto the porch. "You can't just go to my classes and stare at me. That would look really weird."

"Not my concern, baby." Tyr closed the door behind him and strode to the Hummer. He held open my door so I could climb in. "The only thing I'm worried about is keeping you safe. If you're so intent on leaving the protection of this house, then I'll have to bring the protection to you."

"Are you going to put me in a personal glitter bubble?" I fastened my seatbelt as Tyr started the car.

"Kind of." He handed me a lighter as he pulled out of the drive.

"You want me to start a campfire?" I questioned.

"Henrik built this for you. I may have lied when I said I used a device to cloak us on the beach, but it was a pretty genius idea. I had Henrik develop the technology you thought I used when I cloaked us. That little thing distorts the air around you, so you appear invisible. Be careful using it, since people won't be able to see you, and they'll run into you if you're not careful."

"Are you serious? He really did that?" I fingered the lighter. Henrik was even smarter than I'd thought.

"He really did. I'll shield you manually today, since I'm with you, but if we get separated, I want you to flick that thing once. You'll stay hidden until you flick it again. Fenrir won't be able to find you."

My mouth formed a tiny circle. Freaking brilliant—that was what Henrik was. Brilliant, and just a tiny bit scary. If he could build this, who knew what else he could create?

We drove through the woods in silence for a few minutes before Tyr pulled onto the main road. He grinned as he accelerated.

"What?" I asked.

"I've never been to a college class." He chuckled. "This is going to be a first for me. Those are few and far between."

"Yeah, well Art History's a good place to start. We're finishing up paintings of Norse gods. You should feel right at home."

Tyr raised an eyebrow. "They're teaching you about me?"

"They're trying to. I'm finding the entire subject slightly unbelievable."

"I'll be sure to set you straight." Tyr steered into a parking space and jumped out of the car. He opened my door and offered his arm as I climbed out. "Don't be too offended if your friends ignore you today."

"Why on earth would they do that?"

Tyr waggled his fingers at me. "We're cloaked. Just don't go talking to anyone, or you'll freak them out. Watch." Tyr took a few steps sideways and stood next to a brunette getting out of her car. "Hello," he said quietly. The girl whipped her head around, then narrowed her eyes and walked toward the Humanities building. "See?" Tyr asked. "Humans are fun."

"You're awful." I laughed. "Seriously, uncloak us in class. I sit with Charlotte, and she'd notice if I was missing." Or sitting beside her invisible. God, my life had gotten weird.

"Not my problem baby," Tyr said again. "My number one concern is keeping you alive."

"Thanks for that, but I'm equally concerned with not losing my entire identity because of all of this." I waved my hand in a circle in front of Tyr. "And a huge chunk of that identity is *not* getting marked absent from class, and *not* making my friends wonder where I am. I didn't come home last night, and if I don't show up to class Charlotte will worry."

"Or she'll think you're having a really good time with your incredibly hot boyfriend, and couldn't be bothered to get out of bed," Tyr pointed out.

I tapped my foot. "I'm being serious."

"Mia," Tyr moaned. "You're not working with me here."

My fingers rested lightly on Tyr's forearm. It was so tense, his veins bulged. "I'm really going to need you to uncloak us for class." I squeezed. "And maybe for lunch too. I told Heather that Charlotte and I would meet her after Art History. I'm going to tell them I'll be staying at your place for a few days, so they don't worry about my sudden disappearance." I raised one eyebrow. "And I'm giving them my Meemaw's lasagna recipe to master while I'm gone."

Tyr took a slow breath through his teeth, the kind one takes when trying not to make the noise one *really* wants to make. "Fine," he hissed. "But the *second* I sense something off, I'm flying you straight out of there. I don't care who sees it."

"See?" I hid the tremble from my voice. "I knew we'd find a compromise."

Tyr glared at me and marched toward campus. "You're going to be the end of me, you know that?"

I hurried to keep up with him. When I tucked my hand through the crook of his elbow, I glanced up at him with a wink. "Or maybe I'm just the beginning."

* * * *

Tyr was gone all day on Tuesday. He jetted into the woods in the morning, and took the magic rainbow bridge back to Asgard to talk to Odin about the dwarf situation. Apparently they couldn't fit him in for another few days, and if the clicking in Tyr's jaw while he slept was any indication, he was massively stressed about it. While he was away, he left me under the overly watchful eyes of Brynn and Henrik. They followed me to class, to lunch, and Brynn even followed me into the bathroom. When I told her to leave, she pushed out her bottom lip.

"I told you I wouldn't *watch*," she complained. "But if Tyr finds out we let you out of our sight for one minute . . . I told you he had a temper, didn't I?"

"You also told me you weren't afraid of him. That it's Henrik you really have to watch out for," I reminded her. "And I swear, nothing's going to happen if you give me one minute to tinkle. Honest."

Brynn covered her mouth. "You said tinkle."

"Get out." I shoved her through the door.

Tyr should have been home by dinnertime Tuesday night, but at five-thirty there was still no sign of him. I picked up my phone and dialed, not expecting an answer. Even with Henrik's miraculous apps, the probability of my wireless provider reaching Asgard was slim.

"*Ja?*" Tyr picked up on the second ring.

"Hi. Um. Wow. I didn't think you'd answer," I stammered. He must have been back on Earth. Back on Earth . . . jeez, my life was weird. "You almost home?"

"Sorry baby. I'm going to have to stay in Asgard overnight. Hreidmar is being a total pain, and Odin's ready to wage a war over it."

"Hold on, you're talking to me from Asgard? How is that even possible?" I balked.

"Brynn implanted a chip on your mobile."

"She whaty-what now? Did I sign off on that?"

"No." Tyr sounded sheepish. "It's one of Henrik's transistors. You've got reception, and a GPS tracker, that will work in all nine realms." Tyr sounded distracted. I could almost picture him running his hand through his unkempt hair.

"Okay, first of all, let's ask people before installing things on their phones from now on. And second of all, you're *tracking* me? And you have been since when? Seriously, when you get home we have *got* to talk about boundaries."

"Whatever you say, *prinsessa*. Listen, I have to run. Henrik and Brynn are both staying at the house tonight. Do you want me to send Freya back too?"

"No." My answer came too quickly. While I appreciated everything Freya had done to bring Tyr and me together, I still hadn't totally forgiven her for locking me in the house when I should have been out helping my boyfriend fight. Ahlström women did not play the damsel in distress. "Are you okay up there? You're not in any danger or anything, are you?"

Tyr sighed. "Fenrir's on the warpath, and you're worried about me? You're something else."

"You didn't answer the question," I pointed out.

"I'm fine." Tyr's smile sounded in his tone. "We've got the Elite Team surrounding the cabinet room."

"The who?"

"Odin's top assassin team. Don't worry, *prinsessa*. I'm in the safest place I could be. And you are, too. Nothing's gotten past Henrik yet."

"Great." I forced a smile. "So I'll see you in the morning?"

"Here's hoping. Take care of yourself, *prinsessa*. I don't know what I'd do if anything happened to you." Tyr's voice caught. "We can go over some weapons training when I get home, if you still want to."

"It's a date. And Tyr?"

"Mmm?"

"Please be careful," I begged.

I could practically see the twinkle in Tyr's eye. Even though he was trying to talk the lord of the realms out of going to war, he lived for a challenge. He let out a light laugh as he signed off. "I always am."

CHAPTER TWENTY-ONE

"*HEI,* BABY." TYR RAN into the kitchen late Wednesday afternoon, and swept me up in a hug. Thick arms crushed me from behind as I was enveloped in the comforting smell of spruce, pine, and man.

"Hi," I murmured, reaching up to wrap my fingers through his hair. Tyr lowered his mouth to my neck and traced a warm path to my ear, before turning me around to plant a languid kiss on my mouth. When he pulled away, his eyes were hooded. "Mmm, I missed that."

"Me too." Tyr stroked his thumb against my cheek. "I don't like leaving you."

My heart soared at the words, and I couldn't stop the smile that stretched across my face. "I'm glad you're home," I said simply.

"Me too. Now let's get out of here."

Wait. What?

Tyr grabbed my hand and pulled me toward the hallway. He walked to the closet and entered a code in the keypad. The door opened, and Tyr pulled out two space guns, two crossbows, and a sword.

Seriously. What?

"What are you doing? I was just about to start dinner. Should I turn off the oven?"

"Turn it off. We're going outside. I promised I'd teach you to defend yourself." Tyr closed the door with his foot and headed down the hall, laden with weaponry. I hurried to the kitchen and turned off the stove.

"Can it wait until after dinner?" I returned to the hallway. "You just got home. You have to be hungry."

"No time, *prinsessa*. Thar be monsters in them woods."

"Okay, Davey Jones, stop moving and talk to me right now. What is going on?" I untied my apron and folded it in my hands.

"Walk and talk, Mia." Tyr shifted the weapons to one hand and opened the front door. I tossed my apron on the entry table and hurried after him. "I learned two things while I was away. One, Fenrir's working with one of the biggest monsters of all time. He's using him to get to me, and he seems to think it's going to work. His thought is if he can take away enough of the good things in my life, I'll go back to the darkness and fight with him at Ragnarok."

"That's the end of the world, right? Is it coming?" I bit down on my bottom lip.

"It's still looking like it'll be a long way off. Like, centuries away."

Well, that was good news.

"So who is the monster Fenrir's working with?"

"Hymir."

The name sounded familiar, but I couldn't place it. "Who?"

Tyr continued walking off the porch, and into the clearing. He stopped when he was about a hundred feet from the house, and turned to look at me. "Hymir," he spoke quietly. "My birth father."

"Your birth father is trying to make you turn evil? That is seriously messed up."

"I told you I came from darkness." Tyr grimaced. "So that's number one. Number two: this is yours now. Take care of it." He held up a space gun. "And number three: Odin's *this close* to opening a full war on the fire giants, who seem happy to both harbor *and* lend their full support to Hymir. So they could show up in Arcata to come after you, me, Elsa, or just cause chaos because they can, at any moment. Weapon up. It's time to train." He tossed my space gun at me, and I plucked it out of the air with one hand.

Crumbs on a cracker, he wasn't kidding.

"Nice catch."

"I can't believe you threw a space gun at me. Usually you treat me like some delicate little flower." I gripped the firearm. It was lighter than it looked.

"I don't really have a choice anymore. Things could get ugly fast, and I need to know you can take care of yourself. Besides, you're still my delicate little flower. The safety's set."

Of course it was.

"This model has two settings—stun and implode. I keep

them set on stun, because Odin's current order is to capture Fenrir, not kill him. But if you ever find yourself in a position where you don't think stun is going to keep you safe, then push this switch." Tyr pointed.

"But then I'd kill him." I hesitated. I knew what Fenrir had meant to Tyr at one time. "Are you okay with that?"

"I'm a lot more okay with that than with him killing you."

"Oh."

"Hopefully, you'll never have to use this thing. But if you do, and if you're in danger, you do what you have to do to protect my girl. Now, the first thing you do with this one is release the safety." Tyr stood behind me and turned the gun over in my hands. He activated the weapon, then placed both of my hands around the cool metal. His chest pressed against my back as he positioned my arms, and my skin tingled where we made contact.

"What's this made of?" I asked in my most academic voice. It was hard to focus when he was standing so close.

"A titanium hybrid native to Svartalfheim. The prototype was iron, but it was too dense."

"Density matters in this gun?" These were the first things I'd ever actually seen with the technology to make something implode.

"Tremendously. There's a detonator that's activated with a magic capsule Henrik embedded in the chamber. The magic was creating too much reverb in the heavier model, and a few of the, eh, test subjects had some unfortunate injuries. This is the fifth model." Tyr raised my arms to eye level, and placed his knee between mine. Heat leapt through the fabric of my jeans as a warm burn moved slowly up my leg. Tyr shifted his knee slightly and the heat moved up several inches. I sucked in a sharp breath, and leaned into the touch. I had no idea where he was going with this, but I *really* wanted to find out.

"Maybe tonight, *prinsessa*. If you're lucky." Tyr chuckled.

"You said you wouldn't read my mind," I hissed.

Tyr stepped back and doubled over. "Just promise me you'll never play poker. You're entirely too transparent."

Oh. My cheeks burned. "Are you going to teach me to use this thing or not?" I grumbled.

"Sorry." Tyr wiped his eye as he stood. "So this one shoots like a regular handgun, but it's got a killer kickback. I was *trying* to open up your stance; you're going to need as stable a base as possible in order to stay on your feet."

Right. That was why my lower half felt as shaky as if I'd just finished a two-mile downhill course.

"This good enough?" I set my feet shoulder-width apart, with the right set slightly back.

"Wider."

"This?" I stepped back another few inches.

"Spread your legs wider, baby."

I caught the twinkle in his eye, and shook my head. "You are incorrigible."

"I've heard worse. But another six inches will stabilize you more. Try it."

Trying not to blush, I set my stance. Tyr came back to stand behind me, with one leg between mine, and his chest pressed firmly against my back. He leaned over so he spoke into my ear.

"I'm going to fire it with you the first time. I'm not kidding about the kickback. Remember whatever you shoot at will implode, so try to pick something small and far away but still inside the protection." He nodded at the shimmering bubble encasing our property. It stretched around the cabin, all the way to Elsa's cottage, keeping Fenrir, and whatever crowd he hung with, out. "The fire will be silent, but the implosion most definitely will not. So try not to jump. Are you ready?"

I nodded. "Let's do this."

"What are we shooting?" Tyr asked.

I let my eyes roam the woods until I found a small stump roughly thirty yards away—what was left of a fallen tree. "How about that?"

"Looks good. One. Two." He squeezed my hands around the trigger.

"Three." I fired, sending a beam of white light into the stump. The act made the gun jump in my hands, and if Tyr hadn't locked my elbows in place with his arms, the sudden burst of energy would have left me eating titanium.

"Get ready," Tyr whispered. We stared at the stump as it emitted a puff of smoke and appeared to collapse on itself, before sending shards of wood flying in all directions. Tyr wrapped himself around me, bending at the waist to tuck me against his massive form. I felt the impact of the wood chips hitting his arms, and when he released me, I scanned his body for injuries.

"That was intense. Are you hurt?" I held the gun in one

hand, and touched his forearm with the other. "Didn't the wood hit you here?"

"Our skin's pretty much impervious to injury from organic substances," Tyr explained. "They have to hit us pretty hard." He pointed to a cut on his bicep. It was deep, crimson, and oozing a thin trail of blood, but it was also knitting itself back together. In the time it took my jaw to drop, the injury had healed itself. Only the red residue remained.

"What just happened?" I blinked.

"When we are injured, *usually* we're able to heal ourselves. Me especially. I inherited the healing gene with my title."

Of course he did.

"Are there any injuries you can't heal yourself from?" I asked.

"Yes. If a wound comes from a non-organic substance, like a manufactured poison, or if a weapon has been infused with dark magic, I'm out of luck. And if an organic weapon is infused with dark magic, and it delivers a deep enough injury—punctures an organ, severs a limb . . . there's very little chance I'd survive. We can heal, but we can't completely regenerate."

"Fenrir?" I shivered.

"Fenrir or his siblings could kill me, if they had enough dark magic in them." Tyr nodded. "But we don't need to go there. We're safe enough in our little bubble for now, and Odin forbid he breaks through, you'll just shoot him down with that thing, right?"

I fingered the gun in my hand. "Um, yeah. Maybe we'd better practice again."

"Fair enough." Tyr took a step back. "On your own this time."

A tremor danced along my spine, but I found a small shrub thirty yards away and took aim. I set my legs apart, locked my elbows, and pulled the trigger. The gun pushed back hard, sending a jolt into my elbows, but I held them firm and my shot fired straight. The white beam raced for the shrub, and in seconds green leaves flew in the air, resulting in a snowstorm of emerald shrubbery.

"Well played, baby." Tyr clapped his approval.

I tucked a leg behind me and bent in a low curtsy. "I figured leaves were a lot easier to take a hit from than boulder shards or another tree. You can thank me some other time."

"Oh, I plan to." Tyr's eyes grazed my denim-clad backside, and I shot him a grin. He caught me smiling and raised an eyebrow. "Ready to go in so soon?"

"Not on your life. How many rounds can this thing do?" I held up the gun.

"The magic will sustain six shots total, then you need to load up a new cartridge. They're stocked in the hall closet, so be sure to grab extras if you ever need to take your gun out." Tyr raised his arms over his head in a stretch. "Why don't you finish that one out, and then we'll move on to crossbows?"

"That sounds good." The back of my neck grew hot, and I ducked my head so Tyr wouldn't see me blush.

Tyr Fredriksen wielding a crossbow. This was turning out to be our hottest date yet.

* * * *

That night I lay in Tyr's bed, pretending to read *All's Well That Ends Well*. It was impossible to process Shakespeare's prose when a Norse deity was brushing his teeth half a room away. I could see the outline of his arm through the open bathroom door, the muscles of his bicep flexing with each tiny stroke. How could Tyr manage to make dental hygiene sexy? Maybe it was the intimacy of it all. So domestic.

When I heard Tyr rinse his brush and put it in the holder, I gave up and put my book on the nightstand. He came out of the bathroom wearing grey sweatpants and no shirt. His lightly tanned skin stretched so beautifully across a sea of smooth muscles, I nearly forgot what I'd wanted to talk to him about. He yawned and dropped onto the bed, face first.

"Tired?" I stroked his back with my fingertips. Poor thing hadn't slowed down since he'd got back from Asgard. He'd run me through gun training, then taught me how to fire a crossbow, then brought out the second gun and ran me through the paces again. By the time we were done, my arms shook from the effort of stabilizing the space gun. And if the bags under Tyr's eyes as we ate dinner were any indication, he was even more exhausted than I was. It was the first time I'd seen him with dark circles. "You were gone almost thirty-six hours. Did you get any sleep in

Asgard?"

"None. But I've gone longer on less, so it's not a huge deal." Tyr's pillow distorted his voice. He hadn't moved.

"Can I ask you a question?" I hedged.

"Shoot," came the muffled reply.

"Would you ever consider, eh, retiring? Or taking a desk job or something?" I bit my lower lip and waited.

"Why would I want to do that? I like my job." Tyr turned his head just enough to peek at me with one eye.

"Well, what happens if you have a family or something someday? You're not going to keep doing this, are you?"

Tyr stared at me. "If I were lucky enough to have a family, I'd fight even harder to protect them from the monsters hunting our worlds."

"But couldn't you do that from inside an office, or something? Surely Odin has strategist roles?" The inside of my lip grew raw. I stopped chewing.

"What are you really saying?"

"I'm saying"—I closed my eyes—"I'm saying your job scares me. I don't want you to get hurt. And I want to know that if we end up staying together, I won't have to spend forever wondering if this is going to be the day you won't come home."

Tyr tensed beside me. "You want me to quit my job?"

"No. Maybe. I don't know." I threw a hand over my face and opened my eyes. "It's just really scary to think about all the things that can hurt you. And to know you go out *looking* for them. I have no idea where things with us are going, or whether we'd even be able to have a long-term future together, since you're a god and I'm, well, me. But if we *did* end up together in a few years, and things were serious, would you ever, I don't know, be God of Nature, or something?"

"Then who would do my job?" Tyr propped himself up on one elbow.

"Another god?" I asked hopefully.

"That's not how it works, Mia. We're born into our titles. Most of us live indefinitely, but in the rare circumstance a god is killed, his son or daughter is eligible to inherit his post. The Norns selected us for our predispositions to fulfill our duties. I have no desire to relinquish my title, and since I don't have any children, I wouldn't have anyone to pass it on to even if I wanted to."

"What about Elsa?" I ventured.

"She has her own role to fulfill," Tyr reminded me. "And I wouldn't wish this life on my sister. Would you?"

"No," I whispered. My stomach fell. "So you're saying you and your future son, are the only gods of war Asgard's got? Isn't there any way to change that?"

"Even if there was, would you want me to give up what I am?" The look Tyr gave me was devastating. His mouth was turned down in sadness, his brow furrowed in confusion, and his eyes downcast, searching mine with a plea. "Am I not enough for you?"

That was the problem. He *was* enough for me. More than enough. I was terrified the universe was going to take him away. And sending him off into the path of homicidal, dark magic-wielding animals seemed likely to increase the odds of my fear coming true.

"I just don't want to lose you," I whispered. "I'm scared."

"Oh, *prinsessa*." Tyr pulled me to his side of the bed. He lifted my head and slid an arm under my neck so my cheek lay on his bare shoulder. He palmed my bottom with one hand, and stroked the side of my face with the other. "This is who I am. Believe me, doing *this* job is a lot more palatable than what I'd be doing if my dad hadn't adopted me."

"Yeah, but—"

Tyr pressed a finger against my lips. "I get that I'm a lot to take on. And I understand if you don't want to sign up for a life of worrying about me. You aren't the first girl to ask me to quit my job, you know."

"I'm not?" I blinked. *Stupid, Mia. He's a thousand years' old. You're not his first anything.*

"No." Tyr stroked my cheek again. "You're not. Being with me is hard. I know that. But I promise if you stick around, I'll make it worth your while."

He kissed me soundly, the hard, demanding kind of kiss that reminded me how very much in control of himself he was, in every possible situation. His hand wrapped around my head and pulled me closer, and he pressed his palm to the small of my back, driving my hips into his. Blood pooled just below my navel, and I shimmied against him, wanting to close even the tiniest gap between us. As I did, Tyr pulled his head back and looked down at me.

"What do you say? Think you can hang in there with me?"

I took a shaky breath. "I don't know," I answered honestly. "The harder I fall for you, the harder it's going to be to lose you."

"You're not losing me, baby. Get that through your analytical little head. You're stuck with me so long as you want to keep me." Tyr kissed my forehead and rolled onto his back, tucking me against him in the process.

"I want to keep you," I whispered. "I just don't know how to *not* worry about you."

"Then we're even." Tyr turned his head to look me in the eye. "I don't know how to *not* worry about you. Let's take life one day at a time together, *ja?*"

I tucked my head into Tyr's chest and breathed deeply. "Okay."

It was the only thing we could do. Who knew what tomorrow would bring?

* * * *

On Friday, Tyr and Henrik went to the shooting range while Charlotte, Heather and Brynn joined me at Tyr's house for dinner. I'd promised them Meemaw's chicken parmigiana, and Heather sat at the kitchen table and tucked her napkin over her lap before I'd even uncovered the dish.

"Hungry?" I teased.

"For this, yes. It's my favorite of your dinners, and I haven't had it in forever." Heather picked up her fork as I served us up.

"I know I haven't been home in a week, but it's not really *that* long." I smiled.

"One week without Meemaw's chicken parm is pretty much an eternity." She flung her hand to her forehead and pretended to faint.

"It's not good when the one who's *pre-Med* passes out," Charlotte observed drily. "Who's going to revive her?"

"Seriously, Mia." Heather sat up. "When are you coming home? You haven't, like, moved in here, have you?"

"Moved in? Like permanently? No. It's way too soon for that." I kept my tone light. Brynn caught my eye and gave a small wink. She'd coached me thoroughly—the less everybody knew about what was going on, the better. "Truth is, I just can't bear to be apart from this kitchen. Every single appliance is top-of-the-line."

"Right." Heather snorted. "It's the *kitchen* she can't stay away from."

Charlotte giggled. "Even I'm not buying that one."

"Buy whatever you want." I picked up my fork and smiled. "*Bon appétit.*"

"Cheers." Heather took a bite. "Mmm. So good."

"Delicious." Charlotte closed her eyes as she chewed.

"Mmm." Brynn nodded in agreement.

Heather finished chewing and leaned forward. "It was the sex, wasn't it? It was so good you couldn't stay away, even for one night. And now we might never see you back at the house again."

"Heather!" Charlotte threw her napkin at our friend.

"You can't ask that!"

Brynn tilted her head. "But now that the question's out there, how is the sex?"

"Oh my god!" My cheeks may as well have been facedown on a griddle. "We're not talking about this."

"It's that good, huh?" Heather sighed. "I knew it would be. Just look at him."

My arms flew up to cover my head. "Stop it!"

"I have to admit, I've always been a little curious," Brynn chimed in. "How big is his—"

"Stop it!!" I giggled, and peeked out from behind my forearm. "I don't know. I've never seen it."

"You've . . . wait. You guys *are* doing it, right?" Heather looked confused.

"Uh, no. Not yet."

"Why not?" Brynn tilted her head in confusion, and even Charlotte leaned her forearms against the table, waiting.

"I don't know," I mumbled. "It just hasn't been the right time. Can we please talk about something else? Anything else?"

My eyes met Charlotte's, and she gave a small nod. "How about you, Brynn? How's Henrik?"

Brynn blushed right up to the tips of her ears. "We're just friends."

"You want us to say something to him?" Heather offered. "Cause I'm sure if he knew you were into him, he'd be all over you."

"No!" Brynn waved her hands in front of her face. "It's fine. I just, eh, we're good."

"Whatever you say." Charlotte shrugged. "I just want everyone to be as blissfully happy as our Mia, here. Just look at her. She's glowing."

"I am not glowing." I rolled my eyes.

"You'd be glowing if you were having sex," Heather pointed out.

The tips of my ears probably matched Brynn's.

"Oh, this is to die for." Heather pointed to her plate as she spoke through a mouth of tomato sauce. "How do you *do* this?"

"I'll show you next week if you want," I offered. "It's a super-easy dish."

"Sold." Heather raised her fork. "I'm at the clinic on Wednesdays and Saturdays now, but any other evening is good."

"You picked up an extra shift? So your schedules are working for you. That's great!" I took a bite, grateful for the subject shift.

"Yeah. Sorry again for blowing up at you about all that. Turns out micro-scheduling and time blocking was exactly what I needed. I'm carrying a three-point-five GPA, and the time at the clinic has helped my coursework click into place. I'm way more productive than I ever was. So thanks for that."

"I'm glad I could help." I reached over to squeeze her arm. "What about you, Charlotte? How's your boyfriend?"

"Fantastic." She beamed. "I'm going home with him for

Thanksgiving. His aunt lives in Ashland."

"Ooh. Catching any plays while you're there?" I asked. "Or is that off-season?"

"I don't think Matt's really the theatre type," Charlotte mused. "But it's okay. I'm sure we'll find something to do."

"I'm sure you will," Heather teased. "Is everybody ready for the Spirit of the Redwoods celebration?"

"As ready as we can be." I covered my mouth to hide my giggle. Only in Northern California would there be a festival honoring trees . . . complete with two days off school to observe the festivities.

We caught up on the past week while we ate, and when dinner was over we finished the gallon of my favorite cookie-dough ice cream Tyr kept stocked for me. Tiny little Brynn managed to pack in the most, and she clutched her stomach as she walked to the front door.

"Next time, cut me off after two bowls," she moaned.

"No way. Life's short. Eat the ice cream." Heather opened the front door and stepped onto the porch. "Well, hello, hotties."

We stepped out behind her and saw Tyr and Henrik getting out of the Hummer. Henrik shot us a grin as he walked up the front steps. "*Hei hei*, ladies." He threw an arm around Brynn's shoulders. "How was girls' night?"

"It was great," she trilled. "There are leftovers in the kitchen. Mia made way too much."

"She always does." Tyr came up on the porch and planted a hard kiss on my lips. "*Hei* baby," he murmured.

"Hi." The word came on a breath. "You guys have

fun?"

"Always. But we're starving. You really have leftovers?" Tyr's hopeful tone was absolutely adorable.

"Heaps. Help yourself. I'll be in in just a minute." I kissed him again, and he and Henrik walked into the house. Brynn and I walked the girls to Charlotte's car and said our goodbyes. Then I turned to Brynn with a sly smile. "You coming back in?"

"No." Brynn sighed. "Henrik needs to work, and I need to watch Charlotte and Heather. One of our scouts in Svartalfheim said there was some weird stuff going on outside a closed portal. We don't know for sure, but in case they've reopened it, I want to make sure the girls are protected."

"You're a good friend." I gave her a quick hug.

"So are you. Now go in the house before I leave. I promised Tyr I'd keep an eye on you."

"I'm good now. Tyr gave me a space gun," I boasted.

"You mean a nano-molecular particle accelerator?" Brynn corrected.

"Space gun sounds more fun."

"And where is your space gun right now? Do you have it on you?" Brynn raised an eyebrow.

"Uh, no. It's in the closet."

"Exactly. Get inside. I'll see you tomorrow." Brynn blew a kiss as she lowered herself into her car.

"Night, Brynn." I waved, and walked into the house. When I'd shut the front door behind me and peeked out the window to wave again, Brynn started her car and drove off. Henrik jogged by me, headed upstairs as I made my way down the hallway. "Good night, Henrik. Have fun working."

"Night, Mia! I'll have Fred functional soon." Henrik didn't stop running as he spoke.

"You need some help?" I called after him.

"Nope. Just have fun with our boy. See ya!" Henrik reached the top of the stairs and rounded the corner.

"See ya." I smiled to myself. As I walked into the kitchen, I held back a giggle. Tyr sat at the counter, eating the rest of my chicken parm straight from the serving platter. "You enjoying yourself, mister?"

Tyr looked up, guiltily. There were only a few bites left. "Mmm-hmm. That was delicious."

"You missed a spot." I scooped a dollop of sauce onto my finger and held it in front of his mouth. Tyr raised an eyebrow and parted his lips, sliding my finger between them and sucking gently. His tongue slid along my knuckle, licking the remains of the sauce away, and sending goosebumps ricocheting across my arm. As he drew the finger out of his mouth, he swirled it one last time with his tongue for good measure. He didn't break eye contact the entire time.

Oh hot bejeebus.

"Get over here, Miss Ahlström." Tyr pushed the stool back from the counter and patted his lap. I stepped into him so that his long legs straddled mine. His hands palmed the small of my back, pushing up my shirt, while mine flew to his hair. I ran my fingers through the disheveled strands as Tyr leaned forward and brought his mouth to my neck. He massaged my skin with the warmth of his tongue, then moved up to nip my chin. When he reached my bottom lip, he raked it between his teeth, then sucked gently, running his tongue along the sensitive skin at the same time.

Good Lord . . .

"He's back. You need to leave."

In my peripheral vision, I saw the kitchen door fly open and a towering figure stand in the doorway.

"Henrik!" I squealed, tugging at my shirt while Tyr chuckled. "I thought you were working."

"Well clearly." Henrik gestured to my top, which I hurriedly straightened. "But not anymore. Fenrir's back. Get to the safe house now."

Tyr's laughter disappeared. "Where?"

"At the rear entry. He's trying to break through the enchantments. You two have got to get out of here." Henrik tossed a bag at Tyr, who caught it in one hand. "Here's the ingredients from the safe. Take them with you. And get them to the dwarves as soon as you can."

Tyr flew upstairs and returned seconds later, holding a suitcase. Had he found that thing and packed it in the time it took me to fix my shirt? "Where's Elsa?" he demanded.

"Forse and the healers took Elsa to the northwest compound. Brynn's setting protections around the Daffodil Drive house so Fenrir can't go after Charlotte and Heather, and then she's going to the safe house to be with Elsa." Henrik handed each of us a space gun. "You might need these on your way out."

"Seriously?" My mouth opened.

"You bet. Do you want to be unarmed when that breaks through?" Henrik pulled the curtain back on the window and we looked outside. The feral wolf leaped at the invisible shield.

"*Skit*," Tyr wrapped an arm around my waist and tightened his grip on the suitcase.

Henrik nodded. "I'll meet you there at dawn. I'll bring the rest of your things."

Just then, the snarling outside stopped. A crash against the back door confirmed that Fenrir had breached the boundary. My heart leaped into my throat as an enormous wolf came barrelling through the kitchen window. Henrik raced for the weapons closet while I undid the safety on my space gun and gripped it in both hands. I'd thought I'd lined up a good shot, but when I pulled the trigger the white beam only grazed Fenrir's hind foot. He snarled, but the blow didn't slow his trajectory as he raced for us, using only three legs to push off countertops.

Tyr held up a hand and an orb emanated from his fingers. It formed a bubble around us, stopping Fenrir's drive as he leapt from the counter. He let out another snarl and bit at the orb. It disintegrated in a shower of pale blue sparkles, its remains sprinkling the kitchen in a glittery glow. Fenrir took a step back and prepared to strike, and without thinking, I took aim and fired again. And again. I kept firing until the space gun ran out of magic. It never occurred to me the stun setting might not be enough to protect us. In the heat of the moment, I didn't think to switch it to implode. Thankfully, a series of white lights shot out of the weapon, striking Fenrir in the head with enough force to knock him on his back.

"Nice shots," Tyr murmured.

"Oh thank God." My heart thumped wildly and my hands trembled as I lowered the weapon. "I was afraid he was going to—"

"*Skit.*" Henrik returned wielding a crossbow as Fenrir climbed unsteadily to his feet. The animal bared his teeth in a furious roar. "Whatever dark magic they've laced into Fenrir, it's counteracting the effects of the accelerator. You two get out of here. I'll deal with the dog."

Tyr stepped between the wolf and me. He wrapped his arms around me and squeezed, then used his super speed to run us out the back door and into the woods. "Heimdall," he shouted, "open the Bifrost."

A multicolored ray shot through the trees, punctuated by a deafening roar. I threw my arms around Tyr's neck and held on tight, praying the wolf would stay put for just a few more seconds. A wind whipped around us, and I buried my face in Tyr's chest as we were sucked through an invisible portal. I heard snarling in the distance, and I prayed that Henrik would be able to take care of himself. My stomach churned, my head spun, and before I knew what was happening, I blacked out.

The last thing I remembered was Tyr's voice. For the first time it betrayed a hint of fear. "Heimdall, take us to the northwest compound."

CHAPTER TWENTY-TWO

"COME ON, BABY. COME back to me."

Everything was black. I had no idea where I was, or what was happening. The only thing I was able to register was the cool hand stroking my forehead, and the soft surface beneath my body. There was a salty tang to the air, and . . . was that the smell of fish?

I forced my eyelids open. Everything around me looked hazy, but as the seconds ticked by, Tyr's face came into focus. His brow was furrowed, wrinkles lining his forehead. He knelt on the floor, hovering over me. As I blinked up at him, his shoulders visibly relaxed.

"Thank Odin," he exhaled.

I tried to sit up but immediately fell back. "Whoa."

"Stay down. Transports aren't easy for gods. I can't imagine what it feels like for a mortal." He held up a glass while he cradled my head in one hand. "Drink."

I rolled to one elbow and did as instructed. The water disappeared quickly. Tyr helped me lean back on the couch cushions, and I looked around—I was in a living room. It was big, maybe forty feet deep and twice as many feet wide, with a twenty-foot ceiling that stretched over the staircase leading up to the second-story landing. The room was done in creams and whites, with wainscoting covering the bottom of the walls and climbing the wooden staircase. I was on one of two cream couches positioned in front of a stone fireplace. Large windows let in filtered moonlight, and the sound of lapping waves *almost* soothed my nerves.

"Where are we?" I stood slowly, testing my equilibrium. When I wobbled, Tyr grabbed my elbow. He guided me to the French doors that led to the backyard.

"This is the northwest compound. We call it the safe house."

My fingers touched the cool glass of the open door, and I stepped onto the grey planks of the porch. Three steps led to a grassy area, with a longer wooden staircase leading to the ocean. In the moonlight, the sand was a pale silver. "It looks like a beach house."

"It is." Tyr hooked an arm around my waist and walked me down the steps, and onto the grass.

We stood beneath the large tree and looked back at the house. The Cape Cod-style structure had grey shingles, white-trimmed windows, and a white-columned porch that stretched the length of the house. It was big but not imposing—a two-story structure with three, maybe four good-sized bedrooms. I turned around to watch the waves gently lap the silver sand. It must have been high tide—there wasn't much room between the bottom of the staircase and the water. The full moon illuminated the little cove, which hosted a total of four Cape Cod-style houses lined up like sentinels facing the water. The beach stretched about a mile to the right, where a sizable dune marked the delineation between cove and open water. Two miles in the other direction, the water met a mountain—I could barely make out the shapes of the treetops covering the rock. To the right of the mountain a trio of boulders nestled in the water, and from the flashes of light, I gathered one held a lighthouse. Evergreens came right up to the edge of the beach. We had to be somewhere in the Pacific Northwest.

Tyr's arm was still around my waist, so I leaned into him. He rested his chin on top of my head and wrapped his other arm around me. I grabbed his hands and held tight.

"What is this place?"

"Asgard's safe house in this quadrant of Midgard," Tyr explained.

"Why didn't you just take Elsa to this safe house earlier?" I pressed.

"We had planned to. Henrik was in the process of increasing the security in this place, which required a quiet period. But Fenrir struck while security here was down, and Freya got on her matchmaking kick, so we ended up taking Elsa to Arcata, intending to move her here when her condition stabilized. Henrik's only just completed the lockdown on this compound." Tyr shook his head. "*Finally.*"

"Do you have other safe houses?" I glanced around. If they all looked like this one, I wouldn't mind taking the safe house intergalactic tour.

"We do. There are safe houses in every quadrant of every realm, but this is one of my favorites. We've got an Aesir permanently stationed here, though, and now that the security increase is complete, it's probably our safest location." Tyr pointed to the house closest to the open ocean. "That's Forse's residence. He's a close friend. He's God of Justice, and he's one of our primary peacekeepers. Full-time job, these days." Tyr's torso hardened against mine. My thumbs stroked his forearms until he relaxed.

"Whose house is next to Forse's?"

"That's the medical unit. Elsa's there, and Henrik will be staying in the guest wing when he gets here in the morning."

"Did he make it out of Arcata safely? Or did Fenrir . . ." I cringed at the memory of our terrifying departure.

"Henrik's just fine. He used an enhanced weapon on Fenrir and the wolf escaped through a portal. Henrik hurt him pretty badly—Fenrir will probably need some time to recover before he goes on the offense again."

I swallowed down the knot in my throat and pointed to the building directly behind us. "This one's your house?"

"Yes. I don't get to come here a lot, but it's one of my favorite residences. When we're not on the precipice of war, it's a peaceful place to be."

The implication was clear; Fenrir's attacks were a call to arms. Adrenaline surged through my veins.

"What about that one?" I pointed to the house next to Tyr's.

"Ah, that's where Freya's staying."

"Freya lives here, too?"

"At the moment, I do." A musical voice rang out as a willowy figure emerged from the house. The moonlight shone against her long hair and reflected off her sparkling eyes. As always, Freya moved with the poise of a ballerina. Her enviably long legs, slender hips, and impressively toned triceps seemed to float across the grass.

"Freya." Tyr released his grip on me and crossed the lawn to greet her.

"Tyr." Freya hugged him back before giving me a warm smile. "Mia, it's good to see you. Sorry again about locking you in the house. It really did come from a good place; Tyr would have been impossible to live with if you'd gotten hurt. But I hear you've been trained on the basic weapons, so I won't need to do that again."

"Good to know." The space gun and crossbow were *basic* weapons?

Tyr ran his fingers over my arms. That was when I realized I hadn't cleaned up since my blackout-inducing Bifrost experience. I was wearing the filmy top I'd worn for dinner with my friends, only now it sported multiple wrinkles from my catnap on the couch. My hair was in a messy bun, and I could probably do with a mint. I was in no way fit for company. I ducked my head against Tyr's chest.

Freya tutted. "Tyr, she has goosebumps. Let's get you inside, sweetie. I left some things up in Tyr's room for you. When I saw him show up with one suitcase for the both of you, I had a feeling he might have forgotten some of the girlish essentials."

"Thanks." I stared at Tyr's bestie, willing myself to have an *attitude of gratitude*, like Meemaw would say.

Freya beamed down at me, perfect white teeth gleaming against her perfectly tanned skin. She literally could not be any more flawless, bless her heart.

Freya waved her hand. "Don't worry about it. Let's get you all squared away and then we can talk about Elsa. Her vitals were stable when I checked, so her team asked me to let her rest until morning. Though I'm sure you won't relax until you see her yourself, Tyr."

"You know me, eh, old girl?" Tyr cuffed Freya on the shoulder.

"Control freak," Freya agreed.

"Cat lady," Tyr retorted.

"Watch it. My girls are Norwegian skogkatt."

"Norwegian what-cats?" I asked as we walked back into Tyr's house.

"I have Norwegian forest cats. They're like mountain lions. But fluffier. And cuter." Freya's smile was sanguine.

"And a hundred times tougher." Tyr shook his head. "Don't let Freya fool you. If someone crosses her, she'll have her cats bite the guy's head clean off and serve it to the next troll that comes through the dark forest."

"Good to know." I put *Don't tick off Freya or her pets* on the top of my list of Things To Remember About Tyr's Life.

"I'm not that crazy." Freya rolled her eyes. "Tyr's just sore because I can kick his sorry behind in hand-to-hand combat."

"That happened one time. In middle school." Tyr spoke through gritted teeth, and I giggled. Getting beat by a girl during the most embarrassing adolescent years must have been a major blow for the up-and-coming God of War.

"Whatever. It happened." Freya made herself comfortable on the couch, and Tyr guided me up the stairs. "I'll wait down here. There's a bag on the bed—if you need anything else just let me know; I'll run next door and bring it over."

My previous unease surrounding Tyr's BFF was being trumped by her all-encompassing thoughtfulness.

"Thanks, Freya. This is really nice of you."

I followed Tyr up the stairs, past the leather couches lining the landing, and into the master suite.

"Do you like it?" he asked, as he switched on the light.

Like didn't even come close. The suite had an open plan, with an enormous jetted tub sitting opposite a double-headed shower near the entry. A small powder room sat behind a white paneled door, with a vast mirror framing the double sinks and vanity outside. Beyond this area was a plush king-sized bed, swathed in thick white comforters and pillows, and facing two oversized windows. The windows looked out onto the beach below. The whole room was done up in creams and whites, with dark iron fixtures and a cedar dresser. The sand-colored wood floors were warm beneath my bare feet. Were they heated?

"Mia?" Tyr grabbed my hands and whirled me around. "Are you okay? This was the safest place I could think of to take you, but if you don't feel comfortable here we can—"

He broke off when I touched a finger to his lips. "It's gorgeous. I love it. You sure Wolfie can't get us here?"

"I'm sure," Tyr promised. "It's invisible to anyone that doesn't have a residence here, and our bodyguards. And access requires a retinal scan; I overrode that part for you, since you were passed out when we got here. Trust me, this is the safest place in all the realms for you to be."

I let out a breath I hadn't realized I was holding. "Okay."

Tyr drew me in and pressed his lips against my temple. "I promised I'd take care of you, and I will. Always. Now check the bag and let me know what else you need. Freya can bring over more stuff tonight, and Henrik will be here with the rest of your things when the sun comes up."

"I kind of want to take a shower," I admitted. My arms still had goosebumps; standing in hot water sounded heavenly.

"We can do that." Tyr's face lit up. He started to take off his shirt.

I shoved him out of the room with a laugh. "Not with your friend downstairs. Go visit. I'll be down in ten."

"Fine." Tyr sighed. "Towels are on the foot of the bed."

"This place has a housekeeper?" I hoped she'd cleared the security check.

"Better. It has me." Tyr twirled a finger and an extra towel appeared on top of the stack. *Oh. My. God.* He'd left *housekeeping* off his list of magical abilities. If I played my cards right, I might never have to scrub another toilet again. "Soaps and shampoos are already in the shower. Blow-dryer's in one of those drawers. You need anything else, just give me a shout."

He turned and walked out of the room. I grabbed a towel off the foot of the bed and turned on the faucet. Hot water filled the room with steam, and I hung my towel on the hook next to a plush robe before stripping down and stepping into the shower.

The water smoothed my goosebumps almost instantly. I stood under the stream, washing and conditioning my hair. When I was done I took an extra minute to enjoy the water pressure against my back, then I turned off the shower and toweled off.

The plushy robe felt soft against my skin as I padded across the heated floors. It was still dark outside, so I opened the bag and pulled out a soft pair of silk lavender pajamas. Lacy piping at the wrists and ankles gave a delicate touch to the classic design. I put the pajamas on, then pulled out a hairbrush, toothbrush, face cream, deodorant, and a small makeup kit in colors suited to my fall palate. Freya had even included my favorite lavender perfume. How she'd put this together on a few minutes' notice was beyond me. Unless . . .

I froze. Then I crossed to the vanity, put on moisturizer, and blow-dried my hair on autopilot.

Unless Tyr had known something like this was going to happen. Maybe Freya had had this bag packed for weeks, just waiting for my inevitable arrival at the safe house. Tyr said Fenrir went after everyone he loved. And he said he'd do whatever it took to keep me safe. How long had he known we'd end up here? And what was his plan now that we were in the compound? Were we just going to live here forever, or until Tyr figured out how to beat the wolf? Until the wolf was dead? It was immortal, wasn't it? That could take years—what exactly was going to happen to me? And how was I going to pass any of my classes if I was hiding in a secret safe house invisible to *the whole entire cosmos?*

The blow-dryer slipped from my hands and hit the counter with a thud. I turned it off. There were so many questions bouncing inside my head, I wanted to find a notebook or four and work them all out. But these weren't questions I could resolve on my own; I'd need to ask a certain Norse god exactly what his plan was. And I really needed him to have a plan. Because attractive as this compound was, I wasn't about to sacrifice a lifetime of impeccable academics only to flunk out of college my freshman year. There was no way I could live with that shame, not to mention explain my indefinite absence to my family and friends, even if I could justifiably place the blame on the lords of the underworld.

I caught my reflection in the mirror and sighed. My hair was not yet fit for public viewing. My boyfriend and his bestie might have been waiting for me downstairs, but Mama always said it was better to arrive late than to arrive ugly. I finished drying my hair and brushed it until it shone, brushed my teeth, and padded downstairs in bare feet.

"Oh, good. They fit. I was hoping." Freya looked up with a smile as I entered the living room.

I smiled back, feeling more generous now that I, too, had sleek, glossy hair. "They're perfect. And you even packed my favorite perfume. Thanks, Freya."

She waved a hand. "It's nothing. I'm glad you're here. It's been way too long since I've seen this guy. You know, without the weapons drawn."

"So you guys have been friends for a while. How did you meet?" I sat next to Tyr and tucked my feet underneath me. He threw an arm around my shoulders, pulling me close.

"Our moms were best friends, and Freya was born a week after I was adopted. Freya's been trying to keep up with me since day one."

"You wish you were as cool as me." Freya threw a pillow at him. "Or that you had half my skills."

"What's it like being Goddess of Love?" I rested my head lightly on Tyr's chest as he stroked my hair.

"It has its ups and downs," Freya admitted. "It's fun to find the perfect partner for someone and gently nudge them together."

"Shove them forcefully together, more like it," Tyr muttered.

"That was just you. And then you nearly blew it with Mia by being your charming self." Freya stuck out her tongue.

"He's definitely an acquired taste." I squeezed Tyr's arm.

He chuckled. "Oh. Like you could stay away from me."

Freya smiled. "I'm so the best matchmaker ever."

"Except according to Brynn, there were four other girls you lined up in case things with us didn't work out." Tyr stroked the inside of my wrist. "Not so confident in your skills a few months ago, were you?"

"You know how this works, Tyr. I see compatibility, not soul mates. I brought the five most compatible girls to you, but it was your agency that determined who was the best fit for you. Fenrir's a monster, but he did one thing right—he brought out your inner caveman at exactly the right moment. You wanted to club Mia over the head and drag her back to your man cave the minute you saw her in danger." Freya looked inordinately happy. "Don't you glare at me, Tyr Fredriksen. I saw how you looked at her that day, and I see how you look at her now. You're welcome."

Tyr rested his cheek on my head. "Except we're hiding in a safe house, running from Fenrir. Did you ever think there was a reason I didn't want you to set me up? Maybe I didn't want to risk Mia's life."

"It's not my life I'm worried about." I lifted my head so I could look at Tyr. "It's my grades."

"Huh?" Tyr stared at me.

"I don't know if you guys have a plan for how long we're going to be on lockdown, but I've only got Monday and Tuesday off school for that whole Spirit of the Redwoods deal." God bless our friendly neighborhood tree huggers, and their insistence the University observe their holiday. "So unless we can wrap things up here by Tuesday evening, latest, I'm going to need a hall pass to go to class."

"You have got to be kidding me." Tyr blinked.

"I'm afraid that's not going to be possible," Freya spoke gently. "We can't port out of the compound with our enemies looking for it; it would compromise our location. And Fenrir and Hymir are going to be watching Midgard pretty closely. Activating a portal or the Bifrost would catch their attention right away."

"So maybe we don't magic our way out of here." I paused. "By the looks of the trees, we're somewhere in the Pacific northwest, right? That's driving distance from Arcata. Could be a long drive, depending on where we are, but it's doable."

"You want me to drive you to school?" Tyr sounded

incredulous. "And what am I going to do with you when I get you there? I'm not letting you just walk around unprotected. And the cloak isn't enough to protect you from Fenrir anymore—you saw him shrug off the shot from your particle accelerator; he's been laced with enough dark magic to debilitate our weapons."

"Well then, we need to come up with another idea. I realize we're all in danger, and it probably seems silly for me to worry about my grades when I should be worrying about staying alive, but up until now, school has been my life. I've never failed anything, and I have no intention of starting now." I alternated my stare between Freya and Tyr. They exchanged a glance.

"We do have internet," Freya offered after a long pause. "Any chance your professors would let you attend class virtually?"

"You mean like FaceTime a lecture?" I glanced at the high ceiling, trying to recall the RSU handbook. Of course, I'd read it cover to cover when I'd sent my enrollment papers. "I'd need a doctor's note explaining why I'm physically incapable of attending class, but the university allows it."

"No problem." Tyr made a small circle with his finger and a piece of paper fluttered into my lap. "Sorry about your pneumonia."

Really? I picked up the paper he'd magicked out of nowhere, and read aloud. "Due to an acute case of pneumonia, Amelia Ahlström is unable to attend her classes at Redwood State University. Please provide an acceptable course of home study so that she may continue to keep up with her coursework, despite her illness. Sincerely, Dr.

Fredriksen." I turned it over. "It's on hospital letterhead."

"I am nothing if not thorough." Tyr winked. "Freya will send it to the school when we're done here. I'm sure they'll be happy to allow the accommodation. And Charlotte can FaceTime your Art History class with you in case they don't get back to you until Wednesday afternoon."

"Impressively resourceful, and meticulously thorough." Freya smiled. "Just like somebody else in this room. Am I a world-class matchmaker or what?"

I sighed. My college love story was about as far from my parents' considerably less complicated tale as it could get. *My parents.* "Hold on. Are my parents okay? And Jason? And Meemaw? If Fenrir's so hell-bent on hurting Tyr through me, he'd know to go after my family, wouldn't he?"

"They're fine," Freya assured me. "I put cloaking spells on your parents, your brother, and your grandparents just before I came here. And unlike Henrik's technology-based lighter, my spells were created using *älva* dust. So they're infallible."

"*Älva?*" I asked.

"Fairies," Freya explained.

"Shut the front door. Y'all have fairies?" My jaw opened so wide it clicked.

"We do. *Älva* are a particularly magical breed of light elves, found in northernmost Alfheim. Not even the heaviest dark magic can break their spells. I had Henrik incorporate some of the *älva* dust in the protection for this compound, too."

Well, I'll be.

"So Fenrir can't find them? But you still can." I chewed my fingernail.

"Exactly. I also put an aura trace on them, so if they're in any kind of danger, it'll set off a sort of internal alarm with Tyr. He'll know right away if anything's going on with them."

"Thanks." I exhaled. "You really thought of everything."

"I most certainly did." Freya beamed.

A fierce whoosh came from outside. My throat tightened. *Not again.* We jumped to our feet, racing for the back door.

"Stay behind me, Mia." Tyr threw his body in front of mine.

He didn't need to worry. When I peeked around his shoulder I saw a muscular figure walking across the lawn, toting two suitcases.

"Henrik!" I darted around Tyr to hug my friend.

"This is for you." Henrik set the larger suitcase inside the French doors, and left the smaller one on the porch steps. "And this is mine. I'm staying at Elsa's right?"

"Correct. Unless you want to stay at my place." Freya waggled her eyebrows. "Brynn's monitoring Elsa at the moment or she'd have come to greet Mia, but she's going to be bunking with me. So long as you can behave yourself, you can have the second guest room."

"Stop it, Freya." Henrik ducked his head with a smile. He *so* liked Brynn back. "Fenrir's still in Arcata. He took off after you guys when you escaped, so I summoned the taser from the weapons closet and followed him outside. When he realized he couldn't get to you, he turned on me. I got in one good shot before a portal opened up. He got away, but he was limping pretty badly—he'll need some time to regroup, for sure."

"You debilitated the wolf with a *taser*?" I couldn't believe it.

"Well, it was the only weapon I enhanced with the powder leftover from the security beef-up on this place. Freya told me to make sure I enchanted at least one teched-up device with *älva* dust. Good thing, too. Guess I'm starting from scratch on the guns, eh?" Henrik scratched his jaw. "I know the Norns want us to tie him up, and I get that Fenrir's more useful to us alive than dead. But *skit*, I wish I could have just ended him there. Or at least got in a few shots with the crossbow before he fell through the portal. To further delay his healing, of course."

"Of course," Freya agreed.

"Well done," Tyr praised.

"Any time. Have you seen Elsa yet?" Henrik asked.

"No. I don't want to disturb her team any more than we already have tonight, so I'll wait for morning." Tyr checked his watch. "Only a few more hours, by my clock. But you need to debrief Brynn, so you can head over there now, Henrik."

"*Takk.* Oh, before I forget, your laptop and your phone are in there, Mia." Henrik pointed to the bigger suitcase. "You left them back at our place when you, eh, took off."

"Thank you," I said gratefully. "I'd have missed those a lot."

Freya stifled a yawn. "If you will excuse me, I think I'll go catch a few hours of sleep too. Busy day tomorrow, *ja*?"

"Very. Are you going to visit the dwarves with me?" Tyr asked her. "Last I heard from Odin, he'd managed to get us an appointment in the morning."

"You need me to go with you?" Freya asked.

"They do have a weakness for pretty girls," Tyr pointed out. "And there's no way in Helheim I'm taking Mia. She's staying here with Forse."

That was news to me.

"Fine. What time do you want to leave?" Freya covered her mouth as another yawn escaped.

"First light?"

"Make it eight," Freya countered. "And throw in a cup of coffee."

"Deal. Go to bed. Henrik, you good getting over to Elsa's?"

"Yep. Mia, you okay?" Henrik touched my arm.

"I'll be fine. Thanks for looking out for me."

"Any time. You're one of us now." He shrugged. "We take care of each other."

"Call if you need anything. Both of you." Tyr nodded as Freya and Henrik made their way down the porch and to their respective houses. When they were both safely inside, Tyr shut the French doors and scooped me in his arms.

"Upstairs, *prinsessa*. I need to get at least a few hours of sleep before I hit up the dwarves." He carried me up the stairs and set me on the massive bed. He tugged off his jeans and T-shirt, and climbed in after me in his boxer-briefs, pulling the downy comforter up to our chins and tucking me safely under an arm. "You doing all right with all of this?"

"We're safe here? You're sure?" I asked.

"I'm sure," Tyr promised.

"And these dwarves—you won't be in any danger?" I ran my thumb along his chest.

"I'll be fine. I promise. Especially with Freya. They've seen her before; they'll do anything she tells them to."

"Okay." I bit the inside of my cheek, grateful he couldn't see me in the moonlight. My face had to be positively etched with concern.

"The only thing I want you focusing on is taking care of my girl." Tyr's lips grazed my earlobe, and I inched closer to him. "You're not allowed to worry about me. I'll be fine. I promise."

"All right," I agreed, relishing his heartbeat against mine. The pulse, coupled with the rhythmic pounding of the waves outside, should have soothed my level-nine anxiety.

But I couldn't shake the feeling that something awful was coming. Soon.

CHAPTER TWENTY-THREE

THE MINUTE I OPENED my eyes, I fought the urge to squeeze them shut again. Sunlight streamed through the big windows, bathing the cream-colored room in a brilliant light. While I snuggled deeper into the soft pillows, I heard the shower shut off. I turned just in time to see Tyr emerging, wrapped from the waist down in a plush white towel.

My head may have been foggy with sleep, but my nerves were suddenly on high alert.

"Good morning, gorgeous." Tyr ran a hand through his wet hair and shot me a grin that spiked my heart rate more than coffee ever could.

"Morning," I murmured.

"Sorry to dash out on you, but Freya will be here any minute." He crossed to the bed and gave me a very thorough kiss. My breathing came in ragged gasps as he walked away.

Tyr picked up his toothbrush and quickly brushed his teeth, then opened a drawer in the bureau and pulled out some clothes. When he dropped his towel, I had to force myself to look away. His bare backside was even more glorious than I'd imagined.

At the sound of a zipper, I figured it was safe to look up. Tyr stood in front of the dresser, looking every bit the warrior in black cargo pants and a fitted black tee. He crossed to the edge of the bed to lace his combat boots.

"I'll be back for dinner. Steaks are marinating in the fridge, and Forse promised to catch some kind of fish this afternoon. Henrik's gonna man the grill."

"Yum," I mumbled. The gorgeous god and the spectacular suite had me rendered speechless.

"Brynn's next door with Henrik and Elsa, but she's been instructed to shadow you if you feel at all uncomfortable." Tyr finished tying his boots and stood up.

"Wait, shouldn't Brynn and Henrik be going with you? They're your bodyguards."

"Yeah. But like I said, we don't anticipate any hostilities. And nobody's stupid enough to mess with me *and* Freya." Tyr smoothed the front of his shirt. "Forse is downstairs at the breakfast bar. He'll take you out fishing if you want. I know you were disappointed you didn't get to bait the hook last time."

Tyr ducked when I chucked a pillow at him.

"Go." I laughed. "Save the world. Say hi to Freya. And tell the dwarves I said 'Heigh-Ho.'"

"I wish they were that kind of dwarf." Tyr shook his head. "You okay here all day?"

"I'll be fine." I stretched my arms above my head. "Beautiful beach, clear skies, and did you say breakfast bar?"

"I did." Tyr leaned down to kiss the top of my forehead. When he pulled back, he cradled my chin between his thumb and forefinger. "Forse will take good care of you today, and I'll be home before you know it."

"Go on." I stretched to kiss his lips. "Henrik and I will bake something fabulous for dessert."

"Deal." Tyr planted one more lingering kiss on my mouth before I heard the knock downstairs. "That's Freya. See you tonight, babe."

"See you." I waved as he bolted from the room. I didn't want to ask why he grabbed his crossbow on the way out.

The day stretched ahead of me, and somewhere downstairs the God of Justice was eating his breakfast. Much as I wanted to meet Forse, I didn't want to make a first impression with bedhead. I brushed my teeth and took my time fixing my hair, putting on just enough makeup to look presentable.

My phone rang, and I grabbed it off the nightstand, thinking it must be Tyr. Maybe he'd forgotten his Uzi, or his AK-47, or his magic wand, and he needed me to run it out to him. "Hello?"

"Howdy, Sis. How's the big, bad world of Arcata?" My brother sounded typically chipper for a Saturday morning. It couldn't have been much later than ten on the east coast. The sleep-late gene had skipped him.

"Oh, hi, Jase. About that. I'm not exactly in Arcata."

"Where exactly are you then?"

I glanced around the beautifully decorated bedroom,

then to the ocean that sparkled outside the full-length windows, and the coast that stretched all the way to the tree-dusted mountain a few dozen miles off. It was definitely living . . . if you forgot we were here to escape a dark magic-laced, homicidal wolf who was working as the agent of my boyfriend's crazy giant birth father. "Just out of town for a little bit."

"Don't you have classes?" Jason asked. "It's not like you to play hooky."

"Well, it's the weekend," I reminded him. "And then, eh, fall break?" It wasn't a total lie. We had a few days off.

"You coming home for Thanksgiving, or are you going to hang out with the tree huggers and that man of yours?"

"I'll probably have to stay here. You know, um, to study for exams," I hedged. Who knew how long I'd be holed up in this safe house?

"Then I need to pay you a visit. Maybe in a couple of weeks? My exams aren't until the week before Christmas, so I have a little wiggle room in my study schedule. I want to see you. And I want to meet the dude."

"His name's Tyr," I reminded my brother with a smile. "And I'd love for you to meet him." *So long as we're not being hunted by monsters of the underworld. If that's the case I want you to stay far, far away.*

"Good. We need to have *the talk*. He needs to understand that if he hurts my baby sister, I'll crush his kneecaps. You'll notice I'm not asking if he's on this little vacation with you, or what the sleeping arrangements are. Because I am not in a kneecap-crushing mood at the moment . . . but I could get into one if I had to."

I giggled. "I love you, Jase."

"Love you too, Mees. Have fun out there. But not too much fun." He imitated Dad's stern voice.

"Will do. Bye." I turned off the phone and put it in my pocket, grinning. When all of this was over, and I finally got to see him, I was going to give my brother the biggest hug ever. And warn him not to touch the God of War's kneecaps.

With my brother convinced of my safety, I padded downstairs. I wound my way around the floor-to-ceiling stone fireplace, ran my fingertips across the smooth granite surface of the kitchen island, and opened one of the glass-front cabinets to pull out a coffee mug. While I filled it with my morning jolt of energy, I admired the functional elegance of both the hanging pots, and the second island that separated the dining table from the cooking area. Tyr's kitchens toed the line between practical and beautiful *really* well.

When I caught sight of Forse, I nearly spilled my coffee. I didn't know what I'd been expecting the justice god to look like—maybe old and weathered like a Hemingway hero? But I sure wasn't expecting the chiseled Adonis in an ivory sweater and khakis, sitting at the second island and tucking into an apple turnover. He was Hyannis Port chic, with just a touch of naughty footballer in his twinkling eyes.

He was drop-dead gorgeous.

"Do you all look like you just stepped out of a magazine?" My hand flew to my mouth. "Oh my god. That was out loud."

The vision chuckled as he wiped crumbs from his lips.

"What I meant to open with was, hi. I'm Mia. Pleasure to meet you."

"I'm Forse." He held out his hand, and we shook. He had a firm grip, but surprisingly soft hands.

"So you're babysitting me today?"

"You're helping me, actually," Forse corrected. "Our crab supply is dangerously low, and I hear you're a solid fisherman. You don't mind, do you?"

"Not at all." I set my coffee next to the fruit bowl on the island, before climbing up next to Forse and selecting a mango. I cut into it and took a bite. "This is amazing—where'd you find these this time of year?"

Forse shrugged. "Freya handles the shopping when she's in the compound. She probably had one of the valkyries fly them in from Australia. Mangoes are in season there right now."

"Oh." I cradled my cup with both hands and held on tight.

"Our world must seem strange to you." Forse lifted his coffee mug.

Oh, definitely not. A realm of gods is overseeing the fate of mankind, which currently rests in the claws of an evil magic dog controlled by my boyfriend's giant father. Totally not weird. But I kept my words to myself and mirrored Forse's movement, taking a sip of the black coffee. It was hot and strong, and it tasted absolutely heavenly.

"As much as I know of it," I said truthfully. "I know you guys have to be kind of secretive."

Forse set down his cup. "We're usually not supposed to

expose ourselves to mortals, but Tyr's position gives him discretion most of us don't have—since he's charged with evaluating threats to the realm, Odin gives him free rein to mingle with different races."

"Oh. So he's . . . mingled with a human before?" I studied my fingernails while Forse chuckled.

"Nothing like that. You guys are definitely one of the few inter-realm relationships we've seen. But Tyr's aligned forces with friendly factions before—light elf armies, the occasional gnome battalion. His judgment is impeccable, and those interactions have always resulted in increased security for Asgard."

"Got it. Well, I'm not going to bring more security to Asgard. But I won't do anything to hurt it, either. Not on purpose, anyway." I took another drink of coffee.

"I know you won't. Like I said, Tyr's an impeccable judge of character. If he trusts you, so do I." Forse drained his mug and carried it to the sink. "Come on—finish your fruit, and we'll go set the crab nets. I have a feeling we'll bring in a big haul today."

* * * *

"What do we do now?" I watched as the net sank into the water in the small cove. Forse tossed markers after it, keeping an eye on the floating buoys.

"Now we wait." Forse opened a small cooler he kept on the dinghy, and offered me a bottle of water.

"I'm good, thanks." I declined the beverage with a head

shake.

"There are plenty in here if you change your mind." Forse uncapped his own bottle and drank, draining its contents before closing the cooler and returning his attention to the ocean. While he stared at the surface, I looked around. Forse' fishing boat was much smaller than Tyr's. It had an open deck with wooden benches lining the sides, and a small motor at the back.

"Is Brynn still with Elsa?" I asked

"She is. With everything that's going on, we figured an extra set of eyes on our girl couldn't hurt."

"How's Elsa feeling?" I ventured.

"She's doing well. Her vitals have been on a steady rise since she got here last night."

"Are you and Elsa close? I mean were you friends? Before her . . . accident?"

"We were friends," Forse said. He stared at the horizon, a small smile playing at the corners of his mouth.

"Oh my gosh. You like her! Are you together?"

"What? No." Forse shook his head. "I'm not sure how Tyr would feel about that."

"Hmm. Well, have you ever asked him?"

"No."

"He might not be bothered by it," I pointed out. "If you guys are that close, he'd probably love you dating his sister. He'd know you'd never hurt her."

Forse kept his gaze on the water.

"I haven't exactly met her awake, but she seems pretty special," I added.

"She's *very* special," Forse corrected.

"How do you mean?" I studied the gentle waves of the ocean, watching for signs of movement from the net.

"Elsa has an unprecedented gift. But she's only recently come into one of her, uh, talents." Forse paused. I sensed he was evaluating my trustworthiness. I kept an easy smile on my face, which broadened when he gave a nod and continued talking. *Whew. I passed.* "Elsa's a hybrid. She always knew she was a High Healer, and she's been functional in that role for a while. But recently she found out she also has Unifier tendencies. She must have gotten a partial inheritance from her mother."

"That sounds like a lot of responsibility," I said.

"Especially for someone so young. When she found out she had the unifying gift, she asked me to help her learn to use it. She was pretty scared—she'd just lost her parents, and she didn't have anyone to coach her. We started spending more time together."

"And you asked her out?" I nudged him with my toe.

"I helped her hone her abilities."

"But you *wanted* to ask her out."

"You ask a lot of questions," Forse grumbled.

"She wanted you to ask her out too, didn't she?" I guessed.

"Let me check the fishing net."

"Interesting." I thought for a minute. "What does Freya

say about it?"

Forse stayed silent as he leaned over the boat.

"I see. Well, you're going to have to tell Tyr eventually."

Forse finally looked at me. "Relationships make me . . . uncomfortable."

"Why?"

"I had a bad experience."

"Oh." I wanted to ask more, but my companion was back to staring at the water. Somebody had definitely done a number on him. "Well, I hope it works out with Elsa. We don't have to talk about it if you don't want to."

Forse nodded at the buoys. "Here they come."

I watched as he steered the boat around the net, gathering the buoys on the deck.

"Now what?" I asked.

"Help me pull them in."

Forse began gathering the net, and I followed suit. We worked together to pull it in, Forse tying it tight before setting the bundle of scurrying crabs in the boat.

"This is a decent catch," he praised. "Let's get them back to the house."

"Sounds good." I watched the net while Forse steered the boat toward the shore. The crabs scuttled on top of each other, writhing against the ropes. "And maybe we can pay a visit to Elsa."

"Maybe." Forse shook his head. He certainly wasn't a chatty one, but I could hear the smile in his voice.

For all of our sakes, I hoped Elsa woke up soon.

* * * *

"And that's how you barbecue a steak. Boom. Mic drop!" Henrik flipped the meat and threw down the spatula. He'd ditched the fake eyeglasses and wore aviator shades in their place. In his "Kiss The Cook" apron and backwards baseball cap, he looked every bit the frat-boy he could have been . . . if he wasn't biding his time as an immortal bodyguard. He was relaxed and happy, grinning at Brynn as she gazed adoringly at him from her seat across from me at the picnic table.

"These look amazing, Henrik." The valkyrie looked up from under long lashes.

"Why do you think Tyr won't let me move out?" Henrik chuckled. "Just wait until you try my Mississippi Mud Pie tonight."

"*My* Mississippi Mud Pie," I corrected. "It's my grandmother's recipe. He just helped me make it."

"I'm the one who suggested adding the vanilla to the crust." Henrik raised an eyebrow. "I trust you'll find that improves the recipe significantly."

"You baggin' on my Meemaw?" I crossed my arms with feigned irritation. It was impossible to be upset with Henrik over anything—upset with anyone, really. Things were finally looking up. Tyr and Freya had returned unharmed and were changing out of their travel clothes before dinner, and Henrik reported that he'd put the final touches on

Fred, and the arm was fully functional. We could all feel that something good was coming—the end of Fenrir, a break in the fighting—maybe a happy-ever-after for us all.

"I'm sure your Meemaw is lovely. Just as I'm sure she wishes she'd added a dash of vanilla to the butter when she made her piecrust. Just saying." Henrik shrugged.

"Don't mess with her Meemaw, man." A rough voice came from behind me. We turned to see Tyr walk through the French doors. He wore faded blue jeans, and a ribbed white Henley. His feet were bare, and his hair was still damp from the shower. He crossed the porch in four long strides and dropped to sit beside me.

"*Hei* again," he murmured. He put his hands on my hips and pulled me onto his lap.

"Hi." I nestled my head on his shoulder. "How was the shower?"

"Lonely. Wish you'd have taken me up on my offer to—"

I swatted him.

"Did you and Freya get what you needed from the dwarves?" Brynn jumped to my rescue.

"I guess." Tyr scratched the back of his neck.

"What's wrong?" Henrik turned off the grill and removed the steaks.

"It wasn't what I was expecting them to give us," Tyr admitted. "It doesn't seem strong enough to hold Fenrir."

"The dwarves have never gone back on their word," Forse pointed out. He came out of the house carrying a platter of crab meat and a bowl of melted butter. "If they say it's strong enough, it's strong enough."

Tyr rubbed my hip softly. His frown betrayed his doubt.

"Want to show it to us?" I offered.

"You talking about this ribbon?" Freya strolled out of her house and walked across the lawn with something in her hands.

"Ribbon?" Henrik, Brynn, Forse and I spoke in unison.

"Ribbon," Freya confirmed.

"You're kidding me." Brynn's eyes narrowed.

"To hold Fenrir?" Forse stroked his chin.

"Did they think you were talking about another Fenrir? A wood sprite or something? Maybe it's a more popular name than we thought." Henrik put the steaks down on the table next to the potatoes.

"Nope. They swear this will do the job." Freya laid the ribbon on the picnic table and we leaned over to examine it.

"It's pink," Forse said dubiously. "And shiny."

"I know." Tyr's face was dark.

"They want you to tie Fenrir up with a shiny, pink ribbon." Henrik closed his eyes. "Man, those dwarves have a wicked sense of humor."

We stared for a good minute before Brynn broke the silence. She pulled her shoulders back and put on a brave face. "If the dwarves say it'll work, then it'll work. Right?"

"Right." Freya nodded. "They've never betrayed us before, and there's no reason to think they'd lie now."

"Then the matter's closed." Brynn leaned over to light

the candles in the hurricane vases and sat back down. "Steak's done to perfection, we've got fresh crab legs, potatoes are hot, and Mia's Meemaw's Mud Pie is in the freezer. Let's eat."

Tyr shifted me off his lap as everyone began dishing up. The crease between his eyes hadn't eased, so I whispered in his ear. "You okay?"

He nodded. But the wrinkles in his forehead smoothed, and he lifted my hand to his lips for the briefest of moments. I squeezed his fingers, and he winked at me.

"Elsa's doing great today," Brynn interrupted our silent exchange. "Her vitals are improving hourly—must be the sea air."

"Or the proximity to Forse." The corners of Freya's eyes crinkled.

Forse turned bright red.

"Meaning?" I turned to Freya, who'd taken the seat to my left. I wasn't about to out Forse. But if the matchmaker did it . . .

"Elsa's had a thing for Forse for, like, forever." Tyr rolled his eyes. "Only he's been too stubborn to do anything about it."

"Wait. What?" I turned to the justice god. "Tyr knows?"

"I didn't think so." Forse's ears were crimson.

"Mia knows?" Tyr stared at me.

"There's only so much shop talk you can do on a boat," I pointed out.

"True." Tyr nodded. "So what's holding you back, man?

If it's me, don't worry about it. She'd be lucky to have you."

"It's not that." Brynn shook her head. "It's her, isn't it?"

"Her who?" I asked.

"A crazy chick burned Forse forever ago, and he's sworn off relationships ever since. I keep telling him Elsa's nothing like his ex, and this will end happily for him, but apparently *I'm* not an expert." Freya tapped her fingers on the table.

"Can we talk about the ribbon again?" Forse muttered. He was obviously uncomfortable. I felt bad as he fidgeted with his silverware. We shouldn't be talking about his ex.

"Forse showed me some great spots around the cove today," I jumped in. "Did you know that rock just south of here is where the 80s film about the kid pirates was filmed? Do y'all watch human movies in Asgard?"

"We do." Forse shot me an appreciative smile. "And that was a great movie."

"The one with all the Coreys in it?" Freya's face lit up. "I didn't know that was shot here."

"I love that you guys watch human movies. What are your favorites?" I kept the conversational ball rolling.

It turned out Freya liked superhero movies. Brynn liked chick flicks. Henrik and Tyr were partial to action movies, and Forse liked classic films. And *The Notebook*.

"*The Notebook*?" Henrik snorted.

"It's a deeply evocative film." Forse kept his chin high.

Tyr chuckled softly. "My sister loves that movie."

From the wistful look in his eye, it was obvious Forse

already knew.

We finished dinner and moved down to the fire pit, where Tyr lit a massive bonfire. Freya brought out blankets, and we gathered on the Adirondack chairs. From my perch on Tyr's lap, I was pleased to see Brynn and Henrik inching closer together. Maybe the quiet of the compound would give them the time they needed to get together. Things were finally calming down—we were safe in a secret cove with nothing but lapping waves, ocean air, and a gorgeous bonfire to focus on. In this moment, things seemed absolutely perfect.

I should have known it couldn't last.

CHAPTER TWENTY-FOUR

"WHAT'S HAPPENING ON THE dune?" Tyr shifted me on his lap and squinted over the bonfire.

"I don't see anything out of the ordinary." Freya shook her head and speared a marshmallow.

"The sand's stirring ten yards north of the break, and the air above the site is dark. It almost looks like someone's aura . . . oh, *skit*," Tyr growled.

Henrik looked up from his spot on the grass with Brynn. She'd been leaning against him, laughing at one of his animated stories, but now both looked like someone had shoved a ramrod right up their backs.

"Dark's bad for an aura, right?" Henrik asked cautiously.

"What do you think?" Tyr narrowed his eyes and waited. I stared into the distance, but my human eyes couldn't see anything.

Forse rose calmly and turned a slow circle. After he'd assessed the compound, he turned to Tyr. "The protections are in place, but he is trying to break through the west entrance. What do you want to do?"

"Is it . . .?" I rested my palms on Tyr's shirt. Maybe

feeling his heartbeat would slow down mine.

"Fenrir's here." Tyr didn't take his eyes off the dunes. He tilted his head like he was listening for something. "And he's angry. He came back to the Arcata cabin after he ported out, but Elsa wasn't there. He wants to finish her off and then . . ."

"What else? There's something else," Henrik said.

Tyr's chest tensed beneath my hand. "If we don't give him my sister, he's coming after Mia."

"Like Helheim he is." Freya jumped to her feet. She picked up a rapier I hadn't even realized was sitting under her Adirondack chair. An honest-to-goodness *rapier.* "Let's go tie up that monster with our shiny pink ribbon."

"I wish it was that easy." Brynn stood and pulled a set of nunchucks from her waistband. Henrik rose to one knee and reached into a pocket of the blanket. He unearthed two shiny blades that looked an awful lot like real samurai swords.

The entire party was packing, and I hadn't even worn shoes.

"It can be that easy," Forse spoke calmly. Like Tyr, he kept his eyes on the dunes. "Fenrir's judgment is clouded by his anger. He's never had anyone slip out of his grasp before, and he's furious Elsa lived. But he's even angrier Mia escaped unharmed. We might be able to take him down, but . . ."

"But what? What? What?" I tried not to sound like a four-year-old.

Forse spoke without looking at me. "With offspring of

Loki, there's always a price. You know how it is."

No. I most definitely did not know that. Nobody had mentioned any prices on Wikipedia, Art History, or in our little rat-escaping bedtime stories. What was Forse talking about?

"I already said I'll pay it," Tyr muttered. He lifted me off his lap and set me on the grass. "This has gone on long enough."

"What are you doing?" I chased him across the lawn. "Tyr, are you insane? Don't go looking for a fight. We're safe in here; Forse said so." I spun on my heel. "We are safe, right?"

"We are safe," Forse confirmed. "Nothing has ever breached my defenses. Doubly so now that we've reinforced the compound."

"There you go then." I grabbed Tyr's arm and spun him around. "We can just stay in here. He'll go away eventually."

"And then what?" Tyr's voice was thick. "He goes after somebody else in my place? Nobody else is dying because of me."

"You have to stop—"

"No, Mia. This ends tonight. *I* started this the day I begged Odin for Fenrir's life. *I* have to be the one to end it. Fenrir isn't taking my sister." Tyr reached out and touched my cheek with the back of one finger. "And he isn't getting anywhere near you, ever again. I love you."

My breath caught in my throat. I tilted my head, and he cupped my cheek, stroking my jaw lightly with his thumb.

"Tyr," I whispered. The moisture in my eyes threatened

to spill over.

"I love you," Tyr repeated. He pulled my hip into his and tilted my chin up. He brought his mouth down, crushing our lips together with a force that left me breathless.

"You're welcome," Freya called from behind us. "Also, told you so."

Tyr pulled back to glare at his friend. "You gonna give me that ribbon or not?"

"Not." Freya marched over to us and patted her back pocket. "It's in here. And I'm coming with you."

"Wait," I begged. "Let me come too. I can help. Let me be the decoy—I'll reel Fenrir in, and you can fly down and tie him up with the ribbon. Or I'll go get my space gun from the house, and I can shoot him while you bind him and . . ." And what? The space guns didn't work on Fenrir anymore. And there was no way Tyr would let me be the decoy. Or get anywhere near Fenrir. Or . . . or . . .

Tyr's eyes were unreadable as I issued my silent plea. They narrowed infinitesimally, taking on just a hint of sadness. It finally hit me, the point he'd been driving home all along. I was mortal. Destructible. What did I really think I could do to help the gods?

What would I *ever* be able to do to help them?

"I really can't help you with this, can I?" I whispered. "I can't . . . I can't fix this."

Tyr kept my chin in his hand. "I am the protector—I defend the realm against threats. Elsa is the healer, for the rare cases in which I fail. Freya cultivates love, to give us hope in the face of loss. The Norns prophesy destiny, so we know where we fit in our world. Every job, *every single job*, is of equal importance. When one fails to function at its peak, the others fall out of sync, and the realms tumble out of the *perfekt* balance we're sworn to uphold. Do you understand that?"

I nodded.

"Good. I know you want to fight alongside me. I get it. But you weren't born to be a warrior. Trust me, *prinsessa*, there will come a day when you risk everything to protect the realms, but you'll do it using your uniquely beautiful energy in the way *only you* can. Not by shooting some wolf with a gun. You following me into this fight today isn't going to help anyone."

The enormity of Tyr's words sent a tremor through me—could my fate be more entwined with his than I'd dared to hope? I placed my hand on his chest. "Hold on. Someday I'll risk everything to protect the realms, but today you want me to just sit back and watch? And do nothing? How does *that* help anyone?"

"It keeps you alive." Tyr stroked my chin with his thumb. "I know you've been raised to believe you can do it all. That's one of the things I love about you. Midgard is beautiful that way—a human with the right skill and focus can truly conquer your world. Right now, in this battle with this monster, you can't do it all. I'm sorry, but you can't. Not if you're going to live to fulfill your *own* destiny with us. You don't have to like it. You don't have to agree with it. But it's the way it is." Tyr kissed the top of my head, and pulled his hand from my waist.

"Stay with Brynn. She'll take care of you. I'll be back in a few." His eyes didn't quite meet mine.

"Please don't go," I begged.

"I have to. Don't worry, baby. I'll be fine." He walked me to a steely-eyed Brynn and put my hand in hers. "No matter what happens, I need you to promise me you'll keep her safe."

"I promise." Brynn squeezed my fingers with one hand and twirled her nunchucks with the other.

"I mean it, Brynn. Until the day you die. Look after her." Tyr kissed my forehead again and stepped back. My insides lurched, sending a surge of bile into my throat. I swallowed it back down. *Oh god. He's saying goodbye.*

"Tyr." I reached for him, but he jogged into the house. He emerged seconds later wearing the black fatigues from this morning, a crossbow strapped to his back.

"Let's roll." Tyr marched across the lawn and onto the beach. Freya, Henrik and Forse fell in step beside him. Tyr said something to Forse, and the justice god made an abrupt right turn. He ran up the steps to Elsa's cottage and stood sentry on the porch. Tyr must have ordered him to look out for his baby sister.

When the hunting party reached the top of the dune, I held my breath. They crossed over the ridge so I couldn't see them anymore, but I could hear the feral snarl. It made my stomach drop.

"I can't take this." I turned to Brynn. "I have to know what they're doing."

"Absolutely not." Brynn shook her head. "There's no way I'm letting you anywhere near that scene. Tyr would kill me."

"Please," I begged. Tears filled my eyes. "I can't lose him. I have to see that he's okay."

"What if he isn't okay? Do you want to see that, too?"

My insides lurched. Tyr had to be all right. But that wasn't the only problem with my request. As much as I needed to be there to support him, I didn't want to be a distraction. And if Tyr saw me watching him, I knew he wouldn't be able to help worrying about me.

The tears spilled over, and I swiped at my cheeks. "Once they're outside the barrier, can they see inside it?"

"No." Brynn shook her head. "The enchantment works like a mirage—the gods who have access to the compound only see the shimmer of the protection from the outside, nothing more. For everyone else, this place just looks like a deserted cove."

"Good." I wiped my nose with my sleeve. "Then take me somewhere inside the barrier where I can see over the dunes. I'll know I'm there for him, but he won't."

"Unless he picks up on your thoughts," Brynn pointed out.

"He promised he'd stay out of my head." I sniffled. "And besides, my thoughts here are going to be the same as my thoughts anywhere else. I'm worrying about him, either way."

Brynn glanced at Forse, who stood on Elsa's porch. He nodded, and she gave me a stern look. "I'll let you watch. But we're staying here."

"How am I going to see over the dune? It's thirty feet

high."

"Oh, honey. I'm a valkyrie." Brynn put her fingers between her lips and let out a wolf whistle. Out of the corner of my eye, I saw Forse raise and lower his arm, but I didn't pay much attention to the gesture.

Because at that moment, an enormous winged horse landed on the grass. It was white, with long silver hair woven in an intricate series of braids. It easily stood ten-feet tall, with intimidating haunches and silver hooves.

"Mia, Fang. Fang, Mia." Brynn made the introductions. The horse nodded at me while I stared, dumbstruck.

"Your horse has wings."

"Duh." Brynn rolled her eyes. She climbed on its back easily and held out a hand. "She's a pegasus. Now, are we going or not?"

I grabbed her hand and struggled to climb onto the horse. Without a saddle, there wasn't anywhere for me to get leverage, and I didn't want to wedge my foot in the poor animal's leg. Brynn wrapped her fingers around my forearm, and lifted me with an ease that made it clear the valkyrie was anything but human. My arms wrapped around Brynn's waist, and I rested my heels against Fang's ribs. She shimmied.

"Just so you know, I've never ridden bareback."

Brynn stared at me. "Well, have you ever ridden a pegasus?"

Point, valkyrie.

"Just hold on. We'll take care of the rest, *ja*, Fang?" She nudged the animal with her heel and Fang took off. I tried not to scream while we hurtled upward in a tight circle. We came to a stop forty feet in the air. When Fang flapped her wings, we hovered directly above the spot where we'd just been sitting.

A rush of fear chilled me. I wished I'd stayed on the ground.

The gods and the wolf were locked in battle on the sand. Freya kept guard at the perimeter of the compound, lunging with her rapier each time Fenrir got too close. He snarled at the weapon, baring his yellow teeth. Freya didn't flinch. With each growl, she simply squared her shoulders and struck again, jabbing at Fenrir's dripping fangs until he backed up. When he charged, she pulled a dagger out of her back pocket. She swung her weapons at the wolf, the blades moving so fast they blurred. Fenrir let out a yelp. Freya swiped again and Fenrir took two steps back to the water. He pawed at his ear. Freya kept her swords at the ready, but her face was triumphant as she wiped the blood from her blade.

Fenrir stomped the sand with a vicious howl, while Tyr and Henrik closed in on each side. Tyr stalked a half circle around Fenrir in a hunter's crouch, crossbow still strapped across his back. Henrik moved opposite the war god, twirling his Samurai swords in slow figure-eights. Fenrir whipped his head back and forth between the gods.

He lunged for Tyr.

My breath caught in my throat as Fenrir closed the gap between them. Tyr bent at the knees and flew into the air. He met Fenrir ten feet above the ground. The wolf struck Tyr's face with one paw, leaving thick claw marks across Tyr's cheek. Tyr didn't flinch. He grabbed the animal's leg and bit down with his teeth. The sound of crunching bones echoed across the beach.

Fenrir howled again. It was an agonized sound that bounced off the dunes. The god and the wolf crashed to the ground, scrambling apart. Freya saw her chance and lunged for Fenrir, driving him away from Tyr. The wolf was so focused on Freya's rapier, he didn't see Henrik approach from behind. Henrik swung his swords in vicious circles over his head. He swiped at the canine's haunches so quickly his weapons were a blur of silver.

Henrik sliced Fenrir's leg and Tyr held out his hand, sending a beam of magic that shot the animal into the air. Blood gushed from Fenrir's open vein, covering the sand in a shower of red. The wolf hovered over the ground, shrieking in pain, while Tyr, Henrik and Freya shifted positions beneath him. Fenrir was losing a lot of blood, and the minute he touched the ground he'd find himself outnumbered, if not outmaneuvered. From my perch on the flying horse, I allowed myself a moment of relief.

That was when the dragon swept in.

The beast rose from the ocean outside our protective dome like a sunken Viking ship, its head breaking the surface in one smooth movement. Its skin was an inky purple, with sharp black plates along its spine and a wrecking ball-sized orb at the end of its tail. The orb was cloaked in thick spikes.

"What. Is. That?" I clung to Brynn's waist.

"I think it's Hel's guard, Garm. Hel would have sent her lackey when her brother called. She doesn't leave her post." Brynn stared at the dragon in awe. "I've never seen Garm in person. I always figured she was a dog. You know, like 'the hound of Hel'? Guess I should have paid better attention in my Dark Realms lectures."

"The dragon's a girl?" My eyeballs burned as the dragon spewed fire from her mouth. Even at this distance, the heat was debilitating.

"Yes." Brynn gripped Fang's neck with white knuckles. "Mia, you don't need to see this. Let me take you back down."

"I don't want to leave Tyr." The words came out on a sob.

"Mia," Brynn pleaded. "Hel's guard doesn't leave survivors."

"Please," I whispered.

Brynn was quiet, but the way she set her jaw spoke volumes.

On the ground, the gods circled beneath the wolf. I presumed they were working out the best way to tie him up before the dragon got any closer. Blood still flowed freely from Fenrir's leg. His howl caught Garm's attention, and the dragon swooped over the ocean. She was easily forty feet long from nose to tail, with five-inch claws dangling beneath thick legs. She flew effortlessly to the edge of the shore, then blew a stream of fire at Fenrir. Instead of burning his fur, the fire acted as a healing agent. It stopped the flow of blood and Fenrir's legs went from limp and dangling, to firm and strong. *Did the dragon just reset the wolf's broken legs?*

Tyr and Henrik locked eyes and grinned. I had to shake my head. It was so like them to have fun, even in the worst possible situation.

Henrik bolted south along the shore. He swung his swords over his head so the moonlight bounced off their silvery surface. The dragon's head turned toward the moving reflection. She took off after Henrik, shooting fire from her mouth as she flew. Henrik used his blades as shields, deflecting each inferno with a dexterity that left me breathless. It would have been a beautiful dance, if Henrik's life wasn't on the line.

While Henrik drew the dragon toward the rocks, Tyr and Freya prepared to take on the wolf. They took up arms on opposite sides of the beast—Tyr at the shoreline, Freya against the compound's barrier. Fenrir pawed at the ground. He turned in a slow circle.

Tyr drew the crossbow over his shoulder and took aim. "You're trapped, Fenrir. Submit yourself to Odin or prepare to meet your end."

The wolf snarled, a stream of angry sounds passing through his lips.

"He's saying Tyr's wrong. Jörmungandr and Hel will come when he calls them, and together they'll wipe out the gods *and* take down the compound." Brynn shook her head.

"You can speak wolf?" I asked incredulously.

"Can't you?" Brynn whispered over her shoulder.

"No," I muttered.

"Then Odin and Thor will come, and we'll wipe out you *and* your siblings," Tyr countered.

As he spoke, a bolt of lightning shot from the sky. It landed in the sand where Fenrir's blood had gathered, creating a molten-hot pool of crimson glass. Fenrir stared at the pool, then whipped his head from Freya to Tyr and back. His growl came out in a bitter hiss.

"He's saying he won't surrender," Brynn translated. "He knows Odin would have killed him if it wasn't for Tyr, and he doesn't trust the gods. He wants to know what Odin's terms would be for a truce. He knows Thor's bolt could have hurt him if he'd wanted to. The lightning was a warning."

"I thought Thor was the God of Thunder," I whispered back.

"He multitasks." Brynn waved her hand.

"He missed on purpose?" I shouted. "What the hell?"

"We need him alive, remember?" Brynn said.

Cheese and freaking crackers. I shifted my attention to the sand.

"Fair enough," Tyr said. "Odin's requests are simple. He wants you to stay away from Asgard, Midgard, Alfheim and Vanaheim. Is that something you're willing to do?"

Fenrir snarled. Then he nodded once.

"Excellent." Tyr looked at Freya and she pulled the ribbon from her back pocket. "Odin also wants you to wear this ribbon. It's a tracking device. To make sure you comply with the terms."

Fenrir let out a series of growls so visceral, the hairs on the back of my neck stood on end. Brynn tensed in front of me, and even her horse let out a nervous whinny.

"What did he say?" I almost didn't want to ask.

"He doesn't believe Tyr. He thinks it's a trap." Brynn's voice cracked.

Well, it is.

Tyr exhaled slowly. He glanced at the sky, where Brynn and I were cloaked behind the invisible barrier. My stomach clenched as he gave a sad smile. What was he going to do?

"Take my arm." Tyr gave the wolf a cool gaze. "Hold it between your teeth while Freya attaches the tracking ribbon. If anything bad happens to you, you can bite my arm clean off. But if nothing happens, you let me go unharmed. Do we have a deal?"

The wolf let out one sharp bark and opened his mouth. Tyr placed his forearm between Fenrir's teeth.

"No," I whispered. Brynn tensed as I squeezed her torso. "Can't you stop him?"

Brynn shook her head. "He knows exactly what he's doing."

My eyes closed for the briefest of moments. In that instant, I sent silent prayers to the universe, asking God, Odin, Zeus, Buddha, and whoever else might be listening, to protect Tyr from the monster on the sand. When I looked down again, Freya was tying the ribbon around Fenrir's neck. The pink fabric emitted a sharp burst of light as it sealed itself against the wolf's fur. In that moment, Fenrir let loose a terrifying growl.

It was done.

But it wasn't over. Just before Fenrir was rendered immobile, he gnashed his teeth together and jerked his head left, then right. He must have realized it was a trap. The sickening crunch of bones was punctuated by the image of gushing liquid as blood poured from Tyr's arm. And since the ribbon appeared to lock every muscle in Fenrir's body in place, when Tyr's body flew through the air, Fenrir had no way to release his limb.

Tyr lost his arm.

He landed in a heap on the sand, and rolled unsteadily to his knees. As he shifted, he stared with resignation at the exposed sinew dangling just below his right elbow. The jagged muscles were unsettling; the blood gushing from the exposed tissue was downright horrifying.

Tyr lurched to the side. A cardinal pool formed at his feet as the blood flowed freely. Freya dove forward just as Tyr fell to the ground, unconscious. She pulled him away from the now-immobilized wolf. My heart stilled—it felt like someone had dropped a lead balloon on my chest.

This couldn't be happening.

Freya glanced down the beach, where Henrik was locked in a mid-air battle with the dragon. He delivered a well-timed jab to the dragon's chest, sending Garm plunging into the water. Henrik dove after her, taking the battle under water. It felt like an eternity before Henrik rose to the surface, sputtered for air, then dove again. He emerged ten seconds later, sword in one hand and Garm's severed head in the other.

"Heimdall!" Freya shrieked at the sky. "Open the Bifrost!"

The sky parted and a beam of light shot onto the sand, where Fenrir struggled against the seemingly flimsy pink ribbon.

"Heimdall, take Fenrir to the prison chamber. Bring Garm's remains with him. Brynn, get down here. We need to get Tyr to the healers." Freya issued her commands like a seasoned warrior.

An offshoot of the Bifrost beamed in Henrik's direction. He tossed the dragon's head at the light while it drew the monster's body from the depths of the sea. The light pulled back from the sand, sucking Fenrir into the sky when it retracted. As quickly as it had come, the Bifrost was gone.

"Brynn!" Freya screamed.

"Hold on, Mia." Brynn kicked Fang's side, and the pegasus swooped onto the sand. "Scoot back," Brynn commanded, and I moved as close to the animal's tail as I could without falling off. Freya lifted Tyr easily onto Brynn's lap before giving one final command. "Get him to the healing unit *immediately*. He's going to die."

* * * *

"Fenrir's bite was laced with dark magic. Tyr's bleeding out." Freya raced alongside Fang, pulled Tyr off the pegasus' back, and ran my boyfriend into the medical unit while I was still struggling just to breathe. I heard her shout ahead as she ran. "Prep the second bed!"

I followed in a daze, barely feeling the ground beneath my feet. Inside the healing unit, Elsa lay propped up in a queen-sized hospital bed, skin glowing and lips moist, her legs covered in the same plushy white comforters that decorated Tyr's room next door. But this suite lacked the Jacuzzi tub, and in its place sat another queen-sized hospital bed, waiting for a second patient.

It was like the gods were expecting this.

Hold the phone. *It was like the gods were expecting this.*

I surveyed the room. Elsa was coming into consciousness, looking radiant in a royal blue dressing gown. Her hair shone in a mass of blond waves, and her cheeks had the kind of color that didn't come from blush. The machine at her bedside projected her vitals onto the wall, punctuated by one word—*NORMAL.*

She was healthy.

A second bed was set up to the right of Elsa's. Healers stood at the ready, wearing the same white gowns I'd seen back at the cabin. For all intents, the setup looked like Elsa's room had, with one exception: Henrik's mechanical arm sat next to the bed.

What was Fred doing there? My mind started to piece everything together. It was more than a coincidence that Henrik and Brynn had been developing a robotic arm; and it was more than a coincidence that the arm was perfectly proportioned to Tyr's body. None of this was possible, unless . . .

I whirled around. Henrik limped into the ward behind me.

"You knew this was going to happen." I jabbed my finger into his chest. "You knew Tyr would lose an arm fighting Fenrir. You knew he might die! Why didn't you stop him?"

Henrik wrapped both arms around my shoulders, pulling me to his chest, but he didn't take his eyes off his friend. I turned my head so I could follow his stare. Freya and the healers were putting Tyr in position on the bed, and Henrik spoke directly to the medical team. "Once you've stopped the bleeding, we can attempt the transfer."

"Henrik!" I tried to pull out of his grasp, but he was too strong. "What the—"

A hand clamped around my mouth. I fought every childish urge to bite it.

"Don't aggravate them," Henrik whispered in my ear. "Tyr's losing a lot of blood. The healers need all their energy to save him. And Tyr needs to focus on getting better. If he's worrying about you, he won't make it. Do you understand?"

I ground my teeth and took a deep breath before I was able to nod. When Henrik pulled his hand away, I spoke quietly, in the calmest voice I could manage. "You could have kept him from fighting."

"You and I both know that's not true. Tyr has *always* fought his own battles . . . and anyone else's, if he thinks they need him. I've been working around the clock to mitigate the outcome, but what happened today was always a possibility."

"Why didn't you stop it?" I turned in Henrik's arms as healers circled around Tyr, obscuring my view. I wanted to scream, but Tyr couldn't afford that distraction.

"Some things are out of our control. The best we can hope for is to minimize the damage. In this case, there was no getting around the prophecy." Henrik kept his voice low.

My eyes narrowed. "And what exactly was the

prophecy?"

"The Norns saw Fenrir turn on Asgard. They saw the dwarves make a chain to bind him, to slow his path of destruction. They saw the Aesir use Fenrir to bargain with the dark forces at Ragnarok." Henrik lowered his head. "But before that, they saw. . ."

There was a commotion over Tyr's bed. Two healers stepped away, then quickly returned with an oblong device. They ripped his shirt off and held the device up to Tyr's chest. They left a small gap between them, enough that I could see the surge of light shoot through Tyr's body. His chest jerked at the energy running through it. He convulsed violently, bucking against the power coursing under his skin. His body went still, and he turned a ghastly white.

The healers paused, and brought the god-defibrillator to his chest again. Another surge of light struck his chest, and this time his convulsions were more pronounced. His head whipped viciously back and forth while his legs kicked against the hands holding them down. It took a full minute for this surge to pass through him, and when it did his skin was an ashy grey.

The healers tried again, this time firing nine surges into Tyr's torso in rapid succession. With each surge, his body convulsed ferociously, fighting against the power of the light.

Then he went limp. One foot twitched imperceptibly before his body fell completely still.

Freya started to cry.

I felt nothing. No fear. No pain. No sadness. *Nothing*. It was as if my entire emotional center completely shut down.

It felt like I'd died inside.

This was not happening. Tyr was just resting, gearing up for the next phase of his recovery. He was *not* in the same coma Elsa had been in. He was *not* dead. He was *fine*.

"Henrik?" My friend's arms were still wrapped around my shoulders. "What was the rest of the prophecy? What did the Norns see after they saw the dwarves make the chain?"

"Mia, you have to understand. The dwarves said they would require the blood of the Aesir to bind the wolf. We knew one of us would have to make that sacrifice if we wanted to protect the realms from the evil growing within Fenrir. We've tried to cheat the darker prophecies for centuries, and we did everything we could to avoid losing one of our own. We convinced the dwarves to alter the power of the chain so it only required the sacrifice of a limb, not an entire life. It still wasn't ideal, but losing an arm was a lot better than death, right?" Henrik squeezed me gently. "Tyr volunteered to take the hit. We knew the wolf would be more valuable to Asgard alive than dead, provided we could actually bind him. And deep down, I don't think Tyr wanted to kill Fenrir. Even after everything that's happened, a part of him still wanted to believe there was some good left in his childhood pet."

I couldn't speak.

"But there was another prophecy. One that fell between our binding the wolf and our using him at Ragnarok."

"What did that prophecy say?" My words came through gritted teeth.

"It said the God of War would fall."

CHAPTER TWENTY-FIVE

"**I'M SORRY MIA. WE** did everything we could think of to save . . . I'm so sorry."

"No!" I opened my eyes and tried to bolt for Tyr, but Henrik held me too tight. "Let me go!" I thrashed against the hold as my eyes sought out the healers. "Do something. Try it again. If the defibrillator isn't working, give him a shot of something magical. Dragon heart or elf blood or that *älva* dust—I know you have something in here that can help him. Use it! Now!"

Henrik glanced at Forse. The justice god stood at Elsa's bedside, gently holding one of her hands. Something clicked in my brain.

"Wait! Elsa . . . Elsa can bring Tyr back. She's a High Healer, isn't she? That has to be important." My eyes pleaded with Henrik.

"I could do what?" a raspy voice chimed. Elsa had woken up amidst the chaos. She looked around the room in confusion, her silvery blue eyes swimming as they focused on each of us in turn. Forse spoke her name as if in prayer, and hurriedly handed her the glass of water at her bedside. The water sloshed as her hand dipped under the weight of the cup, and Forse helped her steady it. She raised it to her lips and drank, her eyes locked on Forse's in a way that made it clear she returned his feelings, and then some. He took the glass when she was done and placed it back on the table.

"You're okay." Forse's torso practically wilted in relief.

Elsa reached up to touch Forse's cheek before she looked around the room and cleared her throat. When she spoke again, the raspiness was replaced by a melodic lilt. "What's Tyr done?"

Henrik glanced over in relief at the sound of Elsa's voice. Brynn turned away from the window to face the room, her red-rimmed eyes now filled with hope. Even Freya stopped crying at Tyr's bedside long enough to look up. Everyone had the decency to honor the moment they'd been waiting months for.

Everyone but me.

"Tyr's dying! You have to save him *right now*!"

The tiny girl jumped at the sound of my demand. She'd just come out of a coma, and I was shrieking at her.

"Where is he?" Elsa pushed herself to her feet. She swayed unsteadily, and gripped the monitor to steady herself. Forse leaped to her side and guided her to her brother.

"He's here, but he's unconscious. Fenrir severed his arm with a poisoned bite, and he's bleeding out. Is there anything you can do?" Forse's voice was low. He was handling everything with considerably more dignity than me.

Well, of course he was. The person he loved was standing in his arms, and the person I loved . . .

I couldn't even finish the thought.

"Oh my gods." Elsa's blond hair whipped back and forth as she looked from her brother to Freya and Henrik. "How did it get this bad? Didn't you use the—"

"Resuscitator? It failed," Freya whispered. "The healers did everything they could. We don't know what else to do." Freya's tears spilled over. "Please, Elsa. He can't really be gone."

"Stand back," Elsa commanded. "Healers, you too." All nine of us obeyed. Elsa was tiny—maybe five-foot-one if she stretched. She still didn't look a day over eighteen, with her shiny golden locks and cherubic cheeks. But as she stood over her brother in her shimmering dressing gown, she stretched her arms out authoritatively, and a calm settled into her eyes. She looked every bit the magical goddess I needed her to be.

Elsa murmured an incantation in a language that sounded different from Tyr and Henrik's—this dialect sounded ancient, simpler and more guttural than the bits of Swedish I'd picked up over the past few months.

"What's she saying?" I looked at Freya. She stepped back to stand next to me. Henrik tightened his arms around my shoulders, and Freya took my hand in hers. I couldn't tell if they were trying to comfort me or to hold me back.

"She's calling on the High Healers of the allied realms, asking them to join together to heal Tyr," Freya explained.

"Why didn't you guys do that?" I practically spat it out.

"Elsa's the only one who can do it."

"Is it working?" I redirected my focus on Elsa. Her hands moved up and down over Tyr's body. As she continued to chant, a gold glow came out of her fingertips. It covered the bed with a glittery sheen, wrapping Tyr in its shiny cloud.

"I don't know." Freya shook her head.

While we waited, Elsa reached for Fred. She positioned the arm at Tyr's elbow, pinching the limb where it bled. By now, the white sheets were stained red, and Tyr's skin was practically white. *Please, hurry up.* Elsa waved her hand over the metal and it bound itself to the skin. The smell of burning flesh filled the room as sparks shot from Elsa's palm, soldering Fred to Tyr's arm. The odor was cloying, but when Elsa stepped back Fred stayed in place.

We watched in silence while Elsa touched Tyr's forehead, implanting Fred's control panel in Tyr's brain with magic rather than surgery, and then resumed working on Tyr's chest. The tension in the air was palpable—Forse hovered at the edge of Elsa's bed; Brynn had moved away from the window to grip Henrik's shoulder. Freya and I huddled together, hands still tightly clasped as tears rolled down my face.

After a slow eternity, Elsa stepped back. She opened her eyes and stared at me.

"I've done all I can," she spoke calmly. "The rest is up to you."

I blinked. "What am I supposed to do?"

"What do you think?" She smiled.

I had no freaking idea.

"What's the most powerful thing in all the realms?" Elsa prodded.

I stared.

"Give him a reason to want to come back," Elsa said gently. "Are you in love with my brother?"

My gaze darted around the room. I tried to ignore the eyes staring at me, waiting on my response. Of course I was in love with Tyr. He was everything I never knew I wanted, and everything I absolutely needed. But how could I say that in front of a room of gods?

Elsa waited patiently until I nodded. "Then tell him," she urged.

"What if it doesn't work?" I was terrified. Losing Tyr would be like losing a part of myself. It would absolutely destroy me.

Henrik released his hold and Freya nudged me forward. "Try."

I approached the golden glow surrounding the bed. Tyr had more color in his cheeks, and when I pushed through Elsa's enchantment to touch him he felt okay—cool, but not icy. I brushed a lock of hair from his forehead, and stared at his angular jaw peppered with stubble, the strong nose, and the thick lashes I'd have traded my eyeteeth for.

Good lord, I loved this man. This god. Whatever. He'd changed my life in so many ways, and I wanted to shake him awake and thank him for every single gift he'd given me—for the security I felt every time we were in the same room; for the feeling of belonging I had at his side, even in the most unimaginable of worlds; for the adventure I wouldn't have sought out on my own; for letting me believe I might have found the person—the god—who knew all my little oddities and loved me anyway.

There was no doubt in my heart; I'd do absolutely anything for Tyr, anything at all, if it meant saving him.

I bent down and brushed his lips softly with my own. "Please don't leave me," I whispered. "I know we're not perfect. I know we've got, like, the entire universe stacked against us. But we've only just started. Come back to me. Because I love you." My voice broke over the words. They were too true, too right. *And too late.* I lay my head on Tyr's chest and cried. "With everything I have, I just love you."

The hand that touched my back was cold. And hard. It rubbed me stiffly, like it was moving for the first time on its own.

It was Fred.

I lifted my head. Tyr stared up at me.

"You're okay!" I threw my arms around him and squeezed so tight, he winced.

"I'm okay." He pulled me back. "Do you?"

"Do I what?" I blinked back my tears.

"Love me?" His voice was thick.

"With everything I am," I whispered back. Tyr reached up and guided my face to meet his. Our lips met in a rough kiss. It was far too short, and when Tyr met my gaze, his eyes were hungry.

"Gods, Mia. I love you so much. I'd do anything for you. Anything."

"Oh, Tyr!" All of a sudden I couldn't stand the inches between us. I crawled into his bed, careful not to jostle him, and pressed myself to his side. Tyr pulled my head to his bare chest and cradled me with his good arm. He flexed Fred experimentally, moving each finger with care.

"You did it. Nice work, Henrik. Sis! You're awake!" He beamed up at Elsa, who practically wilted in relief. Forse ran over to catch her.

"For the love of Asgard, Tyr, don't scare me like that again!" Elsa leaned against Forse.

"I could say the same for you," Tyr admonished. "Do you have any idea how long you were out?"

Elsa put a hand on her hip. "How would I know a thing like that?"

"Months. It felt like an eternity." Tyr balled both fists—Fred, and the one he was born with. "I am so sorry that monster hurt you. I swear, I won't let anything get near you ever again."

"Ah, Tyr the Protector. Once, now and always." Elsa smiled ethereally. "I adore you, big brother. But you don't have to save everyone, all the time. I'm here, and I'm just fine. A few scratches, is all."

"You gave us a scare." Henrik crossed the room and wrapped Elsa in a bear hug.

Elsa's laugh rang like chimes. "*Hei* Henrik."

Brynn moved to kiss Elsa on both cheeks. "We're so glad you're okay. That *both* of you are okay. Gods, Tyr. That was terrifying! Mia nearly had a heart attack."

"You were pretty freaked out too," I pointed out. "Wait,

the prophecy. Henrik said the Norns saw the God of War fall. Does that mean you're still in danger?"

"I doubt it. The prophecy came true. I did fall," Tyr pointed out. He shifted us so we could sit up in the bed, and he nestled me underneath his arm as he rested his back against the headboard. "For all purposes, that monster killed me. But then you brought me back." He stroked my cheek with one finger. "And now, *mitt hjärta*, I'm afraid you're stuck with me."

I studied Tyr's features, committing every detail to memory. Especially the way he looked at me like I was the only girl in the world. "Thank gods."

"Agreed," Elsa chimed in.

I reluctantly looked away from Tyr. "Sorry I yelled at you, Elsa. I'm usually more well-mannered."

Elsa laughed. "I know. I could hear you all those times you came to visit. I couldn't wait to come out of that void and meet you in person."

"I'm getting you an Elite Team security detail," Tyr vowed. "Henrik, find out who the ranking officer is. I want him reassigned to Elsa immediately."

"I don't need Elite Team." Elsa rolled her eyes. "Honestly, you're so overprotective."

"That's my job. I'm your brother. And we're not done talking about this. But we can table it until tomorrow." Tyr stroked my back while he spoke to his sister.

"I hope he's not this bossy with you, Mia. It's rude." Elsa punctuated her declaration with a wink. She was bubbly—not as perky as Brynn, but more so than I expected of someone who'd shared Tyr's upbringing. She looked out the window with a frown. "So where is Fenrir now?"

"Restrained. Heimdall took him to the prison chamber via the Bifrost." Brynn put her head on Henrik's chest, and Tyr squeezed me tightly.

Freya let out a contented sigh.

"What?" Tyr asked.

"Great Odin, I'm good. Look at you, Tyr. My sweet, stubborn, impossible, irritating, egotistical, stoic, pigheaded friend. Alive. And in love."

"Nice, Freya. How do you talk to your enemies?" Tyr rested his chin on the top of my head.

"As I was saying," she continued, "my friend *finally* met his match. With more than a few gentle nudges from yours truly. Goddess of Love, guru of happiness. Matchmaker extraordinaire. You are so welcome, *kille*."

I couldn't stay silent any longer. "How is this even possible? I can't do any of the stuff you guys can do. I'm not immortal; what happens when the next possessed deific wildebeest or whatever comes after me or one of those jotun things attacks?" My voice dropped. "Or what if you decide it's too much work to have to protect me all the time? I'm not like you are—you guys are going to get tired of doing everything half-speed so the human can keep up." I looked up at Tyr. "I love you. I think I always will. But I can't lose you again. Not like this. You need a goddess who can fight at your side. Maybe I'm not your match, maybe you're stronger without me, maybe—"

"Stop it right there." Freya held up a hand before Tyr

could respond. "I said you two are meant for each other, and it's true. I'm not a Norn—I don't see the future, and I don't know *how* things are going to work out. But I watched as you chose each other. And I know things *are* going to work out. That's all you need to know."

"It's enough for me." Tyr's lips brushed my hair. "What about you, *prinsessa?*"

"*Prinsessa?*" Elsa raised an eyebrow, and the back of my neck grew hot.

"Fine. It's enough. For now. But you know I've got a million questions."

Tyr tilted his head toward the door. "Want to take a walk?"

I pushed myself to my feet, glancing at the enormous blood stain on the far side of the bed. "Are you up to walking right now?"

"I think I can manage it." Tyr stood with care, gingerly testing his weight before taking a step. He took my hand in his good one and leaned to kiss Elsa's cheek. "Glad you're okay, sis."

"Always am," she said lightly. "Now, is anybody going to do something about that or does my brother have to walk around looking like he's part robot?" She pointed to Fred.

"How does it feel?" Henrik inspected the prosthetic as Brynn handed Freya a small pouch.

"Better Fred than dead." Tyr pointed one robotic finger at Henrik, who groaned. "Nice work, man."

"Ahem," Brynn chimed in.

"Sorry. You too, ladies. Thanks for this. I mean it." Tyr grinned.

Freya held some dust from the pouch, and sprinkled it on Fred. "It's the last of the *älva* dust," she explained, looking at me. Tyr waved his hand over the metal, and a flesh-colored sleeve grew over the robotic replacement. It slid down the forearm, and each of the fingers, until the entire thing was covered in a peach coating. Tyr tapped it twice, and the sleeve shimmered, then disappeared. In its place was a highly realistic arm. I reached out to touch it with a finger—it even felt warm. Except for the stiffness in Tyr's movements, I'd never have known it was a prosthetic.

"Much better. And I'll clean up the blood." Elsa raised her palm at Tyr, and the remnants of the red liquid disappeared. By all physical appearances, the past few hours had never even happened.

"*Takk*, Else." Tyr nodded his appreciation.

"Any time." Elsa turned to Forse, who lingered behind her, shifting his weight from side to side. "So what have you been up to while I've been sleeping?"

Underneath his stubble, Forse turned a blazing crimson.

"Let's go." Tyr pulled me out the door. He called over his shoulder. "Don't bother us."

"Wouldn't dream of it, *kille*." Henrik laughed. "Wouldn't dream of it."

* * * *

"You're wondering what happens now." The tide was just

421

starting to come in on the cove. Tyr held my hand as we walked barefoot in the wet sand.

"Yeah," I admitted. "Elsa's healed, and you probably have a laundry list of crises you put on hold to stay here and take care of her. You're going to have to leave Earth, aren't you?"

"I'm sure I will fairly soon." Tyr stopped moving abruptly. Since his fingers were laced through mine, I lurched backward. "But I'm just as sure that I'll come back as soon as I'm able to."

"You're a god. You belong in Asgard."

The words killed me.

He took my hands and dropped to one knee.

Oh my god. What was he doing? I was only seventeen.

"I'm not proposing," Tyr clarified.

"You promised you wouldn't snoop in my head!"

"Didn't have to. You have absolutely no poker face, remember?"

"Oh. Right." My cheeks warmed.

"Listen to me, Mia Ahlström. I belong with *you.* Nobody else. I've never told a girl I loved her, because it's never been true. But I love everything about you. Your eyes. Your laugh. I love the crooked half-smile you give me when I'm being a complete and total *ryck.* I love the way you bite your lip when you're concentrating, and I love that you refuse to leave the house without checking three times for your keys and phone." Tyr smiled. "I love that you refuse to say *butt.* I love the seven hundred pairs of shoes you have to choose between when we go out. I love that you didn't run screaming from my house the night I told you what I was. I love the way the south comes out in your voice when you're tired. Or nervous. And I love the way I feel when I'm in the same room as you. Like my heart is warm, and I'm finally in the right place. Like I'm not all alone anymore." Tyr lifted my hands to his mouth, and brushed his lips over my fingertips. "You're the last thing I was expecting to find when I came to Midgard. I just wanted to get Elsa away from Fenrir. You definitely weren't what I thought I wanted, but you're exactly what I needed. And I don't want to be with anyone else."

I buried my hands in his hair, overwhelmed with joy. The words ran on loop in my brain as I drilled them into my memory—I didn't want to forget a single thing about this moment.

But as much as I loved the sentiment, there was still an enormous problem. "You're a god. And I'm me. Can that even work?"

"I want to try," Tyr vowed. He stared into the ocean. "Being God of War is a twenty-four-hour deal. Asgard's almost constantly under attack, and I've had to run defense pretty much daily for the last millennia. It's not like I can move to Midgard and play house full-time—I have to go where the hostilities are."

"I know," I whispered.

"But it doesn't mean I can't return when the battle's over." Tyr paused. The corner of his mouth was turned up in his typical arrogant expression, but I could see just a hint of vulnerability in his eyes. "This is a whole new game for me. I've never had anyone I wanted to make time for. But I promise I'll always come back for you."

He held my hands gently in his and looked into my eyes. "You're it for me, baby. Will you do me the honor of being my girl?"

In this moment, he wasn't the all-powerful God of War, he was just . . . my Tyr. The one who dried my tears, and proofread my papers, and covered my eyes at the scary parts of movies, and who ate the black olives off the pizza because he knew I hated them. The one who made sure his freezer had my favorite kind of ice cream, and never made me feel like he wanted me to be anything other than exactly who I was. The one who loved me just for being me, imperfections and all.

The one I couldn't imagine living without.

"Of course." My voice cracked. "I will absolutely be your girl."

Tyr stood and lifted me off the sand. I wrapped my legs around his waist and kissed him hard.

"Is life with you always going to be this crazy? Flying horses and feral wolves and killer dragons? Resuscitators and healers and near-death experiences?"

"Quite possibly. You in?"

Tyr brushed his tongue against his bottom lip, then covered my mouth in a fervent kiss. When he pulled back, he eyed me levelly.

"I am so in." I laid a trail of kisses along his jawline until I reached his ear. I took the lobe in my mouth and sucked gently.

Tyr gave a sharp intake of breath and hiked my legs higher around his waist.

"Hold that thought."

"Yes, sir." I kissed him again.

Tyr ran the short distance to his porch, never taking his lips off mine. My hands fisted in his hair as he ripped the French doors open, then slammed them closed behind us. I peppered his jaw with kisses while he took the steps two at a time. When he reached the landing, he tore down the hall. His hands cupped my bottom as he opened his bedroom door with his shoulder, bent his knees and flew twenty feet, cradling me protectively as he landed on his back on the enormous bed. He rolled onto his forearms, and my heart pounded as I stared at the planes of his bare chest. They were firm and smooth and tanned and absolutely perfect.

Oh yum.

Tyr hovered over me. His hips pressed lightly against mine, and he met my eyes with a look that made me shiver.

"You okay, baby?"

"That depends." I raked his bare back with my fingernails. "I can handle the feral wolves, and homicidal dragons, and whatever else you play with for fun. But I'm going to need a whole lot of kisses to make up for all the crazy. Whenever you're around, I need to know there will be heaps of this."

I wrapped my fingers in his hair and brought his head down to mine. I poured everything I had into that kiss, letting go of the pain, the fear, and the absolute agony I'd felt when I thought I'd lost him. We melted together for a delicious moment, and when Tyr pulled back, all that was left was the feeling that I was exactly where I was meant to be.

"What do you think?" I murmured.

Tyr rubbed his nose along my jaw. He flexed his hips gently as he moved, sending the slow throb in my belly into overdrive. I wrapped my leg around him and pulled him closer. When our eyes met, his were crinkled at the edges in his signature half-smile.

"What do I think?" Tyr repeated. His wink sent all-too-familiar heat dancing along my spine. It raced from my neck to my tailbone, radiating across my torso until my entire midsection was warm. Tyr growled as I squirmed beneath him. His eyes darkened and he looked down at me, leaving no doubt as to how very much in control of his world he was.

Double yum.

My lashes fluttered against his nose as I blinked up at him. However crazy a life with the God of War might get, there was no place else I'd want to be.

Tyr raised an eyebrow. "I think . . . that you have no idea what you're in for."

"Is that so?"

"No. Idea." Tyr stroked my cheek with one finger.

Then he hooked the hem of my sweater with his thumbs. With one swift movement, he tugged it over my head and threw it onto the floor, leaving me in my camisole. He rested his weight on one forearm, running his thumb lightly across my lips before tracing a path from my neck, over my chest, and down to my stomach. His hand pushed up the fabric of my shirt so it bunched just below my bra. He spread his fingers outward across my lower abdomen, leaving a thousand burning embers dancing along my skin. I wanted to be his so desperately, my soul ached. He couldn't promise me forever; we didn't even know where tomorrow would take him. But we had this moment. And hopefully, if we were lucky, we had more moments just like this— whenever and however we could piece them together. It would be enough.

It had to be.

I pulled him closer, and Tyr lifted his hand with agonizing slowness, setting his arm alongside my body. Now he had me locked between positively massive forearms. Tyr brought his mouth to where his hand had been, peppering a trail of kisses up my still-burning stomach. I gripped the sheets tightly in a pointless effort to stay still. These kisses were overwhelming—the sensations too intense. He shifted his attention to the neckline of my camisole, and ran his nose along the black lace.

"Mmm." He exhaled as he spoke, his breath leaving a warm trail along my already overheated skin. He nipped lightly at the swollen flesh just above the fabric, then soothed the bite with his tongue. It felt warm, and wet, and when he pulled his mouth away, the cool air sent a shiver down my spine.

Tyr glanced up as I stilled. "You okay?" he asked.

I nodded.

Tyr dropped his head again, and I laced my fingers through his hair as I gave myself over to him. There was nobody else I'd ever trusted with this part of me, and I wanted Tyr to understand—to feel—just how wholly I loved every part of him. The good. The bad. The downright ugly. All the things Tyr loathed about himself were the very things that made him imperfectly perfect in my eyes, and I wanted him to know how completely he owned my heart.

Tyr's mouth made a slow trajectory upward, licking a languid trail along my neck. He took his time, alternating sweet kisses with naughty bites. I squirmed underneath him and pulled at his hair so he had to look up. I met his eyes, and ran my tongue along my bottom lip. His gaze glazed over, and he stirred on top of me.

"Well then, Mr. War God, I'd better not keep you waiting any longer." I gently pushed him off me and rolled so I could remove my cami. I felt incredibly vulnerable, but also incredibly safe. I knew that however overwhelming this moment seemed, Tyr the Protector would take care of me.

Tyr used one hand to wrap long fingers around my wrists and locked my arms in place, stopping me from undressing. "Hold on, *prinsessa*. Remember what I told you—we've got a lot of ground to cover between here"— he kissed my lips softly—"and there." He ran a finger along the still-buttoned waistband of my jeans. "And I want you to enjoy every single second of the journey."

"I'm fairly confident I'll enjoy the trip." I tried to reach for my shirt again, but Tyr's grip was too tight. I looked at him in confusion. "Don't you want to do this?"

"Oh, I want to." Tyr leaned down and took my earlobe between his teeth, the raking sensation making me shiver. "And we will. In good time. But a certain human recently accused me of breaking protocol. And that's a mistake I don't intend to repeat."

"I did what now?"

"I believe your exact words were, 'You might do things

that way in whatever boondocks part of Asgard you're from, but around here there are traditions you have to observe. Steps you have to take.' Or something like that. Sound familiar?"

I squirmed. My brain was *not* firing on all cylinders. "I said that?"

"You were rather upset when I suggested you move in with me. Accused me of moving too fast. Remember?" Tyr positioned me beside him, holding my arms over my head and running his nose along my arm. *Yum, yum, yum . . .*

"Yeah, well. Um. I retract that statement."

"Mmm." Tyr licked a lazy circle along the inside of my elbow, and I turned my head to kiss his stubble-peppered jaw. "I'm afraid there are no retractions. The Norns showed me something today while I was, er . . ."

"Dead?" I whispered.

"I prefer 'regrouping'." Tyr licked my arm again, and my eyes rolled back. "Regardless. The future they showed me. . . it made me realize that this thing between us, it's going to last for a very long time. At least, it will if I do things with you the right way. I promised I'd never hurt you, and I intend to keep my word."

"But—"

"But nothing. This is a big deal, and there's no need to rush into it. I'm not going anywhere. We have forever."

"No, *you* have forever. I'm mortal, remember?" *I'm also a ticking bomb of hormones. Just an FYI.*

"Mmm." Tyr flicked my earlobe with his tongue. *Oh. My. Norse god.* Was he trying to kill me? "Well, maybe we'll have to do something about that."

"Something about what?" The ear kissing was not helping me focus on Tyr's words, and something in his tone made them seem like very important words.

"Don't worry about it, my beautiful *prinsessa*. Just know that I will always take care of you." Tyr *finally* released the manacles on my wrists and pulled my shirt over my head, leaving me in my lacy bra. He pulled me against him so he could cradle me in his arms. Our bodies fit together, his warm skin against mine, which was absolutely, wholly, without a doubt, where I was destined to be.

"I love you, Mia," Tyr growled against my forehead. "I think I always have. And laws be damned, I always will."

"Show me," I whispered. He pulled back to meet my eyes with his signature smile.

"Gladly." He pressed his lips against mine, closing what little distance was left between us. My heart swelled as I realized that finally, I could be Tyr's.

In every way that mattered.

CHAPTER TWENTY-SIX

"TAKE YOUR TIME. JASON'S not going to be here for another two hours." I tucked my phone under my chin so I could transfer Meemaw's red velvet cookies to a cooling rack. "And dinner's not going to be ready for another . . . well, hopefully about the same."

"You said you're making pot roast?" On the other end of the line, Tyr sounded tired. He'd taken a call from Asgard *very* early that morning, then darted out of the house to help the dwarves handle a border skirmish with some dragons. I hadn't expected him back before tomorrow morning, but he was pushing to get home in time to welcome my brother.

"Of course. It's Jase's favorite. It'll be yours, too, once you taste it." I set the baking tray in the sink and turned the oven down to three-hundred.

"Everything you make is delicious, but your lasagna will always be my favorite. It's the first thing you ever cooked for me. I'm nothing if not sentimental."

"True. Because when I think war god, I think sentimental lasagna lover. Oh, and remember, if Jason asks,

I still live on Daffodil Drive. My folks would flip out if they knew I spent my weekends here." I wasn't totally lying to them. I still kept most of my clothes at my "official" collegiate residence. I just *occasionally* happened to enjoy the amenities at Tyr's place, too.

Tyr chuckled. "I'm sure your brother knows how to keep a secret. Now come here so I can kiss you."

"What?"

There was a knock at the front door.

"Oh my gosh, are you here already?" I threw my oven mitt on the counter and raced down the hallway. "I thought you said you were still in Dwarfheim?"

"Nidavellir, but close enough." Tyr's key sounded in the lock, and I skidded to a stop as he opened the front door. His cargo pants were torn, there was blood caked on his black T-shirt, and his hair was matted with a thick black substance that looked suspiciously like tar. But his eyes bore their telltale twinkle, and his mouth was curved up in a half smile. "*Hei hei*, love. Miss me?"

He tucked his phone in his pocket just as I launched myself at him. My arms clutched his neck as my legs wrapped around his waist. I buried my face in his chest and inhaled his sprucey scent, too excited to care that my cheek was probably touching singed dragon bits . . . or worse. "You're home!"

"I'm home." Tyr wrapped his arms around me and squeezed, his large hands pressing into the small of my back. "I promised I would be."

"I know, but . . . well . . ."

"I know." Tyr kissed the top of my head, and I looked up at him. "You don't have to worry about me. I promised I'd always come back to you."

"Yeah." I ducked my head. "But dragons? Come on, that's scary."

"Naw, dragons aren't scary. Now meeting your brother? The one who said he'd end me if I ever hurt you? That's scary." Tyr set me gently on my feet and leaned down. When he stood, he held up a bouquet of pastel pink flowers. "For my girl. Sorry for tracking dwarf dust in the house."

I took the flowers from his hands and inhaled deeply.

Tyr picked up his duffle bag and wiped his feet on the mat before stepping into the hallway. "These grew in the meadow where Heimdall dropped the Bifrost. I couldn't resist bringing my girl a piece of 'Dwarfheim.'"

"Ha ha." I cuffed him on the shoulder and padded down the hallway to put the flowers in water. "You look exhausted. You should just go upstairs and sleep; Jason won't mind if he doesn't get to see you until—"

Tyr gripped my forearm and spun me around. He cupped my cheek in his palm and stopped my words with a kiss. "The only thing I want to do right now is be with you. I missed you."

"Well, you've been off all day slaying dragons. Literally." I shook my head. "You have a really bizarre job, you realize this?"

"I do." Tyr pulled me into his arms and sat on the kitchen stool. "And you're about to have one, too."

I wrapped my arms around his neck and leaned back. "What does that mean? Does Henrik have another robotics project for me? Oh god, you don't need another limb, do you?"

"No, nothing like that." Tyr chuckled. "My limbs are fine." He picked me up so I could sit on his lap. "Do you remember learning about the Keys?"

"Unifiers, Healers, Seers. I know the deal," I recalled.

"Right. Because of my title, my mate will be granted a key role, so long as she's got the inclination." Tyr stroked my hair.

"At marriage. I remember."

"Well?" Tyr tilted his head.

"Well what?"

"Well, do you want to be my Unifier?" Tyr held my gaze with a soft smile.

I froze.

"I'm not proposing, Mia. I know you; you're not ready."

"Are *you* ready?" I squeaked.

"Of course. I've been waiting my entire existence for you. But you're only seventeen. You need to be able to vote, first."

"Gee, thanks, Mom."

Tyr laughed. "No, I'm asking you to start thinking about whether you *want* to take on the Unifier job. Since I have no intention of letting you go, and you've got a steep learning curve because you're a mortal, you have to think about whether it'd be a good fit for you."

I took a slow breath. "That's kind of a big deal. Can a human even be a Unifier?"

"*My* human sure as Helheim can." Tyr winked. "You're something else, Mia Ahlström. I wouldn't count you out for anything."

I kissed the tip of his nose and slid to my feet. "You're learning." I winked over my shoulder as I crossed to the stove to check on the pot roast. It looked fine, but I used the baster to cover it with broth just in case. "I'll talk to Elsa about it. I've got, like, a thousand questions for her anyway."

"I would expect nothing less of you."

I stuck out my tongue. "And speaking of questions, tell Henrik to hurry up and ask Brynn out already. It's driving her nuts."

"Brynn's not allowed to date. Not for a while, anyway. If you want to push anyone, my money's on Forse. He's had a thing for my sister forever. And he's way more impatient than Henrik."

"Want to bet on it?" I checked the contents of the refrigerator. Meemaw's dark chocolate cheesecake was cooling nicely, so I pulled the heavy whipping cream out and brought it to the standing mixer. "If Henrik asks Brynn out first, you owe me a really, really good back rub."

"I do that anyway. You should have asked for something bigger." Tyr came up from behind and wrapped his arms around me. He took the cream from my hands and opened the carton, then poured the contents into the mixer and set it on high. "And if I win? If Forse asks Elsa out first?"

"Well, then you get to pick your prize."

Tyr set his hands on the counter, one on each side of me, so I was boxed in. He lowered his mouth to my ear and whispered in a gravelly voice, "I was hoping you'd say that."

I turned around and smiled up at him. "Want to do me—"

"Yes."

"A *favor*?" I narrowed my eyes as I continued.

"Yes." His eyes absolutely burned with desire.

"Go take a shower? You smell like dragon."

Tyr chuckled and kissed the top of my head. "As you wish, *prinsessa*," he called as he jogged up the stairs.

I smiled as I closed the refrigerator door. By the time Tyr walked back into the kitchen, wearing dark jeans and a blood-free Henley, I'd started to peel potatoes. And for the next hour, I prepared a proper Southern supper with my Norse god boyfriend, while he told me all about his day relocating dragons and negotiating with dwarves.

I'd landed myself a completely crazy, utterly unbelievable life, with a man—a god—who I loved beyond logic or measure. It was a far cry from Mama's fairytale happily-evah-aftah.

It was even better.

This was *my* happy. And I loved every single minute of it.

ACKNOWLEDGMENTS

An eternity of gratitude to my handsome husband for choosing me, and walking beside me on the journey of a lifetime. *Jeg elsker deg.*

Tusen takk to our biggest little blessings, whose kind hearts embody love and *ære* with a light that shines brighter than the sun. We thank God for you every day.

Mange takk to my editor Lauren McKellar, for keeping our gods in check, and always making me smile.

To my lovely friends, Stacey Nash and Kristie Cook, for putting up with endless questions, drafts, and writerly freak-outs. I am so grateful for your friendship. I heretofore bequeath one Gunnar Andersson unto my beautiful critique partner, and one Tyr Frederiksen unto my gorgeous Yoda.

Massive thanks to my 'technical advisor' Lorna Richmond, whose patient explanation of all things energy deepened Elsa's 'magical' gifts. I hope I always do her justice—but please keep the Hiddy pics coming if I don't! And hugs to Heather Brandt, whose tireless enthusiasm and endorsement of all things Norse god continues to blow me away. I'm so grateful you share your talents with me. *Takk* to Antonella Iannarino for providing thoughtful notes on this manuscript, and to Laura Howard and Karen Lynch, for sharing endless support along this crazy journey.

A huge thank you to my RagnaRockstars and our Valkyrie Team for giving me such a supportive place to land on rough writing days. You truly are the greatest street team in all the realms, and I'm humbled that you choose to spend your free time with me, and with our crazy Norse crew.

Eternal gratitude to MorMorMa for making me a part of your family. You're stuck with me forever, and I couldn't be happier with the arrangement.

And *mange takk* to every single reader who's taken a chance on my books. None of this would be possible without you, and I'm so very grateful that you choose to spend your reading time with me. *Tusen takk*, from the bottom of my heart.

MANGE TAKK

Thank you so much for reading the first book of *The Ære Saga*. I hope you enjoyed reading Mia and Tyr's adventures every bit as much as I enjoyed writing them. (Seriously, I had a blast!) If you want to keep up to date on all things *Ære*, hear all about the adventures of Henrik's brother's Norse crew in *The Elsker Saga*, and get a FREE copy of the *Elsker Saga* novella TUR, then sign on up for the greatest group in all the realms. Members of my Reader's Group are the first to hear about fabulous giveaways (I love giving away bookish things!), new releases, and the latest happenings with our Norse crew. I promise I won't share your information, and you can unsubscribe at any time. If you're interested, visit http://eepurl.com/bf9Lff . Hope to see you there. *Skål* y'all!

Reviews are a huge deal for authors, and your feedback means a ton! If you enjoyed this story and have a minute or two, pretty please leave a short review and show the *Ære* crew some love. I truly appreciate it!

ABOUT THE AUTHOR

Before finding domestic bliss in suburbia, S.T. Bende lived in Manhattan Beach (became overly fond of Peet's Coffee) and Europe . . . where she became overly fond of McVities cookies. Her love of Scandinavian culture and a very patient Norwegian teacher inspired the books of *The Elsker Saga* and *The Ære Saga*. She hopes her characters make you smile and that one day, waffles will be considered a health food.

Find S.T. on her website (www.stbende.com), her newsletter (http://eepurl.com/bf9Lff), her Facebook reader's page (S.T. Bende's Ragnarockstars - https://www.facebook.com/groups/548404475215990/?ref=br_tf), or on Twitter @stbende. While you're at it, introduce yourself to @UllMyhr and @TyrFredriksen— when they're not saving the cosmos from dark elves and killer wolves, they love meeting new friends. Especially the human kind.

WANT MORE OF THE NORSE CREW?

Find out what happens to our favorite Norse gods in
THE ÆRE SAGA.

THE ÆRE SAGA: PERFEKT ORDER
THE ÆRE SAGA: PERFEKT CONTROL
THE ÆRE SAGA: PERFEKT BALANCE

And meet the *other* Norse crew (including Henrik's
brother Gunnar!) in
THE ELSKER SAGA.

THE ELSKER SAGA: TUR (a novella)
THE ELSKER SAGA: ELSKER
THE ELSKER SAGA: ENDRE
THE ELSKER SAGA: TRO
THE ELSKER SAGA: COMPLETE BOXED SET
And the bonus Elsker Saga novella…
SUPERNATURAL CHRONICLES:
THE ASGARDIANS

Find out what happens when the valkyrie next door faces her ultimate challenge, in . . .

THE ÆRE SAGA: PERFEKT CONTROL

Rule the realms.

Brynn Aksel is a valkyrie—a battle goddess tasked with protecting both the God of War and the future of Asgard. She fends off giants and dark elves with an iron fist, a glossy smile, and no less than perfekt control. She's focused one-hundred-percent on rising through the valkyrie ranks, and not at all on her lifelong crush on Henrik Andersson—the one guy in all the realms who could be her undoing.

Henrik serves as War's other bodyguard, and he's too focused on protecting their shared charge to realize that Brynn's a girl. When an unprecedented surge of darkness abducts the Goddess of Love, Brynn's already-steely focus is singularly directed on her new assignment—accompany Henrik to recover the realms' source of light before the cosmos descends into chaos.

While battling demons, dragons, and the not-quite-dead, it becomes clear that immortality does not equal invincibility. And when Hel herself puts a hit on Brynn, the valkyrie has to decide if staying in control is worth losing everything . . . or if it's time to rule the realms.

Here's a sneak peek at the next chapter in THE ÆRE SAGA . . .

PERFEKT CONTROL

CHAPTER ONE

"STUFF IT, BRYNN," TYR muttered as he pulled a smoking pan from the oven. The God of War stood in our open kitchen. His girlfriend's frilly pink apron popped against his standard uniform of jeans and a Henley. He glared at me as he dumped the blackened contents of the pan into the sink, where it blended with a sea of similarly situated peers. Our kitchen had morphed into a veritable cake graveyard.

"I didn't say anything." I held up my hands.

"Didn't have to." Tyr threw the empty cake pans at the stovetop, where they clattered loudly in protest. "Your obnoxious little laugh speaks volumes."

I forced my face into a neutral position and tilted my head at the lacy fabric tied around Tyr's waist. "Your cooking attire took me by surprise. That's all."

Tyr pulled the oven mitts from his hands and threw them at me. Hard. My fingertips stung as I plucked them from the air.

"Was that really necessary?" I asked.

"Was cackling like a caffeinated hyena necessary?" Tyr countered with an eyebrow raise.

Harrumph.

"The apron's Mia's. I thought if I wore it while I cooked, maybe this time I wouldn't burn her *förbaskat* birthday cake."

I waited in silence while Tyr scrubbed the big silver bowl clean, pulled a box of cake mix out of the cupboard, and turned to me. With his narrowed eyes and tight-lipped frown, he was the picture of resignation. "Apparently, this apron's not the reason my girlfriend's such a great cook."

"No, it's not." I bounded across the kitchen to rescue the cake box from Tyr's hand. He was squeezing it so hard, I thought it might need saving. "Fred's going to make the packet explode," I pointed out.

Tyr clung tighter to the box with his prosthetic right arm. Mia, Henrik and I had developed it under the guise of an engineering project, and it had saved his life when the homicidal wolf Fenrir bit his original arm clean off. Now, Fred served proudly as Tyr's right forearm, attached by biomechanical medicine, Asgardian magic, and just a touch of fairy dust.

When poor Mia discovered her freshman lab project was actually the saving grace for an Asgardian deity, she thought we'd led her straight to the psych ward. But crazy was the name of the game when you were tasked with protecting the God of War.

Apparently, diplomacy was the name of the game when you were trying to help him bake.

"Okay, fine. Kill the poor mix." My tone softened when Tyr's shoulders drooped. "Look, Mia's a great cook because she loves it. She likes taking care of us. She especially likes taking care of *you*. And the last thing she'd want on her birthday is for you to beat yourself up over something as silly as a birthday cake. You can always order one from the bakery. Want me to call them?"

"No, Brynn. I'm making my girlfriend a *förbaskat* cake. If you're not going to help, then get out of my kitchen."

"I share kitchen custody, you know." I elbowed past him and opened the refrigerator. I pulled out the carton of eggs and set them on the counter, then closed the door behind me. "When Mia started spending weekends here, her bodyguard did, too. Remember?"

When Asgard's resident war god fell for Redwood State University Engineering undergrad Mia Ahlström, I'd been reassigned from my valkyrie post to protect the sweetest mortal this side of Midgard. And when the evil wolf Fenrir made a hit on Tyr's life, Mia and her newly christened bodyguard started spending a lot more time at War's impeccably decorated cabin in Arcata, California. Instead of collecting fallen soldiers for Odin and Freya as I'd done as a battle valkyrie, these days I attended Engineering classes, workouts, and study sessions with my charge. I also got to weekend with the uber-uptight war god, and the hottest bodyguard in the history of the realms, Henrik Andersson.

Immortal life was looking good.

"*Ja*, you stay here sometimes." Tyr ran his hands through his dark blond hair. The normally tousled strands now looked downright disheveled. "But you're useless in the kitchen. I need someone who can fix this. Where's *my* bodyguard?"

As if he'd heard Tyr's summons, the front door slammed, and Henrik's footsteps sounded in the hall. A moment later, the tall frame of the guy I'd had the hots for since kindergarten filled the kitchen doorway. I bounced on my toes—the movement usually distracted me from the unavoidable stomach flutters I got whenever I looked at Henrik's chestnut hair, easy smile, and thick, muscled arms. But there was no avoiding the twinkle in his grey-blue eyes as he looked around the kitchen.

He grinned at the brooding war god stewing over the stove. "Having trouble, mate?"

Tyr let out a growl that echoed across the cavernous kitchen.

"He's trying to make a birthday cake for Mia." I pointed to the sink, now overflowing with blackened culinary rejects. "But it's not going so well."

"Well, did you offer to help him?" Henrik asked.

"We all know Brynn can't cook," Tyr retorted.

"I can too cook!" I threw a nearby dishtowel at Tyr. He plucked it out of the air before it could smack him in his surly face.

"She can cook," Henrik agreed. He walked around the big island in the center of the room and slung an easy arm around my shoulders. An army of angsty butterflies took flight somewhere beneath abs two and three. If I hadn't had *my whole entire life* to get used to hiding my emotions, I probably would have giggled.

"Thank you, Henrik." I stuck my tongue out at Tyr. "Henrik says I can cook."

"Your cooking's fine. It's the baking you're lousy at." Henrik pulled his arm away and moved to inspect the oven. When his back was to us, Tyr turned to me with a smirk.

"Shut up, Tyr." I scowled as I shoved him. Hard.

"Well, there's your problem." Henrik adjusted the dial on the stove. "Your temperature's off."

Tyr's brow furrowed as he scrutinized the box on the counter. "No, it's not. The thingy's at three hundred and fifty. The directions say three hundred and fifty."

"*Ja.*" Henrik walked to the sink and washed his hands. "But you've got the broiler turned on. It's overriding the temperature control and frying your cake." He turned off the water and dried his hands. "You want to keep at it alone, or do you want some help? I don't mind pitching in, but if I'm doing this we're chucking that lousy cake mix and doing it from scratch."

A small wrinkle appeared between Tyr's eyebrows as he weighed his options. Mia would be home from class soon. He'd obviously started early enough, judging by the sea of slaughtered cakes, but now he was down to the wire. He let out a long-suffering sigh. "I'll take the help," Tyr acquiesced. "But I am decorating it myself."

"Whatever you say, *kille*." Henrik pulled milk, flour, cocoa powder and sugar onto the counter. Without even glancing at a recipe, he added ingredients to the standing mixer. "Brynn, grab me the red food coloring, would you?"

"Um, sure." I glanced around the kitchen, my eyes darting from cabinet to cabinet until they fell on Tyr. He gave me a wicked grin.

"You wanted to help, remember?" Tyr said.

"Oh, like you know where it is, Captain Cake Killer." I glared.

"To the left of the stove, just above the spice rack," Henrik offered without turning around. His back flexed as he reached for the oil, the corded muscles straining against his thin grey T-shirt. I sighed. Loudly.

"Uh, okay. Thanks." I crossed to the cabinet, wishing I could wipe the smirk off Tyr's face. My indiscreet ogling hadn't escaped his notice.

It never did.

I handed the food coloring to Henrik then situated myself next to Tyr. Backs against the stove, arms across our chests, we kept ourselves safely out of Henrik's path. It was better for everyone this way.

It was particularly better for Mia's birthday cake.

"Anything we can do?" Tyr asked.

"Somebody want to flour the pan?" Henrik glanced over his shoulder. Tyr and I stared blankly. "Wipe the cake pan with butter," Henrik explained slowly, as if he were talking to a pair of preschoolers, "then dust it lightly with flour. You two master chefs think you can pull that off?"

It took an enormous deal of self-control to *not* roll my eyes as I picked up the butter. "Sometimes you can be a real know-it-all, Henrik Andersson."

"Ah, you love me, Brynnie." Henrik shot me a wink and turned off the mixer. My overworked heart clattered violently against my ribcage. *Bounce, bounce, bounce.* Henrik pulled the bowl from the stand and raised an eyebrow. "Where's my pan?"

Oh. Right. Tyr grabbed the butter out of my hands and rubbed a generous amount into each of the cake pans. I snatched a handful of flour and sprinkled it over the tops. "How'd we do?"

"*Perfekt.*" Henrik gave his easy smile as he divided the batter between the pans. He placed them in the oven and checked the temperature controls. "Now we wait. If we put them into the fridge when they're done, they should be cool enough to decorate about an hour after Mia gets home."

"Not soon enough." Tyr frowned. "I wanted to give it to her when she walked in the door."

"We'll do our best." Henrik patted Tyr's arm. "But a cake needs to cool *completely* before you layer it, or decorate it. So it'll probably be good to go by—"

"It's her birthday." Tyr glared.

"Then you should have asked for my help sooner." Henrik shrugged. "Now if you two can stay out of trouble for the next hour or so, I've got a stabilizer I need to reattach to some grounding cords.

"What are you working on now?" I followed Henrik out of the kitchen.

"There's been some weird activity in the portal behind Elsa's cottage."

"Oh my gods, why didn't you say anything?" I skidded to a stop. "The one Fenrir got in through?"

"One and the same." Henrik kept walking, so I forced my feet to move.

"Why aren't we out there right now making sure nothing gets through?"

"Because I only just noticed it this afternoon. Don't worry, I'm already on it. I've got a halter lock in place, but I'm working on a little something extra to make sure the portal's dog proof. Not that Fenrir could come back or anything; a certain shiny pink ribbon and a little thing called the prison chamber have him on lockdown. This will just be a little bonus security—an early Christmas present for our prince of preparedness." Henrik cocked his finger toward the kitchen.

"Much as I love to make fun of Tyr, this isn't a good time, Henrik." I grabbed him by the arm and spun him around. His biceps were hard against my palm. "Wh-wha . . ." I stamped my foot and forced myself to focus. "What are we going to do if Hymir or one of his minions get through? We all know he's madder than a wet fire giant that we captured Fenrir. And with that vindictive streak, Odin only knows what he's plotting as his revenge." I tightened my grip around Henrik's muscles. "And what about Loki? He's been awfully quiet lately. Hasn't delivered any of us to the jotuns or stolen a treasure in a really long time. Isn't it about time he had an episode?"

"That's the thing." Henrik scratched his chin, where a

smattering of stubble testified to his long hours in his upstairs lab—a technological paradise I called the man cave. "Loki hasn't created a disturbance in . . . it's been a few decades now. It's possible everything's hunky-dory with him."

"Mia's little sayings rubbing off on you, too?" I snickered.

"They are catchy." Henrik paused at the bottom of the stairs with a chuckle. The noise resonated along the hallway, and the space filled with his easy laughter. My lips curved up at the contagious sound. "Point is, whatever he's up to, if it's anything at all, he's not showing his hand. And Hymir's been quiet since Fenrir's capture. If he's got anything to do with the disturbance around the Arcata portal, he's doing it behind the scenes. We just have to make sure whoever's working for him doesn't develop better tech than we do."

"Nobody develops better tech than we do. We're the *perfekt* team." The words were out of my mouth before I realized how they sounded. Henrik's mercifully dense Y-chromosome kept him from picking up on my double meaning. "I mean, our technology's *perfekt*—always way ahead of the game. 'Cause we're so smart. Um, yeah. Listen, if you need anything, I have some of that titanium alloy left over from the robotics backup we started in case Fred didn't perform to specs. If we combined it with some of the *älva* dust we've got left over, we might be able to develop an auto-return glitch to attach to the portal."

"We're out of *älva* dust; used the last of it on Fred," Henrik reminded me.

"Oh. Right."

"We'll figure something out, *sötnos*. I'll give a holler if I get stuck. You might not be able to bake, but you're one Helheim of an engineering mastermind." Henrik pinched the tip of my braid, and my breath caught. I was having a *really* hard time controlling myself today. Muspelheim must be in retrograde. *Stay calm, Brynn. He's just a guy* . . .

Liar. Henrik Andersson had never been just a guy to me. And he probably never would be. I'd been head over heels for the boy next door since he defended my honor in the kindergarten playground roughly six hundred years ago, and my feelings hadn't changed in . . . ever. But it didn't matter. Asgard had survived for millennia thanks to an unchallenged system of rules and structure. Henrik was a seasoned warrior, and I was a junior valkyrie. And our sole priority, for as long as Odin commanded it, was to protect Asgard's first line of defense—the God of War. And on *his* order, we were to protect Tyr's girlfriend, Mia. Personal feelings, and even more so a relationship, would be an enormous liability, notwithstanding the fact that Valkyrie code stipulated I wasn't allowed to date until I made captain rank. Besides, my seat in Henrik's life was planted firmly in the friend zone. I was his colleague, his little brother's classmate, and while we were stationed in Arcata, his occasional flat mate. That was as far as our relationship could go.

It didn't stop the uninvited battalion of butterflies springing to attention every time he looked at me. I might have been an immortal battle goddess, but I was still a girl.

Henrik let go of my hair, and turned around with a small smile. He jogged up to the second floor. The muscles of his backside flexed as he ran, and I permitted myself a solitary inward sigh as I watched pure denim-clad perfection ascend the staircase. When I tore my eyes away from the spot where Henrik had disappeared, I noticed the six-foot, six-inch deity smirking in the kitchen doorway.

"Shut up, Tyr." I grabbed my keys off the key hook Mia had installed in the entry, and ripped the front door open. "If anyone needs me, I'm going to the gym."

"You forgot your yoga mat." Tyr chuckled from inside.

"You know I don't do yoga." I glared at my insufferable friend. "There's a kickboxing class in ten minutes, and my gym bag's in the car. And I need some *space* from *this*." I waved my hands in front of me, outlining Tyr's irritating form.

"Don't be late for Mia's birthday dinner," Tyr warned.

My glare softened. "I wouldn't miss it. She's my friend, too, remember?"

"She's special to all of us," Henrik called as he ran down the stairs and out to the garage. He returned seconds later with a small transistor. "Forgot this." Before we could comment, he'd blurred up the stairs in a display of Asgardian speed.

Tyr nodded to the door. "Have a good workout then." He glanced up the stairs with a half-smile. "I'd imagine you have a lot of frustration to work off."

"Shut *up!*" My glare returned in full force, and I slammed the front door behind me. He might have been my charge, and one of my oldest friends, but if Tyr Fredriksen made one more innuendo about my feelings for Henrik, I might have to kill the jotun-face.

* * * *

"Happy birthday dear Mia, happy birthday to you!"

Tyr's adorable mortal girlfriend grinned, her blush spreading to the roots of her chocolate brown hair. She tucked one loose lock behind her ear and leaned over the coffee table to blow out eighteen symmetrically placed birthday candles. Tyr was as predictable as he was bossy; and he conducted his life with the control typical of most warriors, from his impeccable housekeeping habits to his perfectly organized garage. I, on the other hand, could barely wrangle my nightmare hair into submission, never mind keeping my room clean.

"What did you wish for? More time with your *favorite* roommates?" Henrik slung an arm around my shoulder and pulled me back onto the couch. Benefit number one of the friend zone: Henrik didn't think twice about physical contact. I honestly believed he forgot I was a girl.

So long as he kept on touching me, I was *totally* okay with that.

"Watch it, Henrik," Heather warned. "If you guys didn't have Captain Beefcake all up in here, you know Mia would spend more time at her 'official' residence—you know, the one her mail still goes to. I doubt *you're* sticking to her cleaning schedule."

Mia's blush deepened.

"Captain Beefcake, eh?" Tyr scratched the stubble along his jawline. "I could get on board with that. What do you say, *prinsessa*? Want to call me that from now on?"

Charlotte patted Mia's flaming cheek, then turned to Tyr. "Sorry about Heather. We don't let her out much these days. Her internship's keeping her busy."

"How's it going at the clinic?" Mia diverted the subject as she cut the cake. Heather passed out slices, and I tried not to be too obvious about sniffing Henrik's chest as I turned to watch her. *Mmm. Laundry detergent and sunshine and calm . . .*

"It's okay. I'm having a hard time balancing this unit's Chemistry load with the volunteer hours, though. I might need you to tweak my study schedule." Heather handed plates to Henrik and me. I reluctantly sat up, breaking the blissful contact.

"Consider it done. Anything for my roomie." Mia sliced the final pieces of cake, and curled up on the loveseat with Tyr. She handed him a plate before digging into her own frosting. "Mmm." She licked the cream cheese icing off her fork with a contented moan. "Meemaw's Red Velvet. Tyr, you made it just right!"

Henrik pushed his fake eyeglasses up his nose. Asgardians had *perfekt* eyesight, but he liked to wear the glasses around mortals. He thought it made him blend in. *Snort.* I guessed he wore them for Charlotte and Heather's benefit tonight. "Actually," Henrik began. But he stopped short when I elbowed him in the stomach. Hard.

"Let him have this one," I hissed, trying to erase the mental picture of Henrik's pristine abdomen walking shirtless to the shower *every single weekend*. Why couldn't his room have an en suite bathroom?

Henrik leaned close enough that his beachy smell enveloped my space. Fresh air, and sunshine, and a tang of lime. "Brynnie." He frowned. "I worked my butt off perfecting her Meemaw's recipe."

"And I'm sure Tyr will thank you in the morning," I whispered back. I raised an eyebrow at our friend, who had one hand on his plate and one hand on his girlfriend's behind. The look in his eyes was undeniably possessive.

"Fair enough." Henrik sighed.

"Sorry your sister couldn't make it, Tyr." Charlotte looked up from her cake. "I was looking forward to meeting her."

"You still haven't met Elsa?" Mia shook her head. "You're going to love her. Her friend Forse, too."

"They're still just friends, huh?" I asked.

"Apparently." Tyr shrugged.

"Yeah, we've got a whole lot of stubborn people around here." Mia shot me a pointed look. I snorted. My dating life was not mine to control. Not yet, anyway.

We ate in contented silence, and when the last fork scraped the last crumb of red velvet, Tyr shifted Mia in his lap. "Well, *mitt hjärta*, looks like your birthday is drawing to a close. And I have a gift for you that's not fit for public viewing."

I buried my face in Henrik's chest to stifle my laughter. Beside us, Heather let out a muffled guffaw.

"Well, it's getting late. We'd better get home." Charlotte took Tyr's hint. She stood, carried her plate to the kitchen, and stared at Heather until she did the same.

"Uh, right." Heather scurried to the kitchen and back, then grabbed two jackets from the hall closet. She threw one at Charlotte, then stuffed her arms through the other. "Homework waits for no woman."

"Y'all don't have to go." Mia gave Tyr a pointed look. She gently removed his hand from her backside and stood up. "We have more cake. Anybody want seconds?"

Heather looked like she was about to say yes, but Charlotte grabbed her by the arm and dragged her toward the front door. Mia followed. "Thanks, Mia, but we really should let you, erm, *enjoy* the rest of your birthday. Come *on*, Heather."

As Heather begrudgingly followed her roommate out the front door, she turned with a sparkle in her eye. "Glad to see you finally *glowing*, Mia." With a naughty wink, Heather closed the door behind her, leaving Mia standing in the hallway with flaming red cheeks and a gaping mouth. She stayed very still as the lights of the girls' car flashed through the windows, sweeping across the drive. After a long moment, she pivoted on one riding boot, and returned to the living area. Her eyes darted around the room as she bit her bottom lip.

"Yep. We heard it." Henrik let out a guffaw, and I hit him over the head with a couch pillow. His glasses fell off, and he picked them up and set them on the coffee table. "What? We're all thinking it. You want us to clear out so you two can have the house to yourselves?"

"Henrik!" Mia shrieked.

Tyr looked like he was considering the offer.

"No." Mia glared at Tyr. "No, we do not."

Tyr chuckled as he stood and crossed to Mia. He pulled her into his arms and nibbled on her crimson ear. "You're hot when you're embarrassed."

"Hush your mouth, Fredriksen," Mia protested. But after a minute she leaned into his touch.

"Before you get too into this," I interrupted, "we need to talk about the time freezer."

"Now?" Mia wrinkled her brow. "Is everything okay?"

"Not sure." I paused as Elsa and Forse opened the front door.

"Sorry we're late. Happy birthday, Mia!" Elsa ran to Mia and threw her arms around our friend. Mia beamed, while Tyr tousled his sister's blond waves. Hers were smooth and loose, and not the least bit unruly. Mine took a half-hour to blow-dry straight, and even then they frizzed at the slightest sign of moisture.

Some goddesses got all the luck.

"*Hei*, Elsa. Forse." Tyr held out a fist. Forse closed the front door, before walking into the living room and bumping Tyr's knuckles in the universal male sign of greeting. "You're late."

"Don't be rude." Mia swatted Tyr's shoulder and pointed to the coffee table. "We've got plenty of cake left. Would you like some?"

Forse ran a hand through his hair while Elsa wrung her fingers together.

"What's going on?" Henrik rested his arm on the back of the couch as he studied Forse's face. "It's never good when your jaw twitches."

"Wait." Elsa held up her hand. "First we need to wish Mia a happy birthday. Forse?"

"Right." Forse pulled a small wrapped package out of his back pocket and handed it to Mia. She took it with a smile.

"You didn't have to get me a present."

"Of course we did. You're part of the crew now. And we want to bribe you not to leave us. Odin knows we're a lot to put up with." Forse crossed his arms and tilted his head at Tyr. "Especially this *kille*."

"Shove it, Justice." Tyr growled at Forse, using our nickname for the peacekeeping god. Forse just laughed.

"Open it." Elsa clapped her hands. With a grin, Mia tore open the paper.

"You guys!" Mia squealed, holding up the sporting store gift card. "Thank you! I totally need new running shoes. How'd you know?"

"Hmm, maybe because my brother literally runs you into the ground?" Elsa tossed her hair over her shoulder. "How many miles do you two cover in a week, anyway?"

Mia glanced up at Tyr. "I don't know. Maybe thirty?"

"Closer to forty." Tyr rested his hand on Mia's lower back.

"Mother Frigga." Elsa shook her head. "Cut her a break, will you Tyr?"

"It's me," Mia corrected. "I don't want to be the helpless human you guys lock in the house if something attacks us. Again." She shot me a pointed look.

"I didn't lock you in anywhere!" I protested.

"No, but your boss did. And she's not here, so I'm blaming you." Mia looked around. "Where is Freya, anyway? I saved her a piece of cake with extra frosting."

I couldn't help but smile. Mia and Freya got off to a rocky start, since Mia was under the misconception that Freya and Tyr were an item. But the girl and the goddess spent a chunk of time together on our last lockdown at the safe house, and they bonded over their shared loves of fashion and cooking. Now Mia was just as enamored with the Goddess of Love as the rest of us were . . . and the feeling was mutual.

"That's why we're late." Elsa rubbed her hands on her leggings, nervously. "There's a teensy situation at the portal."

Every god in the room snapped to immediate attention. The mortal simply stopped breathing.

"What do you mean a situation?" Henrik pushed off the couch and stepped slightly in front of me. I jumped up and moved around him so we stood side by side.

"What's happening?" I asked.

"We're not exactly sure." A V formed between Forse's brows. "It's been sparking for the last hour. Tiny electric currents are shooting off the outline of the portal, traveling roughly three meters on due south, then disappearing before they hit the ground. We don't understand what's absorbing the energy. We would have come over sooner, but we didn't want to ruin the party."

"Disappearing?" Henrik's frown matched Forse's. "That's not right. If the portal's being activated, the current should flow to the dirt and ground itself. At least, that's what it did last time."

"I know. I wouldn't believe it unless I saw it." Forse shifted in the entryway.

I tapped Henrik's exceedingly firm shoulder. Great Odin's ravens, how much was he benching these days? "Um, could your blocker be doing it?"

"Huh? Oh! Right." Recognition dawned in Henrik's eyes. "I installed the prototype of a new blocker that should provide an extra level of security." Henrik glanced at Tyr. "But I haven't locked down the tech. Maybe it's short circuiting because of the rain?"

"It's not raining yet," Elsa countered. "Forecast says tomorrow. You sure that's it?"

"No." Henrik paused. "We should go check it out."

The front door burst open, knocking Forse out of the way. He caught his footing and turned, shielding Elsa with his body. Tyr, Henrik and I leapt into action. I threw myself in front of Mia and herded her back into the living room, while Henrik opened the weapons closet and threw a sword at Tyr. Tyr plucked it out of the air and stood *en garde*, while Henrik aimed the crossbow he'd chosen at the intruder.

Oh, skit. Here we go again.

PERFEKT ORDER

PERFEKT ORDER

Made in the USA
Charleston, SC
23 January 2016